TELL HER I LOVE HER

ALEXIS WESTMORE

TDH PUBLISHING

CREDITS

Editor: Heather Flournoy

Cover Artist: Joy Argento

Forever can be found in many different types of relationships. It is a
beautiful tapestry woven of compassion,
personal responsibility, and love.
This book is dedicated to those willing to invest
in a "Forever Us"

CONTENTS

CHAPTER ONE

"**I** WILL NOT ASK her to leave. This is a public library." Layka pulled her focus from the woman sitting quietly in the reading section to the irate woman standing before her.

"She has a cart with garbage bags of who knows what in it."

"She also has two books at her desk, reading and not bothering anyone."

"Well, it's ridiculous! The library isn't meant to be a homeless shelter."

Layka closed her eyes against her own anger. When she opened them, the woman had turned toward the library's automatic glass doors. She sighed as the woman waved hopefully at Sgt. Samantha Corin-Silva entering with a bag of donuts that Layka knew was for Sam's ex-partner—who now managed security at the large library. The gloom and darkness beyond the glass doors fit her mood. Sunrise had been at 6:46 a.m. this morning, but all the color she had watched light the sky was now, two hours later, covered by clouds and the hint of impending rain.

Layka tried to wave her off, indicating she had it under control, but one didn't stop Sgt. Silva once she set a direction of action.

"Hi. Is there a problem?"

"Yes, officer, there is. This librarian refuses to create a safe environment for the public. She's re—"

"Ma'am, I was speaking to my sister, the librarian, who I know loves the library more than her own home."

The woman huffed once, muttered something about reporting to the health department as she moved toward the door, then said loudly before exiting, "If she loved it so much, she'd do something to protect it from vagrants."

Layka cast her glance past her sister, hoping Mildred hadn't heard. If she had, she was unfazed as she continued to read with one hand on her bag of belongings. There was movement from the books on the left as Farrah, her friend and soon-to-be sister-in-law—if she could play matchmaker—rolled a book cart back toward the desk. She turned at the obnoxious squeal of the door behind the shelves to the right, near the hospital side entrance. It didn't always do it, but when it did, it sounded like someone stepped on a pig's tail. It was helpful because you couldn't see the door from the main desk.

"Quiet as usual, I see, sis," Sam said, pulling Layka's attention.

"You know it," Layka said, fighting her interest to see who was coming in from the hospital entrance. "Speaking of quiet. Are you going out again with that pretty, soft-spoken girl, Gemma? She was—"

"Hi, Sam," Farrah said, pushing the cart around behind the desk and reloading it with books.

"Hi, Farrah. I'm just taking these up to Toby." Sam jiggled the bag before heading toward the elevators behind the main desk area.

Layka gritted her teeth against the tension she felt when her sister and her friend were in the same space together. *Why can't they admit they're interested in each other?* Layka made a mental note to talk with her sister when they got together for their weekend tradition of Capture the Queen.

"See you, sis," Sam said from somewhere down the corridor near the elevators.

"I'm taking these reference books downstairs," Farrah said.

Layka registered the sound of the cart rolling but couldn't pull her eyes away from the new development in the broad center aisle of the reading room where Mildred still sat.

"Sure," Layka said to both, now distracted as she stared forward across the expansive entryway to the twenty-foot-wide walk area that separated the floor-to-ceiling shelves of books to the right and left. There were table desks lining the perimeter of the walkway about two feet from the shelves. Mildred sat at one of the rich mahogany-brown tables, but there was now someone kneeling near her. A woman with shoulder-length blond hair ran a hand over a loose strand that hung in her face and pushed it behind her ear as she stood up, lifting a torn, dingy, cream clutch purse and placing it on the desk where Mildred read. Mildred looked up from her book and gave a guarded smile before pulling the clutch to her and placing it in the small cart at her side.

The blonde moved toward the aisle of books, and Layka tried not to stare at how well the scrubs looked on the woman. Weren't those things supposed to make everyone look like an oversized laundry basket? She shook her head to refocus just as the woman turned as if realizing she might need help finding what she wanted. It had to be the blue of the uniform reflecting the light. No one had eyes that blue.

Layka swallowed as the woman turned fully and began walking toward the desk. She tightened her ponytail that sat low at her neck and then ran her hands through the tail of it. She knew it was a nervous habit, but the glossy feel of her hair was calming.

"Hi, could you help me?"

"No," Layka blurted without thinking, then closed her eyes briefly. *Why does my chest feel like I can't breathe?* She opened her eyes to the tilted head of the woman now studying her. Even the lines of her furrowed brow didn't distract from those sky-blue eyes. "Sorry, Sky. I mean..." Layka quickly read her scrub top. "...Dr. Summerhouse. I thought you were going to ask me to remove the lady reading at the desk. I can help you." She realized she was still standing from her previous confrontation with Grumpypants and took her seat, typing her password into the computer. "What are you looking for?"

"Why would I want you to ask someone to leave the library?"

"No reason," Layka quickly said, not wanting to draw more attention to Mildred reading at the desk. She felt the squeeze of her chest release as she opened the resource page for the library. She took a deep, solid breath. That was it—just the lingering adrenaline from the confrontation earlier. Now she could breathe and help the nice doctor. "Are you here from the hospital?" Layka said, trying to regain proper direction as the screens opened up on the computer.

"Yes. There is an old journal I have been unable to locate, and when I saw you watching me like I was in the wrong building..." Dr. Summerhouse laughed. It was soft, drawing Layka's eyes up from the screen just as the woman pushed that strand of hair behind her ear again. Her laugh turned into a full smile before she spoke again. "I figured maybe I was in the wrong building and should come ask for help."

"If you are looking for anything written, you're in the right place. The Library of Congress has access to, or can access, almost anything you need." The computer pinged with the page Layka figured she would need. She was actually really good at knowing what would help someone working on a project, often even before they told her the details. Her sister said she should have been a detective. "And if you're looking for something old, you are definitely in the right building."

"You nailed it. It's a journal article from 1906."

"Wow—okay. Here, I already have the page up to search the microfilm data." Layka turned the screen mounted to the upper counter toward Dr. Summerhouse.

"That was quick. How did you know I would need something old enough to be on microfilm?"

Layka shrugged, enjoying the appreciative smile she received for her efforts. "Just a hunch." The phone at the desk rang, and she pulled her eyes away to reach for it. She could feel Dr. Summerhouse's eyes on her neck as she turned. "Hello, Library of Congress Antiquities building..." She halted in her standard spiel when she realized it was Toby calling from the second floor.

"Layka, can you come up? We've got an issue."

"Yes, sure. Let me ask Alan to come over to the main desk and I'll be up." Layka's instincts said this had something to do with Grumpypants this morning, and she could feel the brightness in her from meeting Dr. Summerhouse darken with dread for another battle with society.

"Will it be all right for me to continue to search here?" Summerhouse said, giving the keyboard for patrons two quick finger strikes before looking up.

"Yes, and I'll be sending Alan up so he will be able to help if you have any more questions."

"Thank you. This has saved me a ton of time."

There was that smile again. Well, didn't that just brighten up a dark spot once more. Why couldn't more of the public be like this—interested in ideas, happy with learning, and eager for knowledge? Looking cute in a pair of scrubs with seemingly no effort at all most likely played a role in her assessment too, but it was secondary. Right? "I'm here most days if you need something in the future."

"I appreciate that, but I was lucky to escape today. I doubt I'll have another free moment for three years."

Well, the universe did what it did. Layka had to deal with the pressing issue that awaited her on the second floor. She nodded and gave a smile.

Layka made her way toward the elevators behind the main desk and offices, stopping briefly to ask Alan to cover the front desk. She turned to check on Mildred reading but saw that she was gone. When she reached the elevator doors, she paused before pushing the button. She wanted to return to the front desk and help Dr. Summerhouse find everything she needed. Her gut twisted at the battle she knew awaited her on the second floor. It wasn't the first time the issue had come up. But, despite the headaches it caused, it was important to her that libraries remain available to everyone. It wasn't meant for her to have extra time with Dr. Summerhouse, but at least her day was brighter for having met her, and she had a renewed energy for the fight by realizing people like Dr. Summerhouse were on her side. She let the happy idea sit with her as she rode the elevator to the second floor.

The elevator doors opened, and Layka collided with Dr. Maya Sudha. "Oh, sorry, Dr. Su—"

"I've told you to call me Maya," she said, twisting smoothly to avoid the impact. Her braids swung with her rotation, and Layka was momentarily mesmerized by the grace of the woman's movement. "I appreciate the respect you afford me for my Pile it Higher and Deeper degree, but we're colleagues."

Layka laughed at Dr. Sudha's standard reply regarding her PhD when she was among friends. She didn't know why she had trouble calling her by her first name but figured it was probably because she so deeply respected the woman's work. "You forget I've read your work and recognize the level of suffering that comes with graduate degrees."

"Noted," Dr. Sudha said, pressing the button to keep the door open as they spoke. "I'm surprised to see that big grin with the news that just came in."

"Well, I haven't heard the news yet, but I imagine I know what it entails." Layka paused, recalling the vision of Dr. Summerhouse tucking that loose strand of hair behind her ear as she lifted Mildred's clutch purse from the floor. "I had a connection this morning with a like-minded soul, and it left a smile on my face."

"That's worth celebrating. I'll bring you back a coffee. Jason, add her order so they don't miss it with the delivery. I'm headed to the first floor to get my planner I left at the main desk and wait for our order from Bean Around the World. Our team"—Dr. Sudha waved her free hand toward the group of people clustered near the security desk while she held the elevator door open with the button inside—"deserves caffeine."

Layka twisted to follow the gesture. Jason—Dr. Sudha's assistant from the antiquities reference department—and Farrah had a laptop open on the corner of the desk to the far right. "I know what she'll order," they said in unison, then laughed when Jason appeared to type in an addition to the order. Farrah nodded. "That's it."

Layka gave them a squinty stare, but they never lifted their focus from the screen to appreciate it. She did drink a lot of coffee. "Doesn't Toby have coffee in the security office?" Layka pointed to Sam and Toby chatting across the highest section of the wooden desk to the left, where it abutted the exterior wall of the security office. They looked like two neighbors talking across a fence.

Dr. Sudha wrinkled her nose. "Sam and Toby drink dirty water. Call me a snob, but I like fine wine and strong coffee."

"That sounds like my ex," Sam said, lifting her paper cup in toast.

Dr. Sudha grinned as if the toast was a challenge. "You dated someone who liked fine wine?"

"No," Sam said, laughing. "She was expensive and bitter."

Dr. Sudha shook her head but didn't stifle her laugh.

"They've already left to deliver, they should be here soon," Jason said, giving Layka a "sorry about that" grimace.

"No worries, I'll drink some dirty water. I'm not picky."

"I ordered a coffee for the Department of Education liaison meeting me after our chat, but you can have it. He's cutting our budget," Dr. Sudha said, winking as she let the elevator doors close.

"Thanks," Layka said to the closing stainless steel, then made her way to the small group.

"Expensive and bitter," Toby said, smiling and shaking his head. The group gave another chuckle. Layka realized she wasn't laughing with everyone else when her sister's eyes caught hers and then looked away. Yeah, she needed to have that conversation with Sam. Everyone saw the flash of comedy and easygoing side of Sam, but she knew the heartbreak that had put walls around Sam's heart—and those walls were getting thicker. She loved her sister, but she was hardheaded and stubborn. Who would think someone from college could still have a hold on her sister's heart? She'd never gotten the full story. She'd been away with the Peace Corps and missed quite a bit of what happened in that time. But with one glance at Farrah, who was trying to look as uninterested in Sam as Sam was trying to act nonchalant about her love life, Layka pushed talking to her sister to the top of her planner for this weekend. "Hey, guys. So what's the news?"

Toby tapped a few keys on his laptop. "Let me close this secondary check system, and I'll give you the scoop."

The security area on this floor, which held some of the oldest and most prized possessions of the Library of Congress, was front and center with an open concept to create improved visibility. Layka closed her eyes and breathed in the space. It smelled different on this level. Despite the specialized airflow system to protect the antiquities, it still smelled like old books to her. *Maybe that's just in my mind*, she thought as she opened her eyes and took in the monitors that surrounded the security area where they all stood.

"Okay," Toby said, clicking the laptop closed. "I'll bring Layka up to speed on the phone call, and then Maya can discuss the protocols we will need to implement when she gets back." There were general nods all around as they each found an overstuffed chair or reading table to collapse at while Toby cleared his throat. "There have been several reports over the last six to eight weeks from the health department to the infectious disease department at the hospital that the library is fostering an unsafe environment for the public. However, it has only been in the last four weeks that those complaints have turned into protocol directives for our security department."

"What kind of protocols? Directives from who?" Farrah asked, lifting her head from the computer she had carried with her to her spot on the vintage sofa near the coffee table.

"The protocols came from our security company, but the directives to put some in place came from the health department." Toby ducked his head and turned toward Sam as if he didn't want to say the next part out loud.

"Today a new one came in, mandating no trash or street debris be brought into the library."

"Trash and street debris." Layka's voice was tight with controlled anger. "That hateful woman is calling another human street debris."

"Hold up, sis. It wasn't the woman you clashed with this morning. Toby showed me the protocol when I came up. Your 'hateful woman' hadn't had time to get to the parking lot probably."

"Maybe not, but I've seen her here other times scowling at people."

"Layka, many of the unhoused population carry trash with them, such as cans to be turned in for recycling cash, and we have to hear these complaints without tinted glasses."

After fifteen minutes, the discussion had escalated, and Layka forced her hands to her side. She often gestured wildly when she was frustrated. She took a deep breath to gather her thoughts. The elevator pinged.

"Four real coffees—three hot, and one ridiculous," Dr. Sudha said, exiting the elevator and lifting the iced coffee from the drink container. She handed it to Jason, who reached for it from his chair.

Layka realized he was still laser-focused on her and Sam as he took the coffee without looking. "Thank you," he mumbled quietly, as if not to disturb the show.

Dr. Sudha looked at her, Sam, then Toby. "I see you've explained the call from the hospital's infectious disease department about closing the library."

"Close down the library? Wait, wait, wait, wait. What?" Layka turned fully to Toby, who was adjusting one of the monitors near the security desk that required no adjustment, but he continued to fiddle with it. "Toby hasn't told me anything yet. And certainly not that the hospital has threatened to close the library."

Toby looked at her. "The health department just asked that the infectious disease team review the risk as part of the new protocol. They haven't threatened to close the library completely."

"I certainly hope not. This is the Library of Congress's antiquities and reference library. You can't just close down that kind of public resource."

Sam piped in as if she felt Layka's growing frustration and anger was unwarranted. "They want Maya to work with the infectious disease team to establish some safety measures in order for people at high risk for communicable disease to use the library. Or she may have to close the library for certain periods of time in order to clean it at a level that will keep the space safe for the public."

Layka searched the faces in the room. All of them appeared focused on their coffee except Sam, who finished her coffee with a smooth swallow and a quick toss of the cup at the trash. Layka hated when she did that. She was effortless in her confidence, and it so often made Layka feel like her feelings weren't valid. Sam was the older sister, and Layka had looked up to her for so many things. It was then that she realized why she found it so difficult to call Dr. Sudha by her first name. She didn't always feel like an equal to people she admired. That thought and the issue at hand combined to make her body feel heavy and drained. She took a seat in the large, oversized chair in the reading nook to the right of the semicircle security desk. "So, they're saying, without any evidence, that this unhoused population is bringing in communicable disease. That's not fair. Some of them do more self-care than some of the stressed-out college students coming through here."

"No doubt," Toby offered. "We had one pass out in the stacks the day you were off. He hadn't slept in four days and probably hadn't showered or eaten in two days cramming for finals. His blood sugar was forty-eight when EMS from the hospital arrived."

"Exactly," Layka said.

"Yes, but the unhoused are the ones drawing attention," Sam said, leaning on the chest-high section of the security desk that started on the left side and stepped down in half-foot increments till it was even with the open part where Toby sat.

Layka noticed the design as she watched Toby start to nod in agreement as if Sam's energy walked down each step carrying her words.

"I'm with Layka about this issue," Dr. Sudha said. "They haven't said it outright, but much of their recommendations are geared toward controlling the number of unhoused people in the library."

"That isn't necessarily a bad thing." Sam held her hand up in Layka's direction.

Layka paused. The flash of memory, her sister lying prone fighting for her life after contracting COVID, made her anger calm but not dissipate.

"Hear me out. We have to be realistic about the risk that each of us poses to the public if we are carrying a communicable disease. I don't think it is unreasonable to think that people living on the streets are a higher-risk population for carrying such diseases."

"Did you feel that way when we were part of that population?" Layka said, watching for the dark shadow she knew would cross her sister's face.

"You guys were homeless?" Jason asked, swirling the ice in his coffee.

He said it as if seeing it as a socioeconomic success story rather than a judgment, but Layka could see Sam's jaw tighten. *Good. Maybe if she feels uncomfortable enough, she'll remember how good some of those unhoused people were to us during that time.* "Yes, we were," Layka said, splitting her attention to look at Jason but keeping her peripheral view on Sam, who moved toward the breakroom where Layka knew she would get another coffee to cover for leaving the space. Layka moved toward the reproduction Louis XV provincial settee. Its long sturdy legs with their feminine curves always made her feel supported when she sat there. "Several of the people, like Mildred, who was here this morning, showed us some safe places and helped us survive till Sam turned eighteen. Sam worked like a demon. We both did odd jobs and saved back the money so that when she became a legal adult, we could rent an apartment and she could apply to foster me since I was still sixteen."

Layka felt Farrah's arm around her shoulder.

"You never would explain what happened after your parents' car accident."

Layka was grateful for the little squeeze Farrah gave her with the acknowledgment of understanding. Now that she had said it out loud, she felt bad. Sam would be embarrassed that Farrah knew they had lived on the streets. *God, I'm an ass sometimes.* "Don't feel bad for us. We had some really great times." *Also, some very scary times,* Layka thought. "Some of those good times were directly related to people like Mildred. I will not have her ostracized from the library like she is an animal."

Dr. Sudha made her way to Farrah's side and sat. "I have the committee information in an email from the infectious disease group." Dr. Sudha sipped the coffee once before setting it on the small end table away from her laptop open on the sofa table in front of them.

Layka watched her lean toward the table as she typed. The woman had a striking beauty about her. Even now, sitting on the low couch, she looked pristine and elegant. Her knees were together beneath her A-line skirt and folded back toward the leather love seat at an angle that allowed her to sit upright on the edge. Sam would have looked like a catcher waiting on a slider ball if she were sitting there, and Layka wondered not for the first time about how different the two women she admired were from each other.

"Here it is," Dr. Sudha said as Farrah leaned toward her and appeared to be reading the email herself.

"Hey. That's interesting. She was in the library today."

"Great," Layka said, leaning toward them. "Don't tell me Grumpy-pants from this morning sits on a committee for infectious disease."

"No," Farrah said. "It's the cute blonde that had you drooling on the counter downstairs."

"I was not drooling. I was being helpful."

Farrah raised an eyebrow. "Hey—I came back from reference for a book I left and thought I was going to have to do one of those training sessions people show on social media with their dogs to get them to wipe their mouth after they drink their water." She made an exaggerated face. "You know, the ones with the big floppy jaws?"

"Shut up and scoot over."

Farrah did, and Dr. Sudha adjusted to create more space on the small seat.

The photos were front and center at the bottom of the email. Six photos with Times New Roman font under each one listing the name. *V. A. Summerhouse, MD. Pulmonology.* Layka read to herself before glancing at the photos of five other doctors with specialty degrees.

"It looks like an intelligent collection of medical personnel," Dr. Sudha said, touching the screen to bring the photos to the middle. "And the email says the committee was formed by infectious disease to address the rising concerns for the spread of communicable disease. That doesn't mean they are going to force us to not allow the unhoused in the facility."

"I don't know," Farrah said, looking at Layka then back to the screen. "That second paragraph changes everything."

Layka switched her focus from the beautiful portrait face staring back at her with those blue eyes and read the paragraph Farrah now pointed at. The paragraph that drew a line in the sand between them. The committee was coming for an inspection next week, and it was highly recommended that no unhoused population be present. Layka tugged absently on the end of her ponytail. Dr. Summerhouse had lied straight to her face. She wouldn't foster anything with a person like that.

CHAPTER TWO

"**S**UMMERHOUSE, YOU GOT A minute?"

Aven didn't turn at her best friend's voice. Instead, she leaned on the hospital lounge windowsill that faced the library. *That failure made me question so much of myself. I'm stronger now. More aware of who I am, what I want, and what I won't accept.* "Do you ever use the library next door?"

"I think I was over there once when we first came here for residency. God, that's been a while back. Why?"

I just felt the absolute clutch of my heart with a stranger who works there. "Just asking. What do you need?" Aven turned from the window.

Aven watched as Reynolds lowered the patient chart she had in her hand and twisted her head in interest.

"Give," Reynolds said with a grin. "You never 'just ask' about something."

Aven followed Reynolds's line of sight out the window as she walked over. The movement pulled them both back toward the glass. The September weather in DC had laid its claim to the landscape on this side of the library.

"You're never in the lounge, and now I find you here staring at the library asking if I ever use it. Talk to me, Summerhouse."

Aven let her eyes follow the strong lines of the maple tree. Its canopy was still full, but many of its burnt-orange leaves lay on the ground. "I've been asked to be on a committee looking at risk for communicable disease since this influx of respiratory patients over the last several weeks here in the DC area, and one of the areas listed as high risk is the library."

Reynolds turned toward her, leaning her back into the corner of the windowsill. Aven watched her with her peripheral vision. If she looked at Reynolds, she knew her friend would read the additional truth in her eyes.

Reynolds tapped her chin. "If you were only thinking about the library in the context of its role in communicable disease spread, you would be in your office on the computer doing research. Instead..."

Aven heard Reynolds's continued self-dialogue like comfortable background music as she watched the wind move the lower bushes in a sway of blended yellow and orange. Her divorce had been amicable. She and Carter were still friends—probably better friends for having realized their marriage had been a rebound retreat for both of them. Carter had been finding their full identity, and she had been rebounding from her first college breakup with a woman and struggling to understand why it hurt more than every other.

"You've met someone!" Reynolds blurted, pulling Aven from her thoughts.

Aven reluctantly shifted her eyes from the autumn landscape and smiled. Her best friend knew her well. Reynolds had decided to pursue research rather than patient care with her MD/PhD, and she was a savvy little sleuth. "I don't know that you could say I met someone. We haven't had a proper introduction, but she helped me find some resources I needed."

"I bet she did."

"Stop." Aven laughed. "I'm serious." She pointed at her laptop on the lounge table. "Simon just dropped an itinerary for our first visit to the library. I came in here so I could open it and think about the process in an open-minded way, not just locked in on the hospital's perspective. I've not had time to look at any of the committee emails."

"Oh, that's right. You're on call today. That's why you weren't on rounds."

"Why were you on rounds?"

"That's what I was coming to talk to you about. The lab identified a new strain of this virus, and Dr. Hindbrook asked me to discuss it on rounds with the students, who saw the patient this morning. This is the patient it was isolated in"—she waved the folder—"and I wanted some pulmonary perspective from you."

Aven's phone pinged. "That's the ER," she said, recognizing the notification tone a second before the hospital intercom announced a code blue in sector G1. "Can you talk on the run?"

"Absolutely. If you're headed there, it's a lung issue and may be related."

"Collapsed lung," Aven said and headed toward the stairs as she read the notification. "I'll probably have to put in a chest tube."

"Damn it, why do you always take the stairs? You know I'm in the fitness protection program and been hiding for years."

"It's quicker than waiting on the elevator, and besides, we're going down. You can handle it. Consider it your first step to a healthier you."

"Fine, but you only get the details my labored breathing allows."

Aven laughed as they hit the landing for the fourth floor and turned down the next flight. "What's the variant?"

"The variant's not unique. It's where it is."

"Okay, where?"

"On the COVID-19 conserved ion channel from SARS."

They hit the second-floor landing, and Aven almost slipped turning to look at Reynolds over her shoulder. Her face said it all. "It's one of the channels you've been researching."

"Yes."

"Shit." Aven picked up her pace and hit the first-floor stairs at a run. "Patients will get septic, and we will not be able to see the virus till it's too late."

Aven jerked the stairwell door open and dodged a radiology tech pushing the portable x-ray. The steady voice of Dr. Totto guided Aven to the correct room.

"Recheck the blood pressure manually after that dose of epi," Dr. Totto said to the nurse just as Aven came through the door. "Summerhouse, we're going to need a chest tube."

"I figured as much."

"The x-rays are up." Dr. Totto pointed, then turned back to the patient.

"Code blue room four," someone shouted from the door.

"God damn it," Totto said.

Aven turned from the x-ray. "Go start the code over there. I'll get a chest tube in and run this one."

"Vein collapsed, doc," Jess said, reaching for the crash cart. The paramedic could run a code as well as any doctor but always followed protocol. "You want her next epi in her intubation tube?"

Aven checked the monitor showing the patient's vitals and heart rhythm. "What was the manual blood pressure?"

"74/48," a nurse Aven didn't recognize said, reading from her records as she continued to document the code.

"Seth, get me an arterial line. Jess, give the next dose of epi in her endotracheal tube, and you take over managing the airway. Sarah, leave the airway to Jess and set up for me to do a chest tube on the left." Aven took a moment to glance at the door. Reynolds gave a nod. "Seth, give one of the blood samples you pull to Reynolds and send the rest to the lab with my protocol seven."

"Blood pressure has increased, 90/75," the document nurse said as Aven made the incision for the chest tube.

The epinephrine is working, but its vascular constriction raising her BP may not hold for long, Aven thought as she felt the tissue separate beneath her blade. "Give me verbal on all activity." She performed the systematic steps, then worked the Kelly forceps onto the tube and slid it inside and past the rib. The hum of the chaos was controlled, and Aven felt herself ease into the familiar as she listened to feedback, gave commands, and finished the procedure. "Connect the tubing to the system, Sarah, and turn on suction." Aven stepped back, not removing her sterile gloves till she could evaluate the tube's effectiveness. The patient's body habitus was overweight but not obese, so she didn't anticipate problems. She checked the patient's status. "Vital signs have stabilized, and we have a normal sinus rhythm. Seth, contact the ICU for a bed while I get the orders in the computer for transfer."

Seth gave a thumbs-up as he sat down at one of three computer terminals in the room. "You'll have to use the computer near the patient to put in orders. IT disconnected the one near the door this morning. There's a ticket in for it to be fixed," he said, smiling like, *Welcome to the circus.*

"All right, thanks." Aven scanned the cluster of debris status post code and tube placement that lay near the computer she would have to use. Still, Seth had taken the worst seat—he was a good kid and a sharp nurse.

"Labs are back from earlier, Summerhouse." Aven twisted her head at the voice of Marcus, the physician assistant that worked the ER. "Looks like the quick code response saved her kidneys. She's got renal insufficiency that may be new, but she's not in failure."

"Yet," Aven added.

"You said it, not me. I'm going in with Totto. Not looking as good over there, and I just sent mine up to the ICU. They're coming in stable and dropping fast."

Aven rolled her neck and looked at the suction machine. It was going to be a long day, but she had helped save one life for now.

"Document the time," she said to the record nurse as she removed the sterile gloves.

"They always come in threes," Jess said, moving to head out.

"Thanks for your help, Jess. You could do this with your eyes closed."

Jess smiled. "Maybe, but you just did. That's the first time I've had a doc run one completely verbal with their hand inside someone's chest."

"Let's hope it all holds. Be careful out there. You are the front-front line, and we need you healthy."

"Got it," Jess said, flipping her paramedic bag over her shoulder.

Sarah slid around the rollaway table and motioned to the opened chest tube kit that lay on it. "I'll bring another kit down for the crash cart. I'm headed to room two. I was down here to do a percussive neb treatment."

Aven nodded. "I'm glad you were here. I can tell when a respiratory therapist has done the intubation."

Sarah smiled. "By the way, I can't do pickleball next week. I'm attending a literary costume ball. You should come. You like to read, and you get to dress up like your favorite literary character."

Aven knew about the event but hadn't planned to attend. "That does sound like fun, but better than pickleball? I don't know."

"Good point. Let's do the morning pickleball and the costume ball that night. It would be great to have someone I know to go with—Steve is playing pool. Maybe you'll meet someone."

Aven's thoughts flashed to the librarian. Why did she keep thinking about her? She had enough on her plate without thinking about relationships. "Yes on the morning pickleball. Maybe on the costume ball, and a hard no on the meeting someone."

"Fair. I'll send you the info."

Aven began picking her way over to the computer near the patient's head. It was hard to see her face with everything in place, but she gave the woman's shoulder a squeeze before she sat down. She rolled the stool back and heard a crunch. "What?" She rolled forward and looked down behind her. "Oh no," she whispered, lifting the small cream clutch purse from the floor for a second time today.

CHAPTER THREE

LAYKA PUSHED THE BEER back to Sam, wiping the condensation on her jeans. "Look, I'd say I'm sorry, but that means little when I did it on purpose." She scanned the room to see who was working. She needed a beer, and Sam liked too much hops in hers.

"I know you did, and I was angry. Now I'm not sure what I feel."

Layka jerked her head back to Sam. Was Sam saying the word *feel*? Something really was wrong. She almost asked who had abducted her sister, but Sam picked at the label on the bottle and kept her eyes on the table. Layka stared, waiting, holding her breath as if air itself might tip Sam back from this important point.

"It makes my skin crawl. Not like creepy, but…"

"Exposed," Layka said, seeing it in the way her usually confident sister had huddled around her beer.

"Yeah." Sam lifted her beer and took a long pull before setting it down.

"Making our way for ourselves when our parents died is not something to be ashamed of, Sam. I'm proud of us, and especially you."

Sam shrugged as if it didn't matter, but Layka knew it did. She just didn't have all the pieces to know exactly why.

"If it means anything, I am sorry for how I said it and for bringing it up in front of Farrah. I know you like her, and that was partly your story to share with her, not mine."

"Farrah's okay."

"Oh, please," Layka said. "You two practically stop breathing when the other is in the room."

"Hi, Layka. Hi, Sam. I wasn't expecting you two tonight. You do know it's trivia night?"

"Hey, Erin. I didn't even think about it. We just wanted to unwind with a beer."

"Well, you're in luck. I saw you from the bar," Erin said, placing a blueberry beer on the table.

"Yes!" Layka lifted the beer in victory. "Thank you for reading my mind."

"Easy enough to do when I've known you forever. You want to order some food, or just have a drink?"

"Food," Sam said. "I'm starving."

"All right, I'll get an order in for your usual. I won't have time to chat tonight like I usually do when you're in here. Wing Night Wed is also trivia night, and it's a madhouse."

"No worries," Layka said. "I need to talk to this one anyway." She pointed her beer at her sister.

Sam pulled her beer in and wrapped her forearms around it, resting them like a box on the table. "I'm not giving any more information till you spill about the blonde Farrah mentioned you drooling over."

"First, I was not drooling. Second, I'm not interested. She may be pretty, but we have very different ideas."

"Such as?"

"She's listed on the committee with the infectious disease team investigating the library for the communicable disease issue."

Sam shrugged. "That sounds like it's part of her job."

"It may be part of her job to investigate, but she doesn't have to form opinions about the unhoused population and ostracize them before she's even started."

Sam grinned.

"What?" Layka sipped her beer and already knew the words that were coming. If her sister needed to open up about her feelings, Layka's problem was jumping to conclusions. She was working on it, but this was different. She had the email, and it clearly indicated the committee had already made a decision about the unhoused population being to blame. What if Summerhouse had been in the library that morning to investigate? The thought made her more irritated. If Summerhouse had just been pretending to be kind to Mildred to get some details for her investigation, then the whole morning was cast in a different light. "I know what you're thinking," Layka said, taking a sip of her beer. "But I'm seeing her whole interaction with Mildred as a way to build evidence for the committee's case against them."

"You don't know that."

She harumphed. "Well, put in perspective with the email they sent out, it makes sense. Say what you will about me being judgy, but I'm right nine times out of ten." She raised her eyebrows, challenging Sam to deny it.

When Sam just lifted her beer, Layka pressed. "Speaking of being right, let's talk about the elephant in the room when you and Farrah are in the same space."

Aven's phone pinged as she reached for the door on the fifth floor. She leaned her head back and blew a breath out, then looked at her phone. The red notification tag told her nothing. She was exhausted. It was almost seven p.m., and she'd been on call twelve hours. The five flights of stairs had helped her process the ER event and all that followed. She had just seen that woman this morning at the library looking perfectly fine. What had happened? She shook her head. She had assisted with one more code, but the rest of the day had been near misses, and eighty percent of them were lung issues that she'd been called for. *Focus, check the notification.* She looked at her phone as the door closed behind her. It was a text from Reynolds.

REYNOLDS: Have some preliminary results, are you available?

AVEN: I'm headed back to the lounge to get my laptop. Can you meet me there?

REYNOLDS: Yes, us normal humans use the elevator so I'll probably beat you there.

AVEN: Wanna put some real cash on that?

REYNOLDS: Not a chance. If you're willing to risk cash, that means you're already there. I know you girl.

Aven laughed, and it felt good. The tension she had been holding in her shoulders relaxed. She typed a laughing emoji and walked to the window in the lounge to view the library again. The sun had shifted and now highlighted a row of medium-sized autumn-red bushes that lined a pathway to an area that appeared to be designed for outside reading. Why hadn't she noticed that before? Sometimes the fast pace of medicine made her feel she was missing too much, that life was passing in a blur. The code had reminded her life could change in an instant. Maybe she should slow down, take some time to date, and even go out with friends more. She checked her watch and already had a message from Sarah in her email about the Literary Ball. It did sound like fun.

What she wanted was more time with the cute librarian. She let her mind wander. The brunette had glossy hair that she had pulled back in a low ponytail. She was dressed professionally in a pair of black-and-white gingham pants and a white sweater. Aven had watched her pull her fingers through the ends of her hair and figured it was a habit. She liked knowing something about the beautiful woman, but what she didn't like was that immediate attraction that had gotten her in trouble before. Not to mention the time it would take away from doing things like this committee, which was obviously very necessary if today's ER events were any indication. She looked again at the library before turning from the window when she heard the elevator ding. She bit the inside of her lip in thought as she listened to the footfalls in the hallway. She had read the email the committee chair had sent to the library and wasn't happy about Simon's sideways recommendation that no homeless people be in the library during the visit. She did not like people bringing preconceived ideology to research projects. Or to anything, for that matter. Her painful breakup in college happened because of preconceived, unfounded bias. She had learned her lesson about people like that. She walked away from them very quickly now. That thought made her smile. The librarian seemed ready to fight tigers to keep the library access available. She shouldn't feel this melancholy concern that there would be conflict. She and the librarian would be on the same team. They could look for answers to this problem together, with intelligence and evidence.

"What are you grinning at?" Reynolds paused in the doorway.

"Nothing. What've ya got?"

"We'll come back to that little lie." Reynolds tapped her tablet and walked toward the table. "Your ER patient has the virus variant. It makes it invisible to many of the screening tools we have. This buys the virus time to replicate at incredible speed and breach the respiratory system into the circulation. It's attacking every organ."

"Have you sent this to infectious disease?"

"Yes. A memo went out to all the departments. They are reporting to their respective channels."

"How contagious is it?"

"That's some good news. It originally didn't seem to be spreading fast."

"Really?"

"Well, that was early data. Today has me concerned that may not be accurate, but we will be weeks into this before we have enough testing completed to reevaluate."

Aven collapsed on the worn sofa and propped her feet on the coffee table corner. It was only then that she realized someone had left the television on in the lounge, on mute. She looked briefly for the remote. It was a politician giving a re-election spiel, and she had no patience for it today.

Reynolds lifted the remote from the counter near the sink and clicked it off. "Barton is going to have a stroke trying to get re-elected." She tossed the remote to Aven, who caught it and laid it on the table. "I've given you the scoop from the lab, now circling back to a happier face." She gestured at Aven's face as if outlining it. "You were smiling when I came in. What was that about?"

"It really is nothing. I just—the woman at the library keeps coming back to my mind." She shrugged. "And when she does, it makes me smile."

"That's not nothing." Reynolds made her way to the sofa and sat on the coffee table edge. "That's something, something." She propped her elbows on her knees and leaned forward, her chin cupped in her hands.

"Shut up," Aven said, laughing. "You sound like your sister."

Reynolds shrugged and leaned back. "True. So, give. What has you so drawn to her?"

"I don't even know. We only talked briefly. Maybe it was the way she read my mind, knew what I needed, and helped me locate it in a matter of minutes."

"Was she cute?"

"You know, I called her that in my mind earlier, but it's more like classy than cute. She has this depth to her. I don't even know what that means, but I feel it."

"And you like it, apparently, because you want to know more about her. That's why you've been gazing longingly at a certain brick building outside the lounge window."

"Apparently. Oh, what am I saying. I don't have time to be thinking about getting to know someone. Especially not a librarian at a facility that is practically under investigation by our committee."

"Eesh. That is not going to go well."

"See, that's what I'm saying." Aven sucked in a deep breath and pulled her legs from the coffee table.

"Wait. If she's the librarian and you're going to be doing an investigation for the infectious disease committee, it will give you time together. You don't have to be enemies. She sounds intelligent."

"Yes, but we both know how quickly things are polarized when opposite ideas collide, and Simon is leading this committee like a witch hunt on the homeless. It is really strange."

"Have you said something to him?"

"I have an appointment with him the first of next week. The day before we visit the library."

"You'll stew all weekend about it. I know that seeing prejudice hits close to your heart, my friend."

"You're right—it had me angry as soon as I read his email. How do people do that? Look at someone or give them a label and decide who they are or what decisions they will make without communicating with them or getting to know them." Aven looked up when Reynolds tapped her leg. She realized she had been twisting the ring she wore on her index finger around.

"Carter gave that to you?"

"Yeah. They said it was to remind me to be myself."

"Ahh. That's why it has both gold and silver."

Aven shook her head but couldn't speak. Carter was her ex, but they had helped each other face a lot about themselves and grow into the people they now were. "Carter trusted me." Aven looked up at her friend. "That allowed me to be my complete self."

"I'll never understand why people want to mistrust someone because they are attracted to men and women. It's not fair."

"It isn't, but I'd almost come to expect it after college."

"Is Carter coming in for Christmas this year?"

"I think so, but I haven't talked to them this week. Work has them in areas where signal isn't always the best."

"Well, when you do, tell them I said hello. I think it was Christmas last year when I saw Carter last."

"It was." Aven snort-laughed, recalling the memory. "You tried to convince us we could still play pickleball in the snow."

"It wasn't a bad idea. We could practice our volleys."

"You're a nut. Oh, but that reminds me. Sarah isn't playing Thursday night next week. I think we might both play Thursday morning. I'll see if she'll bring her husband so we'll have four. I know you play morning and night when you can."

"Why are you bailing?"

"She invited me to a literary costume ball. I haven't looked at the details, but it sounds fun. Why don't you join us?" Aven pulled her phone out and forwarded the email.

"I'll think about it, but you know I don't play as well in the mornings."

"Oh, please." Aven gave Reynolds's knee a shove with her foot. "You play in your sleep."

Reynolds laughed. "Hey, Laney would probably enjoy the costume thing. She reads even more than I do."

"I think it's open to the public, but check the email. I don't even know where it's going to be located, but it would be great if she came. I haven't seen your sister in months. We haven't had a girls' night out in a while."

"She's in Barcelona on a shoot but coming home. If she's here in time, I'll show her the email and let you know."

Reynolds stood, and Aven watched as her friend moved toward the door. It would be nice for all of them to be together. Of course, she was the fifth wheel in the group. Sarah had Stephen, Reynolds had her sister—if she made it in on time—and Aven would be arriving alone. That hadn't felt so lonely just days ago.

She leaned back into the sofa and rested her head on the cushion. Her mind wandered to the brunette with the blue eyes. Not the same blue as her own, but blue—she was certain of that. She found herself smiling again, and that felt nice. Maybe Reynolds was right. They didn't have to be enemies.

Aven closed her eyes and felt some of the exhaustion of the day lift.

CHAPTER FOUR

L AYKA LOADED THE REFERENCE cart with books to return to the stacks, trying to occupy her time before the meeting. It felt like a Monday for sure.

"I'll see you tonight," Sam said, heading toward the glass doors.

"Oh, sure, you leave before the fun gets started."

"I know better than to stick around when you're on a mission. I hope this committee knows what they're up against."

"They'll know soon enough." Layka tapped the computer and a stack of papers beside the monitor.

"No one can say you haven't done your homework on the issue."

Layka gave a broad smile. "Don't send me an email indicating your prejudice against a group of people and not expect me to bring you the facts."

"Go get 'em, baby sister." Sam paused as the doors slid open. "Maybe go easy on the one Farrah said you were making eyes at the other day."

"I wasn't making eyes at anyone, and I'll be harder on her. She lied to my face."

"What? I didn't know about that."

"Yeah, she said she wasn't here that day to kick out the unhoused, then I see the email that says they essentially plan to do just that. You know that doesn't sit well with me. Just be honest. Don't lie to me."

"Ooh. Sorry, sis. Give her hell."

"Not necessary. I'll just give her the facts." She tapped the collection of papers and journals again.

"Yeah, but I know your heart. That open, helpful, smiling girl she met the other day has been replaced by a serious, here's-the-facts, not-letting-you-in girl she will not be expecting."

Layka shrugged. Sam wasn't wrong.

Sam gave a final wave as the glass doors closed behind her.

Layka checked her phone for the time. 10:47 a.m. The committee was scheduled to arrive at eleven. Dr. Sudha had texted that she would be arriving a little late due to an obligation at the White House running over.

"Hello. I realize I'm early."

Layka jumped at the voice that she surprisingly recognized. "Dr. Summerhouse. Yes, you are early. No problem. Saying one thing and doing another is no longer a surprise."

"I didn't mean to startle yo—Excuse me, what?"

Layka pulled her eyes away from the fire in those blue eyes. She couldn't breathe for a moment. She placed a hand at her stomach, pressing against the flutter. This was not the kind of woman she wanted to feel butterflies over. *What's wrong with you?* She took a deep breath. "Look, I understand you're a doctor and I get how important it is to create safety for the public when it comes to disease and the spread of infection, but the data doesn't support increased risk from having the unhoused in the library. I've organized information for the committee's review." She pointed to the monitor then lifted the stack of journal articles on the counter.

"I never said it did, and I'm surprised how quick you are to judge."

"Exactly. You said that wasn't your purpose, but look around. Mildred's not here, nor are two of the other unhoused regulars that consistently show up to read. The committee's first email was clear about its stance, and the second practically outlined a way to make it difficult for the unhoused to have access. Your plan appears to have worked."

"My plan? Mildred—"

Layka watched the anger shift to frustration on Dr. Summerhouse's face. What was she hiding? The thought made her angry. "What about Mildred?"

Voices pulled the attention of both women as the door behind the shelves near the hospital entrance clacked closed and a group of four made their way into the area. Two were in scrubs similar to Dr. Summerhouse's, and two wore professional attire. Only Dr. Summerhouse wore her white coat. It fit nicely, she noticed, and when Summerhouse turned, Layka had a view of the tailored style in the back. *What was she going to say about Mildred?* Layka wondered as Dr. Summerhouse moved away from the counter toward the group.

Layka watched her walk straight to the man the email photo identified as Dr. Simon Burnder. Their conversation was quiet, and Layka watched the faces of the others, trying to read the conversation.

The front glass doors slid open, pulling everyone's attention to Dr. Sudha moving briskly through, briefcase in hand. "Thank you for your patience," she said, joining Layka behind the counter. "We have a study room set up for the meeting, and Layka prepared some resources for your review." She waved toward the hallway behind the counter that led to the elevators, offices, and two of the group study rooms.

Layka tried not to watch as Dr. Summerhouse made her way to the door behind the shelves that led to the hospital while the rest of the team followed Dr. Sudha. She gathered the journals and paperwork, turning to follow the group down the hallway. Disappointment battled with frustration and anger. She did not expect Dr. Summerhouse to run away, but then again, what did she expect? She shook her head, wishing her chest didn't feel a different pang of disappointment.

Layka bounced from her seat like it was a springboard at the Olympics. Dr. Burnder had explained at the beginning of the meeting that Dr. Summerhouse had come early because she needed to round on a few critical patients, and she had just let him know she would not continue on the committee if the approach to collaboration wasn't changed. That had fostered a positive conversation about how to define and tackle the problem. They didn't have a solution, but Dr. Summerhouse had made an impact, and Layka had clearly misjudged her. Layka had twisted and turned in her seat the entire meeting, itching to get to the hospital and apologize. Even the importance of the issue at hand hadn't kept her mind from drifting to the recollection of what she had read in Dr. Summerhouse's eyes. She thought it had been anger, or maybe frustration. In retrospect, she could see hurt. She had so blatantly judged the doctor's motives based on...what? An email from a colleague? "I'm taking my break," she said quickly as she passed Dr. Sudha standing at the door chatting with Simon.

Dr. Sudha nodded, and Layka practically ran the hallway toward the front desk. She'd grab some lunch from the hospital cafeteria to give her time to consider how to find Dr. Summerhouse in such a large hospital. She sprinted the walkway and turned beyond the bushes to enter the breezeway that led to the hospital entrance. She slowed as she approached the rotating door at the main entrance. She brushed the sleeves of her black turtleneck and pulled the cinched waist over the braided black belt of her dress pants. She usually wore jeans on antiquities rotation day because they were in and out of the basement, but she had dressed more professionally for the meeting today. *Not that you acted very professionally,* she told herself as she checked her reflection in the glass door. She and Sam looked nothing alike, and seeing herself in the glass reminded her of how each of them reflected their parents. She had her father's blue eyes and wavy brown hair that she usually straightened, while Sam had their mom's brown eyes and brown hair that had so much curl she kept it in a tight bun most of the time. *I miss you both,* Layka thought as she pushed the door into its rotation.

Layka had to admit Medfirst Washington was one of the most beautiful hospitals she'd ever been in. The lobby on the main floor was expansive, with a welcoming fireplace that was massive enough to block visibility to the bank of elevators behind it, but its light gray stone and white marble created a cozy, welcoming space with the seating area to its front. There was a Starbucks to the right and a long, honey-colored wood information desk to the left.

"Jared?" Layka said, shocked to see one of the unhoused who often visited the library standing at the hospital information desk.

"Ms. Silva, are you here to see Mildred?"

"Mildred is here?"

"Yes, ma'am. They say she's on fourth floor." He handed her the note from the information desk with the room number written down.

She read it. "I'll walk up with you."

Layka stayed by the door as Jared entered the room. Mildred smiled at him, and Layka felt a piece of her heart crumble at the weakness in that determined smile. Mildred guarded her smiles, and for her to make the effort while she appeared to be so weak spoke volumes.

"Ms. Silva is here," Jared said, turning as if expecting Layka to be on his heels.

"Hi, Mildred. I didn't know you were here. How are you doing?"

"Much better now, but I'll be even better tomorrow if my doctor agrees to take this out." Mildred pointed at a tube that ran from her chest.

"Oh my, Mildred. You had to have a chest tube?"

"Yes, but it hasn't been as frightening as it would have been if I hadn't had the doctor I met at the library."

"The doctor you met at the library?"

Layka sat down on the arm of the chair near the bed. Dr. Summerhouse had said something about Mildred. No, she stopped before she said anything. "She couldn't say anything because of HIPAA."

"What did you say?" Mildred asked, shifting in her bed.

"Is your doctor about my height with blond hair and blue eyes?"

"Yes. The one you helped at the library."

"She was there again today, and I think she wanted me to know you were here, but there are protocols in place to protect your privacy, and she couldn't tell me..." *Or defend herself from my verbal assault,* Layka thought, recalling their conversation. "I came here to find her."

"Good luck. She's been pulled out of here twice to assist with other patients having breathing trouble. It seems this virus is hitting a lot of the people in our home space."

Layka leaned back against the upright wing of the wingback chair. "If I leave a note with you, will you give it to her when she stops by for rounds?"

"Sure." Mildred handed her a napkin from underneath her lunch tray.

Layka took it, found a pen next to a Kleenex box in the drawer of the little table near the bed and began to write. *A napkin seems like the perfect place to start to clean up the mess I've made. I owe you an apology. If you are agreeable, I'd like a second try at our meeting. I'll throw in a cup of library coffee.*

She handed the note to Mildred, who folded it as if not wanting to pry into her affairs. "You can read it," Layka said, realizing how much Mildred had impacted her life. She was sixteen when her world fell apart, and this stranger had been there for her when Sam could not. She was family—why had that not occurred to her till now? "I was an ass," Layka said, feeling for the moment that it extended beyond her error with Dr. Summerhouse.

"I've never known you to be such a thing." Mildred folded the note. "I'll read it later, if you want me to."

Layka paused in her effort to reply. Her immediate response was *sure*. Her quick responses had gotten her in trouble once already today. She looked at the note now tucked in Mildred's book. *Sure* indicated she didn't care if Mildred read the note or not, and that wasn't real. She wanted Mildred to read it. Wanted someone to know...know what? Know that she was relieved to find out Dr. Summerhouse might be the good person she had perceived her to be day one, or know how judgmental she had been to forget that first meeting and draw conclusions from an email? *Both*, Layka thought, realizing how strongly she felt about it. "I want you to read it," she said, taking in the brown eyes of the woman now giving her one of those gentle smiles. "I actually want your help, if you are willing."

"If I can help you, sweet child, I will."

The words made tears prick at Layka's eyes. How did this kind, gentle woman survive on the streets, and why? That question put the whole issue at hand in a new perspective. As much as Mildred had been part of helping her and Sam learn the ropes during their time on the streets, she had not had the time or made the time to learn more about the people who shared her struggle. It was obvious whatever this virus was had attacked Mildred, who was homeless. She couldn't discount or ignore that fact, and if something in the environment of the homeless population had changed and put them at higher risk, to not explore it could be deadly to many people. She explained briefly about the situation and how she hoped to talk with Dr. Summerhouse about ways the library and the hospital team could work together without ostracizing the unhoused population. "Have they said how long they anticipate your stay for recovery?"

"Well, I have three doctors, and they've all said something different..." She winked at Layka, then opened her book, adjusting Layka's folded note so she could see the page. "But my money is on the lung doctor knowing what's best."

Layka smiled, stood, and leaned over to give Mildred's wrinkled brow a kiss. "I'll stop by tomorrow and check on you. I'm sorry I didn't take more time to get to know you when you were helping us. That's not the philosophy of life I want to foster."

Mildred squeezed Layka's hand resting on the bedrail. "Philosophical ideals are a luxury of people not trying to survive."

Layka turned her hand to squeeze Mildred's. "I'm not trying to survive now. I'm going to do better."

CHAPTER FIVE

"LET'S TAKE THIS DOOR, it's closer to the elevator," Aven said, pushing on the bar with her elbow as she balanced the cafeteria to-go box of food and her drink.

Reynolds paused, catching the door with her back and darting a look around the cafeteria. "Who is it?"

"What are you talking about? Come on! Stop gawking and close the door."

"You always take the door near the stai—hmm, who is that? Tall, brunette, confident walk, sharp outfit with black on black. Sleek, sophisticated...yeah, you're on the run." Reynolds let the door close and stepped into the hallway. "I'll help you slip away this time, but I want the story."

"I couldn't see from out here. I don't know who you're talking about."

"Come on, I saw the about-face you did to push through the door. You saw sleek-sophisticated and ran for it."

"I don't want to talk about it."

"Hey." Reynolds set her food box on a hall windowsill and pulled Aven's arm. "Whoa. That's a look I haven't seen in years. Can we pause? I'm concerned."

Aven set her drink down on the sill and turned to her friend. Her heart felt so weird. Tight, aching, like she'd lost something and there was nothing to lose. She'd met this woman exactly twice. "She's one of the librarians I met, and I thought it might be nice to get to know someone outside of the hospital for a change."

"Okay, I'm with you. This is the woman you met at the library." Reynolds smacked her forehead. "You had the meeting this morning, asked her out, and she said no."

"No," Aven said. "I wouldn't ask her out at a committee meeting. And if I did and she said no, that would be okay."

"All right, then I'm lost because the look on your face was reminiscent of—"

"Please don't say her name." Aven set her box of food down. She was no longer hungry. That was it. That was what had her stomach feeling like her guts had twisted inside out. She rubbed her eyes with her index finger and thumb. "It kind of feels like that. She looks beautiful, but on the inside, she is judging you without context."

"Ohhhh."

Aven took a seat on the next windowsill, which was lower but just as wide as the center one. "I've avoided people like that as a rule of thumb, and I don't plan to change my policy now."

Reynolds took a seat. "I get it, and I support you in that."

Aven was grateful for her friend's understanding. Reynolds knew her history, and she didn't have to explain.

Reynolds tapped her leg. "Let's take our lunch to my office, and we can make a plan for how you're going to navigate the next few weeks of this investigation without tying yourself in knots."

"Thanks, but I'm really not hungry. Give my lunch to your coworker who likes to take home all the leftovers. I'm going to check on a few patients."

"All right, but now I'm all in on the Literary Ball on Thursday, and Sarah and I are going to snag you a dream date."

Aven smiled. It would be nice to go out with her friends. She would pass on the dream date, as her heart felt threatened already. "Sounds like a plan. Text the group chat so we can plan our costumes with Sarah." That would give her the space to shoot down their dream date plans.

She stood and walked past the elevator toward the stairs. She knew seeing Layka made her think of Mildred, but she had been planning to round on her after lunch anyway, so why not do it now?

Aven climbed the stairs, trying to keep her mind off the librarian. *Reynolds is right—sleek and sophisticated.* But the catch in her chest reminded her of the heartbreak with people who judged so quickly. *It isn't worth it*, she told herself as she passed the door to the second floor. *Yep, keep climbing. Sleek and sophisticated is not the one for you.* But Aven's mind continued to replay the morning's events. As she turned up the last flight of stairs, she mentally kicked herself for the emotional high she had given free rein after their first encounter. That had led to the excited anticipation she had felt when entering the library this morning and made the disappointment after Layka's cutting words feel so much worse. *That part was on me*, she thought, deciding she would guard against letting her attraction to the woman govern her decisions. "Back to my policy of keeping distance between me and people who think it is okay to throw around unfounded accusations and judgments," she said as she reached for the fourth-floor door. A rush of sadness made her hand falter, and she pressed her palm to the door, taking a deep breath. "Regardless of how attracted to them you are," she said as she pulled the door open and walked onto the fourth floor.

Aven knocked on the doorframe. "Hi, Mildred. Did you rest well last night?"

"I did." Mildred laid her book on the lunch table across her lap and scooted herself up more solidly against the raised head of the bed. "I've had some visitors today." She pointed toward a man sitting in the corner. "This is Jared."

"Hi, Jared."

"Hello," he said but didn't look from the window, where he watched two birds. Aven wondered now if Layka had been at the hospital to see Mildred. Probably not. Layka had not indicated she knew Mildred—Wait, had she? Aven held the bed rail as she racked her mind to recall the part of the conversation where her frustration at Layka for thinking she didn't care had almost led to her slip up and disclose that Mildred was in the hospital and that she was concerned about her. She bit the inside of her lip in thought and then remembered where she was. Her focus was Mildred, not the librarian with the penchant for judging people.

"I had another friend drop by earlier. She asked me to give this to you."

Aven watched as the woman lifted her book, pulled a folded napkin out, and handed it to her.

She opened it slowly as her eyes tracked from the paper in her hands to the woman now reading her book.

Dr. Summerhouse,

A napkin seems like the perfect place to start to clean up the mess I've made. I owe you an apology. If you are agreeable, I'd like a second try at our meeting. I'll throw in a cup of library coffee.

Aven found herself smiling but pushed it away when she noticed Mildred watching her. "Thank you," she said, turning toward the sink to wash her hands. "Let me check that tube and we can talk about your progress."

"She's there Monday through Friday, eight till five." Mildred laid her book down again and gave Aven the most penetrating stare.

"She told you what she wrote?"

"No, but she asked me to read it. She realizes you two can be on the same team. She missed that the first go-round, and it sounds like she is sorry about that."

"It does sound like that." Aven hated that her heart betrayed her by the way it felt so happy at the words. She had promised to protect herself, and she wouldn't go back on that. She could work with Layka, but any thought of something beyond that was off the table. At least she didn't have to worry about the awkward part of figuring out if Layka was interested in women. "We have another committee meeting scheduled. I think we can approach the project better this time." *And a project colleague is all I'm open to with Layka the librarian,* Aven thought as she checked the tube and Mildred gingerly leaned forward so she could listen to her lungs. "Can you take a really deep breath?"

Mildred complied.

Aven shifted her stethoscope, and Mildred gave another valiant effort. "I know the tube is more than uncomfortable." She squeezed Mildred's shoulder with her right hand as her left shifted the stethoscope again. She was not pleased with the data Reynolds had brought to her recently. There was a disproportionate number of homeless people impacted by this virus, and they had nothing to go on as for why.

CHAPTER SIX

L AYKA AVOIDED THE MANHOLE as she turned off Pennsylvania
Avenue onto Constitution. She had decided to walk to the literary
costume ball. She was a character from a contemporary romance, so it
wasn't as if she was in full cosplay parading through Washington—even
if the blond wig on her head felt a tad ridiculous. She had her book in
hand, which she thought was kind of a neat idea the event had promoted:
Bring the book your character came from, and that was your ticket to
the event. She rubbed the blue cover and traced over the character's
cream jacket, so similar to the one she wore now. The book reminded
her of Mildred reading in the hospital. Dr. Summerhouse had made no
contact since their conflict on Monday, and Mildred had given her the
scoop on Summerhouse's less-than-enthusiastic reception to the note.
Layka sighed. It had only been three days and they were scheduled for
another meeting, so there was no reason to think Dr. Summerhouse
wouldn't accept her apology and allow them to work together on this
project. *So, why do I feel so anxious?* She made a right to walk in between
the Capitol and the Jefferson Building. Many people didn't realize the
Jefferson Building was part of the Library of Congress, much less know
about the ancillary buildings such as hers that housed specialty resources.
Her phone pinged, and Layka immediately knew that Farrah would
probably be late. Traffic looked horrible.

FARRAH: I'm on my way but traffic uughhh—I'll meet you inside.

Layka smiled at being correct, but her mood quickly dimmed at the thought of entering the event alone. She steeled herself and tried to present a confident air as she entered the building.

She turned in a circle as her eyes appreciated the beauty of the Grand Hall. She read the gold engraved words *Library of Congress* over an archway. The stone and marble created a grandeur that never seemed to fade. She checked the steps leading past the bronze statue, looking for Farrah. Her eyes landed on Purdel, an attractive woman with pixie-cut blond hair and sharp eyes. They'd been out two times, and Layka was certain she had managed to get only two sentences into the conversation at each of them. Purdel was nice and fun, which was why there had been two dates, but Layka didn't have the strength to fight for the floor every time they went out.

"Hi, Layka. How've you been?"

"Great, I've been—"

"You look amazing. I've been crazy busy too. So, I get it."

Layka laid her book on a small cocktail table and settled in for Purdel's update. She would be here for a while. She felt her mind drifting as she scanned the room again for Farrah. *There she is*, Layka thought, seeing Farrah enter through the large columns. She raised an arm to wave her over, but someone with their back to her grabbed Farrah instead. Layka sighed, and the sound of it against the backdrop of Purdel's continued monologue almost made her laugh. She was saying something about being overseas, and Layka thought about her time in the Peace Corps—not that she'd had the opportunity to share that with Purdel—so she tuned in to listen to her. She was a nice person. Layka's mind had just fully returned to the conversation when someone bumped her shoulder.

"Excuse me, I'm so sorry," a brunette said, pulling her phone down from taking pictures and turning toward her. The woman's brown hair was a wig, similar to her own in style if not color, but those blue eyes were ones she recognized immediately. *Dr. Summerhouse*. Her mind leaped to thoughts of the Indian Ocean, which she had seen during her time in the Peace Corps. Her eyes were that same blue. Maybe it was just her mind tying together her previous memories with the physical onslaught of something so beautiful, but her thoughts were tangled and her words came out the same way. "You're beautiful. I mean...it's beautiful there. Your eyes remind me..." Layka closed her eyes and stopped speaking. When she opened them, Summerhouse was staring at her. Her expression was thoughtful, and those eyes were still stunningly blue.

"It looks like we have arrived as the characters in the same book." Summerhouse laid her copy of *Kiss the Girl* on top of Layka's and smiled. "Allow me to introduce myself. I'm Jessica, and you must be here as Brooklyn."

Layka laughed, and everything inside of her felt warm. Then she spotted a redhead moving toward them like she was on a mission. Of course Summerhouse had a date for the event. *A girlfriend?* Only one way to find out. "And, I think your girlfriend might be looking for you."

Layka watched Summerhouse's face twist in curiosity, then both she and Purdel followed Layka's line of sight, looking over the doctor's shoulder.

"Her red hair looks too real to be a wig," Purdel offered.

"It is gorgeous," Layka said. "Oh, and this is Purdel," Layka added in Summerhouse's direction, realizing she hadn't introduced her. "She's a sales team ma—"

"I'm the sales team manager at Treetle's, just a block up the road." Purdel stuck her hand out, but her eyes were still on the redhead approaching.

"It's real all right," Summerhouse said, ignoring Purdel's hand that had no attention connected to it. Instead, she turned the focus of those blue eyes on Layka. "That's Dr. Reynolds, my best friend. She was determined to represent Chelsea Cartwright."

"From *Like They Do In the Movies*?"

Summerhouse nodded, and her smile made her eyes look brighter—if that was even possible.

"I love that book." Layka wondered if some of the exuberance with which she said it revealed her joy that Dr. Reynolds wasn't Dr. Summerhouse's girlfriend. Layka felt a criticism on her tongue about the swagger Dr. Reynolds carried and pulled it back. It was confidence like her sister carried, and her quick critique came from wanting to have it herself. Layka pulled her eyes from Summerhouse's face, trying to regain some composure. *Focus on the good emotions, not the ones you still need to work on,* she thought, turning her mind back to Dr. Summerhouse. She was standing really close. That cranked her heart rate up. She adjusted the belt on her cream coat. Her heart was racing with excitement, and they'd only talked about some fictional characters from books they both enjoyed.

"Will you be at the library for the meeting?"

"Yes, I'm—"

"She works at the library," Purdel interjected.

Layka watched the smile on Summerhouse's face draw into a tight line as she turned toward Purdel. "I feel very strongly about not judging people out of context. I don't want to think that you are someone who disregards the value of Layka's words, so I would like to point out that you have interrupted and spoken over her twice now."

"I did. I have." Purdel looked at Layka with a surprise Layka could hardly believe.

How could she not know she was doing it? Layka thought, then Summerhouse's words about judging out of context sank in, and she felt a little more empathy. *We all have our little habits, tendencies.* She opened her mouth to say *It's okay,* but it wasn't okay, so instead she looked at Summerhouse even though she was speaking to Purdel. "We all have our flaws. We just have to work on them."

"Absolutely. Man, I'm really sorry," Purdel said, running her hand through her hair and looking out at the crowd of people as if she were seeing something completely new. "I'm going to get something to drink. Can I get you two anything?"

"I'm good, thank you," they said in unison as Purdel moved away.

Layka noticed that Reynolds had stopped and was standing in line at the table serving drinks. Layka's stomach flipped like a kid finding out school had been canceled. She rubbed her stomach at the little surge of happiness that hit when you realized you were going to have time to do something you actually wanted to do.

"I apologize for the way I judged your role on the committee. I want to keep the library safe, but I don't want it to come at the expense of a demographic of people who have limited resources."

"Thank you," Aven said, lifting her book from the table, then laying it back down and flashing those sincere blue eyes back to Layka. "Apology accepted. I've had some bad experiences with people who judged me prematurely, and it hits me hard. Can we agree to a restart as two people ready to forge a plan for the community's safety and progress without discrimination?"

Layka liked how that sounded yet also appreciated that it created a very structured outline for their path forward. Two people forging a plan for the community. Work pals. Layka bit her lip, recognizing the little tug of curiosity in her mind that she both did and didn't like. She had been immediately attracted to Dr. Summerhouse on day one. Now, Summerhouse had stepped in and volleyed for her voice in a respectful way to Purdel, and they were going to be colleagues on a committee fighting for something so near to her heart that she was afraid Summerhouse would become someone too central for her to pull back from. That, she could not do—especially with a woman who had clearly drawn a boundary. "Want to talk about that, Dr. Summerhouse?"

"Call me Aven. Can we find a place to sit down?"

"I know a place where it's a little quieter." Layka headed to a hallway off the center floor. She lifted a rope and directed Aven inside.

"Wow." Aven stepped into the long rectangular room that had fireplaces on both ends. "Is it okay to sit here?" She pointed at the ornate table and chairs.

"Yes. It's closed off because it's a meeting room for congressional members, not to protect the furniture. Though, it is antique."

Aven carefully pulled a chair back and took a seat, crossing her legs.

Layka tried not to stare, but Aven was captivating, and the way she positioned her chair and sat forward spoke volumes about her willingness to listen and not just speak. *Finally, someone who wants to hear my voice, and all I'm interested in is every detail about her.*

Layka took the seat at the head of the table because Aven had angled her chair as if she anticipated her sitting there. *Isn't that interesting...* Layka leaned her elbows on the table, propping her chin in her hands and giving Aven her full attention. "I'm all ears," she said, tugging at her own earlobe. "Tell me about it."

"It's only happened twice, but they were significant relationships." Aven ran her finger along the gold line engraved in the red velvet runner on the center of the table. "It has impact when people you care about judge your bisexuality as lack of commitment, or worse—not real."

Layka sat back in her chair. She had asked the question thinking about their new team plan for the community, but looking back, her question had been open to interpretation regarding the bad personal experiences Aven had alluded to. Layka just hadn't expected this calm, reserved woman to open up. She touched her chest at the feeling she had of being trusted with such important information. "That is unfair." She reached out and squeezed Aven's hand as it traced circles on the velvet.

Aven looked up, holding Layka's eyes with a stare that said she had avoided more episodes by avoiding people like her. People who were quick to judge first and ask questions later.

"I meant what I said. I am sorry about yesterday," Layka said, realizing that her hand was still wrapped over Aven's and that Aven had stopped tracing the runner, but she didn't move her hand. She liked the feel of Aven's skin under her fingertips.

"I do appreciate that. I realize this issue is very important to you. I get that."

"I know you do. Mildred told me how wonderful you have been. She trusts you a great deal."

"I don't take that for granted. Which reminds me, you may want to stop by the hospital and talk to Mildred about being on her HIPAA form. If she's agreeable, it would allow us to work together more freely to make sure she heals and is safe when it's time to transition out of the hospital."

"Oh my goodness," Layka said, her hands flying to her face and pressing her cheeks. "How did I not think of that?"

"Why would you?"

Layka thought about her and Sam's period of homelessness, about how much Mildred had helped them both, and about how she could possibly repay Mildred's kindness, and she made a decision. She opened her mouth to share with Aven about their time on the streets, but a noise came from the hallway, followed by a voice. "Mind if we join Camelot?" Reynolds asked, gesturing at the table.

"Hey, Reynolds," Aven said, looking at Layka for confirmation as she spoke. "We'll head out to you."

Layka felt her head bob in assent, but her body was reluctant to leave the quiet bubble they had created together. Would this be forgotten tomorrow when they sat at a table with colleagues and hard decisions had to be made? She was preparing to stand when Aven passed behind her and gave her shoulder a squeeze. She could feel every fingertip create a tingle in her shoulder despite the thickness of her costume coat.

CHAPTER SEVEN

A VEN PULLED HER SHIRTTAIL up and wiped her face. "My God, what's the humidity today? I thought it was September."

Sarah's husband, Steve, shaded his eyes from the sun. "I, of course, unlike the rest of you pickleball rebels, checked the weather. It's eighty-seven degrees, and humidity will hit ninety-one percent before the storms start around lunchtime."

"If you had a true pickleball heart, the weather wouldn't matter," Reynolds said.

"Don't let him fool you." Sarah tossed the pickleball across the net to Aven. "He only checked because he's still dehydrated from his night of food-poisoning celebration."

Aven grimaced. "Yikes. Maybe you shouldn't be out here."

"That's the true evidence of my pickleball heart. Now serve that ball before I pass out."

Aven and Reynolds laughed, but Sarah gave him an eye roll. "Don't worry about him. Somebody passed up their night at the Literary Ball to keep him hydrated last week." She was smiling, but Aven could tell she was disappointed she missed the event.

"Three-seven-one," Aven said.

"Three-seven-two," the other three all chimed at once.

"What did we miss last week?" Sarah asked, shifting her weight from foot to foot in anticipation of Aven's serve. "Did Aven fall and hit her head?"

Aven saw Reynolds grin but didn't offer an answer. Reynolds would chime in and spill the beans only if Aven opened up the conversation.

Steve adjusted his hat. "Yeah, what's up with that? You never forget the score, and you two are usually two points ahead." He looked at his pickleball paddle as if only now realizing his team was ahead.

"You missed a lovely night at the Library of Congress," Aven said. She served the ball with a gentle underhand, causing it to drop just beyond the kitchen with little bounce, and Sarah had to race to get it, popping it up. Reynolds responded with a slam down the middle.

"We're back," Reynolds sang, walking back to the opposite line as Aven smiled and prepared for her next serve.

She stepped back behind the line. "Actually, I restored the work relationship with the librarian spearheading the collaboration with infectious disease on this spreading virus variant. Four-seven-two."

Sarah hit a solid return, and Reynolds volleyed. "And she does mean spearheading. It's clear our fearless leader has, for once, given someone else the lead."

Sarah and Steve both half swung, half retreated, and missed the ball. "Now you're just trying to distract us," Sarah said. "No more of this delicious story till lunch."

Aven laughed but was slightly disappointed. Saying it out loud allowed her mind to be distracted by the muscle memory of the game rather than the other way around—where her body was in the game but her mind was distracted by the muscle memory of Layka's hand on hers or the feel of Layka's strong, feminine shoulder under the soft cream coat.

"Yes!" Steve shouted, winning the point and now the serve.

Aven shook her head, realizing she'd played the entire point with her mind on Layka. She gave her best effort to get back in the game. At least it was Steve and Sarah's turn to buy lunch.

Sarah rubbed her hands together as she sat down at the booth in the large food court, her tray packed with meals for everyone. She handed Reynolds a burrito that was the size of a small rabbit. "Spill," she said, "or this burrito goes home with me."

"See, now that's a threat to my existence. I'm practically bones already. I must surrender the info." Reynolds shrugged her shoulders as if she had no other choice.

Aven laughed, took her bratwurst with mustard and relish, then let her mind drift away as Reynolds told the story—from her perspective—to Sarah and Steve. The committee meeting today was scheduled after five, which was why she had asked Layka about whether or not she would be there. She loved the passion and drive Layka had in her eyes for the issue. She recognized it. Respected it. *Hmm, respect.* That was a word she was careful never to give people who made quick judgments about others without evidence or context. *What am I doing? I've protected myself from this for years. There are millions of people out there who don't judge people so easily. I can respect her passion for a cause, but I don't have to trust her.* The thought was a staggering one, because it made her heart squeeze with disappointment and fear. The only thing between her and another very real possibility of heartbreak was her own policy of protection. She had made an active decision to do something contrary to her natural disposition of being drawn to this type of person. *The type of person I could lose myself in...* The thought of losing herself brought her back to the conversation at the table.

Reynolds was leaning forward over the table, her burrito in hand but only one bite missing. "I'm telling you, when we found them at that majestic table in the congressional meeting room, it was as if there had been an apocalypse and the rest of the world was gone. Those two eyed each other like they were seeing the salvation of Earth itself in each other's eyes. I almost didn't say anything, but Purdel bumped the hook on the rail rope blocking the entrance and the spell was kind of broken."

Aven saw her opening to shift the conversation. "That brings up a new, very interesting point. Maybe it wasn't just my mind wandering from the game today. Do tell us about Purdel."

Reynolds's eyes went wide, and she shoved the burrito into her mouth with such vigor that the entire table laughed.

CHAPTER EIGHT

"**S**COOT OVER. I'VE GOT a break," Erin said, bumping Layka's hip with hers as she took a seat. "I'm glad to see you two back to your regular weekend schedule. Seeing you on trivia night made me think I'd missed a whole week."

"We're back to family night Saturdays," Layka said, lifting her beer in toast to her sister.

Sam took a swig of beer in that way that seemed cooler than when other people did it. At least, that's what Layka thought. Sam looked around the bar and then spoke as if she hadn't found the answer in her search. "Do you all still do the food festival for the homeless?"

"Yes," Erin and Layka said in unison.

"You participate?" Sam asked, and Layka noted the look of guilt she was seeing more frequently on her sister's face.

"I contribute food." Layka looked sheepishly at Erin. "Often the night before the food festival. I'm still the same procrastinator."

"Why do you ask?" Erin stole a fry from Layka's plate.

"Well, we've had some leads about a human trafficking group, and some of the clues have led to some homeless resources. I wondered if you have seen anything unusual. Plus, I want to contribute."

"That's great," Erin said.

"I wanted to find out when the next event will be. I'm not the pro-crastinator my sister is." Sam smiled, so the statement had no sting. "It also appears I'm not as proactive as she is, so I'm changing that." Sam's smile widened, and she bumped her beer to Layka's.

Layka realized she was staring at her sister. Sam didn't hand out compliments frequently, and she was taking that one home with her. Her big sister thought she was proactive.

"We do the festival quarterly, so it's kind of seasonal. You can drop the food off anytime."

"I was thinking about doing something more hands-on. I'm pretty mean on the grill."

"That would be incredible. We never seem to have enough hands those days." Erin's watch dinged with a notification. "Break's over," she said, checking the time and reading the notification. "The date is coming up soon." She tapped her watch screen and brought up the calendar. "It's always on a Sunday, and Jeremy manages most of it, but I know it's not tomorrow. Ah, there it is. It's October sixth and it's Halloween themed, so you've got to choose a costume." She patted Sam's arm, grinned, and closed the calendar on her watch. "Text me and I can send you more details. Enjoy your lunch," she said, snagging another fry.

"Hey, I want a discount on my check for those fries," Layka said, and Erin wiggled her fingers as if to prove there was no evidence as she walked away.

"Can you talk about this trafficking lead? I know you and the team have been working that case for weeks."

"There's not really anything to tell right now. The leads we had turned out to be duds, so I'm just reworking some of the angles to see what comes up. What's going on with you? How was the Literary Ball?"

"Actually, it was great. You'll never believe who showed up as Jessica to my Brooklyn."

"Oh, I've got a guess. It was that hot, blue-eyed doctor that snagged your interest the other day. What's her name?"

"How did you guess?"

"I work with the detective squad. It's an acquired skill."

"No. You've got a mole. You've been talking to Farrah."

"Maybe." Sam smiled, then that look crossed her face and she shrugged.

"What is it, Sam? I know you're interested in Farrah, but every time she comes up it's as if you won't let yourself have that happiness."

Sam turned her beer in a circle, then lifted it. "Have you ever been at a place where you start to look at yourself differently?" She took a sip and set it down, picking at the label. "You know, like you've been wearing these glasses and someone knocks them off and all of the sudden you are seeing things differently?"

Layka picked up a fry. "I don't think I could have explained my week any better than that," she said. "Please tell me this means you're willing to let go of Victoria from college and consider a serious relationship with someone. I'm so sorry I wasn't here for you when that happened."

"Well, that's kind of it. No one was here to witness it but me, and now I'm looking at a lot of things differently. Maybe, for the first time, really looking at my responsibility in a lot of what I've created over the years."

Layka felt the weight of that. She had left for the Peace Corps as soon as she graduated high school at eighteen. At the time, it seemed like the best solution to give Sam her freedom to focus on college and for her to escape all the reminders of loss. Now she realized how alone Sam must have felt. "I'm sure there is blame on both sides when you talk about relationships, but you were so devastated you wouldn't even speak about it. And you've held on to the idea of her like she was an angel, which I'm sure she could not have been if she broke your heart."

Layka watched as Sam's brow drew down and she focused on removing the label from her beer. "I'm thinking about asking Farrah out. I know she's a colleague of yours and kind of a friend. Would you be okay with that?"

"Of course I'm okay with that. Why wouldn't I be?"

"I don't know. You're my sister and I don't have anyone I love more. If she agrees to go out and then I bugger it up, I don't want it to be a strain on your relationship with her. It's always a little strange when you date someone close to someone you love."

"I get it, but you're getting ahead of yourself. You're not going to bugger it up."

Sam laughed. "I am getting ahead of myself. I haven't even given her the chance to turn me down yet. Which brings us back to you. When are you going to ask Dr. Aven...what's her last name?"

"Summerhouse."

"Ooh, fancy name. Are you going to ask Dr. Aven Summerhouse out after the meeting tonight?"

"Ms. Samantha Danielle Corin-Silva, I would never be so forward."

"Oh yes you would, and I love it. Go for it, girl!"

Layka lifted her hamburger and took a bite, letting the chili cover her fingers before reaching for the napkin. She wiped her hands and recalled her napkin note to Aven. Their exchange at the Literary Ball had been different. Something had shifted. Maybe the doctor would be interested in testing the waters.

Layka still felt butterflies in her stomach despite practicing the deep breathing techniques she had learned in a meditation program that had run for a year at the library. Unlike last time, this committee meeting was already into the meet-and-greet phase and had been moved to the large conference room since there were additional guests. They'd chosen a weekend evening to accommodate all the busy schedules. Layka had stayed at the front desk waiting to direct the two stragglers, Simon and Aven, to the new meeting area. She heard the door click behind the shelves. The butterflies in her stomach did a flip, and she grabbed the counter at the actual physical sense of movement. Simon came into view first, but he was looking at Aven as he spoke. Aven, however, was looking straight ahead, and their eyes locked. This was not good. She felt so disoriented when those eyes looked at her. Everything felt enhanced, heightened, and her skin tingled. She looked down at the counter and noticed a legal pad. She lifted it just to have something in her hands and rounded the counter to meet them.

"Everyone is in the main conference room," she said, leading the way as Simon continued to speak.

"I do think what you are describing is beneficial, I just don't know if it is feasible," he said.

"I understand that, but I think if we present it to Dr. Sudha, Layka, and the library team, they may have some insight that would allow us to tackle the feasibility issues."

Layka smiled, enjoying the sound of her name coming from Aven.

The meeting went well, and Layka was proud she had managed two lengthy discussions with Dr. Summerhouse during the meeting that included feedback from the entire group yet still felt very strongly as if the two of them were taking the lead together on a project that would address the health department's concerns about disease spread in the library. She set her legal pad on top of her laptop, picked up the whole stack, and grabbed her coffee cup. She stood nervously, questioning her next step. Did she really want to do this? She did, but she was still uncertain how receptive Aven would be to seeing her outside of the committee. She licked her lips and blew out a breath as she watched Aven shake Dr. Sudha's hand. She moved toward the door, the others still shuffling out, and the mild congestion allowed her to wait without being too obvious.

"I feel that was the most productive committee meeting I think I've ever been in," Aven said, and Layka actually startled. She had been so focused on her own thoughts she hadn't noticed her move toward the door.

"I agree. Are you interested in taking me up on that cup of coffee? I have a few more ideas I'd like to run past you if you have the time," Layka said.

Aven paused, and Layka stepped to the side to wait with her and let Dr. Sudha pass.

"See you on Monday, Layka. Thanks for your insight tonight." Dr. Sudha waved at them both.

"Actually, I'm off this Monday, so I'll see you on Tuesday. And thank you."

Dr. Sudha tapped her temple as if remembering. "That's right. Tuesday then."

"Taking a well-deserved holiday?" Aven asked.

"Actually, I took the day to work on this. The project." She hefted the stuff in her hands.

"Me too," Aven said. "I didn't take off for the project. I'm off because I covered for a colleague last week, but I had planned to go over Reynolds's data on the virus variant, do some literature review and research for the project."

"Which brings me back to my question about coffee and a further discussion about project plans. I want to be completely honest. I like you. I look forward to collaborating with you like we did today to find solutions, but I'd also like to get to know you better. If you don't have time today, then perhaps Monday?"

Aven rubbed the back of her neck. "I don't know if I should spend extra time with you."

"Okay...can you explain that?" After a statement like that Layka wanted to know, because she was fairly certain at some point the project was going to require them to spend a lot more time together—if things shaped up the way they did in today's meeting. "You can tell me you want to work on the project only. We don't have to reach for friendship or anything else beyond a work relationship, if you're with someone or not interested, but I think the project will require some extra time between us regardless. If that is uncomfortable for you, I need to know."

"No, no. I'm not seeing anyone. I just..." Aven blew out a breath, released her neck, and looked at Layka. "I find you very attractive, and I've made myself a promise not to get involved with...with..."

"With people who judge you so quickly," Layka said, knowing instinctively that was the answer, especially after having to apologize for doing just that. *Why do I judge so quickly? Because I'm usually right,* Layka thought, then kicked herself. *You weren't right the first time with Aven.* She had a clear remembrance of the hurt she had seen in Aven's eyes that day, and it was there now. Layka watched as Aven closed her eyes, took another deep breath, then opened her eyes.

"Yeah," Aven said and pushed her hair behind her ear. "It feels really hard to make that decision with you, but that policy has served me well."

"Has it served you well, or just kept you from taking a risk with anyone?"

"No, I've been out with people." Aven had her hands behind her now, leaning her weight on the chair back.

Layka pulled out the seat next to it and sat down. This mattered to her—which she didn't like—but here she was. "What's the longest relationship you've had?"

Aven rocked once and then stepped toward the wall with the whiteboard. She lifted a marker and put it down, then turned to face Layka. "I was married for four years, but we've been divorced now for a little over a year."

Aven turned back to the board and drew two circles overlapping like a Venn diagram. She wrote *hospital* in one and *library* in the other.

"I'm sorry," Layka said, wanting to touch Aven's hand again the way she had at the ball. Layka sensed this was difficult for Aven, so she picked up one of the colored markers and started shading the part of the library circle that didn't overlap with the hospital. She understood what Aven was working on, and she could help her with that while Aven tried to work through this conversation at her own pace.

"Was she the one who hurt you?"

"No. That hurt actually led me to Carter." Aven smiled.

Layka could imagine she was playing out some happy memory of her time with her spouse. She tried to write Aven's name above the hospital circle, but the marker was dry. She lifted the eraser, wiping off the area while she let Aven be with her thoughts.

"I'm going to let you take over while I chat. You appear to be reading my mind."

"My ESP does kick in when I hold a dry-erase marker." Layka lifted the black marker and wrote *Aven* over the hospital circle and *Layka* over the library one, then began listing responsibilities within each circle, leaving the overlapping area blank.

Aven smiled and moved toward the chair, pulling it out and taking a seat. "Actually, Carter and I are good friends. That was kind of the problem. Carter was trying to find their identity, and I was on the rebound. We married too quickly and then stayed together because we kind of worked, but we ultimately agreed to divorce and give each other the space to move forward."

"Have you moved forward?" Layka used the red marker to list the organizations on the right side of the board from which the hospital and the library already had discretionary money for the project, as well as the ones to which they had discussed submitting for grants.

"Yes, in many ways, but you're right about me not taking many risks with relationships since my divorce. I've been out on dates, but work occupies a great deal of my time, and there is a very real part of me that feels safer with the walls I've put in place." Aven's watch pinged. "However, as is obvious by the fact that I've just spent an additional half hour chatting with you, there's a part of me that wants to risk those walls with you."

Layka stopped writing and leaned her shoulder on the wall beside the board, putting the lid on the marker to avoid writing on her sweater when she crossed her arms. She wanted to sit with how warm her body felt with Aven's words, but Aven's phone had pinged, and she wanted to respect her time. "Is that notification something you need to take care of right away?" Layka put the marker down and walked to her things she had put back on the table.

"No. It's Reynolds letting me know the more detailed data I asked for regarding this project will probably take another week."

"It seems we are both passionate about this project and enjoy each other's company. What do you say to coffee at Bean Around the World tomorrow morning? We can talk about the project and leave the rest to progress as it will."

"I'm very afraid of repeating old mistakes," Aven said.

Layka reached out this time and squeezed Aven's hand, then let it go. "I know, but aren't you doing the same thing to me? Judging me without context. I made a mistake. I recognized it and offered to do something different."

Aven opened her mouth, closed it, then smiled the most gentle smile Layka had ever seen.

"You're right. I am, and you have offered that. What time will Bean Around the World be serving us coffee?"

"Way before I get this diagram finished," Layka said.

Aven lifted her phone and snapped a picture of the Venn dia-gram-turned-work of art. "Come on. I'll walk you to your car before I head back to the hospital. Something tells me you will enjoy re-creating this when we can finish it together."

CHAPTER NINE

B EAN AROUND THE WORLD was exactly as Aven remembered it. She hadn't been here in a while, but it was comforting to know there hadn't been any dramatic changes. Unlike her, who was upending one of the biggest barricades she had created. She was both excited and worried. She found a table, deciding to wait and order when Layka arrived.

She scanned the café. The large windows to the left faced the street, but trees planted in large urns gave a colorful display now that it was the last week of September. The thought reminded her of the conversation with the hospital social worker about Mildred's release. Aven had been buying time, hoping a bed would open up in the rehab facility nearby. Aven chose a table off from the center but away from the windows enough to not create a glare on her laptop screen. She took a seat facing the door so she could watch for Layka, as it would be easy for Layka to miss her already seated at the table. *The café is pretty crowded,* she thought, shifting her chair so she could see both doors beyond the line of people. She readjusted the chair when it rocked a little with her. She checked the floor to see if a leg was sitting on something, but it appeared the chair leg was damaged a little, causing it to lean slightly. She looked up just in time to see Layka pull the glass door open. She was wearing a turquoise turtleneck, black slacks, and a black peacoat. "Sleek and sophisticated," she whispered, recalling Reynolds's description of Layka at the hospital cafeteria. Aven licked her dry lips and lifted a hand. Layka removed her black and gold sunglasses and scanned the room. She smiled when she saw Aven's hand, and Aven felt her breath catch. *This is so not a good idea.*

"Hi, am I late?" Layka asked, checking her watch.

"No, I'm an early riser, so I tend to show up to morning meetings early no matter what time they're scheduled. Do not expect that consistency after my day gets started."

"Noted." Layka smiled as she removed her jacket and turned to look at the large chalkboard menu high on the wall near the barista station.

Aven stared. The turtleneck appeared tailor-made to fit Layka like a glove, showcasing the contour of her breasts with her turned at this angle. The ribbed design at the waist gave the simple top a designer look, and she wondered for a moment if fashion was important to Layka or if she could just make simple things look expensive. She looked beautiful and competent. *That's because she is beautiful and competent.* Layka's contributions at the meeting had proved beneficial to helping solve the feasibility problem she and Simon had been discussing on their way into the meeting. It was as if Layka had anticipated it. The thought reminded her that anticipation of problems required knowledge, judgment, and decisiveness. In the case of the project, those traits had been beneficial.

"Have you ordered yet?"

The question pulled Aven from her inner battle. "No, I wanted to wait for you. We hadn't discussed how much time you had available, so I was uncertain if you would want food or just coffee."

"Food, of course," Layka said, grinning. "I can't have you leaving hungry from our second date."

Aven laughed, then paused. "Wait. Second date?"

"Why, yes, Dr. Aven Summerhouse. You chose to spend an hour with me yesterday after the meeting just discussing the opportunity for this date." She winked. "I'm counting that."

"You make a very good point. I chose to stay, and I enjoyed the time with you, so it had to be a date."

Layka smiled, and Aven could see appreciation in those blue-gray eyes.

Aven tilted her head. The turquoise made Layka's eyes appear brighter, more blue.

Layka turned the sunglasses in her hand, then placed them on her head but never broke their eye contact. "What would you like? I'll get in line if you will hold our table."

"I'll join you. I can leave the computer."

"I'd like that. The line isn't long but appears to be moving slow."

Aven used the proper courtesies to sort out who was waiting on orders and who was in line. She'd reached the crowd first when Layka paused to retrieve her phone from her coat pocket. "You managed to get quite a bit of information about me on our 'first date,'" Aven said when Layka joined her. "Have you ever been married?"

"No." Layka took a small side step as the line moved. "And you met my most recent dating experience at the Literary Ball."

"Oh no!" Aven could feel her face flush. "Purdel was your date? I'm sorry if I was out of line to say what I did."

"You weren't out of line at all," Layka said, and once again Aven felt her breath catch at the feel of Layka's focused gaze. "I was grateful. And, she wasn't my date. I came with a friend, like you did."

Aven rubbed her chest, trying to slow her heart rate. *Damn dopamine.* It was like her brain's reward system interpreted Layka's gratefulness as if she'd won a gold medal and was telling her whole body to be happy and excited.

"Are you okay?" Layka asked, covering Aven's hand with her own.

Aven looked down at their joined hands. She had loved the feel of it the first time she did it, but now, with her mind already playing chemical euphoria with her body, she was speechless. Layka must have interpreted her look down as guilt, because she continued to speak.

"Really, you did nothing wrong. Purdel and I went out twice several months ago, but I didn't have the energy to fight for the conversation."

Someone behind them cleared their throat, and they both noticed they were holding up the line.

Layka removed her hand, stepping forward, and Aven moved in sync. It felt like energy circled between them, and she could still feel the touch of Layka's hand.

The person in front of them was ordering for at least four people, and Aven noticed that it had seemed like time had stopped for that moment and now the world had started moving again. Everything felt so intense so fast, and she could sense the fear creeping in.

"What'll it be?" The barista asked the question as if she were exhausted already.

Aven realized she hadn't even looked at the menu. She didn't like being unprepared. "I drink my coffee black, and I'll eat you, yours, whatever you're having." She felt her face and ears heat up and saw the barista grin.

"Two spinach quiche, a large black coffee, and a large dirty chai latte," Layka said, using her phone to pay before stepping to the wait area and pulling Aven close enough to whisper. "At least you made Bad Mood Barista smile."

"I'm so embarrassed. I apologize." Aven stepped back, putting some space between them. She couldn't breathe that close to Layka. Well, she could breathe, but Layka smelled like honeysuckle and lemon, and if she didn't step back, she would lean in. Once again, it was as if her body had decided the smell of coffee and roasted beans were not as important as the scent of this woman.

"Hey." Layka reached for her but paused. "You've asked me to be mindful about making judgments about you, so I'm going to take a page from your book and point out what I see and then let you give me the context. You appear to have an instinct to run."

Aven let her head rock back on her neck, looking up at the ceiling just as the barista called their order. *That was fair,* she thought, grateful for the moment's reprieve while they picked up their food. "I don't like to be unprepared. In school, I would practice procedures step by step from the book before we even reviewed them in class. I panicked when I realized I hadn't looked at the menu and everyone was waiting."

They were at the table, and Aven's chair wobbled when she sat down. She was glad she had set their drinks down first. Layka unpacked the bag of food.

"So, when you panic, you run?" Layka asked, not looking up from unwrapping her quiche and setting it down.

"Can I think about that? It's something I've not been asked before, and it's an important question."

"Absolutely." Layka passed the second wrapped quiche to Aven and sat down. "What do you have for me on there?" She pointed to the computer. "Are you going to be okay to do this on the computer and not have your colorful markers and whiteboard?"

"Hey, don't knock the value of color and highlights," Aven said, glad for Layka's effort to lighten the mood. "It's some preliminary data from Reynolds. You may have to slide your chair to this side to see it."

Layka did so, scooting her chair across the smooth floor. She took a bite of her quiche, then laid it back on her side of the bistro table away from the computer. She scanned the numbers and data analysis.

Aven ate her quiche and watched. After fifteen minutes, Aven realized her quiche was almost gone and Layka's was getting cold. She reached across to retrieve it for her, and her chair wobbled.

Layka's hand grabbed her thigh and warmth spread up her leg. It was only the rocking wobble of the uneven leg, but as she slid the quiche toward her she was acutely aware of the pressure of every finger, as if each one of them sent an individual energy up her leg.

Layka released her leg and settled her quiche next to the computer. "Thank you."

Her voice sounded a little lower, and Aven chanced a look at her eyes. Yeah, her pupils were dilated. At least she wasn't the only one feeling this connection. "You're welcome. I didn't want it to get cold. What do you think about the numbers?"

Layka pushed the computer back and pulled a clean napkin from the bag. "Do you have a pen?"

Aven braced on the table to avoid another chair tilt as she reached into her computer bag on the floor.

Layka covered Aven's hand with her own as if to help stabilize her. Aven closed her eyes at the wash of emotion she felt at the touch. "I admire your passion for helping the homeless. You've put a lot of research and thought into the threat this project could create for reducing their access to resources."

"Thank you for noticing," Layka said. Her eyes locked with Aven's as Aven sat back up in her chair. "It's important to me."

There was very little space between them with Layka's hand still covering Aven's, but Layka didn't move, and Aven took in the crystal-like reflection of light in those gray-blue eyes as Layka continued. "What if we combined resources from the hospital and the library to create a solution that focuses on protecting the public from communicable disease while generating additional resources for the vulnerable unhoused population?" Aven tried to focus. The soft hand on hers was light now as Layka's shoulders lifted slightly when she looked up in thought. The movement made Layka's fingertips drag across Aven's skin, and Aven swallowed and tried to control her breathing.

"The library already gets funding from the education department to create programs within the community." Layka grinned, squeezed Aven's hand, and locked her eyes on Aven.

Aven felt it like a trifecta of sensation. "Go on," was all Aven could manage.

"Dr. Sudha said the liaison for the education department mentioned cutting funding recently because the programs weren't having the level of impact they had wanted to see. He said the plans weren't big enough to make lasting change." She lifted Aven's hand and squeezed it between both of hers. "We could create something that would have impact."

Aven felt her entire body warm with the excitement and passion Layka pulsed through her hand like energy as she cradled Aven's hand in hers near Layka's chest. She could feel Layka's chest rise with her eager animation of ideas.

"We could propose not just education programs, but housing. An actual building that could bring all the resources together." Layka gave Aven's hand a final squeeze before dropping it to gesture further. "We could combine some of the healthcare initiatives you brought up at the meeting."

Aven thought Layka might bounce right out of the chair. They were no longer touching, but Layka's enthusiasm rolled over Aven like a caress. Had she ever basked in someone else's energy? She realized she was grinning, and she was certain she looked smitten to anyone looking on.

Several reality checks passed through her mind about the transient nature of many unhoused people, but she refused to put forward anything that would dampen this new glow Layka seemed to have. How could she say it with a positive spin? "Maybe we create a housing environment that is step-based, kind of like triage, but governed by a balance of what they need and the amount of help they desire."

"That's brilliant!" Layka said, touching Aven's forearm lightly before gesturing and bumping the pen in Aven's opposite hand. "Oh, thanks. You got that out for me. I got distracted..." She smiled gently, taking the pen. "In the very best way," she added. "I'm so excited! Your investigation of the virus risk can help us outline parameters of safety that will apply for any communicable disease."

"True," Aven said, still feeling the tingle in her forearm. Layka was a very touch-oriented person and Aven didn't mind it for once. "Speaking of communicable disease, what was it you noticed in Reynold's numbers?"

Layka adjusted the napkin she had pulled out earlier. "I spoke with my sister last night, and I see a pattern that's very interesting now that I've seen your data."

"Really?" Aven watched as Layka drew out a rough map with some boxes in different spots indicating something, but she didn't name them.

"Each of these represents an organization for helping the homeless. My sister works with the detective squad at DCPD, and they've had these ten on observation as part of a bigger surveillance for trafficking up I-95 into the area."

"So, you have a sister?" *That is not the important question here,* Aven thought, willing her mind to focus back on the project, not Layka.

"Yes, and I can't wait for you to meet her. I completely have big-sisteritis and think she is amazing even when she drives me crazy."

"That's cool, and I'm impressed with what I think you're doing there." Aven continued to watch as Layka added her numbers to the boxes and then drew two large circles around the box now labeled *New Foundations Building* and the box labeled *Chartered Start Building.*

"Those are both areas that correspond to the highest number of people with confirmed disease. But wait—those aren't Reynolds's numbers. Those are numbers she used for comparison in other states."

"Exactly. That's what I noticed." Layka pointed to her rough map. "These are in Maryland. You've been looking for a location zero for your variant based on Reynolds's numbers, but these two meet the criteria for location zero, they're just not in DC."

Aven sat back in her chair. Layka was the brilliant one. This could really make sense with the other data they had about the transfer of the virus, but there were a few problems. "How would homeless people be able to move to another state fast enough to spread the disease without impacting the areas in between?" Aven traced the map in thought where Layka had scribbled in the almost nonexistent numbers of infected people in key areas between the two.

Layka shrugged. "I don't know. I say we check it out."

"Us?"

Layka rubbed her chin in thought. "Sounds like the perfect opportunity to scope out the structure for our own building design and ask some questions that might help make sense of this." She pointed at the map.

"I think someone just planned our next date."

"And you just agreed to a road trip date," Layka said, squeezing Aven's leg excitedly then tapping it lightly before standing. "I'm going by to check on Mildred and fill out the HIPAA paperwork so you can keep me abreast of her progress. I want to help when she's ready to be released."

Aven felt the warmth lingering on her leg from Layka's touch, but her words about Mildred warmed her just as much. Layka was the kind of person doing things to make a difference and not just talking about it. *Is this going to be a mistake?* On the one hand, this attractive, competent woman was exactly the kind of person she was naturally drawn to. On the other, it was also the kind of woman who could break her heart. *The real question is, am I going to run away?*

CHAPTER TEN

L AYKA HAD AVOIDED SAM for almost a week. It seemed longer than that since her café meeting with Aven. *Date*, she thought with a smile, but it was the first Saturday of October, and the homeless festival was tomorrow. She was afraid Sam would know she was up to something and would drag the plan she and Aven had made out of her. It hadn't been easy to dodge her sister, but between texts and messages passed through Farrah, she'd managed it. She was secretly pleased that the effort had landed Farrah and Sam on an impromptu date. It was time her sister went out with someone for more than drinks and a fun evening. Sam hadn't opened up any more about college Victoria, but she was hopeful Farrah would put that ghost to rest.

Tomorrow, she and Aven would take a road trip to Maryland to visit the two organizations operating for the homeless that Layka had circled on her hand-drawn map. The idea of them formulating plans for their own building design for people like Mildred made her excited and scared. She was on Mildred's paperwork now as her emergency contact. The three of them had met one day at lunch in Mildred's room to discuss plans to move her to a rehab facility nearby due to some cardiac complications. Layka smiled at Mildred's enthusiasm for the project, which she and Aven had laid out to get Mildred's perspective. She'd offered to use her time in the cardiac rehab facility to document what resources might be similarly beneficial in the new building design—a Wheelhouse, they were calling it—since it would have a health and recovery sector. They had both been super busy the rest of the week but had met one night with Aven's friends for drinks. They'd almost left together. She felt her center pulse with the reminder.

"What are you plotting, my sweet friend?" Erin slid into the booth seat across from her. "And where is Sam?"

"I'm hiding from her," Layka said conspiratorially. "That's why I'm here early. I need your help." Layka laid out their plan to drive to Maryland tomorrow and then be back in time for the evening events at the food festival.

"What do you need me to do?"

"I can't ask Sam to help because she'll want to know what I'm doing. I need her to have complete deniability about what we plan to do."

"What do you plan to do?"

"We're going to visit two of the organizations that have been under investigation by her team because the areas show a high exposure rate for this virus variant. I need you to be my eyes and ears at the festival. I had planned to be at the festival, but now I can't. It's an event for the homeless you care for every day, so you will recognize new people or notice if something is off."

"Sam will kill me if she finds out I helped you hide this from her."

"Which is again why I'm here early and heading out before she gets here. Tell her I had to leave to discuss the project with Aven."

"Ohh girl, you do want me to die. Hiding this from her is one thing, but lying to her is a whole other issue."

"You're not lying. I am working with Aven tonight, we're just doing it via phone. She's on call at the hospital, and we're finishing up some details on a grant we're submitting to gain some additional funding for the project."

"You two seem to make a good team," Erin said.

"It is so incredible to work with her." Layka closed her eyes, then opened them and let the full smile she felt show. "She's intelligent, patient, fun." She pulled her low ponytail around and played with her hair, then looked up. "I could get in over my head, Erin. I may already be there."

"Yeah," Erin said, and Layka could see her friend's joy for her.

Layka squeezed Erin's hands that were clasped loosely together on the table. "Thanks, Erin. I owe you!" She stood, moving through the growing crowd toward the door.

"Yes, you do," Erin said to her back. "I get half your fries next time."

Layka half turned, gave a salute and a smile, then escaped into the crisp autumn air. Her heart was racing already in anticipation of talking to Aven tonight. They'd agreed to plan on a video call after 8:00 p.m. so that when Aven had downtime in the private on-call room, they would work on the grant application. She'd be home by 7:30 and have time to whip up some food, pour a glass of wine, and settle in to work. She usually wrote grants by herself, so she was happy when Aven agreed to help supply some of the information to save her digging through Reynolds's data blindly.

Layka set her wine down on her kitchen counter when Aven's video call buzzed her phone. She clicked it open. "Hey there, you. How's your day been so far?" She propped her phone against the speaker so she could see Aven and have the paperwork in front of her.

"It would be better if I had a glass of whatever you have there," Aven said, pointing to the glass in Layka's hand.

"I'll save you some," Layka offered. "Dr. Sudha was gifted two bottles from the vice president for her work to add the history of Asian wines to the antiquities department. She and the VP are two of the most knowledgeable people I've ever met when it comes to wine. Sometimes I think they are hundreds of years old when they start discussing its history."

"You've met the vice president?"

"Yes, several times in my role at the Library of Congress when she was a senator, and once at an event at the White House with Dr. Sudha."

"What's she like in person?"

"She's actually very funny, and she has this intelligence that just is...you know, like she's lived a dozen lives and knows things."

"That's incredible. There are so many things I don't know about you."

"Stick around and you'll find them out."

Aven's lips formed a line. Not a hard line, but a thoughtful one.

"What is it?" Layka set her wine down and focused on Aven's face as she pushed a strand of hair behind her ear.

"I asked you to give me some time to answer a question you posed to me at the café. I've really been thinking about it, and you're right. When I'm afraid or hurt, my first instinct is to run. To get away. Find a place where I feel safe and can make a plan."

"That's a reasonable response," Layka said. "Especially if your safety is at risk."

"I thought about that too, and it is, but I don't think I ever stop running." Aven looked into the camera.

Layka felt her breath stop in her chest at the vulnerability in those blue eyes.

"You called me on it, and for the first time in a long time I stopped running and faced my fear."

A knock at Aven's door pulled Aven's eyes from the phone. "Yes? Come in."

The door swung open. Layka couldn't see who stood in the doorway, but she could hear their voice. "We've got a ventilator patient with mild hypoxia in the ICU. The hospitalist is concerned they are going to deteriorate and wanted a pulmonary consult."

"I'll be right there."

Layka could see the heavy wood hospital door close as Aven lifted her white coat from the chair. "I'll be back as soon as I'm free, and we can work on the grant and finalize plans for our road trip tomorrow." Aven grinned. "I've been on Google Maps."

Layka laughed. "Okay, in case I forget or you get tied up and can't come back, I'm dropping by the rehab to see Mildred tomorrow morning. If you want to meet me, we can leave a car parked there while we travel to visit the New Foundations Home."

Layka realized she was touching the phone screen. When had she reached out like that?

"Sounds good. I'll be back as soon as I can. I was afraid it would be busy, but I wanted to talk with you. I sent an email with the grant info I completed to help you with tonight just in case we were interrupted.

I didn't want you to have to do it all." Aven touched her fingers to the screen as if to connect, then turned for the door.

Aven had explained to Layka that each specialty had their own on-call room, so no one would be in there while Aven was away, and the video rolling on the empty space made Layka miss Aven more than if they had disconnected. She replayed Aven's words before the interruption: "I stopped running and faced my fear." Those words had probably been the most honest words anyone she dated had ever spoken to her, and she wanted to be that person. The person with whom Aven could face anything. The person where Aven's running stopped. She wanted to wrap Aven in her arms. *God, I'm moving too fast here,* she thought. She clicked off the video and started a text. She checked the time. Aven would need to rest if she made it back to the on-call room at all.

LAYKA: I'll be up till 11 tonight and I'll be at Mildred's by 8:30 a.m.

CHAPTER ELEVEN

"**T**HIS IS A REALLY nice room." Layka pulled the curtains back to reveal a view of a courtyard behind the rehab facility.

"It is," Mildred said, using her walker to stabilize as she turned to take a seat in one of the two soft chairs near the window. "Fall is beautiful here." She paused.

"What is it, Mildred?" Layka asked, coming from behind the other chair to take a seat and touch Mildred's hand resting on the small side table between them.

Layka studied the woman's features in profile as she twisted slightly to stare out the window.

"This will be my first fall away from the streets in more years than I can remember."

Layka chewed on her lip, wanting to know more but not wanting to pry. "Do you feel comfortable telling me about how someone as smart, kind, and capable as you ended up on the streets? I know from experience that life can change in an instant."

Mildred patted Layka's hand atop hers and then pulled them both back to her when she leaned back in the chair. "Those are all nice words, and I like that I believe they are true, though I would not have believed so years ago."

Layka's phone pinged across the room, but she ignored it.

Mildred smiled that soft smile. "It's Dr. Summerhouse. I recognize the custom ringtone. See what she needs."

Layka tilted her head, evaluating Mildred. She really did seem to want her to get the phone. Maybe she wanted a little reprieve from the conversation. "That's one of the things I'm talking about," Layka said as she stood. "You have a keen sense of observation. Not many people would notice the difference in the ringtone and put together the nuances of interactions to discern it's Aven."

"The streets make you smart that way, but you know that."

Layka nodded and lifted the phone, moving back to the chair as she read the text. "She's asking about you."

Mildred grinned. "Tell her we're discussing the engineering hurdles of creating a courtyard inside a conservatory in the rehab sector of the Wheelhouse building, and we need extra funding from the Department of Housing for irrigation systems to create the proper humidity to maintain the plants and trees indoors."

"See, now, that is book smarts. You've got it all." Layka typed out Mildred's words to Aven.

"That's where you, Aven, and this program are so important." Mildred's eyes went distant, and her smile fell to a resting line as her face turned again to the window. "I couldn't read when I ran to the streets in my late twenties."

Layka silenced her phone before Aven's next text came through, but she saw the words in her peripheral vision.

SHE IS AMAZING!

Yes, she is, Layka thought but didn't speak.

"When my ex walked right through a restraining order and put me in the hospital, my best friend at the time helped me formulate a plan to hide on the streets. The only place he wouldn't expect me to be." Mildred turned from the window, her eyes penetrating. "It's sad when the danger of the streets is safer than your home."

"Mildred," Layka whispered, her heart aching and her anger unrivaled for a woman who had been on the streets now for at least twenty years because the system of protection had failed. Layka leaned into the aching of her heart rather than the anger, because when she touched it, all she could see was red. "Would you like me to help you find your friend? The one who helped you hide?"

"What did Aven say?" Mildred asked.

Layka looked down at her phone to read the rest of Aven's text. "That you are amazing," Layka answered, glad to have something positive to say but hesitant to change the subject. "And, she is on her way. We talk about your skills quite often. We're hoping once you are recovered you will consider being a paid part of the team. I think your friend would be glad to know you are safe, and Sam will help us make sure you're truly protected this time."

"She's gone," Mildred said. "That's what made me ask about Dr. Summerhouse. I see how much you two care for each other. Don't lose that. Do whatever you need to do to be together, or one day you may wake up and find together is no longer an option. My friend's obituary is the reason I learned to read. She would leave clothes, food, shoes, and other items in trash bags at a dumpster near a restaurant we both knew. When a month passed without a drop-off, I tried to find out what happened but I had no resources. One day, I found an old newspaper in a trash can near the library. People often dropped their unfinished food and drinks there before entering the building. When I saw her photo, I tried to figure out why my friend had made the front page of a newspaper, but I couldn't read. I was afraid to ask anyone to read it to me, so I went inside and asked the lady at the desk how I could learn to read."

Layka swallowed. Mildred had said she wanted to know why her friend was on the front page and also that her friend's obituary was the reason she learned to read. The combination of those things and the look of loss in Mildred's eyes told a story she couldn't begin to imagine. Layka let the tears fall as she did imagine the painstaking effort of learning to read on your own with only the drive of panic and pain. Layka suddenly experienced the overwhelming emotion of loss she would feel if that were Aven. It felt so big, and they had only just met. The thought made her look toward the door in anticipation of her arrival. Aven stood in the doorway. Sorrow and grief were evident in her eyes, but it wasn't clear how much she had heard.

Layka tore her eyes away from Aven and refocused on Mildred when she spoke again. "When I could read it, I found out she had been killed by my ex, who then shot himself. I was finally free of him and too devastated to care."

Aven gripped the bed briefly to pause in her movement toward Layka and Mildred when Layka spoke. "You turned your grief into something your friend would be proud of when you continued to read."

Aven admired her effort to bring some peace to the moment.

"Not right away." Mildred shook her head with a look that said she wasn't necessarily pleased with the choices she made for a while. "But yes, when I came through the grief, I committed to reading everything I could get my hands on that would help us survive on the streets. I made it my personal agenda to help as many people who found themselves on the street as I could."

"You certainly helped us," Layka said.

"Absolutely," Aven chimed in, moving again toward them. "You've given us incredible insight..." Aven paused, letting the silence interrupt her. She was missing something. Layka was biting her lip, and Mildred's face was suddenly unreadable.

Layka leaned back in the large chair and looked at Aven with hesitant, gray-blue eyes that made her breath catch.

"I was talking about me and my sister. Pull up a chair." Layka gestured to the plastic chair near the door.

Aven did and took a seat, surprised at the new look of calm, peace, and pride on Mildred's face as she moved her walker to beside the chair and opened up the space between the three of them.

Aven listened intently to several stories of how Mildred's efforts and knowledge guided Sam and Layka's success when they were forced to live on the streets following the death of their parents. She was still a little in shock that this sophisticated, well-put-together woman she was so drawn to and this self-taught pioneer of a woman had both lived on the streets in a cycle of self-preservation that kept all of them constantly moving yet brought them together time and time again.

"But my favorite story..." Mildred said with a twinkle in her eye.

"Oh no, you don't," Layka said, jumping up and plopping gently on the arm of Mildred's chair, blocking Aven's view as she made little attempts to tickle Mildred as she continued her story.

"Those two were so creative," Mildred gasped out, still laughing. "Sam made the hard things about our life comical with her antics, and sweet Layka often tried to save her with varying levels of suc...cess." Mildred finally caught her breath. "Help me here, Aven."

Aven playfully pulled Layka from the arm of Mildred's seat, falling back into her own chair with Layka on her lap.

"Hey," Layka said with a laugh, twisting in her lap. Layka's eyes met Aven's, and the gesture that had been a playful effort to save Mildred became molten heat where Layka's weight pressed on top of her.

Aven smiled, trying to tamp down her arousal. Mildred continued her story about the two of them attempting to retrieve end-of-day-toss-out cinnamon buns from the bakery dumpster unfolded, and Layka made no move to get up.

"Sam was covered in cinnabun icing when she climbed out," Mildred said, slapping her leg.

Aven laughed, and Layka fell back against her, holding her stomach as she tried to speak through her laughter. "She smelled like cinnamon buns even after her shower at the YMCA."

Aven gave Layka a little squeeze as she wrapped her arms gently to keep her from falling to the side. Layka turned her head, and their lips were inches apart. Aven could feel the rapid rise and fall of her chest against Layka's shoulder. Their eyes met, and the world fell away for a moment.

Layka sat up, aware of the tingle of heat in her body. Aven felt so good it was as if she were an actual place she kept getting lost in, not just a person. She took a deep breath and smiled, then tapped Aven's leg lightly so her move wouldn't seem as abrupt as it felt when she stood. She stretched and gave Mildred a you're-in-trouble smile and moved back to her chair. "But, we got the side door of the dumpster open and had bags of fresh bread the bakery had to toss out each evening."

"Yes, we did," Mildred said. "We made a good team when we ran into each other."

"Speaking of teams," Layka started, looking toward Aven. "Aven and I have been talking about a job we would like you to consider."

"I'm listening." Mildred adjusted her cardigan.

"The plan is to build three Wheelhouses: one in DC, one in Kansas, and one in California. The Wheelhouse design is spiral to allow for different levels of use, from those who only desire a roof for the night, to those who are wanting to find a path forward to a life they've lost or a new one. Aven and I are working on the complete proposal, which will incorporate satellite libraries for additional resources. We could use your insight as a consultant."

"I promised Rita the day I read her obituary that I wouldn't leave the streets and the help I could offer there unless I was ever able to do it better somewhere else." Mildred shifted her walker and reached into the large zipper pack that was designed into it. She lifted her cream clutch purse out and opened it, reaching inside.

Aven heard the sound of Velcro and wondered if the purse had a secret little compartment.

Mildred pulled out a small spiral notebook and leaned back in her chair.

Aven looked at Layka as Mildred leafed through the book.

Layka shrugged, and her face held the same curiosity Aven felt.

Mildred found a page and handed it to Layka.

Aven watched Layka as she read. Emotion flickered across her face as her eyes went wide, then soft, before she spoke. "You've kept a list of all the people you helped, me and Sam included."

Aven heard the stories of the previous hour in her head again. Two young girls trying to survive and a homeless woman who always seemed to show up with just the information they needed to survive one more week, one more month, never indicating it was anything but coincidence.

"I'm showing it to you because it is the first time someone has offered me a job that aligns with what I call that book." Layka closed the notebook to read the front. Aven saw the letters *MPFTNL* but couldn't make out the words underneath.

"'My Path Forward To New Life,'" Layka read. She smiled and traced her fingers down the worn blue cardboard front. "As project manager, I've been tasked with naming the project. I've been putting it off, and now it feels right." She stood, laid the notebook on Mildred's clutch atop the table, and took a seat on the opposite arm of Mildred's chair.

Aven could see her face rather than her back this time, and the move made the moment feel so inclusive it took her breath away.

Layka took Mildred's hand, rubbing her fingers along the joints. "I'm thinking about calling it 'My Path Forward Living.' What do you think?"

Mildred laid her hand over Layka's and smiled that gentle smile. "I think you're onto a good thing. My Path Forward is my own, and it is a mindfulness I learned along the way that made it possible. Let me keep My Path Forward for my notebook and continued work. Maybe call it the 'Mindful Path Project,' since everyone's path will be their own."

"I love that," Layka said, smiling, and Aven felt her own head nod in silent agreement.

CHAPTER TWELVE

"THIS IS NOT WHAT I had in mind when I agreed to a road trip date," Aven whispered, tucking her head back behind the small shed that formed an angle with the large barn building. They were hiding about a hundred feet away from the back door of the New Foundations building—a farmhouse that had been converted to residential living for those deemed homeless. The shouts of a woman threatening to do bodily harm if someone tried to take her dog had led them here rather than to the front door. When one of the men loading the vans looked their way, Aven held her breath till she heard him speak to his partner.

"Why are we doing an extra run? We usually get one weekend off a month."

"Kasana's man said to do it, so that's all we need to know."

Aven risked another peek as both men worked to open the van's back doors. This was the second van they had seen them load. She could feel Layka at her back, peeking over her shoulder.

Aven shivered at the feel of Layka's breath near her ear when her words tickled Aven's neck. "It wasn't my plan either, but we can't let them keep forcing those people into vans."

Aven turned and could see the mix of fear and concern in Layka's eyes. She wanted to settle that fear for her, and she had a plan, but would Layka trust her?

"We should call the police," Layka said.

"You said your sister and her squad had checked all these facilities and found nothing out of place, and they had reached out to some Maryland colleagues for surveillance. Right?"

Layka nodded.

"Do you think any diligent surveillance would miss this?"

"No," Layka whispered and leaned her head back against the grooved wall of the shed.

"Exactly. So, either these people have a connection inside the police department, or the department said they were doing surveillance and didn't. Either way, it's a risk to reach out to them without knowing." Aven wondered if Mildred's story was heightening her suspicion and she was not thinking logically, but she was firing on little sleep and lots of adrenaline.

"What do you think we should do?"

"I think we should call your sister and tell her what we've found, then follow the vans to see where they go from here."

Aven twisted in her squatted position to look at Layka when her suggestion was met with silence. "What is it?" she asked. Layka was biting the corner of her lower lip and toying with the ends of her hair.

Layka looked down, lifting a large piece of gravel before looking back up. Aven watched as Layka released her lip. "I didn't tell her we were coming."

"What!" Aven's voice was quiet, but she could hear the incredulity in her own tone.

"Can I tell you in the car? It looks like they've gone in to get the residents. If we're going to follow them, we need to get back to the car now."

Aven took Layka's hand, and the two of them moved quietly toward the back of the barnlike building that created the angle near the shed where they had been hiding. "I'd feel better if we cut through that first row of corn to get back to the car rather than walking the road the way we did coming in."

"Agreed. You say when."

Aven released Layka's hand and walked to the opposite edge of the barn to check that no one had come out of the New Foundations house.

Once again she was grateful she'd planned ahead last night by looking at Google Earth before driving out here. She could see the whole area in her mind. She moved quickly back to Layka. "If we stay in the middle as we walk toward the corn, we should be invisible even if they come out before we reach the field."

"I rescind my sanction of your Google Maps use," Layka said, grasping Aven's hand as they started across the dead grass that marked a tractor's turning radius between the barn and the field. "Your obsession seemed excessive when merely checking for places to park for a casual evaluation of a residential housing hall for the homeless." She ducked to avoid being smacked in the face by a forgotten corn husk at eye level.

Aven reached ahead of them to clear the path of dangling harvest debris. "But now, in light of us deciding to play detective, I regain my planning privileges?"

"Yeah, something like that." Layka picked up the pace to match Aven's. "But I get points for bringing road trip snacks."

"You did bring some delicious snacks," Aven agreed. Sounds of shuffling people complaining loudly came from the house behind them. "Come on, we need to hurry. It won't take them long to load them."

They slipped into Aven's sleek gray Stingray convertible, parked on a hardtop tractor pad beyond the cornfield instead of near the house, where the field sprinklers made the grass and dirt a muddy mess. They'd walked the 150 feet along the road toward the house on their arrival, and it had been the woman shouting at someone to leave her dog alone that had made them get off the road and hide behind the barn rather than continue to the front entrance. Now Aven was rethinking things. Maybe these vans were part of a planned outing, and she and Layka were going overboard. Still, a windowless cargo van full of residents now idled at the side of the house as the men loaded the second van.

Layka tapped the dash. "At least your plan to hit the town in style when we returned means you shouldn't have any trouble keeping up."

"I just hope the gray makes it less remarkable if they happen to notice us."

"You mean you didn't plan for tailing a convoy of vans without being noticed?"

Aven grinned. "No, but you're about to see map planning pay off." She backed off the pad and turned the car onto the road that ran perpendicular to the one they had walked on to reach the house. "This road comes out on the secondary road that brought us in. The vans will have to come this way, and it will not look suspicious for us to pull in behind them. If they do notice, we should appear to be coming from a direction unrelated to them."

Layka reached across the console and squeezed Aven's leg. "I'm impressed. And I should be scared, but I'm kind of excited."

Aven swallowed hard. Heat radiated up her leg where Layka still held it. She couldn't deny her excitement. The adrenaline of their discovery, coupled with the way her heart pounded when Layka was in proximity, meant she was practically ready to jump out of her seat when Layka squeezed her thigh. She focused on the road that now ran in front of them. The vans should be passing by soon.

"There they are," Layka said, pointing at a white van that looked like a rectangle stretched over wheels.

"That's the first one. I'll let them both get past us. You really should call your sister."

"I know," Layka said, pulling her hand back to her side and tapping her phone with her nail as Aven casually pulled the Stingray onto the road a comfortable distance behind the two vans.

The phone rang several times before going to voice mail. Layka hung up.

"You're not going to leave her a voice mail?" Aven asked, keeping her focus on the road.

"She won't have her phone near the grill. She's helping with the food festival today. By the time she gets the message, we'll be at the festival ourselves."

Aven slammed on her brakes when a deer darted from a nearby field.

"Somebody Help IT!" Layka shouted, jerking her head up from her phone and bracing her hand on the dash even as Aven's hand flashed across her chest to hold her back before they both rocked back in their seats as the deer raced across the road.

"Somebody help what?" Aven said, catching her breath and then getting them moving again. Up ahead, a fork in the road appeared, and the two vans slowed with blinkers signaling for opposite directions.

"Nothing. That was the way my mom would say *shit* when she didn't want to say *shit*."

Aven followed the van on the right, since that was the way she would naturally go to get them back home. "Your mom had acronyms for her cuss words?"

"She did," Layka said, laughing and falling toward the door when Aven took a sharp turn trying to keep the van in sight.

"Sorry," Aven said. "I forgot about that turn. Are you okay?" Aven reached over and squeezed Layka's hand.

"I'm fine, but I plan to kiss the ground in gratitude when we finally get out of this rocket."

"I'll slow down. I don't want to get too close anyway."

"Just don't lose them." Layka turned her hand over and laced Aven's fingers with hers. "Thank you for doing this with me."

"I'll do my best," Aven said, feeling the truth of it. She was determined for this project to succeed to reduce the number of serious hospitalizations and death she had seen escalate in the last few days, and Layka was determined to support this population of people that had been so impacted. But underneath it all was this current of absolute want to help Layka, to see her happy. "I have to say I haven't ever had a date like this one."

"I was going for unique," Layka said with a laugh, then traced the back of Aven's hand interlaced with hers.

"Nailed it!" Aven grinned but kept her eyes on the road as she pressed the gas to regain some speed.

"Seriously, though. I'm worried about the people inside those vans."

"Me too, but maybe we're overthinking this. Maybe they're headed to a program event."

Layka tilted her head as if replaying their morning and seeing the same possibility she had considered. "But it seems the last two turns their speed has increased, and why cargo vans for transport?"

"Maybe they've been converted with seating. I've seen it done." Aven was starting to feel silly as traffic took on normal patterns and the van made turns ahead. "If we're right and they suspect something, it will be more difficult to not draw attention as we move through these small towns on our way back. I'll need your help."

"Stop sign!" Layka shouted.

"I've got the road signs." Aven shook her head and smiled. "I need you to watch for turns they make if I hang back."

"Gotcha." Layka scooted forward as much as her seat belt would allow.

Aven laughed. The two of them had to look ridiculous. The incredulity of it made her question their first suspicions more, but they could see where the van was headed. That was reasonable. "What would your sister say about us right now?"

"That we're hopeless, but she'd also be impressed by you using your side mirrors and doing a head check before changing lanes like a pro."

"There could be someone in my blind spot." Aven laughed out loud at her own response. "Fine. High-speed car-chase experts we are not, but safe, thoughtful drivers following a suspicious van to its destination we can be."

"I don't know," Layka said, scouring the lanes in front of them. "I can't see the van anymore."

"Are you sure?" Aven checked the streets as they passed as best as she could, but traffic had picked up and she needed to focus.

Layka twisted in her seat, checking a side street. "No, that's not them. They have to still be ahead. Stay on this road heading back to the festival at Erin's, and if we don't see them, we'll get Sam. She'll know how to backtrack if we lose them."

Aven turned into the side street Layka indicated that ran at the back of Erin's bar. They hadn't seen the van again. Their plan was to find Layka's sister and tell her about the vans, but at this point she was thinking maybe they had judged the whole thing wrong and the van was just transporting people for an event. Hadn't the guy said something about having one weekend a month off, as if they did events or something most weekends? She parked and felt a little twinge of hesitation at this being her first meeting with Layka's sister. She was the most important person in Layka's life, and they were going to barge in and tell her they were chasing vans that had kidnapped homeless people. She sighed. That wasn't even true—the people stayed at the home; they weren't kidnapped. Her panic escalated. "What do you plan to tell your sister?" she blurted as Layka was already unbuckled and jumping from the car.

"The truth," she said easily, and Aven winced.

What was the truth going to look like to a seasoned cop when she found out Aven had been chasing around the unhoused population in vans with her sister in tow after their impromptu stakeout?

"Come on. What's wrong?"

"Nothing. I'm just looking at it a different way. Your sister said they had checked out the house and had asked for some help from Maryland colleagues. Now that I'm thinking it through, if your sister's team didn't find anything, then it fits that the house wouldn't be under surveillance anymore. So my initial thoughts about corruption, I think, were linked more to my heightened state of vigilance after our morning with Mildred." She closed the car door and clicked the lock, toying with the fob. She felt Layka move back toward her, but she didn't look up.

Layka touched her hand, pausing the fidgeting. "You're worried she is going to think we're being ridiculous."

Aven took a breath, appreciating how Layka's touch calmed her. She looked up and took in those gorgeous soft eyes. "I want to make a good impression. She's your sister. Your everything. I know this is important."

"Layka, hey. I thought I heard someone pull in back here."

Layka turned, and Aven smiled at the woman moving toward them. She and her friends hung out here frequently enough that she recognized the owner's face. Aven gave a wave as she neared. She understood the once-over the woman gave her. Layka was one of her closest friends, and she was sizing up the situation.

"Hi, Erin. This is Aven. Aven, this is Erin." Layka pulled Aven to her side and kept their hands joined. She appreciated the connection. How did this woman seem to always know what she needed? "We stopped by to speak to Sam real quick. Is she still on the grill?"

"No." Erin lifted her apron that said: *If The Broom Fits*. She wiped her hands before straightening her witch hat. "Farrah took her home. She wasn't feeling well. I think she got too hot being over the grill all day, but you know she doesn't listen to anyone."

"That's my sister." Layka gave Aven's hand a little squeeze before letting go.

"Although I have to say, Farrah seems to hold some serious sway. I was impressed."

"Really?" Layka's voice squeaked with excitement.

Aven noted the hope in Layka's voice. She'd have to ask about that. *Why are you interested in every facet of this woman's life?*

"Do you think they've had time to get home?" Layka wrung her hands.

"I'd say yes. How was the trip?"

"Lots to tell you. Can I call and check on Sam first?"

"Sure. I'm headed back to the side patio. Jeremy is on the grill now. I have seen some new faces today, so we can chat after you talk with Sam."

"That will be great." Layka scrolled for her sister's number.

"I'll step inside and get us a table?"

"Yes." Layka put the phone to her ear. "If Sam felt bad enough to go home, she will be a bear. We may have to talk to her tomorrow."

Aven nodded and headed toward the front of the building, bypassing the back door Erin had entered. She stepped through the pebbled landscaping to reach the front. She leaned against the rail to clear a stone from her shoe as she took in the festival that filled the parking lot on the opposite side of the building. She paused when her eyes caught a familiar face. She set her foot down, forgetting the stone as she scanned the area for the van. The man she had just glimpsed was one of the residents at New Foundations. She was certain of it, because he had sat on the stairs rubbing at his beard after he refused to get on the first van. He'd been miming dog ears, and Aven had assumed he was afraid of the dog. She never saw if he got on the second van, but he must have, since he was here. She moved closer to the crowd of people. There were tables of vendors from different organizations that provided support within the community, and there was a mix of people. She searched the crowd but didn't see any of the people from the first van. She searched specifically for the woman with the dog, as they would be easy to spot. She paused. The vans had gone two different directions, but had they both been headed here? Or was the other van, the one with the woman and the dog, at a different location? She was glad in that moment that Layka's sister hadn't been here. She cringed at how it would have looked for them to blast in with their accusations only to find one of the vans had been coming to the festival. *Layka's sister*, Aven thought, turning to get back to Layka and tell her one of the vans was here. Hopefully, she hadn't said anything to Sam. She ran right into Layka.

"Hey there, you. I thought you were getting us a table."

"Did you tell your sister?"

"No, Farrah said she was resting. They're at Farrah's place. I didn't speak with her."

"Good."

"What's going on?"

"It looks like we may have jumped the gun. There's a man here who was on the second van. As unorthodox as it was, it looks like they were bringing the residents to events."

"Okay. Did you see the woman with the dog?"

"No, but I suspect the vans were going to different events. Remember, the vans split at the fork right when we almost hit the deer."

"That's right. Hmm. Okay. Well, maybe we could make a trip out there sometime during the week when the residents aren't out at activities." Layka grimaced. "Are you up for another trip so we can get some insight from the residents and the staff?"

Aven smiled. *Why does doing work even seem like fun with this woman?* "Yes, but I want double snacks. I'm starving."

"You got it. Extra snack order noted. Let's get inside and get you fed."

Layka tried to push away the nagging fear in her mind about Sam. Erin thought the combination of grill heat and an unusually warm fall day had led to the problem, but when it came to her sister's health, she always held fear. Speaking with Farrah had helped, and she was determined to enjoy dinner with Aven. It had been a crazy day. "What are you going to have?"

"I think I'm going to have the festival special," Aven said, tapping the temporary paper menu that lay inside the regular menu.

"Oh, that does sound good, but I'll need to add fries."

"Fries, eh?"

"They're my favorite. I have to get a large when I'm here because Erin always snags some of them."

Aven's phone rang, and she turned it over to turn it off.

Layka spotted the name on the screen. "It's your mom, take it."

"I'll call her back."

Layka reached across the table and covered her hand. "That's what I said one day, and my mom never made it home that night."

Aven paused, recalling the history she'd learned just that morning. "I'm so sorry you lost your parents, and so suddenly. What if we order, then maybe we can step outside to the bench out front, and I can video call her so I can introduce you? She's been asking about this intelligent woman I'm working with on the project."

"That sounds like a plan. Service is usually fast here, but today is extra busy because of the festival. We should have some solid time for you to chat before our dinner arrives."

Layka chewed on her lip as Aven texted her mom that they would be calling in a few minutes. She'd encouraged Aven to take the call but hadn't anticipated Aven wanting her to be involved. Now she was nervous.

"Hi, Layka. Does Erin know you're here?"

"Hi, Mary. Yes, I saw her outside. I think we're both going to have the festival special."

"Great. Do you want drinks, or are you set with the water?"

"Water is good," they said in unison.

"Perfect," Mary said, lifting the menus.

"We're going to step outside for a bit, but we'll be back in shortly."

"No problem. Enjoy the festival."

"I'd already forgotten about the festival. Do you want to walk around while we talk with Mom?"

"Sure," Layka said, glad she might have something to discuss if they were at least moving around the festival. It would help settle her nerves.

Aven tapped her phone, hitting the video screen when the phone began to ring. "Hi, Mom."

"Hi, sweetheart. How are you?"

"I'm doing well." She held the phone up so she and Layka both were in the frame. "Layka is here with me. She's the project manager I was telling you about, from the library."

"Hi, Layka. It is so nice to meet you, at least virtually. Aven speaks highly of you."

Layka could feel her face flush. "Thank you, Mrs...."

"Call me Doreen."

"Doreen," Layka said. "It's nice to meet you as well."

"We're at a festival and thought we would walk you around before we have dinner."

"That sounds lovely, dear. Do they have any booksellers there? I always find a good book at a festival."

"I do the same thing," Layka said, then bit her lip to harness the surge of excitement.

"You do? I love the ones when the authors are there. It makes the experience so unique."

"Me too! They have an amazing event here once a year with over a thousand unique books, either by design, printing press technique, or other feature."

Aven handed over the phone as she turned in a circle, looking to see if she could spot any book tents.

"When is that event? Maybe we could plan to come in during that time, Aven."

Layka passed the phone back to Aven and mouthed the words *I'll find out.*

"I'm not sure, but I'll get the details from Layka and let you know. It looks like they have a book tent here. We're going to walk over and check it out. Did you need anything when you called?"

"I just wanted to hear your voice. Your dad said to tell you hello and he loves you. He's on a conference call in the study but says he has a DIY project for the two of you when you come home."

"Greeaat." Aven dragged the word out, but she was smiling.

Layka felt the light tug at her back, guiding her to turn away from the collection of books on the table as Aven lifted the phone to catch them both again in the frame. "We're here, so I have to let you go so you don't see your surprise."

Layka watched the woman's face light up with joy. She knew that feeling for books.

"I'm so excited! See you soon, sweetheart, and thank you for introducing Layka. She seems lovely."

"You're welcome, Mom. I'll see you soon." Aven closed the connection and turned to Layka. "Thank you. She really does love books."

Layka's hand was already tracing one of the leather-bound covers. "I can tell. She may enjoy this one, and the author is here to sign it."

Aven lifted the book and turned it to read the cover. "How do you do that? You're right, she will absolutely love this one."

Layka shrugged, but she could feel her body flush with the praise. "We may want to head back inside after you get it signed."

"I am so stuffed," Aven said, opening the car door for Layka. For the first time in years, she wanted to skip out on work. Her body and mind hummed with both energy and contentment, and it was a kind of balance that made her long for more time with Layka. *I enjoy work and play with you,* Aven thought as Layka spun to put her back to the car and slid in. The Mindful Path Project was in progress and Aven was struggling to keep work and play separated. She was helping Layka with the small-scale model build of the Wheelhouses to identify issues, and the only issue she could see was her growing attraction for Layka.

"Me too," Layka said, pulling Aven back to the present. "I should have skipped dessert."

"What blasphemy is this? No one should skip dessert."

Layka laughed as she closed the door.

Aven slipped around the car like she was on a cloud. Chemistry was an incredible thing.

Layka reached across the console to squeeze her hand. "I can Uber from here to the rehab facility to pick up my car so you don't have to drive back out there. I know you have a long night ahead of you at work."

"No way. I only had one more call after I came back from the ICU last night, so I slept most of the night. I can drop you off and still get into work on time."

Layka's hand was still atop hers on the console, and Aven rotated her hand. Her heart rate picked up and she swallowed when Layka laced her fingers with hers. "Thanks for helping me pick a book for Mom."

"I was glad to do it. Do you have any siblings?"

"No. Mom and Dad wanted more children, but it didn't work out, so they doted on me."

"Ah, the infamous only child."

Aven laughed. "Actually, my cousin lived two doors down, and my mom and her sister were very close, so we grew up more like siblings than cousins. I don't think I really thought I was an only child. My cousin even had her own room at my house, and I had one at hers. It was like having two moms. Her dad left when she was small, so she stayed more with us than the other way around because her mom worked two jobs."

Layka was tracing Aven's palm with her thumb, their fingers still gently laced together. Aven had to focus to keep from closing her eyes at the exquisite sensation.

The conversation was easy and the time passed too quickly, Aven thought as she pulled into the parking lot. She circled around the car to open the door. When Layka stood, Aven realized she was too close. She went to step back, but Layka covered Aven's hand on the doorframe, essentially locking her in place. The soft light of the parking lot or the same ping of arousal that dipped through Aven made Layka's eyes dilate. Aven's lips parted at the sight. "I want to kiss you," Aven whispered and tried to control her breathing. Her body ached with a need she had never experienced with anyone else.

Layka leaned in, and Aven could feel the air brush her lips when Layka spoke. "How long can you wait?" Layka teased, grazing her tongue across Aven's bottom lip. Aven felt the ache become a pulse. She reached to hold Layka's face with her hands and ran her tongue along Layka's lower lip before pulling it gently with her teeth. She released it and captured Layka's groan with a kiss. Layka's lips were soft, and Aven felt a tear prick at the emotion she felt when their lips pressed together. She couldn't get close enough to this woman. A moan slipped from Layka, and Aven pressed for more as Layka's tongue met hers. She tasted like lemon berry cake. Layka's hands tightened in Aven's hair, and Aven growled with need as she deepened the kiss.

"Ahem." The throat clearing was hesitant but clear, and they reluctantly pulled away. "I remember being young," the security guard said, shaking his head. "You don't have to go home, but you can't stay here." He chuckled when Aven and Layka gave him a little wave as he headed back inside the building.

"Did you hear that? We're young," Layka said, reaching into the car for her phone.

Layka's face was flushed, and Aven wasn't sure if it was embarrassment, heat of the moment, or the shift to a cooler evening temperature, but it looked beautiful on her. Aven thought she could hear the walls around her heart cracking. "Would you like to meet me and some friends tomorrow at Erin's bar? Maybe have Sam come, if she is feeling better." Aven began moving toward Layka's car.

Layka still seemed a little out of breath when she answered. "I'll check with her. I think you might be right about us jumping the gun with our suspicions, but Sam would have some good insight. I'll let you know at the meeting."

They were standing at Layka's car now. "Good night, Layka," Aven said, lifting her hand to kiss the knuckles. "Thanks for the most unique date I've ever had."

Layka laughed. "It's going to be hard to top that."

"Oh God, please don't try. I may not survive."

CHAPTER THIRTEEN

D R. SUDHA GRIMACED AT the squeal of the truly dry dry-erase marker as she circled the Department of Education budget number she'd written on the high corner of the board. "With that, I'll turn it over to Ms. Silva and Dr. Summerhouse."

"Thank you, Dr. Sudha," Layka said, and Aven smiled at how she practically sprinted to the whiteboard.

"Thank you, Dr. Sudha," Aven said also, moving to the computer set up on the narrow podium on the left side of the whiteboard that took up the whole wall. She was logging in to access their presentation when Layka's soft voice made her heart race. What was it about the timbre of Layka's voice that seemed to ping through her entire nervous system? She was a little hesitant about their date tonight. They would be out with friends—Layka meeting her friends and Aven meeting Erin, Layka's best friend. She knew Erin as the owner of the bar she and her friends frequented, but little more beyond that. Aven swallowed. She also might be meeting Layka's sister. It was obvious they were close. What if she didn't like Aven? Aven swallowed back the discomfort that actually seemed to have a taste at this point.

"James, can you shift the projector so that our slides only cover half the whiteboard?"

"Sure, Layka, and there are fresh dry-erase markers under the podium if you need them." James's words were innocent, but Aven felt a twinge of something she didn't like in her chest. Was she jealous that James had thought ahead about something for Layka? She pushed the thought around in her mind. She wasn't jealous, and the feeling abated with some rational thought, but there was a distinct primal emotion she would need to consider later.

"Thanks, James!"

Layka's thank-you brushed air across Aven's neck as Layka leaned near her to reach the new markers.

Aven closed her eyes and steeled her body against the visceral contraction of some very important muscles. She blew out a controlled breath through pursed lips. Hopefully, everyone would just think she was nervous. "Thank you, everyone, for squeezing in the time for this extra meeting. Ms. Silva and I spoke with Dr. Sudha about elevating the project from investigation to intervention." Aven clicked to the first slide. She knew Layka was writing out the detail points they had discussed on the residual side of the whiteboard, and she needed to give her a few minutes. Aven had to consciously steer her brain from relapsing to the extra time the two of them had spent in this room going over these details. *Great, my face is flushing.* She could feel the heat in her ears. *And did Layka sound a little overly joyful about the markers?* Aven tried to refocus, but the question gnawed at her—Layka either had a lot of love for dry-erase markers, she was interested in James, or she wasn't accustomed to people doing thoughtful things for her. She'd seen interest in Layka's eyes at the café. She'd felt it in the little touches they'd exchanged since then as they worked together. And it had definitely been in the kiss. She knew what that looked like, so Layka wasn't interested in James, but the latter made her a little sad and she realized she wanted to be the one doing thoughtful things for Layka. And there was a glimpse of what had stirred in her—a possessive streak, that was new. Had her history made her an extremist, to hold things too close or run away? *And that is a reflection for some time other than now.* "Layka is listing two columns on the board." Aven looked over her shoulder to see which column she was listing first. Layka's manicured nails lightly held the marker as her hand moved dexterously across with only a hair's breadth between her hand and the board. So close, but never touching it. Aven licked her lips, then snapped her mouth closed and turned back to the computer. Damn it, she still didn't know which column she was writing first. *How did you miss the actual words on the board?* She cleared her throat. *It doesn't matter, just get your head back on the presentation.* "The funding already available to the hospital and the library that will be directed toward the program are listed in one column, while the funding we recently submitted for is in the alternate column. There are some private funding sources and nonprofits that have expressed interest and will be listed later."

Aven lifted the clicker, stood, and walked to the side of the board where her computer screen was projected. "The public health concern about the exposure of public places to increased risk for communicable disease is not new. However, there has been an increased concern in the last few years since COVID." Aven pointed the clicker at the computer, and the screen animated to turn the display of graphs into active information. "Now, even more recently, within the last ninety days, there have been increased complaints specifically about the risk posed at the library. Ms. Silva has brought forth a valid concern in the approach we were taking initially. It marginalized a vulnerable population based on assumptions about the unhoused population that have not been properly investigated for validity. Ms. Silva." Aven turned to Layka to hand over the presentation, and those gray-blue eyes locked on hers with earnest appreciation. When Layka took the clicker from her hand, the brush of her nails along Aven's palm made a tingle run up her arm and jump-start her heart. *Holy crap, my heartrate must be 175 beats per minute.* Aven rubbed her finger along the side of her neck to slow her racing heart. What the hell?

"Thank you, Dr. Summerhouse." Layka smiled that gentle smile that made the corners of her mouth turn up ever so slightly. "We discussed utilizing the investigation of communicable disease in the unhoused as an opportunity to also evaluate the complexity of the needs for this population. This would allow us to investigate the issue brought forward for the public welfare while providing opportunity for an inclusive, humane solution if the problem is connected to this vulnerable community."

Layka tapped the clicker, and Aven stepped away from Layka and toward the wall when she realized her proximity to Layka meant she was standing in the way of the projected screen on the board.

"The idea is to build three primary locations: one in DC, one in Kansas, and one on the West Coast near San Francisco." Layka clicked again, and Aven smiled as a sketch of the building appeared on the screen beside a computer-generated 360-degree walkthrough video. "Their design is that of a spiral, which is why they are being called Wheelhouses in the grants we submitted."

"Why the spiral design?" James asked, and Aven found herself watching Layka's face.

"Dr. Summerhouse can answer that better due to some of the new data the hospital has collected."

Aven pushed off the wall she'd been leaning against and smiled at James. He didn't seem quite as interested in the answer now. She understood. She could sit and listen to Layka's melodic voice describe a grocery list. "The spiral design will allow access to shelter for those who are transient and not seeking any further assistance from our facility. Our data shows some new variants that are concerning, so it is important that the design be created in a way that reduces the spread of disease. As you move into the spiral, access to resources grows. This facilitates medical evaluation and resource access that allows them to choose their level of cooperation. We are only beginning to understand the myriad causes for many who find themselves on the streets, but for those who have fallen on hard times and need support to transition back to the life they lost, those resources will be available."

Dr. Sudha lifted a hand.

"How will these Wheelhouses be connected to libraries for the educational resources you and Aven described to me in the proposal?" Dr. Sudha looked back and forth between the two of them.

Aven grinned and felt her heart skip a beat and begin its gallop once again when Layka mirrored her look of excitement. "Go ahead, Layka," Aven said, basking in the warmth of Layka's radiant smile.

"The public library connections with the Wheelhouse builds are part of a multi-grant proposal that includes a submission to the Department of Education." Layka pointed to the second column she had listed on the board. "The ones in green marker are grants already in place from the organization listed. The ones in yellow marker are grants that have been in submission prior to the project and we've received notification of funding. The ones in red, like the Department of Education, are modified resubmissions which will most likely be funded with the additional information we submitted. We don't have all the details for how the two will be connected because much of that will be shaped by the resubmissions feedback."

Dr. Sudha tapped her chin. "These will add funding to the money the library already has designated for community enrichment and education, so your initial plan is building on some of the outreach programs, like literacy and ESL, that we already have in place."

"Yes," Layka said, and Aven had to smile at the excitement that glowed in those gorgeous eyes. "We will have to work on the integration of the model, but tentatively the plan is for the Wheelhouses to be built with attachment to a smaller building that will serve as a public library for the community."

Simon lifted his head from his computer, where he had been typing. He must have had surgery this morning because he was in his OR scrubs rather than the shirt-and-tie look he wore on clinic days. "So, the library resources will be used predominantly for the integration of the Wheelhouses with the public library, and the hospital resources will be used to build the Wheelhouses?"

"Aven, you want to take this part?"

"Sure." Aven took the clicker from Layka's outstretched hand and felt the Pavlovian ping when their fingers touched. She clicked it twice to get to the screen she needed, which showed a breakdown of costs. "The Wheelhouse will have a healthcare triage area at the transition between each level of the spiral loop. Most of the hospital resources will be utilized to create these triage areas, which offer expanded healthcare resources as a person or family moves into the next section of the spiral housing. Both the hospital and library contributions will be used in the building of the housing segments, which are created as multiple independent living areas within the structure of a single facility. There are more than a few snags we have already identified, but the core team meets regularly to navigate these as the project evolves." Aven scanned the room. "Does anyone have any additional questions before we move on?"

The room was silent with that good sense of anticipation. "Okay. I'm going to take a seat and let Ms. Silva detail the rest of the project." Aven laid the clicker on the podium. She was reluctant to manage another surge of that electric jolt between them every time they touched. She took her seat then realized she was doomed as she listened, enraptured by Layka's voice as she laid out the time frame for the project.

"As you leave today and head out into the brisk DC October day, imagine a Wheelhouse and new library marking its first day with a ribbon-cutting ceremony in June next year, followed by a celebration of the second one in Kansas around February of the following year, culminating in a grand celebration on the West Coast at the third Wheelhouse in April."

"So, the first two builds have roughly an eight-month window, but the last build will go up in two months?" Dr. Foster's voice was recognizable and Aven didn't need to turn her head, but she did so to see the woman seated near the back of the room with Simon. The incredulity in her question wasn't unkind, but Aven was reminded why so often she and other doctors were seen as abrupt. They were accustomed to having to take charge in life-or-death situations where errors could be disastrous, and sometimes that cut-to-the-core-of-things mindset leaked into other venues. Aven turned back to see the flash of irritation on Layka's face as she physically drew back. Yep. She had seen people look at her just like that—saw the recoil as if she had physically attacked them. She was front and center watching this sophisticated woman flinch as if ambushed when she held in her mind all the detail of the plan the two of them had worked to develop and give real structure. *Why isn't she confident in her knowledge, her brilliance? We all have strengths and weakness.* She herself was unfazed by Foster's words but could be derailed by things that didn't fluster Layka at all. She swallowed hard, thinking again about their plans for tonight. They were two totally different people. Her heart was moving too fast with this woman, but who could blame her? She was intelligent, thoughtful, funny, gorgeous. *Put the brakes on, Fast and*

Furious, she berated herself. *You still don't know her that well, and her sister and friends may hate you.* The thought made her hopes about the evening start to crumble. After all, it wouldn't be the first time people decided not to like her because she was too much or not enough. The look now on Layka's face was a reminder as she forced a smile and answered.

"Actually, we have two teams working on the builds. Both teams will work together on the first, which we anticipate will have the most hurdles and unexpected delays. Then the two teams will move separately to the next two locations, one in Kansas and the other in San Francisco. We've allotted three years in the grant submissions but set our goals aggressively tight to about eight months each so we can identify problems early."

"That's very practical. Thank you. I'll tentatively add notes to those months on my calendar." Dr. Foster lifted her phone.

Layka clicked to the next slide, and her smile became that full, part-ed-lips smile that usually put Aven at ease, but Aven had a distinct sense of unease. Her intuition was confirmed when an email from the DC zoning office pinged on her phone. She watched their fun evening plans for dinner together with friends disappear.

CHAPTER FOURTEEN

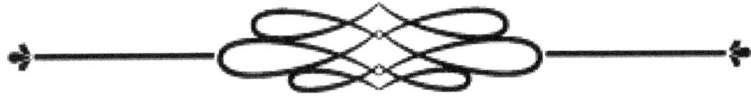

L AYKA WATCHED AS AVEN mimed swinging at a ball with her
hand as she pushed the saltshaker across the table with a grace
that belied the force she had appeared to use. Reynolds was laughing,
and Aven's friend Sarah was rolling her eyes. Layka's cheeks hurt
from laughing, which she had done practically nonstop since they
arrived. Aven, Reynolds, and Sarah played pickleball together, and
apparently their camaraderie on the court often translated to quick
reflexes and reading each other in the ER—and also led to quite a
few laughable stories.

Their original plan to meet at Erin's two weeks ago had fallen through
because additional documents and scaled drawings related to the building's scope and timeline had been requested from the DC zoning office.
Without zoning approval, they could miss the window for the start of the
build and throw the schedule for the entire project off by months. They
had still had time together, but it had been scattered meetings and phone
conferences as they balanced their schedules and juggled priorities. Layka
was on fire from the growing desire to put her lips on Aven's again, but
until now they had been buried in work on the project, much of which
they did via phone and video conference. This was their first opportunity
for another date, and Layka loved seeing Aven so animated and excited.
Aven turned just then, and her laugh became a tender smile. *Dear God,*

when she smiles at me like that, I want to take her face in my hands and kiss her. Layka leaned in to whisper at her ear, "You have a beautiful smile."

Aven shivered and closed her eyes as Layka leaned back. It made Layka's heart feel bigger than her chest to realize she had that impact on this wonderful woman.

Layka twisted back toward the table and placed her head against the high wooden seat, lifting her wineglass to her lips as her best friend, Erin, made her way over to join them. It turned out that Aven and her friends hung out here on Thursday evenings after pickleball and already knew Erin. Layka took a minute to admire the deep ruby color of the wine, enjoying the glow of happiness she felt. She could feel Aven's eyes on her, which made her warm more than the wine did, and that was going down smooth. She hadn't known Erin's place carried a wine Dr. Sudha recommended. But there it had been, right on the list.

"Cheers to Erin selecting the best wine," Aven said as Erin approached.

Layka's heart swelled at how quickly Aven and her friends had pulled Erin into the bubble of their group. She was not good at integrating people in social situations, but Aven had seemed to pull their two worlds together seamlessly. "Sam and I always order beer, so I didn't know you had such great wine."

"Now you do," Erin said, pulling a chair to the end of the table. "How is Sam?"

"She says she's recovering, but her return to work last week set her back. Now she plans to go back to work on Monday, but I always worry when she gets sick. You know how bad COVID hit her."

"You mentioned this briefly before. How bad was her run-in with COVID?" Aven asked.

"She was hospitalized for close to two months..." Layka let her words trail off. She didn't want to talk about how terrified she had been to see her sister fighting for every breath. Aven ran a hand down her arm but didn't speak. Layka appreciated that. Aven seemed to know when she didn't want to talk about something. She had a sixth sense about when Layka wanted words of comfort and when she would rather have the quiet space to put her feelings in order so she could manage them.

"Layka, you have to tell us about Aven's stint as a detective," Reynolds said, lifting her beer.

Layka was grateful for the reprieve from the dark reminders of her sister's dodge of death and was sure Aven's friends were following an unspoken lead from Aven.

"Hear, hear," Sarah said lifting her chardonnay as if in a toast. "Yes, you must."

Layka smiled. Reynolds and Sarah had made her feel comfortable immediately. They welcomed her right into their tight-knit group, and something about all the family she'd lost seemed to heal a little bit with that connection. "You guys are trying to get me in trouble."

"She is sworn to secrecy," Aven said, reaching over and twisting her fingers in front of Layka's lips like she was locking them.

Layka couldn't resist. She nipped at Aven's thumb. Instead of the chirp of surprise she anticipated, Aven made a soft sound, and Layka felt her core spasm.

Aven cleared her throat, but her eyes stayed on Layka's for a heartbeat before she pulled her hand to the menu.

"The sweet Thai Chili wings are excellent if you like a little heat," Sarah said and smiled innocently as she took a sip of her wine.

"I don't know," Reynolds said. "Sometimes you're just in the mood for a Louisiana Rub." She tapped the menu thoughtfully where the wing's name was displayed.

"You're both horrible friends," Aven said, her face still red.

Layka smiled, but it was all she could do to keep from twisting in the seat at the tingle between her thighs. She wanted Aven to touch her. Anywhere. Her hand, her arm, her thigh. *Oh, my*, she thought, feeling a spasm at her core with the vision of Aven touching her thigh.

"Hi, everyone. Are you ready to order?" The waitress tapped the screen on her pad and leaned all her weight on one leg as she stood between Erin's chair and Layka's booth seat.

Layka was glad she had checked the food side of the menu when she ordered her wine. "I'll have the lemon pepper wings."

"That sounds good. Make that two, and can I get a large basket of fries? Extra crunchy."

Layka bit her lip, realizing she'd forgotten to order her fries. *Do I embarrass myself by adding to the order when the waitress has clearly moved on to others or—*

Layka startled when words tickled her ear and she felt Aven's breath hot near her neck. "The basket of fries is for you."

"They are? Did you read my mind?" Layka swallowed at the breathy tone of her answer.

"I remember you telling me about your friend Erin stealing your fries all the time. So, I figured you'd been distracted when you ordered." Aven ran her hand along Layka's thigh.

Yep, and there it went. Layka's core clenched with the touch.

Aven had said this was a favorite hangout for them because of its proximity to the hospital and its panorama of wings, but it was more than that. It was memories and moments, and she was now a part of that. She covered Aven's hand with her own.

Layka's phone pinged, and she checked it with her free hand while Aven lifted a napkin that had fallen to the booth seat.

Layka inadvertently squealed when she read the notification. "We received the grant!" She turned her phone toward Reynolds across the table, then moved it in a circle for each of them to see. When she reached Aven, she held her gaze. "Thank you for your help with this."

"You're welcome, but it was your idea to pivot and add it to the pre-existing grant to get it through faster," Aven said, lifting her wine in a toast.

They each lifted their beverage to Aven's, and she smiled that tender smile before she spoke. "To Layka and her determination to fight for those who might not be able to fight for themselves."

"Cheers!" Reynolds and Sarah chimed in.

"You deserve as much credit as me—" Layka started, but Aven placed a finger on her lip.

"I came with good intentions for the public at large. You came with a plan for both the public as a whole and for the group that could have easily been further marginalized without your voice."

Layka wasn't sure which made her feel more connected—the soft touch of Aven's gentle finger that left her lip still tingling, or the words that seemed to wrap her heart with warmth and gratitude. She sat her phone down and lifted her glass. "Thank you," she said, clinking each glass.

"This is wonderful. When will we be able to start the Wheelhouse builds?" Aven pulled her knee up on the booth as she turned to face Layka.

The movement pressed Aven's knee and shin along Layka's thigh. *Why does every touch of her body to mine seem to make time stand still?* Layka briefly glanced around the room. People stood at the bar, and couples and groups of friends danced while a gaggle of people threw darts near the back of the room. They all seemed to be in slow motion, devoid of the sound she knew they each fostered. She let her hand fall to cover Aven's ankle exposed by the way her jeans had inched up her leg when she placed it on the seat. Her skin was so soft, and she traced the bone. "Tonight, if you're up to it after all of this." Layka waved her other hand out at the expanse of people, but Aven's eyes never left hers. Layka swallowed to get more than a breath behind her words. "We could work at my place for a while. I have all the project details from the contractors and engineers set up for review in my home office."

Aven smiled. "You'll let me put highlights on the whiteboard in your home workspace?"

Layka bit her lip at the reminder of their inside joke. "Maybe."

"I'm in," Aven said, and Layka noted the new low timbre to her voice. "This grant changes everything."

Layka watched the joy shine on Aven's face, and she couldn't define how happy it made her to see it there. Yet, there was a sliver of hesitation in her.

Sarah pulled Layka's attention from Aven when she spoke. "How does this money help? I thought the NIH was funding the project through the hospital's grant for community care."

The hesitation seemed to lift from Aven. "It is part of the funding resource for the project, but when Layka brought forward a feasibility solution that could impact three of the core issues for the homeless, we put together a request for secondary grants to the CDC, the Department of Housing, and the Department of Education."

Layka lifted her phone. "This was the final grant we had been waiting on. It gives us the additional financial support from the Department of Housing to create three independent living facilities called Wheelhouses connected to satellite library spaces to foster tiered living support for the unhoused population."

Aven leaned into the table, and Layka found herself with her elbow propped on the table, her chin in her hand, and her eyes tracing every movement of Aven's animation and excitement as she moved the salt, pepper, and ketchup bottles on the table. "There will be three pilot constructions, one in Washington, one in Kansas, and one in California. We have to work out two final hurdles identified by engineering in the model build." Aven looked to Layka as if to confirm. "I think we can work those out tonight."

Layka smiled and nodded, her head still propped on her hand. She could watch Aven talk all night about something she was passionate about, but now Aven was asking for her input. "The tiered structure started with Aven's idea about triage for reducing the risk of communicable disease, and we built it into a broad structure for housing, learning, and health." Layka watched as Erin, Reynolds, and Sarah took in the idea.

"Wow, you two have really been doing extra legwork outside the committee meetings," Reynolds said.

"I'm glad you said that," Sarah chimed in. "Steve hadn't mentioned any of this from his committee meetings as the engineer consultant. He was going to be in big trouble, but it sounds like the committee is the tip of the iceberg and these two have done ninety percent of the work underwater on their own."

Layka thought about it and for the first time realized just how much work she and Aven had done together. It hadn't even seemed like work. That made her smile. It also meant the two of them were tied to the project. That made her pause.

"I'm proud of you both," Sarah said, scooting toward Reynolds. "I'm meeting Steve at the DC event for the campaign countdown, so I've got to run. It was a pleasure to see you again, Layka."

"Thank you. The pleasure was mine, and I'm in on you teaching me the pickleball ropes before I face off against these two." Layka pointed to Aven and Reynolds.

Reynolds stood to let Sarah out. "Bye, everyone," Sarah said, giving Erin's shoulder a friendly squeeze as she left.

"Thanks for joining us, Erin, we love this place," Reynolds said.

"It was good to have some time with old"—she stole one of Layka's fries from her basket—"and new friends." She popped the fry in her mouth. "I'm glad you love the place. It's my small-business-owner dream come true." She stood and gave Layka a head kiss. "Which also means I should get back to work."

"I've got to run too. Some of us don't have the day off tomorrow," Reynolds said pointedly to Aven.

"Yeah, well, some of us have been on call three nights in a row and deserve a break."

"That you do, my friend," Reynolds said with such a happy smile Layka wanted to tell her how it radiated love for her friend. She watched as the two did a fist bump with three different moves before Reynolds turned to her. "I'm glad the two of you met. If she gives you any trouble, you let me know."

"Hey," Aven said with feigned hurt.

Reynolds just shrugged her shoulders, grinned, and turned for the door.

Layka took a deep breath, realizing they were all alone and she was still absently tracing circles at Aven's ankle. She looked down at her hand, then up at Aven. "Are you concerned if what we're doing now doesn't work out that we will be stuck together on this project?"

Aven covered her hand, pulling it up to her lips and kissing it. "I'm not worried. If this"—Aven tilted Layka's chin, leaning in to brush her lips across Layka's—"doesn't work out, I will be glad I have any reason to still be with you."

Layka leaned into the kiss, then pulled away just enough to speak. "I say we take this discussion back to my house where we can lay out all the options for the project."

"I like how that sounds," Aven said, nipping Layka's bottom lip.

"Are you good to drive?"

"I'm good. I only had one glass of wine." She leaned in for another taste of Layka. "Someone had me distracted."

Layka gently touched Aven's thigh and started sliding her hand up slowly as they kissed. "I'll have to be careful not to distract you while you're driving."

Aven leaned her head back on the wood of the high bench, and her breath stuttered as Layka's hand brushed the center of her pants when she pulled her hand up and lifted her phone.

"We may need to call an Uber," Aven said, then leaned her head forward and smiled.

Layka was on fire, and she didn't know if she could keep her hands off Aven on the drive to her house. She could feel the strength in her leg when Aven's thigh tightened at her touch. The feel of Aven's muscles responding to her touch made her core twitch, and she was wet. She leaned in and bit the very bottom of Aven's ear. "I'll try to be good on the drive home."

Aven followed Layka through the door into her apartment. Layka had not been good, in fact, and Aven thought she might explode with just one more touch at this point.

Layka laid her purse on a small foyer table to her left and pushed the door closed.

Aven shook her head, realizing she had been staring. Now she found herself pushed solidly back against a built-in bookshelf that formed the left side of the archway to the living room. Layka's hand was tracing down her neck. Aven pulled her hard against her body. She couldn't stand it anymore. She needed to feel this woman completely. "God, you feel amazing against me." Layka kissed her hard, and Aven spun them to put Layka's back to the shelf. Then Layka's hands were in her hair, and she parted her lips as Layka asked for more. The feel of her tongue brushing her lips then pressing deeper made her shudder. She ran her hand beneath the ribbing of the fitted turtleneck sweater at her waist. The skin of her stomach was warm, and smooth.

"Yes," came the whisper from Layka, and Aven lifted the sweater, pulling it over her head then tracing down the exposed skin of her wrists still raised over her head. She kissed Layka and gently pushed her hands to the shelf lip above Layka's head. "The perfect place for your hands is near all these books."

Layka's eyes went dark, and Aven ran her hands down Layka's exposed arms from wrist to shoulder, then along the contours of Layka's bra, just brushing the skin that peeked out above the lace. She smiled at the front clasp and leaned in to whisper close to Layka's ear as she clicked it open and ran her thumbs along the inner side of both breasts. "Don't bring your arms down," she whispered and stroked both thumbs over Layka's hardened nipples. Layka's back bowed, and Aven licked each nipple arched toward her.

"Aven."

The sound of her name made Aven almost come herself. She could feel Layka's legs start to tremble. She wanted to lift her, but Layka was rocking and the movement of her body was intoxicating. She'd never used anything like a strap-on, but the thought crossed her mind that she would be able to stroke and please this incredibly beautiful woman while having her hands free to explore. She wanted to be inside of Layka while holding her tight, supporting her as those hips bucked and her hands pressed and squeezed her perfect full breasts. She took one in her mouth and pinched the other as her hand slid down Layka's ribs and traced the waistband of her jeans. Aven unbuttoned them by feel, her lips never leaving Layka's breast. Layka began to roll her hips. Aven licked one nipple, then the other as she slid her other hand to help shimmy down Layka's jeans. They fell to the floor, and Aven caught the scent of her arousal. She kissed up Layka's neck to her ear as she rubbed at the wet lace between Layka's thighs. "I want to taste you." The words made Layka rock her hips harder, and Aven's finger slid back and forth across Layka's clit through the lace. Layka leaned into it as much as she could with her arms above her.

"I've craved your touch. I'm gonna come."

Aven slid a finger beneath the lace. "Hold on. Let me take you higher." She slid the white lace down till it fell to the ground. Layka was so wet. Aven slid one finger inside the warmth and felt Layka's walls squeeze. God, being inside this woman was intoxicating.

Layka let out a sound somewhere between a cry and a moan. Aven felt Layka's weight against her hand. Layka's trembling legs said she wouldn't be able to hold herself much longer. She leaned into Layka's ear. "I'm going to enjoy your breasts, then your center." She slid a second finger into Layka's warmth.

Layka moaned and bucked. "I'm not going to last that long, Aven."

Aven sucked a hard nipple into her mouth, pulled gently on it, and released it. "When I do that again, imagine it here." Aven stroked her thumb across the swollen bud between Layka's thighs.

Layka's "Yes" was a breathy sigh of want.

Aven slid her fingers in and out, then took Layka's nipple into her mouth again and pressed Layka's clit with the flat of her thumb just as she sucked hard on her nipple.

"Aven!" Layka shouted her name.

Wetness coated Aven's hand as she braced it in place with her leg between Layka's thighs to help support her. Layka was still spasming around her fingers when Aven reached up with her free hand and pulled Layka's hands down by the wrists and kissed her knuckles. She released them and gently pulled free of Layka, careful to keep her supported with her leg. She lifted Layka slightly by the thighs, and Layka wrapped her legs around her. Aven straightened, lifting Layka's full weight, and Layka laid her head on Aven's shoulder.

"I'm weak as a kitten, and that came fast, but it's been building in me for weeks." Her soft words tickled Aven's skin, and she shivered.

Weeks, Aven thought, glad to know she wasn't alone in this mounting attraction that had her ready to topple over the edge. "Point me to your room and I'll lay you down."

Layka lifted an arm and pointed at a hallway to the left of the living room.

"Turn on lamp," Layka said as they entered the room.

A robot voice said something Aven was too distracted to hear, and a lamp clicked on by the bed.

Layka's bed was high, and Aven set Layka down and stepped back just enough to run her fingers along the soft waves of her brown hair that she had left down tonight.

Layka looked up and squeezed Aven's hand as it traced through her hair. She leaned her face into it, kissed the palm, and sighed. "I've never come that hard before."

Aven smiled, feeling everything inside her warm. "I've never enjoyed touching someone the way I enjoy touching you. I wish my hands could be everywhere at once." She blushed, recalling her thought about the sex toy.

"What is it?" Layka asked, running her hand along the inside of Aven's waistband and skimming her finger lightly across Aven's skin.

Aven bit her lip. "I can't believe I'm going to tell you this, but I feel so comfortable with you."

Layka paused her movement and stood, lifting Aven's shirt over her head to expose the pink and black bra.

The tingle of her exposed skin made her center draw and a sensation plinked to her core. "I was thinking about how I wished out there that I'd had a, you know..." She motioned her hands down near her zipper. "So I could have my hands free to do more to you, but I've never done that before and would probably hurt myself." She laughed then bit her lip, feeling as exposed as her breasts but also turned on by how good it felt to be this comfortable with someone the first time.

Layka's eyes flickered with new desire. "You've never done that before?"

"What? Had sex?"

"No, used a..." Layka flushed crimson as she searched for the word she wanted. "An accessory."

Aven laughed, glad Layka seemed to be at an equal loss for words. "An accessory." She placed her knee on the bed next to Layka and cupped her face with both hands. "That is absolutely too fun to forget, and I will forever call them 'accessories.'" She leaned in and kissed her. "And even worse, the next time someone asks for an accessory to anything, I will not be able to keep a straight face."

Layka laughed but gave a playful tug and twist that had Aven on the bed beside her and quickly underneath her. "Why are you still mostly dressed?"

Aven grinned. "Because you were too busy coming harder than you ever have before."

"That's true, but I'm recovered now." She started rocking against Aven's center, and Aven was reminded of just how close she was to her own orgasm. Layka must have seen it in her eyes, because she pulled away slightly with a devilish grin and ran only her finger down the zipper of Aven's jeans. "So, tell me a little bit about these accessories."

Aven thought she would laugh every time she heard that word, but right now it made her tingle, feeling the thrum of the pulse mounting at her core.

"It looks like the weak-as-a-kitten novice has your tongue." Layka rubbed her palm up the zipper, and the pressure hit just right.

"I'm a novice too when it comes to that, I've never used one before so I can't tell you...oh, mmm," Aven said into a sigh when Layka's palm rocked gently at her clit through her jeans.

Then Layka was gone, and Aven had to blink a few times to reorient. Layka came back through the door with her phone in her hand. Aven watched, mesmerized, and almost tipped over the edge seeing Layka walk into the room completely naked, her brown waves falling around her tan shoulders. Even in the fall, her skin tone was gorgeous, and Aven watched her breasts move as her arm shifted to scroll something on her phone screen. She was probably going to have to carry extra panties around if she remembered this every time Layka used her phone when they were out.

"Here. This one looks fun," Layka said turning the screen toward her. "Now..." She ran her finger back up Aven's jeans, but this time when she reached the top, she slid the zipper down.

Aven stared at an "accessory" on the phone that looked like it had two ends. One of the ends was curled slightly. She swallowed hard as she imagined one end of it inside her while the other was inside of

Layka. "You've got me so worked up, I can't even read. It looks like it's strapless rather than strap-on." There was a pulsing already between her thighs, and she had trouble breathing when Layka's hands grazed her hips, lifting off the bed at Layka's guidance. She shivered at the thrill of her jeans and panties sliding down her legs. Layka lay directly between her legs, rocking their wetness together. The sensation made her close her eyes against the flow of emotion at the connection. She dropped the phone. *Who needs accessories?* she thought as every inch of her responded to Layka's touch.

Layka slid her hand between them and circled Aven's clit. "All you have to do is focus and tell me how that works. Does it work here?" She pressed Aven's clit. "Or does it work here?" She slid her finger the length of Aven's wet folds.

She knows I don't know, and she is going to tease me with just the idea of figuring it out together, Aven thought, rocking against Layka's hand.

"I'm just toying with you," Layka said, circling Aven's center, pressing then stroking quickly, making Aven writhe.

Aven threw her head back into the soft mattress. "Pickleball score, pickleball score," she muttered under her breath, trying to get the wave at her center to subside, but she was too far gone. *This woman is going to make me come with her smarty-pants ideas and a few touches.*

Layka watched Aven's face. She loved the feel of her hand between them. It felt so good to touch Aven and to feel her body tremble beneath her touch with her words hanging in the air between them. *Who knew sex could be punny?* She realized it was the first time she'd had sex with someone where they were both so hot for each other that even moments of humorous interruption couldn't stave off the want. She was absolutely going to buy one of those accessories. Aven looked so hot and turned on just talking about it. "Talk to me or I'll have to stop," Layka said sweetly, running the heel of her hand over Aven's wet folds then circling her clit again.

"I think, one part fits in me," Aven began. She was panting.

Layka pushed her bra up to pinch a nipple.

Aven lifted off the bed. "And the other is for you."

Layka stopped moving her hand but pressed herself against Aven's center and started rocking gently. She leaned down, licking Aven's neck near her ear. Her blond hair spread out over the mattress. "God, you're beautiful, Aven." The tingle between her own legs as they rocked together had her near the pinnacle again herself. She bit lightly at Aven's ear. "And that sounds really good. You inside me..." Layka said, still controlling the pace as each rock of her hips slid Aven's clit over her folds. "And me inside you."

"Layka, please. I want you inside me."

"Keep rocking against me. From what you've described, it will be good practice."

Aven did as commanded, and Layka pushed Aven's bra off over her head. The movement pushed Aven's hands above her head, and Layka brought them down with their hands laced together then shifted to stagger their legs. Aven bucked at the new pressure of Layka's thigh. Layka took just a moment to take Aven in. Her eyes were so dilated Layka could barely see the blue of them, and her blond hair fell away from her face like a halo around her head. She kept her left hand laced with Aven's and put her weight on that elbow as she took Aven's nipple into her mouth. It was so hard she felt her own clit tighten, and she released Aven's nipple with a moan. She brought Aven's left hand still laced with her right to her lips and kissed it, then slid their laced hands down between them.

"I'm so close," Aven gasped.

"Let's practice working together," she said as she slid Aven's hand over her own swollen clit that was pressed against Layka's thigh. She flicked her tongue across Aven's nipple as she slid two fingers inside of Aven and whispered, "Let's take you over the edge together." She nipped Aven's nipple once then sucked it into her mouth, bracing her leg against the rocking spasms of Aven's climbing climax she could feel around her fingers.

"Yes. Layka!" Aven lifted them both off the bed when she jerked with the orgasm.

They collapsed in a heap on the bed. Layka gently slid from Aven, eliciting a tiny moan as Aven shifted her arm to pull Layka's body tight to her side. She felt like a koala clinging to a tree as she nestled her head to Aven's shoulder. "Now that we've got that out of the way, we can slow down," Layka said, enjoying the comfort of her cheek pressed to the soft skin just below Aven's shoulder as she traced slow circles on Aven's abdomen. The lingering spasms twitched Aven's abs.

"Can I just hold you for a while?"

Layka closed her eyes at the words and snuggled into her tree. *Grounded, strong, gentle Aven. I could get used to this place.*

Aven turned her head and kissed Layka's forehead. "I enjoy the feel of you this close to me." She gave a little squeeze with the arm that was wrapped along Layka's back to her waist.

Layka stopped her circle patterns and stretched her arm across Aven's waist, squeezing her back. "I like being here." She raised up on an elbow and pushed Aven's blond hair away from her forehead. "At this rate, Ms. Principal Investigator of the Mindful Path Project, you are not going to get much work out of me."

Aven laughed, making her abs bounce against Layka's arm. Layka relaxed her arm and traced the faintly defined muscles again, making her way up to circle a nipple that responded with just a touch to the soft skin around it. "If you start that again, Ms. Principal Manager of the Mindful Path Project, I will not be able to put words together for even the smallest conversation."

"Hmm..." Layka leaned in to lick the hardened bud. "That sounds like a challenge." She rolled gently out of Aven's arms and stood. "Stay right there."

"The only other place I'd want to be is following you." Aven rolled onto her side and braced on her propped elbow.

Layka smiled, then walked from the room. She could feel Aven's eyes on her, and it made her body flush with heat. She returned with whiteboard and easel in hand. She smiled as Aven burst out laughing and rolled to her back on the bed. "That ought to slow us down for sure."

Aven sat up on the bed and reached for her clothes.

"No, no." Layka moved to take Aven's hand, causing the black panties to fall back to the floor. "None of those are invited to this meeting."

Layka wrote at the top of the board *MINDFUL PATH LIVING*. Then underneath she began to write *Project*...but Aven was tracing her fingertip across her bare shoulder and down her back. Layka smiled. She lifted a marker, turning to place it in Aven's hand.

Aven smiled and lifted her empty hand to continue the line her other hand had started. Layka twisted, putting herself face-to-face with Aven. Her back still tingled along her spine. "It looks like I'm going to have to keep both hands busy," she said, placing the eraser in Aven's open hand.

Aven groaned and Layka laughed as she reached to finish writing: *Project Goal—s*. She sighed as she wrote out the *s* and felt soft lips at the back of her neck.

"Specific," Aven whispered against Layka's neck.

Layka closed her eyes at the feel of Aven's breasts against her shoulder blades as Aven reached around her to write the word she was breathing against her neck.

"Do you have specific goals, Layka?" Aven asked with a breathy tone that blew across Layka's ear

"Uh-huh," Layka said, hearing the sound like the whimper it was.

"Are they measurable?" Aven asked, kissing Layka's shoulder and pulling the soft corner of the eraser from her naval to circle her breast.

Layka nodded, her words erased by the spark that raced from her core to her nipple.

"Take my marker and write it down." Aven kissed a second spot on Layka's shoulder as she held the marker in front of Layka as the eraser tip continued its spiral around her nipple.

Layka dropped her marker and took the one in Aven's hand. She never even removed the lid as Aven's now free hand slid to her abdomen, then down to circle her clit. "It feels so perfect when you touch me," she said as she traced the long forearm that pressed her back into Aven even as Aven's movements around her clit made her rock. *How am I still standing?* she thought just before Aven's fingers slipped inside of her and she felt the muscles in her forearm flex and the eraser's edge brushed over her hardened nipple. "Take me, Aven!"

"Go to your knees, I'll hold you."

Layka did, and as promised Aven held her all the way down, sliding out only to circle her clit with her own wetness before shifting and rolling her gently onto her back when all she wanted was for Aven to own her. Drive into her with everything she had. *What is wrong with me?* She didn't know, but she had never wanted someone so completely. Aven kissed a nipple still circling her clit, then the other before kissing her way down her stomach. Layka's whole body writhed with anticipation, and Aven replaced her finger with her lips. She sucked once, sliding deep and full inside her. Fireworks lit the back of her eyes, and she screamed out, "Aven, I'm yours!"

The words hung in the room even as her body's residual spasms brought her floating sensations back to the feel of Aven inside of her and the spray of blond hair across her abdomen as Aven's cheek pressed against her and her light kisses grounded her. She told herself the words were the result of a sexual high, but as she ran her hands through the soft hair, her heart knew they were true. "I'll never use a dry-erase board the same again," she said, trying to shift from the feeling of such deep emotion.

"Regardless of where this takes us," Aven said, lifting her head as she gently slid out of Layka carefully and with a tenderness that told Layka she understood—which made it all the harder to deny. "I want us to always be for each other. I like having you in my life."

Layka pulled softly at the hair ends she had toyed with when Aven lifted her head, her hand unwilling to let go. "Kiss me."

Aven smiled and shifted up beside her, kissing her with a soft murmur of pleasure that lit the fire anew.

Aven cracked an eye, then blinked, trying to orient to the unfamiliar room and the sensation that she couldn't feel her left arm. *I'm at Layka's*

apartment. The night's events flooded in, and she smiled. There were so many special moments that her mind wouldn't stay on a single one, bouncing from one to another. She was glad for Layka's steady breathing. It oriented her and grounded her in a way she had not anticipated. She wiggled her fingers and grimaced at the strange feeling. Her arm was asleep beneath Layka's head nestled near her shoulder. *Suck it up*, her brain said to her arm, and Aven chuckled at her own internal dialogue. The sound made Layka shift, and Aven folded her arm around her, drawing her closer and freeing the numb spot on her arm.

"Mmmmm," Layka hummed, tossing a leg over Aven.

Aven kissed the top of her head, then looked up at the ceiling. The night had been the most intimate she'd ever had on every level. They'd discussed a lot of things and finally dozed off talking about visiting Layka's sister today at work to get some more information about the resident houses. Aven grinned, recalling Layka's determined plan to reclaim her whiteboard. They had moved it back into her office space last night and actually managed to create solutions for the building hurdles engineering had identified. They really did make a good team.

The trace of a fingertip at her stomach pulled her from her thoughts. "Good morning,"

"Good morning to you," Layka said, tilting her head up and giving Aven's shoulder a kiss before propping onto an elbow. "I know we didn't sleep long, but I feel so energized."

"I know what you're saying." Aven lifted her now-awake hand to trace along Layka's propped shoulder and arm. "I feel this buzz of energy and I want to do a dozen things with you. Some of which are productive and some that would just keep us here in the bed."

"I would say that can be very productive..." Layka leaned in and kissed Aven's breast. "But someone"—she tapped Aven's shoulder—"has to work tonight, so I have to get my day work out of you. We've got our DC Wheelhouse build planning meeting in a few days, and I do think you were right about us talking with Sam. So, I say we get up, eat the frog first, so that we are motivated to get the work done." She leaned in and kissed Aven's other breast. "Then come home for a nap."

Aven's first thought was *I've never napped in my life,* but her brain quickly remedied the thought as she traced a thumb along Layka's jaw, down her neck, and across the nipple that had tightened with her first touch. "I'm new to naps, but with you leading the way, I'm pretty sure I will be all in."

Layka rolled onto her back and sighed. "God, you make me want to stay in bed."

Aven shifted to a sitting position and placed her feet on the floor. She felt the same, but this was all the beginning and she wanted it to be more. She wanted to hold on to it, so that meant taking their time. They had time. They could learn more about each other and not just spend all their time in bed, but OMG that's what she wanted to do right now. "I'm excited to spend the day with you, any way we do it. Now get that bum out of bed." She gave Layka a playful push before leaping out of range herself.

Layka laughed and rolled out on her side. "Very well. Are you okay with us having breakfast out? Sam loves the donuts from Pastry Palooza. I thought we might grab breakfast there and bring her donuts."

Aven read the slight lifting of Layka's shoulders as she spoke as discomfort. Did she think Aven expected to be served breakfast or something? "Hey." She moved to where Layka stood. "Why do you appear to be uncomfortable all the sudden?"

Layka's eyes flashed with something vulnerable, then appreciative. "I love my sister. Admire her, even, but sometimes I feel a little less when I'm around her. She doesn't say things that make me feel that way. She's just so good at things that I'm dreading to tell her about our little overstep. But I know it's important so that she can help us."

"That's on me, not you. I'm the one that jumped to the conclusion that there was something nefarious going on with the vans. We will explain it to her together."

Layka smiled and pulled Aven in, wrapping her arms around her. Aven anticipated the rush of excitement but instead felt this deep connection as she held Layka. Aven squeezed her. She could so get used to this openness. No games, just two people who could communicate.

A phone pinged, and they pulled apart, searching the room. It pinged again, and Layka moved toward her jeans on the floor. She lifted the phone from the pocket. "It's Sam."

Aven nodded. "I'll hop in the shower, if that's okay."

Layka smiled a devious smile but nodded and tapped her phone.

CHAPTER FIFTEEN

AVEN MOVED A CHAIR to the hospital lounge window as she waited for Reynolds, unable to pull her eyes from the contrast of yellow leaves of the low bushes with their bare spots exposing the red brick of the library.

"Sam is still home sick," Layka had said when Aven exited the bathroom.

Aven ran the words through her mind again, trying to compute the look of fear on Layka's face and the panic in her voice when she canceled their whole day together. It had seemed extreme considering she said Sam had reiterated that she was fine and that Farrah had encouraged her to stay with her to rest, and she was just letting her know because she wouldn't be at work to meet with them today.

Aven had initially felt a little surge at not having to share Layka, and when Layka had wanted to go check on Sam, she had offered to go with her. But Layka had said her sister wouldn't want to meet someone when she wasn't feeling well, so they had ended their first morning together headed in opposite directions. Aven shook off the twinge of sadness. *It all makes sense*, she told herself when an announcement came over the hospital speaker reminding her of the terrible things she put away in that compartment when she wasn't at work. *Layka almost lost her sister to COVID—that creates an extra level of fear.* She was letting her hurt ego at being put aside make her decisions by not texting, and she decided she wouldn't do that with Layka. She pulled out her phone.

AVEN: How is your sister doing?

LAYKA: She is getting better with Farrah's help. I think I overreacted.

The response came so quickly she thought Layka must have been holding the phone in her hand ready to type. Was that the case?

AVEN: I understand your concern. I remember you telling us how hard COVID hit her.

LAYKA: I'm not used to having someone care for her other than me.

AVEN: Her and Farrah haven't been together long?

LAYKA: Are you kidding. She'd never let anyone close. I think she still carries some feelings for an old flame. But, I'm seeing that change with Farrah!

Aven could picture Layka smiling and felt her heart warm.

AVEN: Oh yeah, that's great!

LAYKA: Sam wanted me to bring her back to her house but Farrah's coming over later. Could I cash in that raincheck before you go into work?

"I don't really know what to make of the data." Reynolds's voice startled Aven, and she typed something nonsensical then realized she had sent it.

AVEN: Sorry, Reynolds just came in the lounge and startled me. I don't go on till midnight so let me know a time that works for you.

"The numbers don't make sense. I thought you might have some insight." Reynolds paused when Aven lifted a finger, her back still to the door.

LAYKA: Thank you. I'll let you chat with Reynolds while I get Sam settled, then I'll reach out.

AVEN: OK.

She added a smiling emoji.

"What'cha got?" Aven said, collapsing into the chair at the window where she stared out at the library. She'd decided to stop by the hospital to catch Reynolds for lunch when her plans with Layka had fallen through. Aven closed her eyes against the reality check of her need for Layka. The speed at which her mood had lifted just reconnecting with her was scary. She knew about attachment and early emotions, but it truly felt unique with Layka.

"Not much. That's why I'm asking you. You're the 'I'd rather be single, visit my parents, and binge-watch reruns of old detective shows and new police dramas with my mother' kind of woman. Remember, I know you," Reynolds said.

"Even if I was remotely like one of those detectives—which, by the way, you only know about because you are often there with us—I wouldn't know where to start with the numbers you told me about on the phone. Hey...I could see if Layka's sister could help. Layka wants me to meet her when she's feeling better, and this would be a great way to get two things done."

"Whoa. Did I miss something?"

"What?" Aven asked, turning from the window. *That was a mistake,* Aven thought when Reynolds's eyebrow went up and she smirked.

"You slept with her."

"Really? That's your focus when you have data that looks like viral infection fell from the sky and landed on only a single demographic of people?" Aven was trying to be serious, but she couldn't hold back her smile. "Never mind. You reminded me I've got to call Mom. Her and dad are back from their trip, and she left me a message to come home on my next day off if I could."

"Oh no, you don't," Reynolds said, taking a seat at the table. "Spill."

Aven let her mind briefly drift to the fact that she wasn't single anymore. Was she? They were dating for sure, but where were they now? The thought reminded her that Layka's sister was sick, and she wondered whether to pass on the information Reynolds had just given her or wait till they were together to discuss it. "I want to tell Layka about this, but I want to do it in person so she can let me know if she thinks her sister is up to a discussion about it. If not, then Mom is up to bat with some binge-watching, popcorn-eating, armchair detective work."

As if on cue, her phone rang with the special ringtone she had generated for Layka.

Reynolds raised an eyebrow. "You owe me for letting you off the hook," she whispered and wiggled her own phone near her ear. "Call me if you go see your mom. You know she loves me more."

Aven ignored the eyebrow but gave the "OK" signal as she accepted the call and turned her focus back to the window. Several maple leaves fell and drifted on the wind to the ground. She listened but realized it had stopped ringing. She quickly dialed back and spoke as soon as the line clicked on. "Hi, Layka. How is your sister?" Aven waited as she heard some movement on the other end, and she pictured Layka moving around a room where her sister rested. She grimaced and whispered, "I'm sorry. I didn't think about ringing your phone when your sister might be resting."

"It's okay. I put it on vibrate when I realized I'd butt-dialed you," Layka said, and Aven heard the soft click of a door. "She just dozed off. It's perfect timing. How's your day off?"

"It started off good." She smiled about their morning together and tried to keep the uncertainty about what Reynolds had shared out of her voice. "I have some news about the viral component of our project from Reynolds, but I'll share it when we can talk face-to-face." Aven heard the refrigerator door open and close. "Is your sister feeling better?"

Layka sighed. "She says she is, but she hasn't eaten anything this morning. I'm fixing her a drink flight now of vegetable juice, water, a protein drink, and some kind of sports drink that looks like tropical punch."

"Wow, can I add you to the home health list for patient care?"

"I doubt that," Layka said. "I can only maintain this kind of energy for people I care about. I'd find it difficult to sustain as a job. I admire the people like you who do it every day for strangers."

Aven let the compliment sit with her. Why did it sound so different coming from Layka than it did from dozens of people who thanked her for the same thing? "Thank you. I could say the same for you and the way you've stepped up for the unhoused population. I know Mildred is special to you, but you have stepped up for more than just her."

"We both have," Layka said.

Aven could imagine Layka leaning against a counter or sink, one arm across her stomach bracing the elbow of the arm that held the phone. The vision created a vivid memory of how Layka had looked standing in the café staring at the menu with her hand on her chin. "What does the rest of your day look like?"

"I finalized the meeting with Dr. Sudha for four thirty today to go over the build plans for DC. Until then, I'm going to clean up here some. Sam is a great detective, and she likes everything to have its place in her home, but nothing has seen a dust rag in probably a year. She's agreed to let Farrah come this afternoon about four o'clock, but I know it's bothering her that the place isn't spit-spot for the woman who's finally pulled her heart from a lost love."

"A lost love. That sounds sad."

"Yeah, I don't know much about it, but Farrah has been the first person she has really started to let in. I used to think it was because that lost love still held her heart. Now that they've started using words with each other rather than awkward silence when they're in the same room together, I'm starting to think Sam felt she wasn't worth loving, and that makes me wonder more about what happened."

"Maybe you'll get some time to talk with her today." Aven was hoping to get some feel for whether Layka would be up for the conversation they were going to need to have with her sister in her detective role once she explained Reynolds's data.

"I was thinking that very thing. Do you want to meet for dinner this evening?"

"That sounds great. My treat tonight, I'll pick you up. I have a special place I'd like to take you."

"Now I'm intrigued," Layka said. "Can you make reservations late enough for me to get home, freshen up, and change after my meeting with Dr. Sudha?"

Intrigued, Aven thought, hoping Reynolds's information didn't make that prophetic. The new data that the virus was spreading predominantly through the unhoused population from geographically disconnected places made the van event that had unfolded in Maryland appear to be more of a threat—or at least more suspicious. "Absolutely. Is seven o'clock enough time for you?"

"That will be perfect. What's the dress code for this special event?"

"The restaurant is Maria Andres. Your fashion sense exceeds mine by lifetimes, so I figure it is better to tell you the place and you guide both of us on the attire."

"Wow, that's exciting. I've been wanting to go there for years and haven't made it happen. I'm up for being the fashion influencer for our date. I love dressing up when I get the chance."

Aven laughed. "I'm probably going to have to go shopping just to have something other than scrubs to wear."

"Well, if you do, send me pictures. It will brighten up my cleaning day to see you modeling the latest fashions."

"I'm definitely shopping now." Aven felt her heart leap at the chance to be connected with Layka even when they were apart.

"Are you sure you trust me with this?" Layka said, and Aven could hear the smile she wore just by the sound of her words.

"You did such a great job getting me undressed that I have to believe you will do splendidly getting me dressed."

"Mmm," Layka sighed.

Aven was glad she was sitting down because the sound made her legs feel weak.

"Hey, you, get back in bed."

Aven could tell Layka had turned from the phone because her voice sounded distant.

"I've gotta run. I have a determined, grumpy teenager in a full-grown, sick adult body. Don't forget I expect to see pics."

"I'm on it. Please let her know I hope she feels better soon. It sounds like you have it well in hand, but if I can help you in any way, let me know."

"I will. When she gets sick it scares me, but you know that. Thanks."

The line clicked off and Aven took a deep breath. This was all going to be good. She'd talk to Layka tonight about Reynolds's data, and together they would decide the best way to approach her sister with the details they had from their escapade last week.

She grabbed her keys and headed home. Her sleep cycle was off with the added social activity, so maybe a nap was a good idea if she was going to do dinner before going into work.

Aven jerked at the alarm and fell off the couch. "Ow," she said, rubbing her elbow as she reached for the phone on the sofa table. She realized it was ringing and not her alarm. "Hey, Layka." Aven rubbed at her eyes and squinted at the clock on the microwave in the kitchen through the doorway—5:15.

"Aven, Farrah just called. Sam started getting worse, and they went to the ER."

"Which hospital?" Aven heard the panic starting anew in Layka's voice.

"Washington Regional. They've admitted her, Aven."

"Layka," Aven said firmly but with every ounce of concern she could communicate to let Layka know her feelings were valid. "She is in the safest place she can be. Where are you?"

"I'm at the library. I just finished up my meeting and called Farrah to check on Sam. I felt bad about blowing our plans this morning and then Sam being okay, but now—"

"Layka. I understand. I know my face conveyed my disappointment this morning, but I am okay. Your sister is the priority. I'll meet you there."

"You don't have to do that. I just didn't want to cancel our plans in a text. I really care about you, and part of what I'm struggling with is that for the first time, someone has had enough draw to make me think twice about where I want to spend my time. But it's unfair to pull you to me because I want to be with you both."

"You're not pulling me. I want to come. We can have delicious cafeteria food and chalk it up to another of our escapade dates." Aven could hear Layka's breathing starting to even out. "Imagine the stories we'll have for Mildred next time we visit."

Layka actually gave a little laugh.

"I'm about thirty minutes from Regional with traffic. You are closer. Drive safe and just give me a call when you are there and know her room information."

"Okay, Aven."

The words were so soft, Aven wanted to reach through the phone and pull Layka into her arms.

Aven's phone rang when she reached the parking lot of Regional. She pulled into the nearest lot and yanked her phone from the GPS holder on the dash.

"Sorry it took me a while to call. Sam was being stubborn with Farrah. I sent her to get coffee for the two of us and a specialty tea for Sam's throat so I could put my foot down with Sam. She's trying to push Farrah away like she always does, but Farrah pushes back. I like it, but I was getting frustrated with both of them."

Aven smiled, imagining Layka politely sending Farrah on a mission while she gave her big sister a kick in the bottom. Aven heard a fit of coughing in the background. The reminder sobered her thoughts, and she climbed out of the vehicle and headed inside. "I'm here and will be up shortly. What's the room number?"

"Lay back on the bed and be still," Layka said.

Aven waited. "Is everything okay?"

"Yes, she just won't lie down. She insists on sitting up at the edge of the bed."

Aven bit her lip as she entered the hospital doors and headed for the elevator. She didn't want to remind Layka of her sister's pulmonary history, but if she was trying to sit up, there was a good reason. "Sometimes in people with lung injury, they often can't breathe well when they lie back, and it is more comfortable for them to sit up."

"Okay. The doctor has ordered a nebulizer treatment. Respiratory should be here shortly. We're in room 314."

"I'll be there soon," Aven said as the elevator doors closed. She could tell her words had eased Layka's mind, but the history recollection had raised her own concern. She left the elevator before the doors fully opened and was at her speed-walking pace when she heard raised voices and slowed down.

"You have to stop comparing everyone to your college sweetheart!"

Aven smiled. She recognized Layka's voice before she reached the door. She knocked on the frame just before she reached the opening. "Knock, knock."

The woman sitting on the bed with her back to the door turned but continued to speak to Layka. "I don't anymore, I've gotten over Vickie Strutford—"

Victoria Aven Strutford Summerhouse felt her gut twist. She recognized that voice too.

"Samantha Corin."

"Vickie?"

CHAPTER SIXTEEN

"AVEN, WAIT." LAYKA'S HEART ached at the pained look on Aven's face before she turned and ran.

Layka spun back to Sam, who sat on the edge of the bed, her hands gripping the veneer of the footboard so hard that a cracked portion of it had peeled and curled up. "Dr. Summerhouse is your Vickie from college?"

Sam didn't move, she didn't shift, her body appeared frozen, and she stared right through Layka, who stood in her line of sight at the end of the bed.

"Sam, talk to me! What's going on?" Layka paced in a circle from the bed to the door, her hand pulling repeatedly through her hair. Her heart was so heavy she could hardly breathe. Part of her wanted to chase after Aven, to tell her not to run. The other part wanted to scream at Aven and the universe. She wanted to blame them both for deserting her.

"Hi. I have a neb treatment to help that cough."

The words were spoken by a middle-aged woman who pushed her glasses up with her free hand as she moved toward the bed. Layka watched as she opened the packaging for the pipe similar to the one Sam had at home when she had flare-ups. The woman dumped the medicine into the container just as Sam began another round of coughing. It sounded more wet now, and Sam was audibly wheezing.

"Here you go," the woman said, adjusting the mouthpiece on the pipe so it was horizontal as she handed it to Sam. "There's two medicines in here to help the wheezing and cough. Have you used a nebulizer before?" She pushed her glasses up with her knuckle, careful to not touch her gloved fingertips to her face.

"She has one at home," Layka said as Sam took a careful breath through the pipe.

Slippy glasses nodded when the first few breaths and coughing turned into relaxed shoulders and a solid deep breath. "I'll be back to check on her."

"Thank you." Layka took a seat next to her sister.

Sam took two more long pulls on the neb pipe and then looked at Layka. "Why is her name Summerhouse?"

"She was married," Layka offered, taking her sister's free hand.

Sam took another pull on the nebulizer. "Was?"

Layka paused. She was hesitant. Was this her story to tell? But Aven hadn't stayed to tell it, and her running away hurt as much as she knew it would. Maybe worse. Aven had admitted she ran when she was afraid, but she'd also said she was not going to do that now that they were trying to trust each other. *God, what a mess*, she thought, feeling tears prick. Sam was her family, her sister, all that she had left, and Aven had broken Sam's heart. Yes, it was years ago, but was she not the same person? *She's breaking my heart now by running away.*

"You don't have to tell me," Sam said. "I have no right to know about her life."

"Will you tell me what happened?" Layka asked, then realized she wished she hadn't.

Sam took another pull on the nebulizer and rotated the container with the medicine in it. There was still a good bit of liquid inside. "It was my junior year in college. She was a sophomore but had transferred from another college."

Layka squeezed Sam's hand.

Sam pulled her hand free and untwisted the tubing as if it were kinked.

Layka watched her. There was nothing amiss with the tubing. Sam was just pulling away. *What's wrong with me that people I love don't feel I can help? Am I not enough for them?*

Sam shook the liquid and focused on the treatment.

Layka wanted to yell at Sam for the empty feeling she now had both in her hand and her heart, but Sam had shifted the neb to her other hand and was leaning on the footboard with her free arm. She was sick, and no one made good decisions when they didn't feel well.

"Can you continue, or do you need to rest?"

"There isn't a lot to tell. I was the first woman she ever dated."

"How's it going?" a voice asked from the doorway.

Sam lifted the container, shaking it to show some residual liquid.

"All right, I'll give you a few more minutes."

When the footsteps receded down the hall, Sam turned and looked at Layka. "We dated for six months and never even kissed."

"What?" Layka heard the mix of incredulity and relief in her question.

"I was crazy about her, but it was all new to her, and each time we were close to crossing that line, she would back away." Sam coughed once and set the neb pipe down on the tray next to the machine. "I was young and very sexually active before we met, so it was incredibly tough for me to be so attracted to her and not be intimate."

Layka listened with mixed emotions. A part of her was glad nothing physical had ever happened between them, but hearing how much Sam cared for Aven made her chest ache. She noted Sam's wheezing was gone, but there was sweat at her hairline and her face was pale. She didn't look like she was feeling better, but then again, maybe it was the topic and not the illness causing the visible distress. "Why don't you rest?" Layka could hear conversation down the hall. The voices were muffled, but one had said, "Room 314," which was Sam's room.

"No. This is important." Sam grasped her wrist. Her palm was sweaty and her breathing suddenly became very labored.

"Sam!"

"I failed her, Layka. Don't you do the same."

Sam's hand fell from her wrist, and she clenched the sheet of the bed. Her opposite hand was white-knuckled on the tray she had pushed to the wall. She now seemed to be bracing herself, trying to breathe.

Layka jumped up, scrambling over the bed to the door to get help.

A team of people, including Aven, rushed in. It was a flurry of activity Layka could barely follow as Aven pulled her back. "She's using accessory muscles to breathe. They are going to stabilize her so they can control her breathing."

Layka panicked as she watched them mask her sister and get her flat on the bed. "Stabilize," Layka whispered, recalling the last time she heard that word and she almost lost her sister. Layka rounded on Aven, her voice low and trembling. "You ran! You promised you wouldn't, and you did." Layka braced her face in her hands, turning back to watch through her tears as a team of people intubated her sister and began to breathe for her.

CHAPTER SEVENTEEN

AVEN WANTED TO WRAP Layka in her arms even after her outburst at her, but she couldn't. It felt too connected to a past version of herself she had vowed never to trust again. She closed her eyes, and it all came rushing back. The party, the date, her dressed up to the nines because tonight was going to be the night she kissed a girl. The night she kissed Samantha Corin. She remembered everything down to the shoes she had been wearing. Those especially she remembered because the black, strappy, three-inch heels had been her complete focus when she found Samantha only one pair of jeans away from completely naked with Shanera Brice. She had stood in the doorway, unable to move. When Shanera had made a move to shift off Samantha—*my girlfriend*, Aven thought—she had fled. She felt the pain fresh and now redoubled as she recalled Layka's words tonight about running. She couldn't hold back the memories now, assaulting her in an unstoppable barrage.

First, she had stared down at her shoes for what seemed like hours feeling like a fool, a broken fool, as tears blurred her vision. She'd never seen a woman she was attracted to naked and certainly didn't want the first time to be her girlfriend extracting herself from another woman.

"You didn't want me," Samantha said as Aven continued to watch the floor and Samantha's bare feet move toward her.

Aven ran. She ran as fast as she could in her heels, dodging through people as she heard Samantha calling behind her and telling her to wait.

"Don't run. I thought you were just experimenting with me till your next boyfriend showed up."

Aven had whirled on her at those words. Even in her tear-blurred state she could see the despair in Samantha's eyes. That was when she started to consider staying. That was when the fear gripped her. She would have never given a second chance to any of the guys she'd dated in this situation. Caring for a woman was different for her. She wanted to reach for this woman who had crushed her heart. That was scary.

The thought brought her back to the moment. To the new woman standing next to her. The woman she had seconds ago considered reaching out to comfort despite her harsh, condemning, untrue words. She hadn't run this time, but Layka had blamed her for doing so nonetheless.

The sounds in the room were still a cacophony of activity, but Samantha was stable. Aven took in the scene. Samantha was intubated, and the doctor was listening after an adjustment to ensure proper placement was expanding both lungs. Layka had edged closer, and Aven considered the mix of emotions that warred within her. Samantha was fighting for her life, yet not college Samantha, but Sam, Layka's sister. She had heard Sam's labored words that she had failed Aven as she and the team reached the room. The vision of that recalled despair of a young Samantha, coupled with today's adult Sam, made her realize they had marked each other. She had refused to answer any calls or texts from Samantha after that night. She had run away indeed, on every level. Within three months, she had transferred back to her old school closer to home and her family. She had never spoken to or of Samantha Corin again until she met Carter. And it was clearer than ever now that her marriage had been built on a friendship of two people walking each other through some very difficult times.

Layka was now standing near the bed holding her sister's hand. Aven could feel the tears forming. She blinked several times but let them fall. Her heart was breaking for Sam, who was now in a fight for her life; for Layka, who now blamed Aven the way her sister had years ago; and for herself, for once again having to watch something she had dared to want slip through her fingers.

"You don't have to stay," Layka said, turning from the bed but not releasing her sister's hand.

"What if I want to stay?" Aven said tentatively.

Layka bit her lip and then looked over at her sister. "I can't do this right now," she said quietly and circled her hands between her and Aven.

The nurse indicated she needed to be where Layka was standing as the team made final adjustments.

Layka gave her sister's hand a squeeze and stepped back toward Aven. Layka didn't repeat her previous accusation, but it was there in her eyes. Layka was freely judging her now, based on only the context of her sister's story and what she thought she had seen. But Layka was wrong. She didn't run this time. At least, she hadn't run away. She had immediately recognized Sam's condition and knew she only had minutes to get help. She couldn't run a code here. This wasn't her hospital.

"Oh my God."

Aven jumped at the new voice as a striking dark-skinned woman with panic written on her face entered the room.

"What happened, Layka?" She dropped the drink carrier into Layka's hands and paced to the bed with a determination the nurse seemed to recognize. She allowed the woman to insert herself.

"I'm still not sure what happened," Layka said.

The woman took Sam's hand and spoke in quiet tones they couldn't hear.

Layka and Aven watched but neither spoke. Then Layka turned her focus on Aven. "That's Farrah," she said, giving a nod of her head at the woman now holding Samantha's hand in hers and stroking the top with her opposite hand. "She finally seemed to be making some headway into Sam's heart." Layka folded her arms. "For the longest time, I thought Sam kept relationships at arm's length because she wasn't willing to settle for anyone less than the angel of her college dreams. Now I realize she kept them at arm's length because she felt she didn't deserve to be loved. How did you do that to her?" Layka's usually calm eyes grew icy. "Did you leave her—run away, because you were scared?"

Aven could feel her lips draw into a line. She knew Layka was hurting, but that was out of line. Layka knew nothing about what had happened yet had judged Aven's role in it already. Before she could speak, the team began to exit, and the hospitalist paused to address her.

"I'm Dr. Frankl. The nurse told me you noticed the patient's decline and gave them a more than cursory directive to get the crash cart. Are you in medicine?"

"Yes. Dr. Summerhouse," she said, reaching a hand out. "I'm a pulmonologist at Medfirst Washington."

"Ah. That explains why you told Beth to contact the hospital pharmacy for the additional drugs. You probably saved her life."

Aven barely heard the words. Instead, she watched the emotions play across Layka's face as she began to put together Aven's quick retreat. Yes, she had been shocked when she realized Sam was Samantha Corin from college, but she was well over that and mainly saw Layka's sister exhibiting signs of impending respiratory arrest. It wasn't until Layka blamed her for running, which she hadn't done this time, that she had felt the overwhelming reminder of the hurt of so many years ago. She wasn't going to run now, but she also knew she was putting those policies back in place. No way would she give Layka full access to her heart. She couldn't trust her with it.

CHAPTER EIGHTEEN

L AYKA CLICKED THE COMPUTER touchpad. Hard. "Why doesn't anything just work like it's supposed to?" The computer finally gave a whir, and she flopped back in the chair, rubbing her eyes. It was the wetness on her fingers that brought her back to reality, and she closed the lid on the laptop. She leaned her head down on her folded arms and cried. She was grateful for the sound barrier of the closed wood door in this conference room. It had only a tiny window near the top, and no one was scheduled to arrive for the meeting till ten.

The movie clip of yesterday at the hospital played in her mind on repeat. The stunned look on Sam's face when Aven entered. Aven's hasty retreat. Her own accusation and harsh words to Aven, only to find out she had left to get help, not run away. She would give herself this time to cry, to ache, but she had to pull it together. Her sister needed her. She lifted her head and ran both hands through the sides, pulling slightly. She wanted to scream. Her Aven was the college angel that had held her sister's heart since college. *Only you didn't call her an angel, did you?* Layka's stomach lurched, and she jumped up to run to the bathroom. She was physically sick recalling her words and remembering the line of Aven's lips. She had watched the shutters go up on those blue eyes. She had been the one to do what she'd promised not to do. Layka was grateful she had worn her hair in a low ponytail when another dry heave made her stomach twist like someone squeezing water from a dishrag. She braced against the wall as she retched, then wrapped her arms tight at her waist and leaned back. She could feel the cool of the metal door through her thin blouse. She needed to get back to the grant disbursement outline she'd started, but she was finding it impossible to focus. The wall Aven had immediately erected made Layka's chest ache with loss. She could feel the tears prick again. She wiped at them, then recalled her makeup. She pushed off the door, spun to unlock it, made her way to the sink, washed her hands, and headed back to the conference room. When she turned the corner, Aven stood with her hand on the door.

"Hello, Layka."

The voice was quiet, and Layka bit her lip against the cry she felt in the back of her throat. "Hello, Aven. I'm glad you decided to come. I was concerned after my behavior yesterday..." She let her words trail off. "I would understand if you didn't want to continue to work on the project." Layka struggled to get the words out. She had hoped they would still have this, at least, and she reached for her chest when the thought made physical pain squeeze her heart. She looked up and released her chest. "I apologize for my words yesterday. Actually, for everything."

"Thank you," Aven said, but Layka could see the guarded look in her eyes. "It was a difficult day for everyone."

Layka nodded, pushing back tears at the thought of how quickly everything had changed in just twenty-four hours.

"What are you thinking?" Aven pushed the wood door open and waved Layka in ahead of her.

Layka blew out a long breath as she took her seat. "About how quickly everything can change." She twisted the ring she wore on her index finger, then clasped her hands and set them in her lap. "My sister, who was talking with me yesterday morning, is now on a ventilator fighting for her life against a virus that you and I have been working to curtail." She looked up from her hands. "We've uncovered something very important about how the virus may be being transported, and now we have to balance our work on the project with an investigation, and my sister isn't here to help me." She laid her forearms on the table. "Finally, a woman who I respect and care for turns out to be my sister's college sweetheart.

And as much as I want to see the walls that flash into place behind your eyes disappear, I know it's my fault they are there."

Aven reached for Layka's hands clasped loosely together on the table but paused before touching her. "I promised you I wouldn't run anymore." She tapped the table lightly with a fingertip. "I'm here. I don't know what we can make of us now, but I plan to see the project through."

"There cannot be an us—not that you even want an us after I acted foolishly and forced your guard up again." Layka reached her fingertips to the inner side of her eyes as if she could catch the tears. "Not the way we were originally planning. Not while Sam is in a coma and I still don't know where her heart is about you."

"I understand."

"It makes me physically sick to recall how I acted yesterday." Layka watched those beautiful blue eyes and was surprised how much she could read in them despite the limited time they'd had together. She could see that Aven didn't want to bring back those old "policies" she had in place, but Layka knew she would. Layka bit her lip to keep it from trembling at the evidence that Aven was putting them in place and she had no one to blame but herself. "Do you want to talk about what happened? We've got some time before the meeting of the minds that is important to both of us." She tapped her laptop, where the outline remained incomplete.

"I need some space to breathe and put my own thoughts and emotions into place before I express it to someone else." Aven actually did reach out and touch Layka's arm this time. "The key point is, I'm not running."

"That's good to hear." Layka squeezed Aven's hand atop hers. "I should have given you the benefit of the doubt." Layka watched as Aven rotated her phone in circles on the table. She was fighting herself. Layka could see it as if the idea of accepting the apology and keeping the wall warred with accepting the apology and letting the wall down.

"I appreciate that you see that," she finally said, lifting the phone and turning it toward Layka, a data sheet visible on the screen.

Layka released a breath when Aven smiled. It was genuine, but Layka could see the hesitancy in it.

"I'd like to go over this data that Reynolds gave me. It seems really important in light of the van transport we uncovered."

It was the new hesitancy and change of topic that made Layka realize how deeply her words had cut, or perhaps she had just hit a wound that was easily opened. "Will you tell me your side of the story?" Layka asked, not wanting to hear how this woman she cared about had loved her sister first, but also not willing to leave dormant an action that would speak of how she valued knowing Aven, valued understanding both her joys and hurts. They were in a different space now. This type of intimate, outsider space that felt like a planet orbiting a sun, feeling the pull but unable to move closer. Her stomach twisted again, and she took a slow, deep breath to stave off the roll of nausea. She had lost something very real with her quick words and certain judgment.

"Thank you for asking," Aven said. "It means a lot that you are giving action to your apology. I will tell you, but I'd like to do it on some downtime rather than when we have the press of this responsibility." She tapped her phone.

"That makes sense," Layka said. "And I'd like that." *What do you mean you'd like that? You've told yourself there can be nothing intimate between you, but you're going to sit alone with her on some downtime?* "So, what do you have there? It looks like two screens collaged. The one is the data, but what is this?" She pointed at the second photo on the phone screen. "And what does it have to do with the van trip of the homeless residents to the festival?"

"There has been an explosion of the virus from the same areas. The hospital ICU is at full capacity since last weekend. Reynolds's data shows comparisons of the virus strain are identical to the ones from the hospital in Maryland close to that residential home and not at any of the hospitals in between."

"So, it's a pretty good indicator that the virus is moving via these unhoused people who were brought to the festival."

"That's part of it, but there's another component that has a more nefarious look about it, which is why I told you I wanted to tell you in person and ask your sister to join us."

Layka watched as Aven closed her eyes. She imagined she was revisiting all that had transpired and wondering how it would have been different if the three of them had met at the restaurant the way they planned before they were aware of the severity of Sam's condition. "You think we really were onto something about trafficking the unhoused, not just a resident's trip to the festival."

"Yes. I mean, where did the other van go? Remember the woman with the dog they loaded in the other van? She never appeared at the festival."

Layka thought about it. She leaned back and tapped her chin. "You're right. Does Reynolds's data give us any clue?"

"It does, but it's outside of my short-lived detective phase to chase leads and investigate campaign fraud."

"Campaign fraud?" Layka's head jerked back, and she stared at Aven.

Aven just shrugged. "Reynolds is very active politically, so she's always up on the news of what's going on in that realm. She pointed out to me that Barton misrepresented information in his campaign about the program to assist the homeless. In his last term, he privatized ten of the twenty resident homes that were in place—which isn't inherently a bad thing. So why lie about it?"

"So, how does that relate to us?"

"It appears that Barton has been under some political scrutiny about how ineffective the privatized sector of the pilot program has been at creating any real change for the unhoused population in those areas. The resident home we were at is one of the privatized ones."

Layka sat back as understanding started to work its way through her thoughts. "The ten facilities you are talking about are the ones Sam's team had been investigating."

"Correct. It's just too many loose strings that appear connected for me not to feel that we need to let the police know about what we saw with the vans."

"Hey, you two. You're here early." Dr. Sudha placed her laptop on the table and pushed several braids to her back.

"Good morning," they said in unison as Dr. Sudha turned toward the whiteboard and began to list information.

"So, that's where you get it from," Aven said to Layka with a grin.

Layka laughed just as Dr. Sudha turned from the board.

"No, she did this to me," she said, pointing the white erase board marker at Layka. "It started out simple, but now I'm addicted." Dr. Sudha turned back to the board.

Layka took a relaxed breath and was grateful for the reprieve of laughter. Aven had done that. With a simple remembrance of something unique to her, she had brought out the one thing Layka thought she would not have again for a long time.

The wood door opened again, and two more of the team entered.

Layka leaned toward Aven, and for a moment she both regretted it and soaked it in. She smelled like fresh linen when you climb from the shower. She wanted to bury her face in Aven's neck. Instead, she just breathed her in. "I'll ask Toby for the number to the lead detective on Sam's team. I've met them all and know a few that Sam hangs out with, but I always called her on her cell, so I'm not sure of the proper channel to reach out to them about the vans. I should be able to have a connection for us by the end of the day."

"That sounds good," Aven said. "Maybe we can meet at the hospital cafeteria and go over everything. I know you will want to get to your sister as soon as you can, and I agreed to do a cross-hospital consultation with the pulmonology team that is providing her care."

Layka took that in. She knew the hospital team at Washington Regional was excellent. If they were asking to meet with Aven, then... "They want your expertise because of your work with the virus," Layka said, feeling the shadow of death like a cold hand on her face.

"Yes," Aven said, touching Layka's knee then pulling back.

The move reminded Layka of the part of those whiteboard memories that was lost. Still, she was glad Aven didn't say more. Aven didn't try to tell her everything was going to be okay. Layka should have felt panic. Her sister had so much lung damage from COVID that they had warned Sam about her risk should she get exposed and require ventilator treatment again. But somehow, knowing Aven was helping—that her expertise would be contributed—seemed to warm that cold feeling of impending death, and she wished Aven's hand could have stayed. Wished all the chaos wasn't real and Aven's hand could have lingered for her to cover with her own. "Thank you for still being here." She looked up, realizing she was staring where Aven's hand had briefly touched her leg. "Meeting in the hospital cafeteria sounds good, and it gives us some downtime for me to listen, if you're ready by then to talk about what happened between you two."

"I think we're all here," Dr. Sudha said, pulling them back into the hum of the room as it quieted from individual conversations.

Layka sat back in her chair and once again missed the warmth of Aven's hand that had gently lifted from her knee. The sensation was one of loss, but she didn't feel the anger at herself from this morning. It was a step back for both of them, but life didn't always give you what you wanted, much less what you needed.

CHAPTER NINETEEN

*G*IVE US THE DOWNTIME *to talk. What was I thinking to ask for that?* Aven's thoughts circled. She had told herself she would keep distance between them. Now she had agreed to share something very personal and painful and on downtime. That meant some time separate from work, separate from their project. She had essentially asked for personal time with Layka when she had said she needed space.

It was six o'clock, and they had agreed to meet at six thirty in the cafeteria. Aven had never dreaded and longed for a meeting in equal parts as much as she did this one. Not once in a million years would she have dreamed she would walk into that hospital room and find out that the woman who shattered her young heart was the sister of the woman who now had it wrapped around her little finger. She was working through her own hang-ups with Layka's quick assumptions and cutting words, and Layka was asking to know her side of the Samantha story, but it still left them at a dead end. She shivered once at the words, but a romantic relationship with Layka was absolutely that—a dead end.

Reminded of the fact that death was a real possibility for Sam, she increased her pace. She always enjoyed contributing her research knowledge to real cases, and she wanted to spend the half hour before her meeting with Layka with the Washington Regional Hospital pulmonologist to discuss a new approach that had proved beneficial in patients struck by the virus variant. She reached to push through the rotating glass door and smiled at the blue line on her thumb. She'd never been marked with a dry-erase marker before. It may rub off easy from a board, but not human skin. She stutter-stepped at the door, remembering the brief moment between her and Layka as the two of them drew on the whiteboard to explain to the committee how the funds would be dispersed for the project. The mark had been an accident as they worked side by side, but the flash of recollection of their night together was as clear in Layka's eyes as she knew it had been in hers. Dr. Sudha had noticed the mark at the close of the meeting and joked that Layka had escaped the whiteboard war unscathed, but Layka's abrupt reach for the wall as if she needed support said the reminders of their precious intimate time together being snatched away was accumulating. Aven noticed her face reflected in the glass as she pushed through the doors. No one came away unscathed when the universe twisted your world, but she wasn't running. She stepped through the doors and breathed in the familiar scents of a hospital.

Aven made her way to the bank of elevators and pressed the button for the ICU floor. Dr. Frankl wanted to meet in Samantha's room. This was one of those times she was grateful for her ability to compartmentalize.

"Hi, Farrah," Aven said, giving a wave to her from the door and a nod to Dr. Frankl, who was speaking to the nurse at the desk just outside the room. She walked to the bed to check the ventilator numbers. "How's she doing?"

Farrah sat next to the bed in a chair facing Sam and the ventilator. She had her hand laid over Sam's on the bed. "Dr. Frankl backed her down some on the ventilator this morning, and she has tolerated it."

"But she didn't tolerate the next step-down," Dr. Frankl said, entering the room.

Aven nodded but saw the crestfallen look on Farrah's face. "We've been using the protocol I sent you for many of our patients once they are confirmed positive for the variant."

"I appreciate you sending the information earlier. It is what we did for her when she failed the extubation attempt, and she stabilized."

"Good," Aven said and pointed at the ventilator. Dr. Frankl leaned forward to see which dial she was pointing to. "This can be adjuste—"

"I didn't know you were coming up here." Layka's voice once again held that edge of accusation. It wasn't fully there, and Aven reminded herself that she had a perspective of hurt that could be coloring the words, so she smiled respectfully.

"Dr. Frankl asked me to meet here."

"They've reduced some of the ventilator usage," Farrah said as if she thought the words would alleviate some of the stress Layka was visibly wearing on her face. Her furrowed brow relaxed some, but not much.

"The planned extubation failed," Layka said as understanding turned to disappointment.

Aven saw the weight of it sink Layka's shoulders.

"Yes," Dr. Frankl said. "But we have a new protocol Dr. Summerhouse shared with our team, and our first step with that was a success."

Aven watched as Layka sat on a love seat that was pushed against the glass wall. She pointed out the ventilator features that were part of her protocol, and Dr. Frankl made some notes in a small notebook he slipped back in his white coat pocket.

"I'll email you if we have any snags. Thank you. The team is eager to see if the other steps will be as successful as the first. We've had an uptick of cases and are grateful for every success."

"Really? When would you say the uptick of cases occurred?" Aven asked, chancing a glance at Layka, who caught her eye and pulled out her phone. Her thumbs were now in ready mode, hovering over the phone.

"I'd have to check my hospital log to know exactly when. Actually, one of them I planned to ask you about. I know you mentioned you're already scheduled for a meeting this evening, so maybe we can review her case tomorrow. I can use our encrypted email to send you her information. She came in with her dog. The animal wore a service dog vest, but with the patient in a medically induced coma, hospital policy would not allow it to stay. I considered whether the dog could be a carrier. She is very sick. Have you seen animal-to-human transfer with the variant?"

"I'll speak with my colleague Dr. Reynolds. Her work in the lab extends beyond the work we do together, and I'll let you know tomorrow. Where is the dog?"

Dr. Frankl pulled the notebook back out from his pocket, and Aven saw the discomfort he was trying to hide play across his features. "He was picked up by the Three Legs Animal Shelter."

"None of her family would take the dog?" Aven asked.

"We don't even have an ID for the patient. I'm going to finish my evening rounds. Let me know a good time for you tomorrow once you review the email. I'll send it before I leave tonight."

Aven nodded as he headed for the doors. She locked eyes with Layka, still sitting on the love seat. "You think it's her?" Aven asked, taking a seat next to her.

Layka didn't answer immediately, and Aven could see her moving pieces around in her mind as her eyes tracked back and forth but never focused on anything in the room until she spoke. "Farrah?"

Farrah turned from the bed, which she now leaned over, rubbing lip balm on Sam's lips. "Yes?"

"Aven and I were going to grab dinner in the cafeteria before I come up to stay with her tonight. Would you like to go get anything before we do that, or I can bring something back for you?"

Farrah twisted the lid back on the balm. "No, you go ahead. I'm going to go home and shower once you're back. I'll grab something then."

"Okay."

Layka stood and Aven followed. Once in the hall, Layka spoke. "I do think it's the woman from the van. I have zero evidence, but my gut says it's her."

"I agree. It's a pretty good indicator that she is one of the unhoused if they were unable to find an emergency contact for her that would take the dog."

"I know. And God, that's horrible."

"It breaks my heart. Animals are like family when you bring them into your life."

"Do you have any animals?"

"Not since Kiri died. It was really hard when I lost her, and then I was in residency, followed by an almost twenty-four-seven fellowship. I didn't think it would be fair to bring an animal into my life and not have time to be with them. You?"

"I have a cat. I found her as a kitten curled up behind one of my planters in late fall last year. She was too weak to even be afraid. Now she's a fireball but loves to cuddle with me on the couch. She's a recluse when I have guests. How hungry are you?"

"Not at all. I'm pleased our variant step protocol allowed Dr. Frankl to see some progress with Sam, but I'm still worried, and I know you are. I don't think I could eat much." Aven bit the inside of her lip. She wanted to tell Layka her side of the story, wanted her to understand why she felt the way she did about relationships, but she wasn't going to lie about being hungry just to have that time. "You can tell me the information you have for connecting with the detectives on the way downstairs, and we can coordinate schedules to meet with them. I know you have a lot on your plate."

Layka reached for Aven's hand and squeezed it once. "I haven't forgotten that I owe you an open-minded sit-down discussion about what happened with you and Sam in college. It's a weird place to be for me, but I don't want to lose the friendship we've started even if there can't be anything else."

They reached the elevator, and Aven pressed the button. Her arm felt like lead, or maybe it was just a heaviness that consumed her whole body. She had been hurt and angry with Layka, but she had apologized and put action behind that apology, which made Aven's wall crumble only to be faced with Layka's reluctance. "I understand, and I appreciate you being open to seeing how what happened between Samantha and I impacted who I am. Where would you like to go if you're not hungry?"

"I'm texting Farrah to ask if she can give us two hours."

"Two hours? Where are we going?"

"Three Legs Animal Shelter. I know someone who will let us in. I worked there in my last few years of high school."

Aven saw a shadow cross her face and made a mental note to ask about it when Layka didn't look so vulnerable. Something told her it was too close right now.

CHAPTER TWENTY

LAYKA TAPPED OUT A thank-you to Farrah, then put her phone away. "I'm parked in the garage. I know we're going in separate directions when we finish at the shelter, but I can bring you back if you want to ride with me." This new dynamic, this whole crappy situation, made her feel alone even when Aven was with her. "I know it isn't the sit-down dinner time we planned, but I'm willing to listen whenever you're ready."

"Sure," Aven said and fell in step with her as she walked. "Let's do it."

Layka pushed away her own reluctance. She wanted to find the proper amount of support to help Aven open up. Meanwhile, part of her wanted to just let it go. Pretend it never happened. But, she knew ultimately that would result in making it harder for all of them. She felt Aven wanted to talk about it, but she'd been wrong about Aven before, and with two strikes against her, she wanted to prove herself to this woman she so deeply cared for even when it would twist her heart to hear how Sam had known her first. *Suck it up, you owe her this*, Layka thought. "So, how did you meet Sam? Oh wait, was 'Let's do it' just an answer about riding to the shelter?"

Aven rubbed the back of her neck and blew out a breath. "Yes and no. I want to explain, and I want to run away. I promised I wouldn't do the latter." Aven shrugged. "Maybe if I start by explaining the circumstances when Sam and I met at college."

Layka listened and felt her heart wrenching with the struggle Aven described as she dealt with a difficult breakup with a long-distance boyfriend who felt they'd grown apart and a budding relationship with a woman that had her feeling things she'd never felt before. Aven paused when she realized Layka had stopped moving. "This is me," Layka said, pointing to the blue Subaru Legacy. "But I didn't want to interrupt your story."

"It's okay. This is good. I don't feel like there is this beam of focus on me. It's more casual." Aven looked away from Layka as if considering how to say something. Then she looked back and held Layka's eyes with her own. "You're really listening, and that's what matters to me, not where it happens."

Layka felt the weight of the words and swallowed back the swelling grief that this woman, who in so many ways helped her be a better person, was now ripped from her while still standing only feet away. She absently rubbed at the doorframe, trying to soothe herself with the tactile sensation.

"I love these cars. They will run forever," Aven said, lifting the door handle and spurring Layka to click the lock.

"That's true. I wish everything lasted as long as they do." Layka bit her lip as soon as the words were out.

"You can say that again, which kind of brings me to the crux of the story with Samantha."

Layka turned the car on and cracked the windows, then turned it off.

"Are we not going to the shelter?" Aven asked.

Layka twisted in her seat. "I want to listen to you without distraction," she said, bringing her knee up against the console so she was facing Aven. "The last thing my sister said to me was, 'Don't fail her the way I did.' I don't know what that means yet, but I know I failed to listen to your side of the story when everything hit the fan on two occasions now. I'm not perfect, but I'm trying to actively do something different when it comes to you."

Aven looked down at her hands, and when she turned her head, Layka could see the wetness of unshed tears reflected in the low glow of the garage parking lights.

Layka reached out and took Aven's hand, lacing it with hers. "I want to listen to you."

Aven squeezed her hand and propped their arms on the console, tracing over Layka's knuckles as she spoke. Layka forced her focus to Aven's words, but the sensation of Aven tracing her hand made her heart flutter. She didn't want to interrupt because she was talking about a party where she'd planned to kiss her sister for the first time. Layka swallowed hard when Aven described how she had avoided intimacy with Samantha because everything was new and she always liked to be prepared. Layka gave the hand holding hers a gentle squeeze just to say *I know this about you, and I see the truth of it*. She could imagine Aven feeling like she needed to do a complete training on how to love women before she took the first step. She loved that about her. *Love... Be careful there, Layka,* she warned herself. She couldn't love little things about this woman. She'd have to draw the line somewhere because she was already emotionally in over her head. She could at least manage the physical between them. As far as she knew, Sam was still hung up on—if not in love with—Aven. She couldn't let her wake up and find out she had been making out with her the whole time she was fighting for her life. *Focus,* she reminded herself. Aven was describing a room at the party, and she had come in and found...

Layka literally felt something in her chest rip as Aven described the pain of finding Sam with another woman. *It can't be true*, she thought. But Aven would have no reason to lie.

"Layka...Layka."

Layka lifted her head, realizing it was leaned back against the glass window. Aven was saying her name, and she was holding her chest. She wanted to cry and her chest ached, but she was not certain who she felt the most pain for in the moment—Aven for the betrayal she had faced, Sam for the love she had lost with a stupid decision, or herself because she felt trapped in a limbo of wanting to hold Aven close and fearing her sister still loved her.

"I'm okay," Layka said, squeezing Aven's hand still holding one of hers. She pulled it away and wiped at the tears. "I am so sorry that happened to you."

"It wasn't your fault, and I don't blame Samantha anymore. We were both young, and I can see now why she thought what she did about me."

"That doesn't make what she did right," Layka said.

"I know. It just helps me understand it. For the longest time, the combination of not being able to manage a long-distance relationship with my boyfriend because I wasn't physically there, and then my first girlfriend cheating on me because I wasn't physically available, made me feel I wasn't worth the wait. I pulled back from dating altogether, which, funny enough, is how I met the woman I married. Only to realize that, yes, we were friends, and as good as that was, something was missing. I've just not been willing to risk the pain again to have that missing piece. Not until you."

Layka leaned forward and wiped the tears from Aven's cheeks. "It also wasn't right how I blamed you. I am sorry for that, and I wish more than anything that Sam was at home in her bed safe and I could take you home with me and hold you till you believe you are worth every minute of waiting. Or not waiting," she added with a smile when she saw Aven's eyes darken even more in the dim light. Her smile fell away as if pulled by the weight twisting in her gut. "But my sister isn't home safe in her bed. She's fighting for her life, and as far as I know, she still cares for you." Layka pulled her hands away from Aven's face and buried her head in her hands. "For God's sake, she asked me not to let you down the way that she did, and now I understand." Layka wiped at her face and looked at Aven. There was sorrow there but also understanding.

Aven squeezed her shoulder. "I understand. Let's focus our energy on the project and getting Samantha well."

Layka nodded. "Mackenzie texted she would be at the kennel side of the shelter to let us in at seven." She lifted her phone to check the time. "I'll tell her we will be about fifteen minutes late."

"Or I could drive," Aven said.

Layka appreciated her effort at levity, which made her smile, but her heart still ached. "Fat chance. I'm not letting Fast and Furious drive my Subaru." She turned the car on and backed out, making the turn to follow the exit out of the garage.

"So, I know we're only going to the shelter to confirm if the dog is the one from the vans, but I have a question."

"Okay, shoot." Layka looked both ways before pulling onto the dark street.

"Are we taking the dog to your house, or mine?"

Layka smiled, and a little of that weight lifted. The plan to take the dog home with her had been in her mind already, and for Aven to instinctively know that felt like a connection when they couldn't have one in so many other ways.

CHAPTER TWENTY-ONE

"Brillo." Aven laughed and pulled back away from the tub as the small, sandy blond dog shook vigorously, sending soap flying. It had been about two weeks since they brought her home from the shelter. She was grateful for the routine they had settled into that allowed them both to have time with her. "I thought the bath on Monday night would have lasted at least the week." It was Sunday night, and Layka was coming over to review some glitches in the DC Wheelhouse build and would be taking Brillo back to her place. Brillo whined and Aven leaned in, scratching the dog behind her ear. "You're a good girl," Aven said with the singsong voice that made the dog's ears perk up.

The shelter had bathed her when she arrived, but Aven now realized soap and water was an affront to this dog. As soon as she could, she would roll in the dirt or grass and return with what literally looked like a dog smile. "You really dressed up for me this time," Aven said, lifting a front leg to pull caked mud from the dog's long hair that made it appear she was wearing dark brown boots. She had to have some terrier in her, but she was definitely a mix of some type because her color was a sandy blond all over. Her hair hung straight like that of a Yorkie, but it had a wave at its roots—like a poodle, maybe. "I'm no dog expert, but you're beautiful."

Brillo's mouth dropped open and her tongue lulled out with that doggie smile again, which was adorable, except she had squatted like she was ready to pounce and shuffled her feet when Aven reached for one of them. "Layka will be here soon, and I'm going to be in big trouble if you're dirty." When the dog continued to play, Aven was forced to use a tool she and Layka had discovered the second night the dog was with them. They had been at Layka's house, and the dog was still refusing to eat or respond much to their efforts. "Mommy will be home from the hospital and will be sad if you haven't eaten." The dog's ears had lifted at the word *Mommy*, and those deep brown eyes had focused from one to the other of them as if waiting. They had encouraged the dog to eat—and even take some cuddles—with *Mommy* added to different commands till they found some familiar to the dog.

Aven chewed the inside of her lip. In the past two weeks Brillo's mom had not improved, and Aven wondered what they would do if she didn't make it out of the hospital. Would there be a day when the dog stopped believing this was temporary and returned to mourning the woman she had been with for long enough to have a tag with Brillo engraved on it? "She will get better," Aven said. "Mommy says paw." Brillo bounced from her crouched position and sat her bum down in the tub, lifting her paw.

The doorbell rang in the townhouse, and Aven wiped a hand on the towel, then reached for her phone on the pedestal sink while the other hand worked the mud on the offered paw into a soapy lather that could be washed off. She pressed the microphone and said, "Come in, I'm in the upstairs bathroom bathing Brillo." She tapped send. Layka had the code to the lock on the door but was being polite as they navigated their new dance within the dynamic Aven had started calling the no-touching zone. They were still working on the project and, in many ways, were closer due to the constant interaction that was shrouded in both of them caring about the well-being of Layka's sister while never speaking about the elephant in the room. Sometimes, the tension of wanting to comfort Layka, hold her, be held by her, or touch her intimately required a vigilance of restraint that was exhausting, but she refused to give up what she had with her.

She heard the beeping of the code being put in, then a shuffle as she imagined Layka putting her things on the dining room table before climbing the stairs.

"Again, Brillo?" Layka's voice was melodic and laughing, and it was music to Aven's ears. Samantha was making some progress with the step-down protocol she had shared with Dr. Frankl, but she'd had a small setback yesterday, and it had put Samantha's risk back into perspective. It had been increasingly difficult to find the balance between comforting Layka and maintaining the appropriate distance to respect the boundary Layka had established to honor the unknown of her sister's heart.

It had been harder than she had anticipated it would be. Her heart was racing at the thought of Layka being here and soon only inches away as she knew Layka would want to help with Brillo. Technically, Layka had adopted her, but they had agreed she would be the mascot for the project and they would both pitch in for her care till her mom was better and able to take care of her.

"Hey there, you little rat. What did you do?" Layka knelt, kissing Brillo's wet head on her way down.

Brillo pulled her paw free from Aven and danced a circle in the tub, her wet, soapy paws slipping as she spun.

Aven watched as Layka began scrubbing behind Brillo's front leg, and the dog pushed into her hand. Aven smiled, grabbing the sprayer she'd laid in the tub and turning it on low as she softly sprayed some water to rinse the lathered pup while Layka worked her hands through the residual dirt.

Layka wrapped a towel over Brillo as Aven began wiping down the tub. "I like baths at your house. I get the cuddles while you get to clean." Layka bumped Aven's shoulder with her leg as she stood with her happy bundle.

Aven turned toward her just in time to see her perfect butt strolling away with her head buried in the towel bundle she held in her arms. *Put those thoughts away,* Aven told herself, wondering if it would be harder if they hadn't had intimate physical time together before all this happened. The thought reminded her of the purchase she had made after that night. She had never considered using a sex toy in her relationships till their night together. Now a brand-new one sat in her drawer, and she might never be able to touch Layka again in intimate ways at all, much less ever use that for the new experiences they had joked they would do together.

"I bought takeout," Layka said from the dining room that opened up to the right of the foyer stairs.

Aven finished her task and gathered the laundry, tossing it in the hamper and laying the two wet items on top to dry. She washed her hands. "I'm going to change my clothes real quick, and I'll be down." She stepped toward her room down the hall. She had a minute of panic where she worried about what to put on but reminded herself of their new dynamic and chose her sweatpants, tank, and hoodie.

"Wow, that smells delicious!" Aven said when she reached the bottom of the stairs.

Layka had the to-go containers opened on the table and was topping off Brillo's bowl from her water bottle. Aven had already put food and water down in the portable fold-and-go system that sat inside the dining room, but Brillo must have gobbled it up. "It's my favorite restaurant on Underscore Street."

Aven settled in at the table as Brillo circled on her dog bed in the corner. "Thanks for this," she said, waving at the food.

"No problem. It gives us more time to focus on the project with our limited time, and it's amazing."

Aven poked the fork through its plastic. "Any information from the detective we spoke to earlier in the week?"

Layka wiped at her mouth with the napkin, set it down, and touched Aven's arm resting beside her to-go container. "I've been dying to tell you but wanted to do it face-to-face."

Layka didn't remove her hand, and Aven could feel her arm tingling where manicured nails contacted the inside of her wrist. She squeezed her legs together at the ping in her core. *Focus—that is not an option right now*, Aven thought, then felt a longing in her chest she had never experienced. *What if Samantha never comes off the ventilator? Would Layka ever consider being with me without her sister's blessing?* The devastation of that scenario, both for the grief it would bring Layka and the reality of it being the end of any hope for them, made Aven's stomach turn, and she realized she was just rotating the food in the container.

"Is your food okay?" Layka asked, removing her hand and lifting her bottled water.

"Yes. It's incredible." Aven shoved a large forkful into her mouth, hoping the turning in her stomach would settle with her effort. "Go on. I'm eager to hear what they said."

"They've found some additional evidence that supports the possibility of there being involvement of campaign fraud. The FBI has come into the investigation because of it."

"You're kidding."

"No. I'm not. Agent Sebastian asked me if we had taken any pictures. I told her we had, but that in the calamity of Sam's decline, I hadn't looked at them and wasn't sure what we had." Layka twisted the cap off the water.

"I took a few pictures, but like you, I'd forgot about it when we thought the van had just been bringing the residents in for the festival."

"That's a key part. None of the residents we were able to describe could be positively identified, so it's weak for building a case on, but there are only four residents at the house now, and Agent Sebastian is fairly certain none of them are from the group we saw go to the festival."

"So those people never went back to the resident house?"

"That's the way it looks."

"Where did they go?"

"That's the problem. There's no way to track them. If they were just dropped off at the festival, then they could be anywhere."

"And if they are carrying the new virus variant, they could be spreading it among the local homeless population as they try to settle in among the unhoused here."

"Yes."

"Dr. Frankl said they had an influx about the time of the festival, but the festival at your friend's bar is closer to our hospital. What if they used the festival as a distraction, a ploy because they knew they had been followed?"

Layka picked up on the thought. "They could have loaded those people up again and carted them closer to Washington Regional after the festival. We had left thinking it was a dead end, and we needed to check on Sam."

"Possible. If they loaded them up and carried them to a final destination closer to Washington Regional, that may be why we saw a smaller influx of patients." Aven ran several scenarios in her head. "There are too many variables to know for sure. We had nothing like what Washington Regional saw, but we have still had an increase. My first inclination is the festival is where they left the people from that second van because I remember looking for the van when I saw the man, and I didn't see it."

"I hear you, and it would be like herding cats to try to pick them back up later."

Aven agreed. Discussions with Layka were insightful, and their different perspectives always created unique ideas and solutions. She tapped her chin. "But, Erin's bar is walking distance to Medfirst Hospital, so why didn't our numbers increase more similarly to Washington Regional? Or worse, even, with the festival having so many in a concentrated area nearby?"

"Oh no, Aven," Layka said, bringing her hands to her face.

"What is it?" Aven reached out to touch Layka's elbow where it was propped on the table while her hands covered her mouth.

"Survivor bias," Layka said through her hands still cupped over her mouth.

Aven's heart twisted at the words, and the last vestiges of the wall she had put in place to protect her heart fell away with the horror in Layka's eyes. She would be lying to herself if she pretended to keep it in place when this woman stood on the other side with her transparent emotions and tender heart. "I hadn't even thought of that," Aven said as she saw a tear roll down Layka's face. "I'll have Reynolds check with the coroner at the medical examiner's office to see if your theory is right."

"That would make sense because we didn't see Brillo's mom from the first van at the festival, so their drop-off may have been a less concentrated area near Washington Regional."

"Yeah, but we don't have any way to prove that because we didn't follow that van." Layka stretched from the table to drop two blueberries from her dessert into Brillo's bowl. Layka frequently wore turtlenecks to work. Today's version was an emerald green that fit her perfectly, tapering down from her breast to a well-fitted ribbing at her waist that lifted as she stretched. Aven felt a sudden awareness of time's transience with the somber possibility of survivor bias. It seemed to heighten her need for this woman that was now out of reach both figuratively and physically as her stretch pulled her away from Aven but revealed a patch of skin visible between the green of the sweater and the braided brown leather belt. A flash of memory at the belt on the toy in her drawer made Aven wince at herself, but death was always a stark reminder to be present. To be alive today.

Layka sat back up in her chair and lifted her water, still smiling at Brillo.

Aven pushed thoughts of Layka away and forced her eyes from the perfect curve of Layka's smile. She considered the possibility that the Medfirst numbers, where she worked, were lower than Washington Regional because Washington Regional was taking care of the survivors exposed to infection from residents in van one, while van two intensified the exposure level to severe due to the festival. *That scenario could lead to death outcomes rather than treatment.* Aven rubbed her forehead, feeling the weight of the thought. That would make Medfirst numbers lower because the dead didn't come to the hospital.

The consideration of this new possibility sobered her mind, bringing it back from the new flash of skin at Layka's waist where she leaned again from the table, now petting Brillo. Her body still felt stirred by the need to express that it was alive amid the reminders of life's frailty. She swallowed and turned back to her food. She had eaten most of it while she listened to Layka tell her about the detective's information. *This is ridiculous*, Aven thought, realizing how far her mind had drifted from the work at hand. *Was this how Samantha had struggled when I was taking my time to start our physical connection?* It was the first time she'd really thought about how hard it may have been for Samantha. It didn't justify her actions, and she felt nothing for Samantha except hope that she would recover. But she decided right then, if Samantha recovered, that part of facing her fear would be to have the conversation she hadn't had with Samantha when she ran away so many years ago. Maybe if she had chosen to have that conversation, she would have known then that she was worth waiting for and desired, but that Samantha's choice was her problem, not something wrong with her. It would be a step of resolution since her own behavior of running away created a pattern she had only recently faced and still hadn't managed.

"You're such a good girl," Layka said, rubbing Brillo's head.

The sweet words and cute "puppy talk" voice pulled Aven's eyes back to focus on Layka as she sat up and Brillo bounced. Layka reached out yet again with another blueberry, this time stretching over a jumping Brillo, which just made the shirt ride higher. Aven closed her eyes and took a deep breath, trying to recall the thread of the conversation. "Brillo's mom had been on van one, which is the vehicle we are presuming was taken to a less concentrated place closer to Washington Regional. Right?

"That's what Agent Sebastian said was their working hunch." Layka sat back up and reached out, wiping a bit of sauce from Aven's lip.

Aven kissed at the thumb that seemed to rest on her lip.

Layka started pulling away. "This is so hard."

Aven closed her eyes. *You have to stay focused. People are dying.* She could feel her nose flare, trying to capture the scent of Layka's hand before it pulled completely away. Aven swallowed. *Stay on task.* "Maybe we can go through our pictures to see what might help the detective's case once we finish with the building issues. Then if Reynolds confirms..." She didn't want to say "the homeless deaths," so she left it unsaid. "We can share that with Agent Sebastian as well."

"Yeah, I think that will really help," Layka said, her voice choked with emotion.

Aven understood. She looked at Brillo, curled up and sleeping peacefully in her dog bed, her feet jerking from time to time like she was running in her dreams. Such a dramatic change from her playful bath time. Aven couldn't help but feel the parallel with her emotions. She was comfortable, even calm and peaceful amid these somber moments with Layka, but inside, her desire to touch that swatch of skin under Layka's sweater was jerking Aven's libido like Brillo's legs. "Okay, I'm focused," she said as if willing it to be.

"We know that Brillo's m-o-m was at the house and was on the first van." Aven spelled the word *mom* to be sure to not wake Brillo from her sleep. "She will have some answers."

"If she survives," Layka said thoughtfully, and Aven knew Layka was seeing the similarities between Brillo's mom and her sister.

Aven had no words of confirmation that Brillo's mom was going to succeed with the taper they were using for her as well as for Samantha. She squeezed Layka's knee and released, careful to respect that boundary.

Layka stood and moved to stand beside Aven's chair.

Aven pushed her chair back, uncertain what Layka wanted but glad the chair had no arms when Layka sat sideways on her lap and laid her head on Aven's chest. "Do you think this is okay? It is so hard for me not to be close to you."

Aven wrapped Layka in her arms. "I'm holding a friend who is, number one—worried about her sister both in body and heart, number two—carrying the missing pieces for an investigation that could blow up a campaign, and number three—planning the future for a program that will change the landscape of opportunity and support for the unhoused population. I think this is okay." *Just tell your body and your heart to stop wanting more*, she thought as she felt the press of Layka's forehead at her neck.

CHAPTER TWENTY-TWO

"**I**T'S BEEN ALMOST A month since we contacted the DCPD, and they still don't have enough evidence?" Layka pinned the phone between her shoulder and her ear as she plucked dead leaves from the plant in the windowsill of her private office and listened to Agent Sebastian. She closed her eyes against the irritation she felt. Sebastian didn't deserve her angry tone, but did she have to do everything? The Board of Directors had promoted her based on a recommendation from Dr. Sudha. The Mindful Path Project was officially funded, and she was the principal manager. The new personal office space was a perk, however, the increased workload, right as her sister was nearing her last step-down to extubation, was an added stress. Aven explained every step Sam had faced from the tracheotomy to the medically induced coma and how they would reverse it, but she was still exhausted with worry, and her nerves were on edge.

"The depositions you and Dr. Summerhouse gave were helpful, but it's not enough to move on at this time."

The FBI agent's mention of the depositions brought her thoughts back to the conversation at hand. They had been called in on the resident home case, and their little escapade with the vans had them more entangled than she had ever imagined civilians could be in a case. She tried to stay focused on the agent's words about some delay with the photos she and Aven had sent, but she was worried about Brillo and a hundred other things and just wanted off the phone. "Okay. Thank you for explaining that. I'm glad the pictures and medical examiner information helped. If we think of anything else, we will let you know." Layka clicked the phone off, laid it on the desk, and wrapped her arms at her middle.

She squatted and rubbed Brillo's exposed stomach. Brillo had been with them nearly a month now. "I'm sorry your belly hurts. We're going to go see Dr. Mehr today." The words reminded her Aven would be here soon to pick Brillo up and get her to the vet. Brillo's mom had not had the same success as Sam had with the step-down, and part of her wondered if Brillo's illness was somehow her knowing that fact, connected somehow to the woman who had cared for her. Aven was taking it hard that the viral variant step-down she had helped create wasn't enough to help Brillo's mom. That thought made her stomach tighten. It was getting increasingly difficult to keep from blurring the lines on the no-touch zone between them. It seemed like a betrayal to Sam to be intimate with Aven, but it felt like a betrayal to herself to have the intimacy they had shared pulled away. Samantha still wasn't off the ventilator completely, and though Aven had indicated the reports Dr. Frankl had shared were promising, she had also explained how tough a transition it would still be for Sam. She might have to practice simple things like walking again, Aven had said. Sam would not handle that loss of independence well at all, and it certainly wouldn't be the time to do a deep dive into where Sam's heart was regarding her old flame.

There was a soft knock at her door. Brillo didn't budge. Her ear gave a little twitch but fell back, and she closed her eyes. "Come in," Layka said, rubbing the bottom of a paw and standing.

Aven pushed the cracked door open, and Layka tried not to catalog every nuance of her features, but it was hard. The world still seemed to stand still for her every time Aven entered a room. Aven ran her hands along the back of her neck underneath her ponytail before looking at her, and Layka held back her groan of frustration. They were both struggling, and they had been avoiding the conversation about Sam coming off the ventilator this week.

"How's Brillo doing this morning?"

"She actually ate a few bites from my hand and drank some water but hasn't had much change since I called you last night. Thanks for offering to take her to Dr. Mehr today."

"Absolutely. I'm just glad you have vet connections." Aven squatted near Brillo's bed. "I was surprised you were able to get in touch with her last night to get her on the schedule for today." Aven was sitting fully on the floor now in her perfectly fitted jeans, her legs folded like she was prepared to meditate, Brillo cradled in her arms. Brillo licked Aven's hand twice as she stroked the dog's face. The licks were short-lived, and Brillo closed her eyes again. "I'm not a vet, but her heart rate feels fine and she doesn't feel fevered. I'm hoping Dr. Mehr can sort out the problem. I'm really worried."

"I know," Layka said, kneeling and not fighting the soft ping at her center when her knee pressed Aven's thigh. "Me too. Dr. Mehr asked me last night if I had recently lost another pet."

"She thinks we're going to lose her?" Aven's shattered look made Layka reach for her.

"No. Actually, she thought she might be grieving and wondered if there had been a loss of someone the dog might be attached to. It made me wonder if she senses her m-o-m isn't doing well."

Aven rolled Brillo close to her chest. Layka recalled being held like that by this woman, and she couldn't move or breathe as she watched a tear make its way down Aven's cheek. It could have been her own tear—she felt it. Felt every complex meaning of it. She wiped the tear, kissed Aven's forehead, and stood. This week was going to be hard, but they had a strong friendship, and they could lean on that if they couldn't have anything else. *Even if that's forever?* The question cut through her mind, and the pain of it made her stumble. She grabbed the corner of her desk and doubled over.

"Layka, are you all right?" Aven was up and at her side before she could straighten, one arm cradling Brillo and the other at her back.

"I am. I'm just tired and worried." Layka twisted slightly, leaning her weight on the desk. The movement caused Aven's hand to slip away, as she knew it would. If she let Aven's hand stay on her back, she would be in her arms. She leaned forward and kissed Brillo's wet little nose. "You make sure she drives safe," Layka said, rubbing Brillo's pink belly.

"I've only driven fast once, and we were on a mission then. Don't you listen to her." Aven rubbed a paw, then placed her in Layka's arms. She walked to the far corner of the office where Brillo's plush carrier bag and two toys sat. She lifted the bag and placed the ragged rope toy inside, turning back to Layka. "Besides, I've got precious cargo." She patted the fluffy wool that lined the bag where Brillo liked to sit when she was riding.

Layka kissed Brillo's ear and stage-whispered, "I've been that precious cargo. Don't let her go over forty-five."

Aven snort-laughed. "Hey, I got you back to the festival safe."

"Yes, you did." Layka smiled. They were back on solid friend ground again. It felt both good and painful. "Which reminds me, Agent Sebastian said they're still looking for some links to tie all the pieces together but that the pictures and medical examiner's data we sent have been helpful. If you think of anything we might have forgotten to share or that might give them an additional lead, let me know, and I'll reach out to her."

"Will do." Aven set the carrier on the desk. "I know you're staying at the hospital tonight." She bent down and lifted Brillo's blanket from her bed. "Would you like to have dinner before you go in and relieve Farrah?"

Layka watched Aven preparing the carrier for Brillo. She seemed to want to say more but didn't. "That actually sounds good. I'd like to run a few solutions by you that I have for the Wheelhouse buildings. I need to submit the Mindful Path Project update in two weeks."

"You have some solutions for connecting the Wheelhouse buildings we designed to libraries?"

"Yes. To get the additional funding to do what you and I originally planned, we will need the funding from the Department of Education that was originally denied. For that grant, we need to demonstrate a consistent connection to the library and some form of educational opportunity."

"If you managed to work out that glitch, that means you've turned your feasibility skills on high. I'm excited to hear your ideas."

"Thanks, I appreciate your confidence. All three solutions work for the library's connection for an occupational independent living model. I'd like your input about which one will give us the best data for analyzing diversity, function, and effectiveness of the project, and to include communicable disease safety."

Aven lifted Brillo from Layka's arms and nestled her in the carrier. "I'll be glad to do that. How about dinner at Pazel's?"

"Pazel's is perfect."

"I'll pick you up at six thirty?"

"I can just meet you there." She couldn't risk being alone in a vehicle with Aven. It was too easy for little touches to turn to lingering ones, and with days stretching into weeks since they had made love, she was dry kindling near a forest fire.

Aven folded the blanket over Brillo. "She's sleeping now, and I need to head out to make the appointment on time." Aven turned to Layka. "I know better than anyone how difficult Sam's recovery will be without the stress of this." She circled her hands between them. "I'm not expecting her extubation to create an immediate resolution for us, but please don't push me away."

Layka held her breath. Aven was so close, and she was on a razor's edge, ready to pull her in and kiss her just for the release she knew it would bring. Layka released her held breath with a groan and moved to the front of her desk, adjusting the monitor that didn't need adjusting. "You've quickly become my best friend, but you're the one person I can't talk to about this. You're right about the resolution for us." Layka looked up and held Aven's eyes. "I don't want to push you away, but I do need to create some physical space so I can focus on Sam's recovery without wanting to bury myself in the woman she may still love."

"I don't think Samantha still holds that flame for me, but I understand the confusion of your conflicted emotions." Aven's smile was gentle but pained as she lifted the carrier and walked to the door. "I'll text you once Dr. Mehr gives me some information," she said from the door, then clicked it shut behind her.

Layka closed her eyes and sat down on her desk, her hands tracing the wood edge on either side of her. Her anger and irritation from earlier were gone, replaced by a calm despite the chaos. It was as if Aven left a wave of peace in her wake. She wouldn't give that up. She wasn't going to give up Aven. She just needed some time. When Sam came out of her treatment in two days, she'd give her a week to orient, then she would tackle the subject of Aven.

Her phone rang, and she turned to read the ID. *The hospital.*

CHAPTER TWENTY-THREE

AVEN TICKED OFF THE list of Dr. Mehr's recommendations on her fingertips, tapping her pinky with the last and hardest recommendation. "Let her say goodbye," she said, wishing Brillo was in her arms and not with the vet tech. She turned her head to look out the single window in the room, contemplating a plan.

"That last one is only if you think it will help Brillo. It sounds like you and Layka have a good handle on her baseline behavior and should be able to determine what will be helpful."

Aven nodded. "I'm relieved her physical exam was okay, but my heart breaks that she's grieving." Aven rubbed the back of her neck. Because of patient privacy, she couldn't tell Dr. Mehr that Brillo's mom was scheduled on Friday for her last step-down attempt to come off the ventilator, but Dr. Mehr knew Brillo's original owner was in the hospital because of the medical history listed from the shelter. Aven brought her eyes from the leaves falling outside back to Dr. Mehr. "I'll speak with Dr. Frankl. I think we can work out some type of visit before Friday." Aven rubbed her chin.

"That may really help. Everything otherwise looks good. Let me step out and check the x-ray just to confirm everything."

The door clicked open, and the vet tech entered with Brillo. "She perked up a little when I put her in the dog park enclosure with the other dogs."

Aven reached for her, pleased that some of her lethargy had lifted.

The vet tech scratched behind Brillo's ear before pulling away. "Her x-ray looks pretty good, doc. She has a migrated microchip beneath the small mass on her leg, but it's otherwise unremarkable."

"Thanks." Dr. Mehr thumbed over her shoulder at the door. "Sofia is headed back to college soon and plans to be a veterinarian. I'm going to go review the x-ray with her and then be back."

"Wait!" Aven held up a finger, asking for a minute as she ran through her head what she knew about microchips.

"Are you okay?" Dr. Mehr asked.

"Yes. Are you sure it's a microchip? They scanned her for one when she was brought to the shelter and didn't find one. Matter of fact, they gave her one before we, I mean Layka, could adopt her, and she's had that little bump on her leg since we brought her home."

"I'll take a look," Dr. Mehr said, raising an eyebrow at Sofia as if asking her to reconsider if she thought it might be something else. "But Sofia is really good with x-ray interpretation. I doubt she got it wrong. It's common for chips to migrate to the leg and no longer work."

"Hmm," Aven said thoughtfully. "So, she could have had the chip and it was not able to be read because it had migrated and now it's broken?"

"Yes, or it does work, but because it migrated, they didn't think she was chipped at all. It's a requirement for shelters to check, but chips are put in standard places, like between the shoulder blades. Shelters are so busy that if they check the standard placement areas and don't find anything, they chip them."

Sofia chimed in. "I think that is what happened. There is a chip at her shoulder blade, so when I saw the one in her leg, I checked her history and saw she was a rescue. The chip in her leg is a little unusual compared to most microchips, but I have seen one similar."

"Are you able to tell what kind of microchip from the x-ray?" Aven rubbed Brillo's soft fur.

Dr. Mehr paused in the door. "Not necessarily, but our scanner can give us all the information that is on it."

"That's great. Can we do that?" Aven was excited. Brillo's mom would finally have a name, and maybe it could give them information about her next of kin if the chip listed an emergency contact.

"Certainly, give me just a minute."

Aven nodded and stepped toward the window, nuzzling Brillo, who seemed energized by Aven's excitement. "Maybe we've been part of the problem," Aven said, recalling the tension she and Layka had been feeling. The thought reminded her of their plans for dinner. Layka had indicated honestly that she needed some space to deal with the Sam issue, and seeing Brillo's mood so impacted by her excitement made Aven think maybe she and Layka should work on being happy separately till everything worked out. That led her to the conversation she had planned to have with Layka tonight at dinner. The buzz surrounding the Mindful Path Project had done a lot to boost both their careers. Layka was now the program director over the entire project, which was now aligned with a developing presidential mandate, and Aven had been offered a job at UCSF Berkeley to assist the infectious disease team with the component there and become the pulmonary team lead at UCSF Medical Center.

Brillo's ears twitched against Aven's hand, then perked, and Brillo turned her head toward the door just as it opened and Dr. Mehr entered.

"X-ray looks good. Let's get that chip scanned."

Aven handed Brillo to Sofia and pulled her phone out to text Layka.

AVEN: Brillo's checkup good. She is feeling some better already and Dr. Mehr has given some directives to help with her grieving. Give you details tonight and some news to help identify Brillo's mom.

Just typing the text made her feel better. She did not want to lose what she and Layka had. The thought of moving to the West Coast had felt overwhelming, but now she was seeing it as a short break. A time when she and Layka could stay connected as friends and wouldn't have to struggle with the physical tension while Sam recovered. Layka didn't quite believe her when she said it could take a year, but it could—and that was if her transition from ventilator down to stable care in the ICU

went smoothly. She didn't get a response right away but knew that Layka
had meetings scheduled all day.

Layka swallowed back the bile she tasted in her throat when she saw the
hospital number on the phone screen. She answered and lifted it to her
ear. "Hello."

"Layka, it's Farrah. They had to extubate Sam early. It was traumatic."

"Is she alive?" Layka shouted in panic. "I'm on my way." Layka
dropped the phone on her desk, then realized she couldn't hear Farrah's answer. She pushed speakerphone as she slipped on her jacket and
grabbed her purse.

"They have her sedated now, but she is breathing on her own."

There was a pause.

Layka moved behind the desk to close the computer, her mind starting
to calm the panic with Farrah's words. She shoved the purse straps onto
her shoulder when they kept slipping. "What is it, Farrah?" she asked
when the pause lingered.

"She's disoriented. Each time she wakes, she asks for someone named
Vickie."

Layka collapsed into her chair and dropped her head into her hands.
Her purse slipped to her elbow braced on the desk. She unfolded her
arm and just let the purse fall. It smacked the ground, turned over, and
everything spilled out. She just stared at it, feeling the same way. She
rubbed her eyes, which were wet with tears she didn't realize she was
shedding.

"Layka. Are you there?"

Layka pulled the phone to her. "Yes, I'm here. I'm closing things up
and I will be on my way." She enlarged her phone screen to see the time
that was blurry through her tears. She could do her next meeting at the
hospital if she needed to. She did the time difference calculation. She
had an hour. It was her first meeting with her assistant project manager
on the West Coast at the public library near UCSF. "I'll be there in

thirty minutes." She needed half an hour to get to the hospital through traffic. Farrah made a sound of acknowledgment and clicked off. She didn't want to have to put off her meeting with the California project team connected with UCSF, but her sister was priority. She tapped the screen for notifications. Nothing from Aven about Brillo. She'd get to the hospital and do the meeting from there if possible. She pushed her chair back and began putting everything back in her purse, slipping every item back into its place. *God, if it was only that easy to do with my life*, she thought. She took a deep breath. She had a lot to be thankful for. Samantha was off the ventilator, she had a new position she loved, and she was scheduled today and tomorrow with the assistant project managers under her for the two other pilot sites, and she had Aven. *Oh, Aven. What are we going to do with us?* She checked again for a text. Aven would let her know as soon as she knew something about Brillo. For now, she needed to focus on Sam. She stood, dropped her phone in her jacket pocket, and slid her purse up her arm one more time. She'd have time to see how Sam was doing, then make a decision about whether to cancel the UCSF meeting or not. The Kansas meeting was tomorrow, and she could do them back-to-back but preferred to have a day to deal with each. *God, I look forward to dinner with you, Aven.* The thought had circled in her mind before the weight of how it had all changed twisted her stomach, and she braced herself with her hand on the door. *Breathe deep, pull the door open, and head for the elevator.* One step at a time. It was all she could manage.

Layka's phone pinged with a text notification as she pulled into the garage to park. She could see it was from Aven because her phone was seated in the GPS cradle she kept on the dash. "Let me check on Sam and I'll get to you," she said to the notification. If there was something seriously wrong with Brillo, she couldn't deal with that while facing the issues with Sam, and if it was good news, she would need it after dealing with Sam's situation.

She parked the car, then toyed with the thought of opening the text. "One problem at a time," she told herself. "Brillo is with Aven. She is safe." The words made fresh tears start. Aven was also where she felt safe.

"Layka," Farrah said, wrapping her arms around her when she entered the room. "Thank God you're here. She's resting now, but it was horrible."

Layka held Farrah and let her own tears fall with Farrah's. She could see the steady rise and fall of Sam's chest over Farrah's shoulder, and the sight of that without tubing and ventilator allowed the constriction of her chest to release enough to take what she felt was the first deep breath in weeks.

Farrah pulled back, wiping at her eyes. "They sedated her." She turned and moved toward the bed, reaching for a Kleenex and extracting one for both of them.

Layka accepted it and wiped at her eyes and nose as Farrah adjusted the blanket.

"They still will only let one of us stay with her. Do you mind if I stay tonight?"

Layka ran her hand across her sister's forehead. She wanted Sam to have Farrah there when she woke, but her mind questioned her own deeper motives about postponing time with her sister. "That's fine. I'll sit with her now. You go home, shower, eat, and take some time for yourself."

"That would be great. Thank you, Layka." Farrah headed for the door before pausing. "Do you know who Vickie is?"

Layka felt her heart slump with her shoulders. She raised her head and turned from the bed. "I do. If you're okay with it, let me talk with Sam when she wakes, and I'll answer all your questions when you come back."

Farrah nodded, grabbed her coat, and headed out.

Layka sat down in the chair pulled next to the bed. "I love you, Sam. Thanks for not leaving me," she whispered as she squeezed her sister's hand.

Sam moved her fingers beneath Layka's hand but didn't wake. "I'm right here, Samkins." She leaned over and kissed her sister's head, then pulled her phone from her purse, hooked the purse strap on the back of the chair, and sat back down. "I'm going to do my meeting while I'm here," she said, pulling open her Zoom app on her phone. She didn't know how much people could hear or process when they were sedated for sleep, but she felt better telling Sam what she was doing. She had seven minutes before she was scheduled to meet with the new assistant project manager Mildred had hired for the California Wheelhouse build. The committee had agreed with her idea to hire an assistant project manager to be boots on the ground at each site. "I'm meeting with Naomi," she said to the sleeping Sam. She hovered over the text notification from Aven. She didn't want to wait to find out about Brillo but also didn't want to manage emotions if the news wasn't good. Sam would tell her to open the damn text. "I should open the damn text, shouldn't I?" Layka said, not expecting a response.

"Lay..." Sam said with a puff of air.

Layka dropped her phone on the bed. "Sam, I'm right here." She lifted Sam's hand, cupping it with both of hers.

Sam smacked her lips and relaxed back into sleep.

Layka released her hand and scanned the area for the lip balm Farrah kept handy. She found it on the table near the head of the bed and lifted it. "I'm not going to be as good at this as Farrah is," Layka said, applying the soft Vaseline-based balm.

"Farrah," Sam whispered.

"She'll be right back."

There was a slight curve of Sam's lips, a quick flutter of her eyes, and then her lips parted with a sigh before returning to steady breathing.

Layka felt something in her relax at the small gestures of normalcy she thought she might never see again. She knew there was still a long road ahead but was grateful for this moment. She had shared with Aven Sam's battle through COVID, and they had discussed the possible outcomes for Sam following this illness. The thought brought her back to Aven and Brillo. She lifted her phone. A second notification from Aven appeared. She could read the first part of it. "Good news and..." She couldn't read the rest without opening the text. She glanced at the time on her phone. One minute till her meeting. She started the meeting so Naomi would be able to join, then tapped the texts from Aven. She read through them quickly. Then read them again slower, pinching her lip as she thought. She could keep her dinner plans with Aven and get the details then. *Farrah is staying tonight with Sam. We'll have some much-needed time to talk,* she thought as she read through the texts again and her Zoom app pinged.

She typed out a quick text telling Aven where she was, that Sam was stable, and that she was starting a Zoom meeting and would meet her at the restaurant.

She closed her text and opened up the Zoom app. She took a deep breath and clicked the button to bring Naomi into the meeting.

Sam stirred several times during the thirty-minute meeting but never woke, and a nurse came in once. Naomi knew about the situation with Sam and had been gracious about the impromptu setting. "I appreciate your time today, Naomi. I look forward to staying connected with you as we prepare for the sequential Wheelhouse builds. The ribbon-cutting here is set for sometime between April and June of next year, with Kansas to follow, and then the final build in California with you. My plan is for the four of us to coordinate the work for all of them between us to lighten the load for each of us."

"I think it is a great idea. It will create opportunity for us to all be part of the process from the first effort."

"Exactly, we can enjoy the successes, see the hurdles, and face the pitfalls together."

"I like that you give us the room to lead and provide the experience we need to do it well."

"Thank you, Naomi. It helps to hear that." Layka could feel her mood lifting as pieces of chaos in her life were gradually coming back into calm. She would work through the details. "I know Mildred and the hospital liaison are still building the teams at the Kansas site and yours."

"Yes. I'm very excited that Dr. Summerhouse may be joining us out here."

Layka froze. She gripped the bed rail her hand had been resting on. If she held it tight enough, maybe she could hold her world together.

CHAPTER TWENTY-FOUR

L AYKA TWISTED THE NAPKIN in her hand. She was pleased she
arrived before Aven. She needed the time to settle her racing
thoughts. Aven was bringing Brillo, so she asked for a table outside. She
tried to push the last part of the meeting with Naomi from her mind
and concentrate on the fact that Sam had opened her eyes twice, and the
second time she had even managed to look around. Layka was glad Farrah
had been back by that time. They each took a hand, and that seemed
to help Sam orient. She was groggy but managed a smile before falling
back to sleep. Dr. Frankl said it would probably be morning before her
sedation dose was low enough for her to be alert more often. She had
said both Layka's and Farrah's names a few times. There had been no
mention of Vickie this time, but Layka had been waiting for the shoe to
drop.

She could handle this new development with Aven. She could. She
would, but why hadn't Aven told her? *Maybe she's been trying to*, she
thought, running through their interactions the last few weeks. She now
regretted her words this morning. She'd asked for space to grapple with
her big emotions for Aven while navigating Sam's connection to her and
her recovery. Now she wondered if Aven would take that as a cue to fly
to the other side of the country. She didn't want her to leave, but it was

unfair to ask her to put her career and opportunities on hold when Layka needed to work through the complications with Sam. She wiped away a tear. Why did she feel so much for her? What made Aven Summerhouse different from everyone she'd ever dated? She gasped. She was struggling to breathe. She was sitting outside, and yet it felt as if there was no air. If Aven left, it would rip open that hole in her chest. Aven was as much a part of her as her family had been. In only a short period of time, this stranger had become her world. *I want her in my life. I want her to love me.* The thought ripped open the scars of her past, and she let the tears roll. Every loss of her past mounted like a wave. She wanted this beautiful, kind, patient woman in her life. She wanted Aven as that one thing that wouldn't be taken from her, but she already had been. A move across the country would just be the physical evidence of it. She propped her elbows on the table and covered her face with her hands till she could stop the flow of tears.

"Layka, what happened? Is Sam okay?"

Aven was at her side, her arms wrapped solidly around her and Brillo whining with her paws on the low rung of the café high-top chair.

Layka pulled back slightly from the hug, but the look of concern in Aven's eyes almost made her surrender to it again. "She's stable right now, but it's been a tough day." She leaned down and scratched behind Brillo's ears. "You look better, little one."

"Dr. Mehr gave her some IV fluids. She thinks she has been grieving, but after seeing her in the vet office, I think she is also feeling some of our tension." Aven didn't move from her spot next to Layka. "I'm so glad Sam is stable, and I support you taking some time to work through everything."

Layka closed her eyes at the comfort she felt when Aven squeezed her shoulders before moving to her side of the table. She equally felt the loss when Aven chewed the inside of her lip and stared down at the menu.

"What is it?" Layka lifted her water, hoping it would relieve her dry mouth. She didn't really want to know.

Aven looked up, and the sorrow in her eyes broke Layka. This was killing them both.

"The hospital liaison has asked me to consider a position at UCSF Berkeley Medical Center." Aven looked down at the table, dragging a finger through a ring left by her water glass. She lifted the straw from her glass and added more water to the table, then spiraled it with her finger. The design mimicked the spiral design they had discussed with the engineer and builder. When she looked up, there were tears in her eyes. "It's a promotion. I'll be the lead attending pulmonologist at the hospital and an adjunct faculty at the university." She drew another spiral wheel near Layka's side of the table. "It's the only offer that allows me to maintain a direct connection with the project. I know you need some space—"

"Hi, ladies. I'm Meghan, your server. Angie said she brought you waters, so can I get you anything else to drink while you check the menu?"

"Water," they both said, and Layka let Aven finish for them. She couldn't breathe over the knot in her chest.

"The water will be fine. Could you bring us an extra water?" Aven said, lifting Brillo for a squeeze as she pulled the mini collapsible bowl from her pocket and poured some water into it before setting it and Brillo down and hooking the leash handle on her chair.

Meghan nodded, and both of them watched as Brillo drank. When they looked up, their eyes locked. Layka felt the weight of those soft, determined eyes.

Aven reached out again toward the circle of water on Layka's side of the table. She pulled a line of water from Layka's circle to her own. "I know you need space," Aven started again.

Layka tried to release the death grip she had on the lapel of her light jacket, but her heart was pounding so hard she felt her hand there was the only thing holding it in place. She wanted to scream that she didn't want space, that she didn't need time to let her sister heal enough to have a long overdue conversation with her. But that would be a lie, and Aven already knew the truth of it. Asking her to stay for this no-romantic-connection limbo would only hold Aven back from her dreams.

Aven tapped along the water line between the two spirals. "This offer lets me stay on the project in the same capacity I have now, working with you and the teams put together by Mildred and Michael." Aven covered the hand Layka had on the table. "I want to stay on the project. I want to stay a part of your life, even if it is only this. I don't want to lose you."

Layka lost it. Everything in her broke, and she didn't care that they were one of several full tables out on a patio near the street. She was losing Aven, even as she offered to stay a part of her life.

"Hey, hey." Aven was up and moving toward her.

The next few moments were a blur to Layka as Aven left cash for occupying the table, lifted Brillo and her bowl, and pulled Layka from her chair. The crowded patio was shrinking to a circle with blackness collapsing from the rim.

Aven felt Layka's weight when she went limp in her arms. They had made it to Reynolds's Escalade. She'd driven it today and parked in the garage near the restaurant. She stooped and took Layka's weight on her shoulder and back for long enough to set Brillo down, pop the hatchback, and shift her foot over the end of Brillo's leash.

"I've got you, Lay-lay." Aven shifted her position and lifted Layka into the open space. Reynolds had removed the seats so they could carry their portable pickleball gear, complete with net and poles. Layka stirred, and Aven took in this woman she loved. *Love,* she thought, touching the patch of color that was returning to her cheeks. "I guess the future will tell us," she muttered. She didn't know if she could do it. Take the leap to move to the West Coast. They hadn't discussed it fully yet, and she wanted it to be something they decided together. She could take the job in California, but it would kill her to be physically away from Layka. She cherished the light brushes of contact, the hugs, and the episodic cheek or forehead kiss that snuck in occasionally. The move would force their physical separation, which they struggled to manage every time they were close, and she knew it made Layka feel guilty. Now that Sam was in a place to recover, Layka could work through those things with her sister.

Aven lifted Brillo into the truck with Layka. She wanted to touch her cheek again, run a hand along it, kiss her forehead, but knowing how Layka felt, she leaned on her to set the line for their physical connection, and "passed-out" Layka couldn't do that. "Thanks, Brillo," Aven said when the dog started licking Layka's cheek and Layka shifted. She was coming to. Aven braced her hands on the Escalade bumper and let her head drop between her shoulders. She was so happy Layka was in her life, and at the same time, her chest ached with wanting more. She'd given a lot of thought to the Sam issue. It was strange how life twisted and turned. She stood here now feeling the physical draw for Layka that Sam had felt for her years ago. It was frickin' hard to want someone this bad physically. And at least for her, she knew Layka wanted her. The younger version of Sam had lost her parents to a car accident, her sister to the Peace Corps, and wanted physical touch to prove she was loved. Aven knew it didn't justify what Sam did, and Sam's words to her sister before her decline indicated she knew that too.

Layka's breathing became nasal, and Aven lifted her head to see Layka's nose flare. She was taking in her environment. Aven felt no draw to Sam, and she was fairly sure Sam was over her, but she had to let Sam and Layka sort that out.

CHAPTER TWENTY-FIVE

T HE SMELL WAS THE first thing Layka noticed. It was oil, stale air, and gasoline. She blinked her eyes and felt wetness lick her cheek as she tried to place the soft gray fabric above her.

"Hey there, you." It was Aven's voice, and it soothed her like soft blankets in the fall.

"Whose SUV?" Layka asked as her mind pieced together that Aven had managed to get her into the back of somebody's large vehicle. They must have removed the seats because the space was huge. Aven's beautiful face came into focus, and Layka registered the wet licks were Brillo. She was about to ask what happened when it all flooded back, and tears leaked from the corners of her eyes like someone turned a faucet. Brillo licked at them as they trailed toward her ear. She pulled her close, trying to sit up.

"Hold on, Lay-lay, I'm right here. Rest for a minute." Aven lifted her legs, elevating them again. Layka had pulled them down from the side wall near the window of the SUV in her effort to get up. "You almost made it to the vehicle before you passed out. Keeping your legs up will get the blood back to your brain." Aven gave a little laugh, but her eyes were red-rimmed and belied her effort at levity.

Layka let Aven adjust her body in the extended open area of the SUV. She blinked to clear the tears at every gentle touch. Layka wanted to tell her it wasn't blood missing from her brain. It was the piece of her heart that was missing. Instead, she watched Aven move at the rear of the vehicle, the hatchback open as she removed her jacket and rolled it into a pillow that she placed under Layka's head.

"Reynolds asked me to put some air in the tires for her while I was running errands today. She and Purdel are taking a road trip, so I've got to drop it back at the hospital and get my vehicle. How are you feeling?"

"Hopefully their road trip is less eventful than ours was," Layka said, wanting to avoid the question about how she was feeling. She let her answer be pulling her legs down and twisting up into a seated position with Brillo in her lap. She was proud of herself for that much, because she still felt a little woozy.

"True that," Aven said, sitting down and sliding back to be next to her. "That brings me to some better news." Aven pushed Layka's hair off her shoulder.

Layka felt the touch as deeply as if Aven had kissed her bare shoulder. It was the little gestures they had now. Never getting too close, practically holding their breath, hoping the cards would fall in their favor.

Aven's hand lingered for a minute, then fell away. "Dr. Mehr found a microchip in Brillo, and we may have information about her m-o-m and family."

"Really? That is good news." Layka pulled Brillo tight and kissed her head.

"Mom's name is Amelia, right, Brillo?" Aven said.

Brillo's tail thumped.

"It's an unusual chip. Only the owner's name can be read with the scanner Dr. Mehr has in her office."

"Can we take her somewhere else to have it read?"

"That's why I said 'may have information.' The chip requires a special fob to read it. Without it, the only other way is to remove it and send it to the company to get the information from it. You're her parent on Dr. Mehr's paperwork. If you're agreeable, Dr. Mehr can remove it and send the chip to the company for information recovery. It's a long shot, but if there is information, such as an emergency contact, then we can forward that to Dr. Frankl."

Layka read the connection Aven had with patients in the silent plea of her eyes. "You're hoping to find Amelia's family," Layka said, running the back of her hand along Aven's cheek. "It is beautiful that you care so much for someone you've never even spoken to."

Aven's cheeks flushed, and Layka's heart twisted again at what she was losing. "Is the surgery to remove it complicated?"

"I asked Dr. Mehr about that, and she said they are superficially placed, which is why they can migrate so easily. She said the procedure was simple and had very low risk for problems for Brillo. I had her email me the form you would need to sign for the chip to be returned to the company along with details about the procedure for you to review if you had questions."

"I have to sign something for her to send it?"

"It's required for this chip. Apparently, it's a newer product, very expensive, and requires a transfer of documentation if owners change."

"Really?"

"Yes, that was the other good news. It appears Amelia Kangadams may have a brother. Dr. Mehr recognized the name, saying it was an old DC family with some very deep pockets, which she thought might explain the expensive microchip. We'd need the chip information to give us an emergency contact number, but if Dr. Frankl can connect with them, they can give us more information about her medical history." Aven paused. "I'm not sure it will change her outcomes, but it's worth a try."

"Of course I'll sign it. Can I do it now? I want Dr. Mehr to send it as soon as possible." Then realization hit: If Amelia had family, they may want Brillo. She squeezed Brillo close and buried her head below the soft ear where she could nuzzle her and let the fresh tears fall.

Aven's arms wrapped around both of them, and Layka let herself be held.

Aven savored the moments of Layka in her arms. Layka didn't allow it often, and Aven understood why.

Layka pulled back. "Can you pull up Dr. Mehr's email? I want to do that before we leave, and then I want you to take me home."

Aven pulled her phone from her pocket and found the document. She handed the phone to Layka.

"Have you read it?" Layka asked, scrolling through the three pages.

"Yes. I wanted to be able to tell you about it if you had questions without you having to spend energy on it." Aven absorbed Layka's appreciative smile and wondered when they had started leaning on each other's strengths. Each did their fair share but allowed the other's strength to shine when it expended more of their own energy than was reasonable or comfortable.

"There," Layka said, passing the phone back to Aven. "Now will you take me home?" She looked down at Brillo, snuggled in her arms, then back up to Aven. "And, stay for a while?"

Aven shifted in their seated position and placed her hands on Layka's shoulders. "There is nothing in this world I would rather do than be with you as much as possible. Are you going back up to the hospital later tonight?"

"No." Layka dropped her head.

Aven mentally kicked herself. She'd just thrown cold water on Layka's plans for the night. No matter how platonic they planned or kept them, they both knew that time alone at home led to cuddles and touches that exceeded what they normally allowed themselves. Without meaning to, she had indirectly reminded Layka of the one thing that stood between what they had started.

Layka began scooting toward the bumper. "The hospital will only let one person stay in the evening, and Farrah asked if she could stay with her." Layka reached the edge and stood. She gave Brillo a squeeze as she set her down on the ground, then looked up to Aven. She bit her lip. "And then when Naomi told me in our meeting that you might be coming on board there, I knew I wanted to be with you tonight." Layka covered her face, and Aven scrambled to get to her, unable to bear seeing shame in this woman who did more to be good to others than anyone she had ever met.

Aven wrapped her in a tight hug. "Please don't feel guilty for caring about me. I know I will always care about you." Layka pulled back enough to see her face but didn't pull out of her arms. Aven locked her eyes on Layka's blue-gray ones. "The decision to go to California isn't one I plan to make alone."

Layka leaned to put her head on Aven's shoulder. "It will be good for your career and will give me time to help Sam recover. I know it's the right choice, but I don't want you away."

Aven felt Layka's arms lace round her waist. It was comfortable, warm, intimate. And not for the first time, she wondered at how gestures of human connection that she had with people every day, such as hugs and hand touches, were enhanced with Layka. These close-proximity happenstances had a layer of heat and longing when they came from Layka. She understood about chemistry, dopamine release, and all that occurred in the limbic system with attraction, but it exceeded defining when something as gentle as this hug had her heart soaring and her core molten. She pulled Layka tight to her. "Let me take you to your house. You can get Brillo fed and our whiteboard ready."

Layka squeezed her waist and nuzzled her cheek into Aven's shoulder.

Aven could feel Layka smiling against her shoulder at her words, and she memorized the moment. "I'll take Reynolds's vehicle back to the hospital and get my car. If you order us dinner, I'll stop and pick it up on the way home."

Layka adjusted in Aven's arms, and for a moment Aven thought she might kiss her shoulder, but she didn't. Instead, she whispered, "That sounds wonderful," giving Aven's waist a squeeze before withdrawing her hands. The movement was slow, as if she were tracing every inch before she stepped away. Her eyes were thoughtful, and Aven imagined her marking the memory like a favorite quote in a book, the way she had done with so many of Layka, eager to return to it time and time again.

CHAPTER TWENTY-SIX

L AYKA FLEXED AND RELAXED her sister's feet as Sam pushed against her hand. Sam was almost ten days out from her extubation.

"Exactly. Do those and the other exercises four times a day, and I will start your physical therapy with staff tomorrow."

"Thank you, Dr. Frankl," Sam croaked.

Layka swallowed at the painful sound, but she was so happy to hear Sam speaking and moving. Her muscles were still weak, but the doctor said her neurologic exam was finally normal. That had not been the case when she first came out of sedation. A little—or rather, a lot—of hard work now, and she could be back to herself.

"You're welcome, but I was only part of a larger team for you, Sam. Your friend Dr. Summerhouse played a key role on the team."

Sam only nodded, and Layka wondered if it was because of the soreness of her throat or if it was emotion at the reminder of Aven.

"Speaking of Dr. Summerhouse... ask her to call me, and I can give her an update on our mutual patient. I can't give her medical information to you, but I can tell you the patient's family wants to meet with you and Aven. They are grateful someone is caring for...Brillo, I believe they said was the name."

Now it was Layka's turn to nod. Aven had told her that the hospital had been able to use Amelia's name to reference old medical records and had reached out to the emergency contact on record. She was grateful Brillo hadn't needed the surgery to remove the chip, but she didn't trust her voice to respond while the emotion of possibly losing Brillo soaked into her.

"I'll see you on rounds in the morning," Dr. Frankl said, then turned for the door.

Layka and Sam both gave a little wave, and Layka took a seat on the bed at Sam's feet. Sam had made steady gains mentally and physically, and Layka was champing at the bit to tackle the hard issues. Aven's family was visiting and scheduled to travel with her to Berkeley to help get her stuff moved in over Thanksgiving weekend. Layka would be spending Thanksgiving here at the hospital with Sam, and as hard as it was for Aven to be leaving, she knew they had made the right decision. Sam had several episodes while coming out of sedation where she asked for Vickie. She never did so when awake, and Dr. Frankl's mention of her, along with Sam's reaction, told her it was time to talk about the elephant in the room. "Do you want me to pass on a message to Aven? Farrah should be here this evening, so I'm going home."

Sam picked at the sheet. "I've been able to separate the past and the present recently." She looked up at Layka and pushed herself up higher on the bed. "I've been talking with Farrah about it. I felt that was where I needed to start."

Layka nodded.

"I know you said Aven was going to California because it is a positive step for her career, but I realize our college history played a role in how that evolved, and I am so sorry."

"Do you still have feelings for her?" Layka asked, needing to face this head-on. Aven was leaving. That wouldn't change regardless of the answer, but she needed it.

"I want you to be happy with her," Sam said.

"That isn't what I asked."

Sam rubbed her forehead. "I've been talking through it with Farrah because it's an old wound that was born of my failure, then twisted over years of suppression and festering. You deserve to be happy with her, and

I know that what we had wasn't love, but to describe what I feel is too complicated for me to do right now."

"That's honest," Layka said, blowing out a breath. She knew it wasn't going to be easy to hear, but she hadn't anticipated how conflicted she would feel as her heart held both understanding and frustration. Aven wasn't perfect, but she was a good person who was liked by everyone Layka knew, so it would be unbelievable if Sam had said she felt nothing. Sam said what they had wasn't love. It may not have been forever love, but it was young love—and that left its own mark. Sam's response was probably the best answer she could have expected. She had encouraged Layka to foster a happy-ever-after with Aven, and she had been honest about her emotions being a complex maze *she* had to navigate. Sam was leaning on Farrah and using this difficult time to build a strong relationship with a woman she did love. Layka could see that, but where did that leave her now? "Aven and I have a meeting, and I hope we can connect with Dr. Frankl and Amelia's family here at the hospital this afternoon. You never said if you wanted me to give her a message or not."

Layka felt Sam's feet rubbing together under the blankets, a habit she had since childhood when she was nervous. Layka laid her hand on her sister's leg and rubbed up and down.

Sam pulled her eyes from the window and looked at Layka. She opened her mouth, then closed it. "Do you think..." Sam picked at her thumbnail. "Do you think she would come by so we could talk?"

Layka heard her own gasp but closed her eyes against the pain in her chest.

"I'm not interested in her romantically, sis. Please know that. Farrah says she thinks I need to have the conversation we didn't have years ago. She thinks that's part of why we both carried only the tragedy of it. There was never closure."

Layka nodded once again, not trusting her voice as she swallowed the ugly feelings of jealousy and inadequacy. "I'll let her know you asked for that." She could feel the black veil of not measuring up curling around her heart. She'd always felt she could never do anything as well as Sam. Her bigsisteritis had a dark side when she viewed the insecurities she held about herself compared to her sister, especially when her sister had known Aven first. She faced for the first time the truth that some of the hurdles to having a full relationship with Aven were about her own flaws. She tapped Sam's leg. "I'm going to get another coffee in the cafeteria. Do you want anything?"

Sam reached for her sister, and Layka placed her hand in Sam's. "I love you, Lay-bear. I want you to be happy. I think Aven can do that for you."

Layka tried to smile, and she hoped it touched her eyes, but her heart felt twisted with the grief of recognizing she had new challenges to face. "I know you do, and I love you. What lies ahead are my own battles. You work on you, and I'll work on me." She squeezed Sam's hand. "And, we will have each other as we do."

"There's my two favorite ladies." Farrah stood at the door, a familiar bag from the local bakery in hand. "I hope you still have your coffee," she said, shaking the bag.

"I'm just headed down for a fresh cup. I'll be back up to hang out, unless we are able to meet with Dr. Frankl and Brillo's original family this afternoon." She was careful not to mention Aven by name. It was weird that she thought about that. And it would have to change, eventually, if the four of them were going to have a future together. *One piece at a time.*

CHAPTER TWENTY-SEVEN

A VEN WATCHED AMELIA'S BROTHER, Barcephe, place what looked similar to a key fob in Layka's hand.

"There is a website that tells you all the extra things the chip can do with access to the fob."

Layka turned the black and silver fob over in her hand reverently. Aven could read each emotion as it crossed her face: relief, sorrow, determination.

"We'll make sure to review it in detail," Layka said, and Aven warmed at the soft look Layka gave her before placing the fob back in its engraved silver case.

Aven knew the look was one of comfort at having another small thing they could share across the distance. She knew because she felt it too. Brillo was an unspoken connection for them. They had freely discussed their fears that the family might want to take the dog who had wagged her way into their hearts. The conversation had been laced with their underlying proximity loss of each other in this strange turn of events that had them dancing around their emotions.

"We're grateful someone is caring for the dog. We travel constantly, and there would be little rest for her." Barcephe took his wife's hand and kissed it.

It was nice to see two people still enjoying each other's company late into their years. Barcephe had explained the two of them met at his sister's high school graduation. His sister and his wife had been classmates, and he'd come home from his first year of college to support his sister's success. Her learning disability had made school difficult, and her severe depression had often caused her to miss class, but Aven could see Barcephe had always seen his sister's strength.

"We were traveling when the mental health facility that was housing Amelia closed its doors." Barcephe touched the silver fob box Layka had placed carefully on the tray table at the foot of Amelia's bed, then shifted to take in his sister still on the ventilator.

Aven harnessed the ping of guilt that her protocol had been unable to help Dr. Frankl wean her from it.

"Our last report was that she was doing well and eager to head into independent living."

Barcephe's wife moved to stand behind him, her arm and hand rubbing his back as he held his sister's hand.

"That's when we bought the fob and microchip for Brillo. We were surprised to find the fob in such good condition among her things when Dr. Frankl explained she had possibly been living on the streets. Our last interaction was when her case worker had sent us a video of the two of them taking Brillo to the vet to have the chip placed. We were out of technological contact for three months but set up a delivery service to send her flowers each week that represented our locations."

His wife turned toward the side table that had been pushed askew from the bed to make way for the ventilator. She stabilized the vase of roses as she opened the drawer, pulled free a Kleenex, wiped her eyes, then took a seat in the chair facing her husband. She leaned forward as if to keep the closeness to him but was unable to watch the machine continue to breathe for Amelia. She smiled a weak smile. "We always did that when we traveled." She turned the Kleenex to use a new side on her still-watering eyes. "She would write down her guesses for where we were each week, and when we came home, we would show her pictures, and she would see how many of the places she had guessed correctly."

Barcephe reached out and touched her shoulder. "It was a way for us to stay connected with her when we were away and out of contact."

She covered his hand. "It was when we were back in the area that we were contacted by the delivery company, saying the hospital had shut down and they needed to reimburse us for not making the last month of deliveries. We had no idea if Amelia had an early transition to her independent living or had been transferred to another facility. We had to submit our request for information on a government website that has been managing the consolidation of mental health hospitals across the country."

Barcephe's grip on the bed rail tightened, and Aven could sense his pain. *How long did you search, wondering where your sister was, only to find it was too late?* The thought made the sorrow and struggle of all that the virus had wrought well up in her chest and start to suffocate her. Barcephe and his wife had spoken with her and Dr. Frankl earlier in the day and made the hard decisions.

Aven breathed in and closed her eyes against tears when Layka's hand slipped into hers. She hadn't registered Layka's movement into her space, but her body had because she didn't startle at the touch. Layka must have seen the emotion on her face and had broken one of the unspoken touching laws between them to hold her hand. It wasn't a friendly squeeze or brushing contact—which was the mainstay for them—but she had laced their fingers together, and it was absolutely exactly what Aven needed.

Barcephe stood between the bed and his wife still seated in the chair. His tall frame and broad shoulders meant he blocked Aven's view of the machine now.

"Thank you for the information about the investigation that is ongoing. I'm hoping Amelia kept the recording feature on for the microchip. You'll know when you read the chip with the fob."

"We'll keep you posted as things develop. The FBI, a Maryland squad, and my sister's team have been working on separate pieces of the puzzle."

"The card I gave you with the fob case is our business phone and information." Barcephe rubbed his wife's back. "Venetia wrote both our cell numbers on the back."

Layka released her hand and stepped back toward the tray table, lifting the business card and taking a moment to pull her wallet from her purse to put it away, followed by the fob case.

Aven stepped to her, lightly touching her hand to Layka's back. "We'll leave you to have some time with Amelia. Please let us know if we can do anything for your family."

Venetia stood and lifted the vase of roses from the side table where she'd retrieved the Kleenex. "Will you take these home for Brillo? Amelia always said they were Brillo's favorite, and we ended every trip by bringing roses to our picture-sharing time with them."

"Brillo," Layka started, then paused.

Aven felt her shift her weight and lean into Aven's hand that still rested at her back when Venetia placed the vase in her hands.

Aven rubbed Layka's back with her thumb, keeping the support of her hand unwavering as Layka found her words.

"We will keep Amelia a part of Brillo's life."

Barcephe moved to his wife, almost a mirror of her and Layka. "Thank you."

Layka turned toward the door.

Neither spoke as they moved toward the bank of elevators. Layka held the vase close, and Aven didn't speak as quiet tears rolled down Layka's face. She knew not to wipe them away and felt the prick of tears herself when one dropped on an open petal near Layka's nose as she breathed in their fragrance.

When the elevator doors closed, Layka started to speak but changed her mind and Aven preserved the quiet of the space, letting their physical contact be, for once, unguarded as their bodies pressed close in the support every small touch ever represented.

CHAPTER TWENTY-EIGHT

L AYKA STIRRED HER COFFEE and stared at the flowers on her counter. She'd not been able to tell Aven that Sam wanted to open a conversation about their past. Sassy meowed her judgment from her cat-shaped food bowl beside Brillo's. She and Brillo had failed to become the bosom buddies she had hoped for, but they tolerated each other, which meant giving each other a wide berth most days. Layka leaned over to rub an ear. The moment had seemed wrong last night to tell Aven, but then again it was probably her own discomfort with it all that made her reluctant. She put the spoon in the sink and moved toward the sofa. Aven and her family were leaving today.

They had discussed taking Brillo in to see Amelia, but when they arrived at the house, Layka had set the vase on the floor, and the two of them had sat on the couch. Brillo had circled the vase, then nosed through the flowers as if searching for a special one. She'd pulled a single rose from the vase and made her way to the couch. She nestled between them and laid the rose across their legs where they touched at the peak that created a triangle of space for her. If Layka ever believed a person's energy could inhabit the environment around them, she believed a part of Amelia's energy rested in that rose.

It had been an effort of will for the two of them to separate last night, but they'd made some tentative plans for the upcoming months. Layka sighed. She'd need to tell Aven about Sam's request today. It was only fair that Aven have a choice as to whether she met with Sam and, if so, when to do it.

Brillo jumped into her lap and nuzzled in close. "If I knew how that flower energy worked, I would bottle some of Aven's to keep here with us," Layka said, setting her coffee on the sofa table and cuddling Brillo with both arms wrapping her tight.

"Are you ready to go see Avee?"

Brillo's tail lifted. "I know, baby. Me too."

Aven sidestepped a box and reached for the large, framed artwork wrapped in moving blankets. She squeezed it into the space she'd left that would keep it upright and protected. *Protected*, she thought, shaking her head. She was still having a hard time believing her dreams were both coming true and being destroyed simultaneously. How was she going to navigate this move and protect her heart from cracking like a frame around a work of art?

"Layka, dear. Come here." Her mother's voice held a singsong quality, and Aven turned. The butterflies soared and fell, her heart fluttering at the sight of Layka and her mind reconciling reality with the moving van walls around her.

Aven smiled when her mom wrapped Layka in a huge hug, then they bent together as if in sync to pet Brillo.

"Did you get any snackies this morning, you pretty little thing? What? No snackies? The horror! Come with me."

Aven's mom grinned and lifted Brillo, heading back into the condo for the special peanut butter treats she made for her. She refused to divulge the recipe. Aven watched Layka's eyes follow her mom, then felt the weight of those gray-blue eyes when they turned their focus to her. She stepped down on the bumper, then jumped the remaining distance to the ground.

"A doctor would tell you that's bad for your knees," Layka said.

"Yeah, but who listens to doctors?" Aven leaned against the bumper, and Layka moved to stand in front of her, watching her own hands as she rubbed them together in the cool of the November morning. Aven wanted to reach out, to pull her in, but today was a new day, and Layka's stiff posture and distance said they were back to their baseline. "Layka," Aven said softly and waited for her to look up. "Talk to me."

Layka held her eyes and took a deep breath. "Sam wants to have the conversation the two of you didn't have years ago. There." She blew out the rest of her breath. "I said it." She rubbed her fingertips on her forehead, then circled them down to rub her temples.

"It's okay." Aven touched Layka's elbow. "I've been thinking about that myself."

"You have?" Layka's hands paused in their movement, applying pressure at the temples in a way that pulled the corners of her eyes.

Aven shrugged. "The coping mechanism of running away is evolutionary and normal, however I turned it into a permanent answer. I think it would be a good step for me and Sam to have that conversation." She pushed off the bumper, knowing the movement would put her in Layka's space. She didn't step back. "I understand and respect the difficult place you're in." She cupped Layka's shoulders. "For us to have a hope of an us somewhere down the line, Sam and I will have to find a way beyond our history." She lifted Layka's chin. "The one thing I do know Sam and I have in common is the absolute desire to see you happy." Aven held Layka's eyes with hers, rubbing the soft skin of her chin. "She and I will work through our issues, but only you can put our history to rest for yourself."

Layka bit her lip. "And there it is," she said, wrapping Aven's wrist with her hand and stroking along the bone. "I've kept the focus on Sam, but the truth is I've seen some ugly feelings in me."

"Do you want to talk about them?"

Layka shook her head. "They're too fresh and muddled."

"Very well, let's focus on the project, Brillo's microchip, and be there for each other at a distance."

Layka locked eyes with her, and Aven breathed in the depth of the moment. She could see forever in those blue-gray eyes, but it might never be the forever she desired. They seamlessly moved into each other's arms as if they had been given one pardon for this moment and they had to take in every second of it. Aven's body hummed with the feel of Layka pressed to her at every point of contact along her body. There was no sound but Layka's breathing near her ear, no smell but that of pumpkin spice body spray along the line of Layka's neck, no taste but the crisp air blowing wisps of Layka's hair across the corner of her mouth.

As seamlessly as they joined, they parted without speaking.

"I'll reach out to Farrah and Sam after Thanksgiving. I need to discuss some project details with Farrah that Naomi mentioned in a phone call this week, and I'll give Sam some dates for sitting down with her the next time I am in town. Farrah has already approached me and indicated she wants to keep our communication on the project open. She is a brilliant, kind woman."

"She is. Sam said she's helping her wade through the mix of emotions she's locked away for years." Layka reached out and gently touched Aven's arm. "That's not a blast at you. Sam's always been kind of a loner, but when our parents died, she put part of herself in a panic room with the door locked and walked away to do what she felt she had to do."

"I get that. Do you want to head inside and warm up?" Aven pointed to a vehicle pulling in on the other side of the truck. "Dad did a breakfast run. I'll help him. He'll have more than he can carry."

Layka smiled. "I'll know if one of the donuts is missing. Your dad and I talk," she said, moving her finger back and forth between the visible front of the car and herself.

Aven's heart seemed to stretch one more time with her admiration for Layka's beauty, not just the physical beauty but that deep beauty of who she was as a person. Layka had to surmount the understandable concern of Aven's parents, who had watched their daughter navigate the pain of Layka's sister, yet she had done it with the transparency of her kind, open heart. "That's not fair. He'll eat one and blame me."

Layka shrugged and gave a "then you better protect the donuts" look and headed inside.

"Hi, sweet child." Mildred's voice from the house behind her sounded excited as Aven lifted bags from her father's arms as he fought with the car door. Even with Mildred and Layka beyond her view because of the moving truck, she could imagine their interaction. The bond between the three of them had grown. Mildred had found a home on Butternut Street where the owner offered a rent-to-own option, and the three of them had celebrated with a painting party. The place looked great. She was still considering the option of living on-site in the assistant project manager apartment at the Wheelhouse once it was built, but it had been important to her to have the option of owning. Mildred had placed the letter indicating her employment with the Mindful Path Project, signed by her and Layka, on the wall in her little house office. The letter, along with a paycheck stub, had sealed the negotiation, and Aven hoped Mildred decided to keep it. It was not a completely altruistic hope. The place already had memories of her and Layka, and she wanted to hold on to each memory like a tether to her personal dream as she leapt across the country to make her career dreams come true.

CHAPTER TWENTY-NINE

L AYKA SPUN IN EVERY direction in her kitchen. She picked up
her coffee cup, then put it down and moved to the toaster to
get her bread to butter it while it was hot, then remembered she
only wanted to warm the bacon for fifteen seconds and the timer
had automatically set to one minute, so she raced to the microwave
knowing she was too late with the smell of burnt bacon permeating
the air. She read twenty seconds left on the microwave and let her
shoulders sag as she popped the door to stop it. December had come
both too slowly and too quickly. She was dying to see Aven, but it
also meant the first real meeting of Farrah, Sam, Aven, and herself in
one space. "I know I burned the bacon," Layka said as Brillo came
into the kitchen. She knelt, rubbing her soft ears. "Aven's coming
home." She wished it was completely true. Brillo's tail wagged. "I
know. Me too, girl. Me too."

Her phone rang on the counter. Sassy strolled past both of them
with her nose and tail in the air. Layka used her toes to pet her, gently
squeezing the silky fur of her tail between her bare toes as she checked
the caller ID. "Hi, Agent Sebastian."

"Hello, Ms. Silva. I'm calling to confirm the meeting tomorrow
with you, Sam, and Dr. Summerhouse."

"Yes. Dr. Summerhouse is arriving today, and we will meet you at Sam's police headquarters at ten."

"Perfect."

Layka clicked off the line and leaned against the counter. Aven and Sam were doing drinks tonight at Erin's. Hopefully, the meeting with the feds tomorrow wouldn't be awkward after they had their "closure conference," as Sam called it. Layka was uncertain what she expected from Sam and Aven's time together. She had dinner planned for the four of them here at the house tomorrow evening, so apparently she was secretly hoping things would go well. But then what did that mean when she was still struggling with how she measured up? She huffed and headed for the bedroom to dress. She bit her lip. Aven loved seeing her in black and white. Then again, she couldn't recall a time when Aven's eyes hadn't lit up when seeing her. She smiled—she had that look memorized. Regardless of the crazy way things were right now, she still had butterflies at the thought of seeing Aven. Brillo hopped on the bed and watched intently as she pulled three outfits out and held them up one at a time. "It's not reasonable to think Sam will fan an old flame up in Aven, right?"

Brillo tilted her head.

"I know it doesn't make any sense, but why do I feel this way?" Layka folded the dress in half and sat down on the bed. "Sam is so charismatic and likable. How would Aven not like her?" Layka sighed, letting her head fall back as she stared at the ceiling. The decorative silver rim of the ceiling fan reflected three shades of purple to her left. Layka stood and walked to the nightstand. She ran her hand along the arrangement of flowers that arrived the first of the week. She lifted the card as Brillo moved to stand on the pillow, her nose leaning into the single rose amid the collection of greenery, pansies, and asters. "I want Brillo to have new memories with us," she read as Brillo sniffed the arrangement and circled on the pillow. Layka bit her lip. "What does 'us' look like right now?" she asked, lifting Brillo and her dress and heading to the bathroom to shower and change.

Aven rubbed her eyes, then scanned the bar again. She was exhausted from the travel. It hadn't been the smartest thing to schedule this meeting with Sam the evening she arrived, but she had wanted to get it out of the way. It had hung over her for way too long. She was headed toward an open barstool to chat with Erin while she waited for Sam when she saw the familiar face holding up a hand. The gesture was similar yet different from the confident wave she remembered Sam making many times when they had met out somewhere. It was strange meshing the two times together, and she rubbed at her eyes again.

"Hi, Sam," she said, reaching the table and taking a seat in the booth across from Sam.

"Hi, Vi—"

"Call me Aven." Her words weren't harsh, but they were firm, and she was surprised at how relaxed she felt now that she was here. When she came in, she'd noticed the difference between the Samantha she had known in college and the Sam she saw across the room. Now she was seeing the similar changes in herself. An older, more confident version of herself, more self-aware. Someone smarter from the scars, but less pained by them.

"Certainly. First, thank you, Aven—Dr. Summerhouse, even—for being part of a team that saved my life."

"You're correct about it taking a team, and you're welcome," Aven said, accustomed to patient thank-yous for things she had done because she wanted to do them. "You had an excellent team, my role was more collaborative, but I'm glad you are doing well. I know you are everything to Layka."

"She's everything to me as well." Sam twisted the bottled beer on the table, then looked up. "She is part of why I wanted to do this."

Aven nodded but didn't speak. She felt they both needed this, but Sam had asked for the time, and she would let her manage the lion's share of it.

"Would you like something to drink or eat? It's on me. I asked you to come."

"Thanks, but I'm fine. I grabbed a bite to eat after I picked up my rental car. To be honest, I'm more tired than anything. So, maybe I should start so we can move through this and get to the other side." It was Sam's turn to nod, and a waitress showed up at the table.

"Can I get you something to drink?"

Maybe she should have something. She'd been a little gruff, but she was tired and surprised at how much empathy she felt for Sam now that she herself had grown and she understood more about the girl Sam had been back then. "I'll have the house Pinot Noir. No food for me. And, two tabs, please."

The waitress nodded and left.

"I'm wise enough now to know I'm not responsible for other people's actions, but for a long time I blamed myself for what happened—"

"I'm so sorry for that. I hated that the most. The look in your eyes that night was burned into my consciousness and turned you into this ideal that never happened. I don't know if, even now, knowing that you are doing okay, I can ever forgive myself for the betrayal and pain I saw in your eyes that night. I wanted so badly to make it up to you, to explain that I was in a bad place, but that wasn't your problem or responsibility."

"I took away your chance at redemption when I ran away. That is on me."

"I wouldn't have deserved it then, but I would like to try for it now." She lifted the beer and picked at the label, then set it down. "I love my sister, and I know this"—she circled her index finger between them—"has been hard on her."

Aven watched the slight lines at Sam's brow relax as she focused on Aven, and her eyes held hope and strength. "I want to support her relationship with you, and that starts by me taking responsibility for my actions years ago. I'm deeply sorry for hurting you."

The waitress chose that moment to drop off Aven's wine, and she couldn't have been happier for the opportunity to have a legitimate reason to pause their conversation. Aven's younger self had wondered what she would feel, what she would say if her path ever crossed with

Samantha Corin, but she was certain what she felt right now had never been a consideration. She felt respect for this woman who loved her sister so fiercely and was facing her demons with accountability. Aven lifted her glass of wine, sipped, and set it down before looking at Sam.

"Thank you for your honesty and remorse. I believe you, and I accept your apology. I know we both want Layka to be happy, so I think we have a wonderful foundation to build a friendship." It was the smile that broke across Sam's face that answered the niggling question in Aven's mind. Sam wanted only a friendship from her. "So, I have the eldest's blessing to date her sister?" Aven asked, a smile forming for the first time.

"You do. And I will tell her myself. It was shame that kept me tied to Victoria. It took that moment of seeing you again for me to realize that truth. I never forgave myself for the hurt and betrayal my actions brought to you. I can do that now. Thank you."

Layka fidgeted with the zipper on the attaché case she carried today for their meeting at the precinct as she waited for the officer to take her back to the meeting room. She'd been on edge all morning and most of last night. Erin had sent a text with a picture of her, Aven, and Sam at the bar closing out their tabs. She'd sent a response to the group text but hadn't texted any of them individually. She knew it had been sent to make her feel included because they each knew differently about how she had struggled with the situation. Sam had texted her when she made it home and said she and Aven had officially cleared the air. So, why did she feel more isolated and alone? She took a seat beside Sam. This put Agent Sebastian across from her and Aven to her left, but there were several empty seats between them. Two of Sam's buddies were seated to Sam's right, forming the round edge of the table, and Sebastian was on the opposite side with the two Maryland officers seated to the right of the agent.

"Thank you for being here today," Agent Sebastian said, starting the meeting and causing the quiet chatter between the two squad teams to fade.

"I'm going to ask Ms. Silva and Dr. Summerhouse to elaborate on the microchip information they've shared in the document."

Layka looked at Aven.

Aven gave her a supportive smile before she spoke. "You are the most knowledgeable about the recording information. Please, you take the lead."

Layka took a deep breath. Aven still had the ability to ground her. Even with the new dynamic, no one made her feel more understood. "The recording component of Brillo's microchip was activated and recorded the transition of Amelia, Brillo, and most likely the other residents in the van to a known area of unhoused people in DC near Washington Regional Hospital. Agent Sebastian and the FBI team have the recording data and are analyzing it further."

"This is unusual for a microchip," one of the Maryland officers said.

"Amelia's family had the financial resources to purchase a new type of microchip that has some very advanced features," Layka said.

"Why was she homeless then?" Sam's colleague Jonathon asked.

"The family shared Amelia's history, which has been detailed in a new document we brought today. Between what they shared with us and what Agent Sebastian and the FBI have been able to determine from the government resources managing the shutdown of mental facilities across the US, Amelia was one of many who was functioning at a level for independent living. But without the support system for transition to that independent living, she and many others fell into decline for multiple reasons."

"Multiple reasons meaning we have some direct connection to the resident house under investigation?" This question came from the second Maryland officer, and Layka was grateful when Aven stepped in to answer.

"Actually, Officer..." Aven paused, waiting for the name.

"Roark."

"Officer Roark, the reasons are more commonly related to medications running out and patients not having the support they need to secure follow-up visits with new providers, or having limitations with transportation, which makes the pickup of medication impossible. Many of them can deteriorate quickly without their meds, which leads to a cycle of decline."

Agent Sebastian leaned forward with her forearms on the table to leaf through a paper document. "We did confirm from the hospital that she was discharged to independent living and prescribed medications. However, she never picked up the prescribed medications sent to her pharmacy of record at the time of her discharge."

Sam piped up when the conversation settled with everyone in thought. "We were able to track and confirm Amelia's movement that led to her arrival at the New Foundations Resident Home from our investigation follow-up on some of the recorded data from the microchip."

"So, this gives us a definite link of Amelia to the New Foundations home we were suspecting, Matt," Roark said to her Maryland partner.

"Yes," Agent Sebastian said. "But it only gives us correlation with the transport. It is not enough for a causation connection with Barton, which we suspect."

"Sam's team submitted a new document, which I reviewed this morning. It was well done and identified an area where some of the recorded data may offer some crucial evidence to warrant further investigation," Aven offered.

Layka tensed, then chided herself for the jealous thought that had slipped in unbidden. She listened peripherally till Agent Sebastian closed the meeting. She should be glad that Aven and Sam were developing a complementary working relationship. Layka lifted her attaché case and placed the documents back inside as the meeting began to wrap up. She could sense Aven moving toward her even as she leaned over her bag, looking down at the table. Her heart was pounding. God, she could barely breathe sometimes when they were in proximity.

"Thanks for reviewing the document, Aven," Sam said just as Aven reached the chair behind Layka.

"You're welcome," Aven said and then squatted next to Layka's chair, her voice softer. "Hi, Layka. Are things still a go for games at your place tonight?"

Layka closed her eyes and swallowed. She wished her heart wouldn't beat so hard. It was one thing to beat fast, but this pounding made her chest hurt. She realized she was gripping the attaché case close to her chest, and she relaxed it but didn't turn to meet Aven's eyes. Would Aven be able to see the jealousy there? It was such an unwelcome emotion, but she couldn't shake it. She breathed in once and let her mind focus on the sounds nearby. Farrah and Sam were talking to her right, and there was a hum of chatter around the room. "Yes," she said tentatively, not trusting her voice.

"Okay, what time?"

"Six thirty."

"Six thirty," Aven repeated. "I'll probably see if I can catch up with Reynolds, Sarah, and Steve before then. Can I bring something?"

Layka could hear disappointment in Aven's voice. Was it because she hadn't offered for her to come on over now?

Layka closed her eyes, took another slow breath, opened her eyes, and turned to the woman who was now "officially" available to her but felt farther away than ever. "No, I have everything I need."

Aven sidestepped some uneven pavers in the walkway up to the brownstone apartment. She pulled her coat tighter, wondering if the temperature was dropping or if she just felt colder the closer she came to Layka's front door. She'd brought a bottle of wine despite Layka's weighted answer earlier in the morning. She was still feeling off-balance from the exchange. She'd felt so excited about the possibilities for them after having drinks with Sam and feeling they could put that part of their history behind them, but Layka seemed almost angry. *Maybe something happened at work and she brought it with her to the meeting,* she told herself. They could both be abrupt sometimes when they were working. She rang the doorbell and felt some of her anxiety lift with the laughter she heard in the background as Farrah opened the door. Then felt her hope plummet when she stepped through the door and met those blue-gray eyes, and Layka's laughter cut off when she bit her lip and turned for the kitchen.

"Hi, Farrah," Aven said, trying to ignore the commotion that started in the kitchen as she heard Sam and Layka in a low conversation.

"Hi, it is so good to see you." Farrah wrapped her in a hug, and she squeezed her back.

"Thank you. How are you doing?"

"Overworked and underpaid, of course." Farrah said it overly loud and with a laugh, but it managed to do what neither she, Sam, nor Layka had been able to do, which was to bring them back to some form of normalcy.

"I heard that," Layka said from the kitchen, still not visible.

Farrah winked, and they moved toward the table, which was set up with the game already.

Aven felt her excitement newly restored. She loved playing this game with Reynolds, Sarah, and Steve. It was a game where you worked together against the game itself rather than in competition with each other.

"I'll take that," Farrah said, lifting the wine from Aven and heading for the kitchen as Layka and Sam came back into the room.

Sam walked over and offered her hand. "I'm glad you could make it. Can you play this game?"

Aven shook the offered hand, even as she felt her stomach drop when Layka took a seat on the other side of the table. She wanted to hug her, tell her how much she'd missed her, but it was as if the conversations and texts they'd had over the last month did not exist. "I have played before, but I think Sarah is our best strategist when we play."

"How are they doing?" Layka asked, and Aven immediately dropped into the chair across from Layka to be eye to eye when she answered her. *What is wrong with you?* She berated herself for the Pavlovian response to the small gift of Layka's words. Aven forced herself to take a breath and relax her shoulders before she spoke. "They are doing really well, and they asked about you. Steve and Reynolds said they don't see you as much now that you've taken on the additional responsibilities for the project."

"It's true. Please tell them hello for me." Layka looked up for the first time from separating the cards, and when her eyes locked with Aven's, everything stopped. It was still there. Aven could see it. Whatever was going on, Aven still mattered to Layka. She could see it in her eyes.

Layka handed Aven her cards, and when their hands touched, she saw Layka close her eyes as if to blink back tears. She didn't want to hurt her. *What's going on?*

Sam plopped down in the chair by her sister and bumped her shoulder, essentially breaking the moment and causing Layka to smile when she began a review of the snacks on the left and right edges of the table. "I made my first cheeseball ever, so that's your public service announcement regarding the snacks." Aven was grateful for the reprieve. Farrah came from the kitchen with a tray of wine-filled glasses and passed them out, then took her seat beside Aven.

They lost once but beat the game twice, and by the end of the second game, the tension had shifted to a more familiar camaraderie. When Layka stood to go to the kitchen for the desserts, Aven lifted her wineglass and followed her. "Does anyone else want some more wine?"

"Yes, please." Farrah lifted her glass.

"I'm good," Sam said, waving her beer she'd brought in during the last game.

Aven carried the two glasses into the kitchen and just dodged Layka coming from the right with a tray of desserts and plates. Layka startled and tilted toward the island. Aven stabilized her with her forearm at her waist and the wineglasses still in her hand. The rectangular tray between them was stable because it pressed into each of them with their proximity. Layka's eyes drifted from Aven's eyes to her lips. She licked her lips, and when they parted, Aven leaned in and pressed her lips gently against them. Layka's eyes said yes, but she wanted her to have the space to say no.

She did. Layka pulled away and shook her head as if she'd walked into a spider web. "Aven, no."

Aven quickly placed the wineglasses on the island and stepped back. "I'm sorry." She grabbed the counter to help her stand. Why did everything feel so heavy? The room seemed gray, like all the color of the moment before was gone. There was something visceral for Aven in the rejection, but she had to accept it. "I just need to sit down." She heard herself say the words but didn't recall finding the banquette bench she realized she was now sitting on by the kitchen bay window and breakfast table. She tilted her head, feeling as though she'd been transported through time. She blinked and realized Layka was kneeling, trying to get her legs up.

"I'm okay." She hadn't passed out, and apparently she had moved herself smoothly enough that they hadn't drawn the attention of Farrah or Sam from the other room.

"Are you sure?" Layka asked, carefully standing and pulling the bistro chair close but not taking a seat.

"Yes, I think I was just overwhelmed by emotion. Part of me feels disoriented and shocked, unable to follow what's transpiring between us. I'm fine now." Well, she wasn't fine, but she was functional. She would be fine again one day. "You don't have to give an explanation. You said no. I will respect that. I'm going to go." Aven stood and stepped toward the back door.

Layka's arms lifted, cupping Aven's face with both hands, and this time Aven saw Layka blinking back tears as she leaned in and pressed her lips to Aven's.

Aven backed up, bumping the wall, but didn't pull free. "What are you doing?"

"I don't want to lose you." The words were a whisper, and Aven could feel Layka's tears reach her lips.

"Hey, hey, hey. Please don't cry." Aven rubbed her thumbs under Layka's eyes, wiping away the tears as she pulled back to see her. "You are never going to lose me. I am your friend. I am here. I just won't ask for this anymore." Aven brushed her thumb over Layka's lip.

"But I don't want you to stop asking for this," Layka said, leaning her head into Aven's hand. "I just can't pick up and zoom our relationship forward because you and Sam have made up." Layka covered her face. "It's almost like it's worse."

Aven pulled Layka's wrists, and Layka's hands slid away from her face to prop under her chin. "I can see that the hurt of Sam and I is old pain for us, like rubbing over a scar that doesn't hurt anymore and all you really remember is the lesson learned." Aven traced along Layka's knuckles where Layka had made little fists under her chin. She imagined Layka holding this new pain that Aven didn't quite understand, but she was trying. "For you, the pain is recent. When I look back, I wasn't physically ready for a relationship with Sam, but honestly, if she had come to me and opened up, I probably would have had something physical with her before I was ready. But it would have been out of fear that I would lose something—not out of love." Aven pulled Layka's wrists, causing Layka's head to tilt forward. She kissed her forehead. "I'm your friend first. Let's start there. I don't want fear of loss to be the reason you kiss me."

CHAPTER THIRTY

A VEN PACED THE LENGTH of the ceremony hall. "Why did I even tell her about it?"

"Because you love her, and you want her here," Reynolds said.

"Hush, no one asked you."

"You asked the universe, and I happen to be here. Now stop pacing."

"I do want her here." Aven didn't dare use the L word. The visit home in December had been a mixed bag of ups and downs. "I want her to be proud of me, but having her here makes me nervous at the same time. What if I make a mistake in my speech and she's embarrassed?"

"You're not going to make a mistake, and she looks at you like the genius you are, so she wouldn't be embarrassed even if you did make a mistake. If I know you, you've rehearsed it so many times that an internationally renowned pop star on her world tour is more likely to forget the words to one of her songs than you are to forget your speech. Where are things with you two?"

"Hi, Dr. Summerhouse. You look beautiful today. Good luck on your speech."

"Thank you, Arianna."

Reynolds started adjusting chairs that were already properly placed as Arianna paused and stepped a little closer.

"Hey, I was wondering if you'd like to do coffee one morning. I've got two days off from the pharmacy this week and don't know what to do with myself."

"I'm..." Aven paused. Dr. Daniels, her teaching partner at UCSF and colleague at the medical center, had said she thought Arianna was interested in her, but Aven had blown it off. She was working through what she felt for Layka, but suddenly Reynolds's question needled right through her chest. *Where are things with you two?* She almost doubled over with the thought of someone asking Layka out. Had it happened? It was March and they texted every day, video chatted at least twice a month, but there was still a distance between them they hadn't regained since she stepped into the hospital room that day and forced their relationship to deal with her having dated Layka's sister. She had been surprised to learn Sam had carried this ideal of her around for years like a measuring tool that now made her, to Layka, both a stranger and a familiar bit of her sister's history at the same time. "I'm interested in someone," Aven blurted when she realized she had created an awkward silence. "Sorry, that sounded weird. I would enjoy coffee sometime. You can never have too many friends."

"It wasn't weird, and someone definitely has your heart. I saw it in the panic of your eyes. I hope she knows you're interested. We can still do coffee sometime, but it looks like you've got a lot on your mind right now." Arianna gave a wave as she headed across the room.

"You're interested in someone? That's where you all are at?" Reynolds asked, giving a final nudge to a front-row chair.

Aven slumped into a nearby chair. "Honestly, we avoid talking about it." Aven rubbed her eyes.

"Well, I think you need to remedy that. The woman is flying across the country for this ceremony to celebrate you."

"So did you."

"You know it's different. Talk to me, Aven."

"I'm in over my head with her, Reynolds. It's been three months and I miss her every day. We text, we video chat..."

"What do you talk about?"

"We work on the project, talk about Brillo, our other work, but we haven't talked about us. Remember as a kid where you would hold someone's hands to make a ring and dance around till you were dizzy and couldn't stand up? That's us. Holding hands, spinning around, but forever pushed apart by the force between us."

"I thought you said at Christmas you and Sam had made a real leap."

"Sam and I did. We had a few drinks at Erin's the first night I was in. It was actually very cathartic, I think, for both of us. It was a little surprising, but afterward I was excited. I felt she and I had put the past behind us and could honestly become friends."

"So, what's wrong?"

"It's almost as if us being friendly is harder for Layka." Aven shrugged. "This is old history for us. The part that hurt and impacted us happened years ago. Running into each other in October was just a reminder of it. But for Layka, that was the first wound. I can't expect her to process all of that emotion in just a few months. I also can't be the person she talks to about it."

"Why?"

"She's said as much."

Reynolds tilted her head and squinted. "What did she say?"

"She said it was too hard to talk to me about it." *Or rather, her actions said that,* Aven thought, tentatively touching the memory of the pain she felt when Layka had pulled away from her kiss.

"Did she say why?"

Aven looked up, suddenly realizing she hadn't asked. She'd just assumed, tried to understand, and given Layka that space. "I figured it was because it involved me."

"So, when it comes to this situation, she's lost her best friend and the person she was starting to love."

"She's never said she loves me."

Reynolds rolled her eyes.

"You can roll your eyes, but she hasn't, and this is huge. Sam is all she has left of her family. They're close. This has been hard for her."

"I get it. I've just seen the two of you together, and now there's this issue that has shaken her, and she's lost the person she talks to about everything."

Aven hung her head. Reynolds was right about that. She'd let Layka push her away on this because she felt it was her choice to make—and it was. But as a friend, she needed to ask the why, not assume she knew it already.

"Maybe the two of you should discuss seeing other people instead of hovering in this limbo. Maybe right now she needs her friend."

"I do have a horrible track record with long-distance relationships." Aven felt sick at both the reminder and the idea of relinquishing the last thread of an "us" she had been holding on to like a lifeline.

"You're not bad at LDR. This would just give a clear line in the sand that you are friends and free to see other people."

The look on her face must have conveyed her discomfort at the idea, because Reynolds backed off.

"Look, you've got a big event today. Focus on that. Layka will be here." Reynolds knocked Aven's shoulder. "I'm going to go get spiffed up. You can talk with her about it in person."

Aven felt anticipation and smiled. Maybe this was it. The time to confront the issue head-on with Layka. *What if she's not receptive? What if she's seeing someone? Would she be seeing someone?* Arianna's invitation earlier had her head spinning. She was so hooked on Layka that she hadn't stopped to consider where Layka's heart was amidst the chaos. Was Layka going to become another Carter in her life? Someone who saw her as a friend but could see nothing more? Her heart ached at the thought. That had been a mutual feeling with Carter. Layka was different. She fit every role like a glove, was everything she wanted: friend, lover, instigator, prankster...

Aven's phone pinged with a notification. She opened the text.

LAYKA: Is my favorite doctor ready for her big speech?

AVEN: I think so. Will you be here soon?

LAYKA: I'm riding to my hotel now. I can be there as soon as I drop off my luggage and change.

AVEN: That will be great.

Aven rubbed her temple. Layka had said she was getting a hotel when they spoke on the phone, but now it made the distance between them feel exponential. Her mind rolled over their first night together. Their last night together. How could that be? She felt closer to Layka than even Carter, and they had been married. She wanted to tell Layka to take her things to her condo, but she was trying to respect the boundaries Layka had put in place. Aven bit her lip.

AVEN: Get here as soon as you can. I can't wait to see you.

LAYKA: You got it—speed round shower and dress!

Aven closed her eyes against the image of Layka in her arms with water streaming over them from the rain shower in her condo.

An hour later, Aven checked her watch. Traffic was always bad, but at 3:00 p.m., Layka should be able to get here in reasonable time. She'd texted her to meet at the event because Aven had to be there for the final rehearsal at five. She turned to head back into the auditorium to get the pad and pen she'd brought down in case there were any last-minute changes at the rehearsal. Drawing things out helped her remember if there were seating changes. Then she saw the flash of black and gold sunglasses catching the sunlight as Layka stepped from her ride. She was wearing an off-the-shoulder V-neckline red dress fitted from her waist to her knees. Her heels were black, and Aven appreciated the shape of her legs as she walked gracefully to the doors to Aven's left. She had gorgeous legs. Aven absently rubbed her bare shoulder. Her own dress was a black one-shoulder A-line sheath dress with a soft ruffle that just touched her knees. Aven's eyes locked with Layka's when she made the turn inside the door of the auditorium lobby and removed her glasses. Aven's fingers tingled where she rubbed her shoulder, and she dropped her hand and walked toward Layka. They both paused when they met in a cozy seating area. Layka's eyes tracked from Aven's eyes to her lips, then back to her eyes, and Aven wanted to believe it was for the same reason that she felt every inch of her body tingling. "You look stunning. I'm so glad to see you." Aven waited once again, letting Layka take the lead on their physical contact.

Instead, Layka stood frozen, her lips parted, a sudden pain in her eyes Aven could hardly bear.

"Layka, what is it?"

Layka swallowed and took two stuttering breaths as if she had been crying. Aven searched Layka for an injury, her medical mind and skilled hands racing for an answer, when a tear leaked out at the corner of her eye.

"Can you just hold me?" Layka whispered.

Aven wrapped an arm around her waist and pulled Layka's head across her bare shoulder, never releasing her hand from the back of her head as their bodies melded together. "I'm right here." Aven closed her eyes and breathed in the lavender scent of her hair.

"I'm sorry. I've missed you so much. I thought it would be easier." Layka pulled her head back enough to see Aven but didn't step away.

"Please don't say you're sorry for missing me. I've talked about you to everyone who would listen today."

Layka gave a little laugh.

"I'm serious. Ask Reynolds," Aven said, touching a strand of hair at Layka's forehead and tracing the length of it along Layka's face to push it behind her ear. "I wanted to talk about us while you're here anyway. This is the perfect segue."

"We shouldn't do it before your speech. You should be focused on that. I just needed to feel you in my arms." Layka leaned her face into Aven's hand where it still rested near her ear. "And I wanted to be in yours. It was selfish."

"The most important thing about my speech tonight is that you are here to share it with me."

"I wouldn't miss supporting you for the world."

Aven squeezed Layka's hands together between them and directed them to the sofa in the seating area. "That's it. We've been doing that. You showing up for me and me showing up for you in the big events of life, but there is one place where I haven't shown up for you, and I want that to change while you're here."

Aven traced Layka's hands, which she now held in her lap. Their bare knees were touching with the angle, and it was all she could do to manage the explosion of sensation everywhere her body touched Layka. "I want to talk with you about Sam. Or rather, I want to listen."

Layka bit her lip and looked down at their hands.

Aven pressed on. "I honestly think it has been easier for Sam and me because the issues for us were old ones, and we had already worked through much of it. But this was a new hurt for you. I get that, and I want to give you the lead on us." She reached up and ran her thumb along Layka's cheek. "I just want it to be an us. If that means friends for now while you process, I'm here for it, but let me be a friend for all of it."

Layka shook her head, and Aven felt her heart crack. Suddenly, Layka's words about not doing this before her speech had a different meaning. Her stomach lurched, and she felt her body follow it.

"No," Layka said, reaching out and grabbing Aven by the shoulders.

Aven was glad for the unexpected support. With her arms wrapped around her stomach, she had no way to hold herself up.

"It's not what you're thinking," Layka said. "Look at me."

Aven tried, but her vision was blurred with unshed tears. How had the tears come so fast? *They'd been on standby,* she thought, realizing how much she'd kept this fear bottled up. She blinked, clearing her vision. Layka traced her thumb across Aven's lip.

"I'm no longer processing you and Sam. I'm processing me. Listen to me. I am here because there is no one more important in my life. I still think there can be an us, and I want to navigate it. Please feel that and bring back that smile I saw when I turned the corner."

Aven let the words soak in, and she could feel it as if someone poured warmth into her soul. How could one person have the ability to bring her so much joy?

Layka startled when two arms grabbed Aven from behind before releasing her, and a body materialized at Aven's side sporting a tailored suit, an undercut, and a mischievous smile. The auditorium was a buzz of sound with independent conversations now that the event was over, so neither she nor Aven had heard her coming. Layka watched the woman laugh, then give Aven a broad smile. Layka realized the woman was the same height as Aven and probably hadn't seen her when she approached from behind.

"Hello, Aven. I saw Arianna stop by and chat with you when I was helping Stewart check the microphones before the event. Did she finally ask you out? I told you she was interested."

Layka watched emotion play across Aven's face and settle on a "pretend you didn't hear it" decision.

"Layka, this menace is Dr. Ramera Daniels. Dr. Daniels, this is Layka Silva, my—"

"This is your best friend from DC!" Dr. Daniels cut Aven off before she could finish her sentence, and Layka gritted her teeth at the missed opportunity to know how Aven would introduce her. "Hello, Layka Silva. It is a pleasure to meet you. Aven has told me so much about you."

Aven looked as though she was grateful for the interruption that meant she didn't have to label her relationship with Layka. The thought made Layka's gut twist yet confirmed what she knew she had to do. Dr. Daniels's mention of someone wanting to date Aven made it feel more necessary. She was still struggling with her feelings of inadequacy, and it wasn't fair to ask Aven to give up entire swatches of her life waiting for her to be a better person. The person Aven deserved. Someone like Dr. Daniels, with her laughter and easy camaraderie.

Layka smiled and waved as Dr. Daniels backed away with a bow and a flourish. She had to admit she was fun.

Aven was laughing too but cut it off when she turned to Layka.

"Please don't ever stop laughing," Layka said when Aven's face turned somber.

"I'm sorry I didn't correct her about you being my best friend. That really is what she knows about you. I'm very private about my personal life."

"You don't have to apologize. I'm honored to hold that spot, and we did leave things clearly in the friend zone when you left DC this last visit. Tell me about this pharmacist that is into you. Have you been out?"

"No, absolutely not, I wouldn't do that..." Aven let her words trail off as if she realized she didn't have any support for the rest of the sentence.

"What were you going to say?" Layka prompted.

Aven's eyes looked everywhere but at her, and Layka's heart ached at seeing Aven frustrated at herself, but this was exactly why she had to do this.

Aven's eyes finally settled on Layka's, then she looked down and folded the program in her hand. "I was going to say that I wouldn't do that to you, but that doesn't make sense when we're just friends."

Layka reached out and took the paper Aven was now folding repeatedly. She laid it on the stage just to the left of where they stood, then took Aven's hands in hers. "You were right about me being scared of losing you. I don't feel that now. I know that you will always be here for me." She lifted one hand and kissed it, then the other. "I will always be here for you." God, she felt like her heart would shatter to do this, but she wanted to be fair to Aven. "You gave that to me. That security. I want to give something to you. Sam said something that I'm only starting to realize is not true. She said you both wanted me to be happy and she thought you could make me happy. The first part of that is true. You both want me to be happy, but you can't make me happy. I have to be happy with myself, and I'm not."

"Why not? You're incredible. You're kind, you're intelligent—"

Layka halted Aven's words with a fingertip to her lips. "You're not the one who has to believe those things about me. I do. And I see those things sometimes, but I also see that I'm jealous and insecure. I never realized how much I struggled with this until now, but then I've never dated anyone who dated my sister, who I idolized most of my life. This is a me problem, not a you and Sam problem. You deserve to live your life, to date Arianna or see other people, while I work through this. You said you didn't want me to kiss you because I was afraid of losing you. I'm not afraid of that now—you gave that security to me. I know you are a forever friend."

Aven's features dropped at this.

"Please don't misunderstand." Layka lifted Aven's chin. *This is so difficult,* she thought when Aven's tempestuous blue eyes locked with hers, reflecting the same conflict. She wanted Aven to have the best. *I'm nowhere near my best right now,* Layka thought, wanting to scream at the struggle she felt. It was unfair to hold Aven to some unspoken tie between them while she became that complete person who could be a real match for Aven. "My absolute desire to be in your arms is the same as when I fell into them when I arrived. Yet, now it is my turn to tell you I don't want your desire to make *me* happy to be why you kiss me. I'm going to work on being happy with myself, and if an us is meant to be, I can share with you a whole person."

A person you deserve.

CHAPTER THIRTY-ONE

L AYKA LIFTED HER BURGER, then laid it down. Again. Her stomach was rolling. She needed to eat but had tried to eat the burger three times without success. Aven was coming to visit, and she was dating someone. How was she supposed to handle this? Aven was still her very best, closest friend. A woman she had slept with and never fully recovered from, an absolute jewel of a person. Layka lifted the bun and watched the cheese stretch between the burger and the bread. "I want her to be happy and not held back by my hang-ups. Why am I talking to my burger?" Layka surrendered the bun to the pull of the cheese and turned her plate. But if it had been the right thing to do to encourage Aven to date rather than wait for her to work through her crap, why did it hurt so bad?

She reached for the hamburger again but lifted a fry instead with her plate turned. She could always manage a fry. She chewed and thought about all the good things she still had with Aven. They texted practically every day, video chatted at least once a month about little pieces of the project, and she'd been a supportive sounding board as she worked through some of the tragedy, grief, and coping mechanisms she'd developed following her parents' death. Aven frequently reached out for her opinion on a protocol she was revising and ninety percent of the time used Layka's recommendations for structure. Layka smiled. It was amazing how their strengths complemented each other.

"Hello, daydreamer." Erin stole three fries from Layka's plate in one swoop. "Thanks for the food donation. Is Sam going to help on the grill for this quarter's festival?"

"I'm not sure. I'll ask her when she gets here, if you have to steal back to the bar. I can't believe it's June."

"Thanks, and I do need to get back over there. It's been crazy busy these last two months, but I can't complain. I stepped over here to see what time the ribbon-cutting ceremony starts."

"Ten a.m. Monday. I've been so busy with the project, Sam and I haven't been able to keep our weekend visits here, but I've noticed the increase in business when I travel home in the evening. The parking lot is always full."

"It is, and I am riding the wave, but I have missed you."

"We are officially restarting our 'meet at Erin's' tradition tonight."

"Awesome," Erin said, snagging another fry. "Stolen fries just taste better."

Layka laughed. "God, I've missed you. I'm so glad you will be coming on Monday. It will help me feel less nervous."

"You know I'll be there. Is Aven coming in?"

"Yes, she'll be in tomorrow." Layka bit the inside of her lip.

"What is it?"

"We talked the last time I was in California. Mostly about all the crazy emotions I've been working through." Layka picked up a fry but used it to make circles in the ketchup on her plate before looking up at Erin. "I told her she should date other people while I work on me."

"Go on," Erin said suspiciously.

"I explained that I needed to work on me, and it wasn't fair to ask her to wait in limbo while I do."

"Is that what you really want?"

"Not really." Layka dropped the fry, making the ketchup splatter on the plate. "But it felt like the right thing to do. We're still really close, and it felt good to be able to share with her some of what I was feeling." Layka stopped fidgeting with the napkin under her glass and looked at her friend. "She's been so understanding."

"Okay, apart from the obvious problem, which is that you've told a woman you are over the moon about to date other people, what's bothering you? You just neglected a fry."

"This is the first time the four of us will be together for a public event."

"Are you concerned because it requires the two of you to be publicly together?"

"Sam is so much better with crowds. Farrah will be there as the library liaison, so Sam will be there supporting her. I've always been nervous when Sam watches me do something, and now I'll have both Sam and Aven present. I like being director of the project for all the behind-the-scenes work, but I get really nervous with crowds."

"Look at me. Just because Sam and Aven are more comfortable with crowds doesn't mean they do better with them. I've seen you manage meetings and events. You do really well!"

"Thanks," Layka said, trying to place the compliment. She didn't feel she did well, but with the work she was doing to understand herself and evolve, she was now able to step away from the inner judgment of everything she did. This helped her appreciate herself more. "I know you have to get back to work." She didn't know how to say what was really in her heart. She was feeling the inadequacy that plagued her when her sister was present, and by extension, seeing Aven and Sam beginning to form a friendship of sorts made the inadequacy sensation bleed into her feelings with Aven. She and Aven had been talking about it more openly in their communications since her visit to California, but this would be her first time face-to-face with Aven since opening up to her during a video chat about her struggles with jealousy and inadequacy that made her feel like she was a less exciting version of her sister. It was a long-standing fear of hers, and finding out Aven had cared for Sam before meeting her had stamped that fear in a way she couldn't truly explain. Aven had tried to reassure her while asserting that her feelings were valid, but that had been on the phone. What would it be like when she saw her tomorrow? What would Aven think when they were face-to-face?

"I do need to get back to the bar, but are you serious that Aven is dating someone else? You two just had this beautiful chemistry."

Layka closed her eyes against the vision that flashed in her mind of Arianna and Aven. "We haven't talked about it since I video called her in the middle of a basketball game date with Arianna, the pharmacist." Arianna had been gracious at the interruption, but Layka's heart had been a flux of emotions for a week.

"Do you plan to talk about it when she comes in?"

Layka shrugged and shifted in the booth. She used the movement to place her eyes on the door beyond Erin's shoulder. "I don't know. Aven said to meet her at the dog park with Brillo tomorrow at noon." She smiled at the little thrill she felt that Aven had wanted to do something special with her, then felt the weight of Erin's question. Sunday at the dog park would be busy, and she had racked her brain for what Aven might be up to. She'd offered to pick her up at the airport, but Aven said it would ruin the surprise. She had to admit she was feeling much of her discomfort and self-doubt dissipate with her new openness with Aven, but was that happening just as Aven was settling into a more comfortable fit with their friendship-only arrangement? "I'll let you know how things go, but now get back to work before there is anarchy at the bar."

Layka parked the car. She hadn't slept at all last night. Both anxiety and excitement kept her mind a tennis match of questions back and forth till she had finally dozed off in the early morning hours. "What do you think Avee is up to, Brillo?"

Brillo's tail thumped as Layka lifted her from the carrier. "I guess we just have to go find out." She put Brillo on the ground and hooked her leash to the harness, then scanned the park. She immediately spotted Aven waving from a picnic table. Brillo cleared the landscaping mulch surrounding the parking lot in a single leap, and Layka tried to keep up as she jogged toward Aven. Aven was already down on her knees as Brillo barreled in. "Hi there, my beautiful girl," she said, rubbing her from head to bottom and lifting her as Brillo licked and nuzzled her. Layka felt her smile growing with every second as she took in the table behind Aven.

There were decorative clips holding the corners of the red-and-white gingham tablecloth, but the table was bare except for an empty basket.

Watching Aven with Brillo made her heart squeeze with the reminder of what they had before the move. What she had let go, by telling Aven to date other people, in order to become the complete person she felt a relationship warranted. She had done that and was proud of the leaps she had made. She still occasionally struggled to see some of that growth, and now was one of those times. She wanted Aven for herself. She needed to remind herself Aven was with someone else now. "How is Arianna?" Layka blurted.

Aven set Brillo down and moved into Layka's space. "My friend Arianna is doing well and dating a new pharmacist that joined the hospital."

"That's grea—" Layka's preplanned reply fell short on her lips. "Oh, I'm sorry?" The questioning tone was honest. Was Aven upset about it? *She doesn't seem to be,* Layka thought, watching the sunlight hit those sky-blue eyes that held a piece of the smile that lifted the corner of Aven's beautiful lips as she tilted her head watching Layka's changing expressions.

"It was a mutual decision. I respect her, and she is a fun person, but we are so much alike, it was like dating myself."

Layka felt a rush of excitement.

"Besides, I'm wanting to date someone new."

"Oh?" Layka tried to keep the disappointment out of her tone.

Aven took Layka's hand and lifted it to place a soft kiss at her knuckle. "I have missed you so much that I daydreamed about ways to show you. In a moment of weakness—a.k.a., one glass of wine too many at a colleague's wedding—I shared one of those daydreams with Daniels, who promptly pointed out that it was one thing to be patient and another thing to be complacent." She took Layka's other hand and pulled both of them to her chest. The movement brought Layka just inches away. "It's hard to date someone else when you are the face I wish I could see when I wake in the morning and the voice I want to hear at the end of my day." She reached up to push a wisp of hair that had escaped Layka's low ponytail back behind her ear.

Layka closed her eyes at the touch. Did Aven know how much those words made Layka feel wanted, necessary, needed? Her heart raced, and she wanted to lean in, wanted to taste those lips.

"I want a second chance at all our firsts," Aven said. "In all my daydreaming, I realized I've told you why you are so special to me, but I haven't shown you, and I wanted to do that. You've shared with me your plan to find happiness, wholeness, with yourself. Can I show you what I see in you?"

Layka nodded, unable to speak.

Aven smiled. "Brillo has your first clue."

Layka looked down and saw the ribbon tied to the harness. Aven must have put it there when she was loving on her. She detached the piece of paper and began to read. She grinned and began to walk till she reached the sundial up near the parking lot where they had come in. She lined up with what would be the eight o'clock point and walked twenty-five steps away. There was a box with a ribbon that she untied, and she lifted the lid. There was a single champagne flute with a note folded inside.

I met you for the first time at 8 a.m. It took me twenty-five steps to reach you. Layka read the words and looked up. "You counted the steps?"

"I did. It was the only way I could get my heart to stop racing."

Layka smiled and pulled the paper to her chest.

"Your second clue is on the bottom of the box."

Layka slid the note back into the glass and into the box before turning it over. She smiled and set off toward the large maple tree near the enclosed dog park area. She knelt, searching a low bush beside the tree before reaching her hand inside and pulling out a second box, larger and a little heavier. "It's a plate," she said with an eyebrow raised as she opened it and flipped the plate over to read the note she could see attached through its clear glass.

I daydreamed about you from the hospital lounge, staring at the brick of the library wall through the bare spaces left by falling autumn leaves, eager—for the first time—to maybe let my walls down.

Layka made her way around the park, following each clue and placing her gifts in the basket Aven carried. The last clue brought her back to the picnic area, where a large box and two smaller boxes sat as a tiered gift with a large bow behind the table. She knelt to lift it from where it lay.

"Wait," Aven said, taking Brillo's leash and clipping it to the rotating clasp in the ground that would let her roam in the shade of the overhanging tree without getting tangled. She placed the basket on the table before kneeling, and Layka took a moment to look at this side of the table. There were little words taped to form a place setting on the gingham cloth. She began to read them as Aven stood. "What are these?" she asked, reading one that said *Willingness to grow.*

Aven stepped to the basket and traced the handle. "I wanted you to know what I see in you. I know I've said it, but I didn't feel like you believed me sometimes. I admire your fearlessness in being open with me about emotions so close to your heart these last few months. I wanted you to know that in that process, it has made me admire you all the more." Aven tapped the table gently. "I thought I would use a different approach to show you just a few of the remarkable things about you." Aven leaned into the table, pointing at what Layka noticed earlier as a pattern for a place setting, marked by little pieces of colorful paper with writing. "Each of these," Aven said, pointing at the collected clues in the basket, "goes over one of those." She gestured at the colorful tabs on the table.

Layka read the one she had first noticed and knew exactly which item went there. She reached into the basket and pulled out the napkin that said, *I apologize.* She recalled the day she had scribbled those words on a napkin in Mildred's hospital room. She smiled and laid the napkin over the words *Willingness to grow.* She had been willing to grow, willing to evolve, become a better version of herself with this woman. She smiled at Aven and lifted another item. Each of the nine objects had a specific memory she could place, but it wasn't until this moment, when she had to set the item over words like *intelligent, funny, tenacious,* that she saw herself through the eyes of this woman she respected. There it was. She respected, even admired Aven, and a part of her had been afraid she wouldn't measure up to have that respect in return, but Aven had said it. Even more than that, she had shown it. She laid the ninth item over the last word, and her heart felt as if it took its first real beat since that terrible day in the hospital.

Aven stepped next to her and took her hands again the way she had earlier. "Do you see now how incredible *you* are, not just to me, but as a person?"

Layka nodded, watching Aven trace her knuckles with her thumbs. Her heart felt like it was kicking in her chest with this happiness she couldn't contain.

Aven smiled that gentle smile, squeezed Layka's hands, then knelt and lifted the three-tiered package onto the picnic bench. Its rectangular base would have taken up half the table. "This is the last one before we eat."

Layka balanced it on the bench, recognizing immediately what it was by the feel of the bottom edge that stuck out slightly. She glanced at the two boxes on top. One was just large enough for a set of dry-erase markers, and the other one the exact shape of a... She swallowed with the perfect memory. An eraser.

She opened each with a reverence and anticipation that made her hands shake. She turned the eraser over in her hand to read the note.

I want to erase your fears and hold you forever, the way I held you that night.

Layka pulled the eraser in close to her chest, her eyes brimming with tears as she closed them, as if to hold the memory. She remembered that night like it was yesterday, burned into her mind. She had felt so connected, so loved, so entirely Aven's. The single thought seemed to wash away another layer of her self-doubt. Aven had wanted her so completely that night, and now she had patiently waited for Layka to find her way back to them through a messed-up world of unexpected tragedy and her own issues. She could sense Aven just inches away now, even with her eyes closed. She laid the eraser down on the edge of the table and opened her eyes. "I'd like to have a new first kiss."

Aven's mouth crushed to hers like a tsunami had been mounting. Layka took it all. Took the passion, the need, the hope, and the peace.

CHAPTER THIRTY-TWO

"**W**E ARE NOW CRUISING at thirty thousand feet, and with this tailwind, we anticipate arriving ten minutes early to Dulles Airport. We have turned the seat belt sign on due to turbulence. Please remain in your seats with your seat belts fastened."

Aven felt the flip in her stomach just as the pilot's announcement ended and the plane seemed to fall from the sky, then stabilize, over and over again. She had traveled so much since leaving in November two years ago. She'd returned a month later in December, then June for the ribbon-cutting in DC, then traveled to Kansas in February. They'd had a few days again this past April, but Kansas had been special. She closed her eyes and took a deep breath, letting her mind find something calmer than being 30,000 feet in the air with her stomach doing somersaults. What it found was a similar episode of her stomach flipping during an extended visit with Layka. They were in Kansas for the Wheelhouse ribbon-cutting ceremony, and Layka had talked her into going to the "toy store" for something new. Their first attempt with what she had dubbed the two-headed dildo Layka brought with her had been a laugh. She smiled, recalling the memory. Neither of them had the skill or, apparently, pelvic muscle strength to manage it properly. She leaned her head against the window, remembering how special it had felt to lie in bed laughing with Layka after their failed attempt. Then falling asleep with Layka in her arms. She'd always felt she needed to be prepared before trying something new. She still felt that way, but somehow Layka made her feel safe outside of that comfort zone. Layka had done so much to help her find comfort not only with her emotions but also with her sexual expression. The realization of how far she had come, from a naive college student waiting six months to even kiss a girl, to a woman who appreciated—even lauded—the history of sexuality in women...it was a leap she owed to Layka.

"I don't think I could have done it with anyone else," she whispered to the clouds. The problem was the thought of Layka at 30,000 feet and a plane playing ping with her gut just made her both aroused and nauseous. She laughed, then stifled it as she gazed out her window at the cluster of clouds that were creating the present havoc in her stomach. She watched the clouds wisp by like scenes from a montage of her sexual growth. She'd been incredibly embarrassed when they entered the toy store in Kansas. It was their first time in one, but they had been met by a museum of history and a lesbian determined to remind the world that women needed orgasms. Layka had taken her hand, and like so many other things, they had experienced it together. Aven closed her eyes and let the memory play out in her mind.

"Here is the advertisement from the Sears & Roebuck catalog for a medical device to alleviate hysteria in women." The woman standing near the door, wearing a T-shirt with the store logo, was speaking to a customer and pointing at a shadow box display of old news advertisements, medical journal articles, and yes, a Sears & Roebuck catalog.

"So, you're saying for years doctors traveled all around giving womb massages to women to alleviate hysteria?"

"Yep."

Layka had continued to walk, but Aven had stopped. She was familiar with the issues of women being called "hysterical" because the Greek word for uterus was *hyster* and the male-dominated world of science and medicine for centuries had blamed many female ailments on her uterus, often diagnosing them as hysterical. This woman knew what she was talking about and, blast herself for her prejudice, Aven hadn't expected to find this information in the sex toy shop.

Layka, halted in her momentum by Aven's abrupt stop, turned and moved back to Aven, wrapping her free arm around Aven's waist. The gesture was simple but made Aven feel like she could rule the world with this woman by her side.

The customer talking with the employee had noticed them and shifted to open up the space for Aven and Layka to see the museum-like displays where the employee stood, but she continued to speak as she reached for a device on one of the shelves. "And the doctors were frustrated because the pressure, technique, and time it took to relieve the hysteria was different for each woman, so a device was developed so a woman could do womb massage herself?"

"Yes." The employee smiled and leaned a long arm along the shelf as she propped herself confidently while she spoke. "There were medical and scientific articles written on the effective techniques of womb massage, technological advances to create equipment to provide the womb massage when doctors found it tedious, and advertisements in catalogs like Sears & Roebuck for vibrators."

"What?" Layka's shocked one-word question made Aven both smile and startle.

The employee smiled as if that was the most frequent word she ever heard. "Uh-huh. That's right. For years, rubbing the clitoris of a woman was a procedure performed by doctors to alleviate hysteria. Technology was developed to self-treat it, and advertising promoted it until around the 1920s, when it was realized that 'womb massage' was essentially an orgasm for women. At which point, of course, it was shunned."

Layka had moved closer to one of the shelves and was reading a display in a glass frame. Aven read over her shoulder.

"You can take that off the shelf to read it. There's sometimes a glare from the lighting," the employee said, then explained to the other customer what they were looking at. "Sears & Roebuck recalled the printing of their entire catalog just so they could remove the advertisement once the device was considered a means to alleviate a woman's sexual need and not a womb massage for her hysteria."

Aven bit the inside of her lip at the blatant effort to shame women for sexual release and how the continued promotion of that shame had not changed. Hadn't she carried it herself into the store just today?

"This is incredible," the customer said from behind Aven. "How late are you open? I want my wife to see this."

"Here, I'll give you a card with our store information. I'll be back to help you two," she said, tapping Aven's shoulder lightly before heading to the cash register with the other customer.

Aven gave her a nod, and Layka set the display back and turned to her. "Can you believe that?"

"Yes, I can," Aven said. "And, I'm a little disappointed in myself for neglecting an education of our sexual history as women."

"Me too," Layka said, then gave that sideways smile that made her look like a dream to Aven. "But, I'm excited to start my education with you." She ran her thumb along the back of Aven's hand as she pulled Aven close.

"I'm Meiomi. What can I help you two find today?"

Aven startled. "I have a strap-on I ordered shortly after we first got together, but we've yet to use it. I put it on once." Aven felt her ears warm and her face flush. What the hell was that?

Layka laughed and leaned in, kissing her flaming ear. Aven could feel her anxiety calm. How had she survived without this woman? And even worse, what would she do if they never made it to a forever "us"?

"Don't lie," Layka said, bumping her. "If I know you, you've put it on and taken it off a dozen times like it was a timed event so you could make things seamless for me once we have the chance with it."

Aven grinned at the truth of it. She could laugh at herself with Layka, even with this need she had to be prepared. "She's right. I have, but it doesn't feel comfortable and makes me feel like I'm prepping for a skydive. I'd prefer..." She looked at Layka, who smiled knowingly. *God, it feels good to read each other's minds this way sometimes.* "...a strapless, but I'm not very good at stabilizing it."

"That's common. I never recommend a couple try a strapless the first time."

"We did," Layka said, laughing, and Aven felt the smile on her face reflect the joy in her heart at the shared memory.

"How did that turn out?"

"Just like you imagine," Aven said, laughing.

Meiomi smiled with a kindness and connection that did something to Aven's heart. This camaraderie of women enjoying an open discussion about putting themselves and their relationships in the most honest light of shared experience and growth together made her feel renewed.

"Let me have you try on a pair of the boxers. If you like the comfort of that, we can pick out the rest."

Something rattled, like ice in a glass, and Aven tried to orient. She wiped at her lip, and her eyes flicked open. She blinked several times.

"Would you like something to drink?" The flight attendant was waving an ice-filled cup above the seat, and Aven realized the woman had probably asked her the question more than once.

"Please, just some water, thank you." She'd been "on the slip," as Reynolds called it, when you weren't quite asleep but your thoughts slipped around through memories. And that had been a good one. Now it was December, and she was headed back to DC for a visit. This would be longer than the four days they had in Kansas for the ribbon-cutting, or the five days for the April groundbreaking ceremony in California. Things got behind schedule when Anthony, one of the lead contractors, had a heart attack. The delay had kept them busy, and they hadn't talked about the unresolved issue of their future that still hung over them. It was as if they had decided to avoid it by diving completely into either their sexual intimacy or the project while keeping any possible "forever us" discussion on the sidelines. She was a little nervous about bringing it up. She didn't want to jeopardize what they had, but she was starting to want a forever, and Layka had not been ready for that the last time. She took another deep breath as the pilot made an announcement about their descent. *It's your first Christmas together as a couple, don't ruin it!* She repeated *Don't ruin it* like a mantra till the wheels touched down.

Aven raced across the asphalt, her luggage wheels rolling over the uneven surface between cars. One thing she could say about a long-distance relationship with Layka—it made reunions a Pandora's box of emotion.

She was happy, excited, horny, and about seventy-five other things all at once. Apart from snatching single nights together between meetings across the country for project hurdles, they had seen each other only two extended times in the eighteen months since their new first kiss, and those had been at the Kansas City ribbon-cutting ceremony and the San Francisco groundbreaking ceremony. Aven looked forward to every snagged moment they could grab before they had to return to their work on opposite sides of the country.

"Thanks for picking me up," Aven said, grabbing Layka in an unrelenting hug. "It always feels so good to hold you." She breathed in the smell of Layka's vanilla noel lotion and thought again that she adored how her fragrance shifted with the seasons, but that there was always the familiar scent of Layka wrapped in it. Horns began blaring from the other cars pulled up to the arrivals curb. She quickly tossed her luggage in the back of Layka's car as the curb police headed their way.

"You're getting me in trouble already," Layka said, laughing as they both raced to their respective sides of the car and hopped in.

Aven's body hummed with excitement. She'd been on call last Christmas, so this would be their first Christmas together as a couple. She had shipped all her gifts to Sarah's house, and she couldn't wait to celebrate the holiday with Layka. She was a little anxious about the busy schedule with their families and friends, but she had planned everything out so everyone would have quality time with them, and they could still have alone time together.

"Are you running through the two-week itinerary in your head?" Layka placed her hand on Aven's leg and grinned.

Aven smiled, laid her hand over Layka's, and stroked the top of her fingers. "I am."

"Then where do we go first?"

Aven lifted Layka's hand and brought it to her lips. "I'm so happy, and I just want to have some time with you today. Can we stop by Sarah's? I've got a key. I can pick up all my Christmas stuff while they're at work, and we can go to your house and spend the day in front of the fireplace watching Christmas movies, wrapping gifts, and playing with Brillo."

"That will put us right on track for you to open your early Christmas gift." Layka turned those gray-blue eyes to Aven and gave an impish smile before putting her eyes back to the road.

"Maybe we should skip Sarah's," Aven said.

"No, no, no," Layka chided, pulling her hand free to wave a single finger back and forth. "No changing the itinerary."

The soft white lights of the Christmas tree, the gold glow of the fireplace, and the strewn remnants of colorful wrapping paper and bows were a blurred background as Layka wiped at the happy tears. She hadn't laughed this hard in a long time. "It is so good to have you here," she said, pressing a kiss to Aven's lips and watching the furrowed look of concentration relax. She wished she had a picture of Aven's face when she had handed her a present to unwrap amidst all their efforts at wrapping. "So, technically, the early Christmas is me, as you suspected. I just come with a little extra." She nodded at the box in Aven's hands.

"So, this is the curved strapless Meiomi mentioned?" The curious furrow returned to Aven's forehead.

Layka ran her thumbs along Aven's brow, feeling a deep connection when the furrowed lines relaxed. She'd never realized how good it felt to bring someone else that calm until she'd done it for Aven. "She said when we feel we have some success with the boxers then maybe try one of the curved strapless."

"Yes, I remember, but do you think numerous single nights between meetings across the country and two extended weekends makes us ready?"

Layka slid a finger over Aven's lips, stopping her words as she laughed. "They were very busy nights."

Aven persisted. "You know I don't know how to use this one."

Layka laughed again when Aven turned the box over as if to read the instructions. Layka placed her hands on either side of Aven's face and lifted her head. "You don't have to be perfect at everything the first time." She pressed her forehead to Aven's, knowing this was one of those moments where understanding how important it was to Aven to be prepared made this more intimate than just two people having sex. "And you don't have to prepare for anything alone anymore." Layka felt her heart open to a new place when Aven enveloped her in those strong arms. She kissed her softly. "We can practice as much as you like." She bit Aven's lip and smiled into another kiss. "And, I'll give you honest feedback."

Aven laughed, and Layka heard the box land on the couch as Aven lifted her off the floor. Layka wrapped her legs around Aven as she carried her a few steps and pressed her back against the wall.

"I want to do everything with you," Aven said, and Layka could feel her weight completely supported on Aven's hips and thighs as she gently ran her hands through Layka's hair, then paused at her neck and made circles on her cheeks with her thumbs.

The doorbell buzzed.

Aven groaned. "Whose idea was it to order food?"

"Yours," Layka said with a sigh, leaning her head back against the wall and hoping the delivery person would just leave the food at the door.

It buzzed again.

"Well, I'm firing myself," Aven said, supporting Layka's thighs with her hands to lower her to the floor as she stepped back. "I'll get it."

Layka followed her to the door. If she knew Aven, it would take both of them to carry in all the food.

"Sarah?" Aven said when she pulled the door open.

"Hi," Sarah said, smiling and lifting the packages in her arms. "Steve had placed these on the shelf in the mudroom when he came in the other day, so they weren't with the others."

"Come in," Layka said, seeing the delivery guy coming up the walkway. "I'll get our food. Aven, if you will take Sarah to the kitchen, I'll bring it in."

Aven's look of relief told Layka how grateful she was to avoid the endless ribbing she would get from Sarah if she found their fun in the living room.

"That sounds great. Let me take one of those," Aven said to Sarah as she backed into the arch of the living room entrance and directed Sarah down the foyer hall to the kitchen doorway.

"Your house is so beautiful," Sarah said. "I had an early day and left after lunch."

"Thank you," Layka said, pushing the front door closed with her hip before heading toward the kitchen with the two bags of food. "I remember asking you to stop by sometime and see the decorations."

"Exactly," Sarah said. "When I saw the packages in the mudroom and the others gone, I knew Aven would be in a panic when she realized they were missing, so I thought I'd kill two birds with one stone."

Layka set the food on the counter. "Aven, I'm going to get the wrapping paper up off the floor in the living room so Brillo doesn't wrap herself in it while you and Sarah get the food out. Then we can give her a tour of the house after we eat."

Aven gave her a deer-in-the-headlights look before relaxing when Layka said, "I've got this, babe."

Layka turned to enter the living room from the other doorway in the kitchen. She smiled as she picked up the wrapping paper and tucked Aven's present under her arm. She bit her lip at the thought of missed opportunity, but they had two weeks together. She smiled as she made her way back to their bedroom.

"Happy New Year," Aven whispered, pulling from the kiss only because she needed air in her lungs.

"Happy New Year to you." Layka twisted her finger in the single blond curl that fell around Aven's face. Aven reveled in the feel of Layka in her arms.

"I can't believe I have to fly back tomorrow. I'm so not ready to leave."

"Can we not talk about it today?"

Aven ran her hand along Layka's face, memorizing it anew. She understood. It was getting increasingly difficult to be apart, but they both had significant commitments where they were located.

"Hey, you two lovebirds. Happy New Year!" Sam raised her beer in a toast to them, then looked at Farrah, who stood by her side, arms wrapped around her as Sam squeezed her close and kissed her forehead.

"Happy New Year!" Aven and Layka said in unison as they both opened their arms and embraced the other couple. It was such a solid feeling to hug Sam like this, as if she was in the very spot she had always been destined to hold in Aven's life. The four of them had spent Christmas Eve together, and it had been a blast.

"What's the latest lead on your Barton case?" Aven asked when they stepped back from the hug.

"We've actually had a positive turn on that, but there are some small pieces we need in order to make an airtight case. We'll know more when we bring together all the details we have with the information from the FBI and the squad that helped out of Maryland at our next meeting near the end of the month."

"That's great. Oh—hey, Mildred! Happy New Year," Aven said as Mildred slid under Sam's arm.

"Yes, it is. And, I plan to keep it going all year. I'm making this year one to remember. What about you two?"

"I think we may do the same," Aven said cautiously. She paused to look at Layka for her response to the idea. They had remained very focused on the physical intimacy of their relationship these last two weeks, and the *don't ruin it* mantra still played in her head on repeat, but she had to push if they were going to move forward. After all, these brief periods of time together were all they had if she wanted to deal with this face-to-face. And she did want to do that. It didn't seem to be a conversation Layka wanted to have via video chat.

"That's what I like to hear," Mildred said, and Aven felt Layka wince in her arms.

"Would you like some more champagne?" Aven asked Layka, hoping to give them an out to avoid discussing any details about what making the year one to remember might entail.

"Yes. I'll walk with you over there." Layka's response made Aven feel conflicted. The ease with which they read each other was a positive, but it was clear to her that Layka was struggling with what might constitute a "year to remember" for them. *Why is she still struggling with the idea of an us?*

"Maybe we *should* talk about me leaving tomorrow?" Aven said, lifting two new champagne flutes from the table as Layka sat their old ones on a tray.

Layka took a sip of her champagne, and Aven pressed on. She'd been toying with this idea, so she might as well put it out on the table. "What if you come to San Francisco? The build of the final Wheelhouse there is eighty-five percent complete, and the library build connected with it is ninety percent done per Naomi."

Layka bit her lip, and Aven felt the hesitation like a punch in the gut. Was Layka getting tired of her after being in each other's space for two solid weeks? Reynolds had reminded her when she was visiting with her and Sarah that she and Layka hadn't spent a lot of solid time together in the same physical space. She had blown it off, saying they talked every day despite the physical distance between them, but the nudge from solid friends for that next step had her stressing again about where they were and if they were on the same page for their future. She let her mind race back through the rush of events, people, and Christmas activities. Had she been present enough? One of her flaws in past relationships had been not being present in one form or another. Hadn't that been ultimately why those people had found someone else? Aven pushed back at the thought. It wasn't that it was wrong, just that it wasn't a complete analysis of what had been wrong in those relationships. She and Layka were different. Weren't they? The question arising in her mind made Aven panic. "Never mind, it's silly for me to ask that. You've got your whole life here. I mean, your work and family."

Layka still hadn't spoken, and Aven felt her tumbling words would strangle her. She'd been so worried about failing at a long-distance relationship that she hadn't considered that she might fail at being present when she was right here. How many calls had she accepted from the hospital these last two weeks?

She was ravenous for Layka, but that wasn't the same as being present. Was Layka seeing a venture to California with a doctor who worked too many hours as a bad long-term decision?

Layka bit her lip to stave off her immediate response of yes. Was she ready to move to the other side of the country to be with Aven? Could she be enough for this intelligent, capable woman? Aven's understanding and love had healed parts of her she didn't know were broken, but was she a whole person? Was she bringing a heart that was happy with who she was to this relationship, or was she still leaning on Aven to accept the imperfections? And would those imperfections be magnified when they were no longer working on a project that pulled them together? She looked up at Aven, searching her eyes. "Can we see the project through before we make those kind of plans?"

"Sure." Aven cleared her throat when the word came out a little too high-pitched. "That's reasonable."

Layka felt the slightest distance open between them with the words, despite Aven's arms wrapped around her.

CHAPTER
THIRTY-THREE

"YOU THINK YOU CAN make it?" Aven could hear the need in her own voice as she watched the San Francisco rain pelting the window in her small office inside the West Coast Mindful Path Wheelhouse overlooking the courtyard connecting them to the new Library of Congress Antiquities building. Things had been a little strained between them, and Aven's old fears were trying to creep back in. She was determined not to let them. They'd both been extremely busy with their individual work as well as the press of bringing together all the final pieces of the project.

"Absolutely. I'll make it happen. I wouldn't miss an opportunity to see you."

"Hmm," Aven hummed, trying to keep things light. She tapped her chin even though she realized Layka couldn't see it. "The event is at the new LOC Antiquities building. I'm thinking that has more draw for the librarian I know than anything."

"Not more than anything," Layka said, and the husky sound in her voice made Aven ache. It was the first of February, and it would be April before she would see Layka at the event.

Aven could kick herself for the blatant need for Layka's reassurance in her teasing, but she was in deeper than she'd ever been with anyone. The thought made Daniels's words flash through her mind: *It's not healthy to be pining or continuously waiting for someone who isn't interested in a next level of relationship.* To be fair, Aven had only recently explained that the person she was "interested in back home," a phrase she had used generically to avoid matchmaking when Daniels had tried to set her up on dates, was also the best friend she talked about constantly.

"Well, I'm excited for you to see it." The line went quiet. "I'm excited to see you." Daniels didn't understand the depth of their relationship when she told Aven she couldn't "wait forever." God, what a crazy turn for her to be the one not wanting to wait.

"I miss you too, Aven. It's okay to say it."

"I know, it's just there is a part of me that feels if I'm too excited to see you or want it too much, the universe is going to flip everything on its head. I'm so proud of what we've accomplished in under thirty months. Even with the delays, the California Wheelhouse ribbon-cutting is planned for April, and the entire project will have been completed in just under three years. I've enjoyed capturing moments with you across the US as we worked on this project together. Now we even have a Library of Congress branch in California."

"Which is great," Layka said. "But it also means the project is almost over."

Aven let the words sit with her. What they had was growing, but where would that lead them when they were still on opposite sides of the country? She loved the stolen moments they had, but she wanted more. Their relationship was stronger than she had ever had with anyone, but her fears from past failed relationships were starting to wear on her emotionally more than she had admitted to Layka or herself. She wanted something permanent with Layka; she wanted a forever us with her. Yet, it wasn't fair to pressure Layka about a move to the West Coast, and she still had time on her commitment to the university hospital. Could they manage long distance for another year? Could her doubts battle another year of that emotional strain? Her thought became a spoken question before she could consider it. "Are you up to managing another year long distance?"

"Can we talk about it when I get there?"

Aven paused. The words were innocent and reasonable but seemed like a way to deal with an answer she was not going to like. "Sure. When are you planning your flight?"

"I'm helping Sam tie up some loose ends, these things take forever, but Brillo is a little hero. You remember how Barton's campaign was funding those two ghost companies we discovered?"

"Yes."

"Well, it turns out they weren't just ghost companies. The chip recording from Brillo showing their transport across state lines gave the FBI what they needed to get a warrant to search New Foundations and all of its subsidiary connections. He was using them to transport the homeless out of his region and into the DC areas so he could show reduced homeless numbers for his project 'Clean Streets' going into the election."

"He was shipping them out without their consent?"

"Yes, and often in numbers that are unimaginable using the transportation vehicles the FBI has confiscated."

"That explains the high numbers of the homeless population testing positive for the infection. Close proximity for extended periods of time increases the risk for infection."

"Right—which probably also explains why people like Mildred had such severe cases."

"Yes. Being brought into the DC homeless population so abruptly would mean no time for immunity to develop naturally."

"That makes sense. Which reminds me, Mildred said to tell you hello. She'll be excited to keep Brillo while I travel out there. I'm almost afraid to leave him. Sassy still refuses to come home since Mildred kept them both last time."

"Oh no!" Aven laughed. "We can video call her once you're here, and I can say hello to her, the traitor cat, and Brillo. Are the charges going to stick? Barton is a slippery politician, and Reynolds says he has connections with a Separatist party that is on the rise."

"I don't have all of those details, but I do know Sam says the receptionist had copied secure documents that show Barton giving directives for the homeless to be taken to the DC region. It looks like she was planning to blackmail him but now prefers to look like a hero by turning them over to the FBI."

"So, all the dots for the communicable disease issue link back to this illegal transport rather than from the homeless in general spreading disease in public places?"

"Yes. Your friend Reynolds helped us confirm it was too great a distance for the virus to leap with no connection of infection in between."

"She mentioned working on some comparable data for the FBI she was going to share with me when it was released," Aven said. "She asked me about any pulmonary mechanisms that would incubate a virus beyond what she understood of the virus itself. I figured she was addressing the issue of the possible direct transport system from a county in Maryland to the DC region, but she wasn't allowed to share the FBI details."

"She did?"

"Yes. Why?"

"I was at the interdisciplinary meeting where Sam, Reynolds, the Maryland detectives, and Agent Sebastian were discussing this issue because the Mindful Path Project was creating its first Wheelhouse in the DC region. You were leaving, and I was struggling with that. Reynolds seemed very protective of her sources. Now I know she was keeping your name out of the mix. It feels weird and prophetic to realize you were there with me all along, giving us your voice through Reynolds. Your insight was key to the investigation."

"I'm glad to hear that, and even though it appears the reason that fostered us beginning this program was unfounded, the results are beneficial."

"The homeless can have a room, a shower, a meal, a health check, and access to books and tools to rebuild their lives."

"And we've increased the number of library resources across the US."

"Definitely a win-win for the two camps we represent."

"Yes. And now we get to celebrate that with the first Library of Congress Antiquities branch opening on the West Coast."

"And I get to steal another special moment with the woman who makes my heart feel like it is home."

That sounded positive, Aven thought. Then she replayed Layka's words in her mind. Was it always just going to be little moments they could snag? They had overcome the hurdle of the emotional distance between them, but now it was physical distance. It seemed all the distance pulled their hearts closer, but she was too scared to believe it could ever all come together. "How are Sam and Farrah doing?"

"Great. Oh—I was so focused on the project, I almost forgot. Farrah wanted me to get your condo number since you moved within your complex. She will be sending some 'special invitations' out soon, but I'm not allowed to tell you what it's for."

"OMG, they're getting married!"

"I said nothing and fully expect you to surrender your condo number so I can find you when I arrive, and I will pass it on to Farrah very secretly."

"Secretly indeed," Aven said, laughing. "But let me know when you are arriving, and I'll pick you up."

"Thank you. It looks like I will be arriving at four p.m., but that may change if the flight is anything like my last three. Regardless, I'll see you in just a few months!"

"That isn't nearly soon enough, but I'll take it." Aven continued to hold the phone after Layka clicked off. They were at the end of the project, and Layka had asked her to wait till then for them to talk more about their future plans. Now that they were there, Aven didn't like the uncomfortable stirring in her gut that Layka was postponing the conversation.

CHAPTER THIRTY-FOUR

A VEN WATCHED THE VIDEO call as Layka shifted her carry-on bag to sit on her rolling luggage. Her yellow spring dress spun just above her knees like a dancer's as she twisted back and forth, corralling her multiple pieces of luggage. "My flight's been delayed. I'll meet you at the event."

"Oh no. Okay, I'm sorry you will be rushed. Is there anything I can do to help?"

"No, you've got enough on your plate getting prepared for the event. Mildred said Naomi has had her hands full and you've taken some of that load. That should ease up once the new head librarian is there next month. At least I'll have the heightened anticipation of seeing you with hundreds of people around and knowing I can't touch that beautiful body till we get through the evening."

"You sound a lot stronger than me. I've already been scoping out the new facility in my mind, thinking about places I could squirrel you away to have my way with you."

"Oh my, Dr. Summerhouse, you sound very determined."

"Determined doesn't even touch it. I haven't seen you in three months!"

"I know. My body aches for you. It sounded like sweet torture to see you at the event and know you are untouchable for two more hours, but I like your idea much better."

"Well, now that I know what it does to you, I may need to play hard to get."

Layka laughed, and Aven thought her heart might overflow with joy. How did that happen? Just some chemical release at the sound of her lover's laughter created this incredible sense of happiness. "I look forward to seeing you and having our talk. I haven't forgot about that," Aven said, hoping to get some more detail from Layka about how that would play out for their future. The nagging reminder of her failed past relationships was increasing with the delays in them moving forward to a forever us. The failures had played in her mind unbidden in an unending loop since her conversation with Dr. Daniels last week. Was Layka not at the same place in their relationship? Was she holding on to something that would never become a forever? *You're not getting any younger,* she thought, recalling Daniels's quip after recommending she not put all her eggs in one basket.

"I'm glad, because it's important. Let's enjoy our evening and let that happen later, when it's just us. Besides, I have a surprise for you in the twist of my costume for tonight."

Aven bit her lip. Layka's tone was happy and positive. She would lean into that. It was reasonable for that conversation to happen organically, and the thought of a surprise related to how Layka was showing up at the Literary Ball made heat flush her entire body.

Aven's breath caught when she saw Layka enter through the columns of the new building. The high ceiling and marble columns mimicked, in many ways, the Jefferson Building in Washington, and seeing Layka pass through the columns brought flashes of memory from that night at the Literary Ball when she had sat in a quiet room and opened up to this woman, who at the time was practically a stranger. They had agreed on a classic book for this Literary Ball, but Layka had put some serious spin on her costume. The black sequined gown was strapless, and from here, the holes and tears designed to make it look tattered only made it sexier. Their eyes met, and Aven's heart set a new record pace. She took a slow, deep breath as Layka smiled and made her way over to her. It was then that Aven realized she was frozen in place. This woman absolutely made time stand still for her when she entered a room.

"Hello, beautiful," Layka said, leaning in toward her ear but not touching her.

Aven almost groaned out loud. It was Layka's grin that pulled her to her senses, and she recalled their earlier conversation. How long could they manage this torture of not touching?

"God, this brings back memories," Aven said, knowing she would have to refocus if she was going to win this little challenge between them. They stood in the center of the room at the new LOC Antiquities branch. It was the library of record with the third Wheelhouse in the Mindful Path Project they had initiated together. She turned a full circle and observed all the people dressed as literary characters. She raised her glass and passed Layka the flute of champagne she had been saving for her. Layka plucked at the golden thread that held a balloon tied to the flute. "Why do I get the champagne with a balloon?"

"Not just any balloon." Aven smiled. "There were twelve balloons as part of the pre-event auction."

"Only twelve at an event this large?"

"Of course, supply and demand, you know."

"Oh really. So how many gold ones?"

"Only one," Aven said, excited to see Layka light up the way we all do when we feel special.

"To the first Literary Ball on the West Coast." Layka took the flute and tapped her glass to Aven's. "It does bring back memories," Layka said, running her hand along the double-breasted lapel of Aven's white jacket.

Aven relaxed at the feel of those dexterous fingers near her chest. It was nice to know Layka wanted to touch her. She had found the vintage lab coat in pristine condition at a secondhand store and had the long jacket tailored to fit her curves, knowing Layka would appreciate the

Dr. Frankenstein lab coat with the black ribbon tied around her neck. If the dilated pupils checking her out from only a breath away were any indication, then the look layered over her pleated, pressed silk dress pants and accented with stiletto black heels rather than boots was a winner. She wrapped her hand over Layka's as it moved across the buttons at her stomach. This woman's touch made the butterflies within circle like a swarm of Monarchs migrating south. "I'm struggling to remember I'm supposed to see you as Frankenstein's monster when you look so sexy," Aven said. Layka had surprised her with the idea of coming this year as characters from the science fiction classic *Frankenstein*.

"I did take some artistic liberty, but then again I have every intention of seducing you and rewriting the entire story."

"You're well on your way to that," Aven said, letting her eyes trace the mermaid-style fit-and-flare black evening gown that appeared torn and ripped to expose areas of beautiful tan skin across Layka's chest, shoulders, abdomen, and legs. She let her eyes linger on the split along the left side that showed a toned thigh. "Maybe I can see that these heal well." Aven traced one of the painted but realistic-appearing suture lines that ran across Layka's taut stomach toward her navel.

Layka shivered with the touch, and Aven closed her eyes with anticipation. Layka stroked her finger across the back of her hand, and Aven opened her eyes. She pulled a set of keys from her pocket. "As lead principal investigator for the Mindful Path Project, I've been asked to evaluate the office for the head librarian coming in next month." She smiled. "Want to help me see if anything might be needed in the office space? I could use your expertise."

"Hello, Dr. Summerhouse. It's great to see you." The voice was elderly and soft.

Aven recognized the voice as the NIH liaison, Mr. Sanders. She bit back her sigh of exasperation. He was a nice man, but she wanted—needed—to feel Layka against her. Needed to kiss her long and deep. She smiled and turned. "Oh, hello, Mr. Sanders. It's good to see you. Thank you for your work and your recent donation to the Mindful Path Project here in California. This is Layka Silva. She is the principal manager for the entire Mindful Path Project. She's visiting from DC."

Layka extended her hand. "Hello, Mr. Sanders. It is a pleasure to meet you. I've seen your name appear several times in connection with the facility here. It is nice to put a face with a name that has been so generous to the community."

Sanders shook her hand, and the wrinkles around his eyes softened with his widened smile. Aven understood why. Layka had such a quiet way of making people feel seen and appreciated. He ran his hand through his wisp of gray hair and nodded toward a small group of people near the food table.

"With that kind of encouragement, I better do what I do best and convince my colleagues to do their charitable duties."

Layka smiled that winning smile, and Aven took a moment just to take in her face as Sanders moved away. Her blue-gray eyes were bright, and the red lip gloss accentuated the cupid's bow of her lip and made her smile irresistible. When Layka turned those beautiful eyes on her, Aven reached for her hand. "You up for that escape to evaluate the office for our new head librarian?"

Layka's smile made Aven's breath catch when her tongue ran across her teeth. "I'm excited about our plans for the week, and I'm very pleased with how it is starting out, Dr. Frankenstein."

Aven was already moving through the crowd, Layka's hand in hers. She tried to keep the pace casual, but she had missed everything about being with this woman. She slid the key in the door once they had discreetly stepped into the hallway, and with the click of the door shutting behind them, she took Layka's face in her hands, studying it before leaning in to brush her lips across the soft red gloss.

Layka's moan and parted lips were the only invitation she needed to deepen the kiss. When she pulled back to catch her breath, she noted the room around them. They were standing in the open space with only the light of the moon coming through the floor-to-ceiling glass on the far wall. They were on the sixth floor of the building, and all the buildings immediately nearby were two stories or shorter. The sensation was one of both privacy from and connection to the world as the soft light of the moon streamed into the space. She pulled Layka in for a hug before extending her hand to the room. "What do you think?"

Layka's response was to give a gentle push with her hands that were undoing the buttons on Aven's white jacket. The momentum made Aven take a step back toward the wall with solid wood floor-to-ceiling bookshelves.

"I think your head librarian should be happy with the extensive shelving space that is provided."

Aven's back was now pressed against the fluted divider between two shelving units as Layka pushed the jacket from her shoulders, running her nails gently down Aven's arms as the jacket fell to the floor. Aven smiled at the little pout Layka gave when she saw the black tank top underneath.

"I wasn't prepared for layers," Layka said, sliding her hands beneath the tank.

Aven groaned and let her head fall back with the heat of Layka's hands tracing a line up her stomach and cupping her breasts.

"I like how that sounds," Layka said, kissing up Aven's exposed neck as she pushed Aven's bra up to cup both breasts.

"Layka."

"Oh, yes." Layka pinched both nipples as she pressed Aven's lips for a kiss, then pulled back, teasing. "The shelves have the project manager's approval. What's next?"

Aven's mind was a blur of arousal, but she loved the playful arc Layka was taking and tried to remember what was in the space. "There's a desk near the opposite wall." She managed to get the words out, but her voice was low and laced with the need she couldn't hide.

Layka squeezed her breasts and slid her hands away, whispering near Aven's ear, "Take your bra off but leave your tank on."

Aven did so and watched as Layka weaved through some small boxes on the floor. Every move accentuated her perfect ass in that dress. Aven swallowed, then felt her nipples harden against the fabric of her tank when Layka leaned over the desk, that bum in the air as she opened the drawers on the other side. Aven was across the room in seconds, her body pinning Layka between her and the desk as she ran her hand up the thigh-high slit. Layka stood and pushed back into her as Aven slid her hand inside the slit to rub across the wetness at the front of her bikini panties. "You're so ready," Aven whispered, her voice husky with her own need. She slid underneath the panties to the silk of Layka's center. Her breasts were so sensitive, and the fabric of her tank rubbing them sent pings of current to her core, where Layka rocked back into her in a slow rhythm that soaked Aven's fingers now teasing along Layka's wet center and clit.

"Yes." Layka moaned, her arms braced on the desk as her movements sped up and rocked her butt against Aven's clit. Aven pressed into her. She was so ready to go over the edge with her. She slid two fingers inside, letting her thumb press Layka's clit.

"Aven, yes! I'm so close."

Aven could feel her own climax mounting with the rub of Layka against her through her thin dress pants. "God, I've missed the feel of you, in my arms, on my body," she whispered against Layka's shoulder as her right hand splayed over that exposed taut abdomen from behind. She could feel every rock of Layka's body.

"Aven!" Layka cried out with release as she pressed her hand to her dress over Aven's left hand beneath her panties.

Aven bucked, her climax triggered by the sound of her name on Layka's lips, the feel of Layka's hand pressing her own hand into the heat of Layka's sensitive center, and the pressure of that evening-gown-clad bum jerking in spasm against her clit.

Layka released her grip on Aven's hand and placed it flat on the desk to join her other hand. Her head hung between her shoulders, and she was panting. "Oh my God, that felt good. I knew it would be fast. I've missed you."

Aven leaned into Layka's back, placing her own hands beside Layka's and feeling the pressure shoot current that spasmed her clit a second time. "I take it the desk is approved?"

Layka laughed and turned, seating herself on the edge and pulling Aven in for a kiss. "I'll have to make a note to have this desk reappointed. I'm sure they can get the new head librarian a different one."

"We better get back to the party before you claim everything in here." Aven smiled through the kiss that followed her words. Most of the stuff in the room was new, brought in by the facility team, but a few of the soon-to-be head librarian's boxes had arrived earlier in the week marked as personal, and she wanted to steer clear of those. She was certain she didn't want to explain breaking something.

Layka ran her finger along Aven's collarbone, then over the thick strap of the tank to make circles at her shoulder. "Do we have to go back to the party?" Layka slid a single finger down each strap and circled Aven's nipples, which peaked in immediate response.

Aven groaned and felt her core pulse anew. *We could go one more round*, she thought. "I think I still have some work to do to heal these wounds," Aven said, kissing the fake stitches along Layka's neck. "I do prefer our retelling of this classic story." Aven's phone rang. She recognized the custom ring and instinctively reached for it in her pocket before pausing. Her eyes searched Layka's face. "It's one of the residents."

"Take the call. I understand your responsibilities to the hospital."

Aven accepted the call and hit speakerphone so she could set the phone down and continue to hold Layka.

"Dr. Summerhouse. There's been a huge pileup on Interstate 580 and Dr. Daniels's vehicle was involved."

"What?" Aven said, lifting the phone. "Is she okay?"

"They flew her and three others out from the scene."

Aven ran her hands through her hair. Dr. Daniels was a good friend and must have been headed to the hospital for her shift.

"One of the paramedics called me, saying Dr. Daniels was concerned that she wasn't going to make it in for her shift and made him promise to notify us."

"That sounds like Daniels."

There was a pause. "He said she had lost a lot of blood. They flew her and several burn victims to Saint Francis. The rest are piling up here. It's bad. There must have been a gas leak from a tanker truck."

Layka was rubbing Aven's arms near her shoulders, and she was grateful for the soothing gesture. A gas leak meant fire, which people often recognized meant an increase of burn patients. However, they often overlooked the increased smoke inhalation, which meant the pulmonology team—her team—would be taxed, and now she was down the doctor scheduled for call. Aven quickly ran through the protocols she had created. "Initiate our disaster readiness plan C, and I'll call you back in five minutes with coverage for Daniels and some modifications based on my review of the accident."

"Thanks, doc. Will do."

Aven clicked off and saw her night with Layka disappear before her eyes. Was this one of the reasons Layka was unwilling to move forward? Her job was often as detrimental to relationships as any mistress.

"Hey. I'm here all week."

Aven closed her eyes against her frustration. She loved how medicine gave her the ability to make a difference at times like this, but she was beginning to feel the cost of that more tangibly than ever before. Her time with Layka was limited, and each day was precious to her.

"I could call Dr. Johnson, who's scheduled for the day shift, but that would mean I'd need to cover his shift tomorrow. In fact, it would change the whole schedule at work, making me lose more time with you. If I do this one night shift, I can reach out to Dr. Luken, who does locum tenens work and will cover Dr. Daniels's schedule this week."

"You are the lead pulmonologist. Part of what I love about you is your commitment and passion for what you do."

Love. Aven liked how that sounded, even if only mentioned in the context of her work. "Ultimately, the structure of dealing with any pulmonary crisis falls to me, and this is the best way to manage it and still have the week off I planned with you. I don't want to lose that."

Layka cupped Aven's face between her palms. "Check on the accident details, plan to go in tonight, and call your resident. I will be here."

Aven tilted her head to lean into a palm as Layka's thumb stroked her face. Layka's touch brought her so much peace, and she marveled, not for the first time, at how much this woman made her better at her job. Perhaps just better on every level. She nodded and pulled up the data access she had to the first responders' news feed, sent a text to Jeff on the Firstnet med flight team, then prepared to call her resident when she had Jeff's response. She propped her hip against a box, Layka's arms wrapped around her middle and her cheek softly pressed to Aven's bare shoulder, exposed by her tank top. Her phone pinged with a response from Jeff. She blew out a breath and dialed her resident.

"Dr. Fields. Firstnet has a helicopter in the area and will bring me into the hospital." Aven paused, listening to Fields give some directives on his end of the line. She felt Layka's arm fall away from her waist and she watched her toy with the balloon string tied to the champagne flute base.

"Yes, Jeff said he was headed your way to pick up that patient for transport to Saint Francis," Aven said, touching Layka's cheek before placing it on Layka's lap where she now sat on the desk. She knew what Layka was worried about, so she shifted the phone and added to Layka, "He isn't headed to the bridge fire."

Layka removed the balloon attached to the glass and tied the string to Aven's finger. Aven rubbed at the string as she waited for Fields to finish confirming a discharge to free up a bed before speaking again. "Is the protocol keeping triage moving?"

"Yes, we're doing okay, but we're starting to see the strain."

"I'm on my way." Aven clicked off the line. She wiggled her finger, and Layka slid off the desk, making her way back to the shelf where Aven's costume jacket lay on the floor.

Aven reached her in time to take the jacket as Layka stood.

Layka tugged the loose loop of the balloon string from Aven's finger, but Aven closed her hand to hold it in place. "It will remind me of what is waiting for me. I'll put it in the lounge." Aven said, then tied the string through the buttonhole of her jacket and slipped her phone into the pocket. She tossed the jacket briefly over her arm and handed Layka her bra with a smile. She kept a set of scrubs and a change of clothes at the hospital.

"I've got a surprise for you tomorrow, so don't be away too long."

Aven smiled and ran her hand along Layka's jaw as she kissed her. *How long can we keep waiting to be together?* she thought, pulling away and turning for the door. She only had a few minutes to get up the stairs to the roof. As often as she had run the stairs in one hospital or another, she'd never felt the weight of it so personally. Could she keep waiting for a life together with Layka? The thought made her legs feel like lead. Hadn't that been the very thing she had so often asked for, someone to wait for her? "Well played, Karma. Well played," she whispered to only

the whir of blades in the air as she exited to the roof and the specialized helipad for Firstnet, which shared the building with the LOC.

Aven tossed her jacket inside and climbed in just as a message
crackled through the headgear Jeff had pulled from his ear. "They've
got a thready pulse on the passenger they cut out of the car beneath
the tanker. We're the closest flight team," he said, gesturing between
himself and the paramedic in the front seat.

Layka leaned against the shelving unit as the door clicked closed.
She had all week to be with Aven—she could occupy herself for one
night. She turned in the room, taking in the furniture purchased for
the office. She could start by organizing the space for the head librarian coming in next month. She'd almost told Aven her surprise—that
she was considering the position—but she wanted everything to be
perfect. She bit her lip at the thought. Wasn't that her problem all
along? Wanting every piece of her life, every part of herself, to be
perfect before asking Aven to be a part of it? Maybe she should have
just told her, but she'd wanted to say *I love you* first, and the timing
didn't feel right. Layka huffed at herself. What was she even saying?
It wasn't like she needed a special setting to love Aven. She loved
Aven everywhere. In fact, she had loved her practically from the East
to the West Coast. So why was she waiting to say it? The thought
almost made her race from the room to catch her and tell her, but
tomorrow would have to be soon enough. If she stepped out of here,
she'd be pulled back into the party, and Aven was probably already
on the helicopter.

Time dragged by with Aven away. She tugged at the bubble wrap
around the large fainting couch that took up a massive area of the
room. That was next. She was halfway through the job of organizing
the room and took a break, ready to scan her results, when she heard
a knock at the door. She moved toward the door and pulled it open.
"Naomi."

"Hi, Ms. Silva. I saw Dr. Summerhouse head for the stairs earlier and just heard a conversation near the punch bowl that there was a terrible accident on the 580. I thought you might be in here."

"Sorry I've been away so long. How are things going with the event?" Layka asked, unable to muster too much energy for the question.

"Everything is running smooth. Do you need a hand? I'm about all peopled out."

Layka smiled. "Sure. I'm just unwrapping the fainting couch. I could use a hand." Layka bumped the TV on its stand as the two of them tried to squeeze through some boxes.

"I had Justin bring that up yesterday. It was in an office not being used."

"It's bigger than the one in my office back home."

"All the more reason for you to take the position," Naomi said, bumping Layka's shoulder with her own.

Lakya smiled and pulled her dress up slightly so she could squat to lift it.

"Here I'll help," Naomi said. "If we set it in the center of the shelving unit, I think the cords are long enough to reach the cable hookup and the electrical outlet."

They shuffled together to get the TV in place. "What time is it?" Layka asked, realizing she had piddled around in here for quite a while before tackling the bubble wrap on the couch.

"I think it's close to ten."

"Can you get the local channels on so we could see if anyone is still reporting on the accident?"

"Yeah, sure. I'll go to my desk and get the Wi-Fi password after I hook the TV up."

Layka sat down on the deep seat of the couch. Only the legs remained wrapped. Naomi hooked up the TV and left to get the password. What was she doing? The boxes in here were hers. She had shipped them with the idea that what was in them could be used by anyone taking over the office—a stapler, tape, extension cords. Except for one box, all of the boxes marked "personal" were anything but. Naomi probably thought she was insane, unwilling to commit to accepting the position but dancing all around it with boxes of items for the office space. Layka stood and moved toward the single box that was truly all hers, the last box she'd packed to ship. She opened it and pulled out the frame on top, turning it over. It was a picture of her, Brillo, and Aven in the car. It was one of the many road trips they had taken when Aven had been in for a visit. She sat the photo down and lifted the next one. The door opened behind her, and she turned to see Naomi enter, reading a Post-it Note. Layka turned her attention back to the second photo.

It was her, Sam, and their parents. It was one of the few things she had taken when they left the house in a hurry when the CPS people and the police showed up where they were living alone in the apartment their parents had rented. That was the day she realized nothing was guaranteed. Was that part of the problem now? She wanted to be perfect so she could guarantee success for their relationship. She slumped onto the stacked boxes beside the open one as the TV flickered on and Naomi searched the channels. The revelation seemed to lift a weight from her chest. She traced the next picture in the box. It was her and Aven at Christmas. The tree in the background was beautiful, and Aven's smile was as bright as the lights that decorated it. The cacophony of sirens from the TV forced her head up.

"I had trouble finding the volume on this thing," Naomi said, lifting the remote. The earlier report showed the far-right lane clear and traffic moving again over there." Naomi pointed at the screen with the remote. "But this looks like a recap from earlier." Naomi sat on a decorative column brought in for the space as Layka saw the volume line escalate at the bottom of the screen, as if mimicking the escalation of activity that appeared very critical on the screen. There were two trucks and a car visible, obstructing the road. There appeared to be more cars behind the truck, but she couldn't make them out. One of the trucks was a tanker. There was commotion everywhere, but most of it was focused on putting out the fire near the second truck. For some reason, in her mind it had been the tanker that was on fire, but clearly it was the other truck on fire, and the fire trucks were in a race to keep the flames from reaching the car between the two trucks. Then there was a spotlight lifting into the air like a beacon to a helicopter flying in. The reminder of Aven leaving to board a helicopter made her stomach lurch, and she was glad Aven was headed to the hospital, not the bridge. She realized she had lifted the frame of her and Aven when the edge of it cut into her finger. She pulled the frame to her chest as she tilted her head to try to see through the smoke at what the searchlight was focused on. The helicopter was trying to turn to avoid the smoke.

"It's a backdraft!" Naomi shouted at the screen as if the helicopter pilot would hear her.

Naomi's words were distant as Layka watched the windshield on the truck shatter. Smoke billowed out, making the screen darken for several seconds before the helicopter tipped in a flash of fire from the burning truck. But it was the eerie incongruity of a balloon attached to a white jacket drifting down toward the water in the spotlight that made Layka leap toward the screen and scream, "Aven!" The backdraft caught the helicopter propeller. "No!" Layka watched her own hand grasp at the tilting aircraft before it dropped from view like a stone, toward the river below the bridge.

"Aven?" Naomi twisted Layka toward her. "Was Aven on that helicopter?"

"I've got to get down there." Layka looked down at the frame she still held tight to her chest as she paced to the desk. She spun in a circle, unable to think. She laid the frame down and lifted her phone, refusing to look at the faces in the photo. The thought tugged at her brain that this picture was their last Christmas. She shoved the thought away as she pushed off the desk and headed for the door. She covered her mouth at the cry that escaped. She'd wasted so much time.

"Ms. Silva…"

Naomi was saying something from behind her, but her brain couldn't process the words. Aven was in the river. She had to get to her. The vision of the helicopter dropping flashed in her mind, and she reached for the wall as her legs buckled.

"Layka!" Naomi's use of her first name and the tight grip at her wrist jarred her from the spiral of her thoughts. Layka realized she was halfway down the hall and almost near the ballroom where the event carried on, oblivious to her heart's destruction and her life's worst grief.

"There is a back entrance to the building. Come this way. I called an Uber to take us to the hospital nearest there."

"She's at the hospital...is she okay? How do you know?" Layka couldn't think. Naomi looked away, and the grip on her wrist relaxed. "You don't think she is at the hospital."

"I'm going with you," Naomi said, but what Layka heard was: *An Uber won't take us to the scene of an accident where smoke still licks the air and a flight team crashed into the river.*

"The hospital. Right," she said, turning. Her body wasn't hers as she pushed their pace from behind Naomi and her mind played through scenarios of her hiding inside an ambulance as it left the hospital to make another run to the scene. Layka shook her head as they pushed through to the stairwell. She had to focus.

"Be reasonable," she whispered to herself as yet another irrational plan claimed her mind for a moment from its racing thoughts. They slid into the ride waiting when they reached the exit at the bottom of the building. Naomi laid a hand on hers as she twisted her phone in a constant rotation. The gesture felt heavy with permanence, and Layka jerked away. "I'll call her. She could be on the riverbank unconscious...a call might..." Naomi let her hand fall away, and the gentle recoil made Layka angry as she tapped the screen.

The ominous sound of the unending ringing phone in the silence of the car made Layka swallow back nausea. It pushed into her chest and made her double over in pain when Aven's voice mail answered. Naomi reached for the phone, but Layka gripped it and pulled it to her chest. "Her phone has a locator," she said, her voice sounding too loud as she tried to see the screen through her blur of tears. "I can see where she's at and the driver can take us close." She was tapping the screen, and there it was—the beacon. She wiped her tears so she could see. It was still a blur. "Where is she?" Layka screamed, not caring anymore as she shoved the phone toward Naomi because she could no longer see with the pounding behind her eyes and the flow of tears.

"Where is she?"

"She probably lost the phone in the crash."

Naomi's words were placating, and Layka pulled the phone back around, enlarging the screen so she could see. "She usually keeps it in her back pocket." She pinched the screen with her trembling fingers, then widened it again and forced her eyes to focus. "It's in the river. She's still in the river." Layka dropped the phone, clasping and unclasping her hands, then pulling at her dress. It was too tight. She couldn't breathe. "Take us to the bridge," she shouted at the man driving as she reached for the split in her dress to tear it off. It was too heavy for the water.

"Layka, the scene we saw on TV was a recap." Naomi paused, and the hesitancy made Layka scan the car for anything to avoid the rest of this conversation. Naomi laid a gentle hand on Layka's exposed shoulder. "They will have already taken her to the hospital."

The words knocked the last scaffold of hope from Layka's house of cards. If Aven's phone was still in the river with Aven, she had been there too long to be okay. Layka dry-heaved between sobs, and only Naomi's efforts kept her upright as she crawled from the vehicle. The hospital was a buzz of chaos. There were people everywhere. Layka looked away when her eyes caught the charred arm of a man standing outside, smoking a cigarette as if he realized, despite the severity of the burn to his arm, he was not the worst off. Layka followed in Naomi's wake through the sea of people in the waiting room, and as Naomi spoke to the desk clerk, Layka made her way back into the belly of the beast that would either save or destroy her heart. She heard voices calling after her, but she just moved faster. She rounded a corner and pressed a handicap button that opened two large wooden doors. She raced into the cacophony, her eyes darting to every space, searching for the woman she had waited too long to say *I love you* to.

Layka's eyes connected with exhausted, familiar blue eyes across the expanse of the busy ER. She didn't hesitate, she didn't pause, she didn't ask for the people in the way to move. She was done waiting for perfect.

Aven rolled her neck and waited for Luken to type in the notes she'd given him on the pending tests and labs for the patients remaining in the ICU.

"It sounds like you had a long night," he said, dropping his phone into his shirt pocket. The gesture reminded her she had left her phone in her jacket pocket on the helicopter when she jumped out so the flight team could head to the bridge. The drive had taken longer, but the hospital needed her. The bridge needed the flight team.

"Yes," she said, not stifling a yawn as she covered her mouth. She let her eyes rake across the ER as she took in the controlled chaos. She knew she was exhausted because she was starting to see familiar people in the busy crowd of worried friends and family. Her mind was creating a mirage of Layka moving toward her. She couldn't see the woman's face, but the hair was nearly identical. She followed the movement of the Layka look-alike as she barreled through the crowd like a wave. Each muffled cry, cough, or painful moan created the soundtrack to this woman's determined gait. The endurance and resilience of the injured humanity and the loved ones surrounding them reiterated what was in her heart. There were forever people in your life. Layka was who she would want standing by her side if it were her in one of those beds. It was Layka she wanted to love her, and Layka was everything she loved—all she wanted—friend, lover, confidante, supporter, accomplice. She loved her, and she would wait forever. She would take sex once every three months, phone calls, texts, and video check-ins for another year if that was what it took to have forever with the woman who...

"Layka?" Aven's eyes connected with Layka's gray-blue ones now ten feet away at the corner of the three-quarter triage wall, with eyes red-rimmed, bloodshot, and determined. Aven shook her head and focused on the woman. *Why would Layka be here?* As the thought formed and merged with the woman moving toward her, the TV screen behind the nurse's station broadcast a recap of the accident, only the spotlight of the responder team was no longer on the accident but focused on a white jacket tied to a balloon drifting slowly away from a helicopter blown onto its side in a wave of smoke just before it fell toward the river. *My phone, my jacket...* Aven's eyes locked with the gray-blue eyes now only feet away. Aven recalled an earlier report from Dr. Fields after stabilizing their second code blue of the night—that they were down a flight transport because Jeff and his paramedic were at Saint Francis after an incident at the bridge.

That Jeff and his paramedic were the injured hadn't registered at the time.

Aven knew empathy in that moment. The sheer terror in Layka's eyes would haunt her dreams even as the relief of the welling tears in them tried to wash it away. The arms that wrapped her in an embrace had never held her so tight, and the whispered words at her ear almost made her knees give way.

"You are worth waiting forever for, but I can't wait till I'm perfect to tell you I love you, Aven Summerhouse."

Aven let Layka's momentum and the swell of her words back her into the lounge. She kicked the door closed with her foot and pressed Layka against it, kissing away the tears that now freely rolled down Layka's cheeks. "I called Luken to come in early..." Aven pressed into Layka, sensing the urgency between them. "...because I couldn't stand being away from you." She kissed possessively down Layka's exposed neck. "We have such little time." Aven's heart clenched with the truth of that as Layka's hands in her hair tightened and pulled to tilt her head back with a primitive need. Their gazes locked, and Aven could see it all in Layka's dark, hooded eyes. Aven's words came out as a breath. "I love you." With Layka's lips only a lick away, she did just that. "I want *you*, and only *you*, till forever is ours." Aven pressed her lips to Layka's and swallowed the cry that escaped from her, then tasted each word as Layka spoke them.

"Take me home. You are my forever."

CHAPTER THIRTY-FIVE

AVEN KEPT HER EYES closed, but she could feel the warmth of the dappled light through the shutter slats that shaped the light of the rising sun into warm and cool patterns along her exposed skin. Only her hips and ass were covered by the tangled sheet, and she savored the feel of Layka's finger trailing a slow, curving line down her back as she lay on her stomach. They had finally managed to slow things down last night, but that had only lasted for one round before they were back to climax frenzy. They simply couldn't get enough of each other. This felt relaxed, and she wanted to be present in the moment of it.

"What are you thinking? I can tell you're awake."

Aven felt the curve of her lips at Layka's words. Every muscle seemed to respond to Layka. "I was thinking about how nice this feels." She rolled gently onto her back, allowing Layka's finger to follow a natural path to her abdomen. She lifted a hand and stroked Layka's jaw with her thumb. "How happy I am to wake up with you. I have these few days with you, and I want to be present for every second."

"That's perfect," Layka said, kissing Aven's thumb, which had moved to her lips. "Because I've got a surprise for you today."

Aven's phone rang, and she reached to the nightstand and gave it a shove, pushing it off the stand into the wicker basket of folded towels and rolled washcloths she kept there for the bathroom.

"Aven!" Layka laughed.

The second ring was muffled.

"No one needs me as much as I need you right now." Aven pushed Layka's hair away from her face, making it tumble across her back and off her opposite shoulder. Layka settled her body against Aven, laying her head against Aven's chest.

"I love hearing your heart beat."

Aven shifted her legs as much as she could in the tangled sheet to allow Layka's body to fit like a puzzle piece atop her.

A click like a door lock being tripped made Layka startle.

Aven wrapped her arms tight around Layka. "I have a landline answering machine system in my office space." She thumbed at the small sitting area with a desk in the open alcove where the shutters still braced against the light. "It's a backup in case something goes awry with my phone. Oh no! That was your phone I shoved off the nightstand. Mine is in the river!" Aven half sat up. "I'm so sorry," she said, reaching toward the basket.

"It's fine," Layka said, laughing, then traced a trimmed nail down the flexed ab muscles that had Aven somewhere between a crunch and an oblique twist as she reached for the phone in the basket.

The click came again, followed by a familiar voice. "Aven. Hi, it's Naomi. I tried Layka's phone but didn't get an answer, and your phone is in the river, I believe, but I found this emergency number in your file. The new head librarian has arrived. Can you call me as soon as possible?"

Aven's head fell back against the shifted pillow.

"It's fine, my love," Layka said, kissing along Aven's stretched neck. "We need to get up and start our day. We've got a full schedule of events today."

Aven hummed out a breath of pleasure as the words were whispered along her neck. She liked the kisses, and she let the words *my love* settle in a special part of her brain, but she was uncertain about the rest. Their trip to the amusement park wasn't scheduled until tomorrow. She didn't recall making plans for today, and staying right here sounded like a great plan to her.

Layka stuck her head in the refrigerator to cover the smile that crossed her face when Aven put the call on speakerphone and Naomi's voice came through the line. It had been all she could do to keep the excitement out of her voice when she convinced Aven to call Naomi back on her phone. Naomi was great to help her with this, but then again, she was a gifted project assistant and, after last night, a very good friend. She'd texted her before Aven woke up about helping her with the surprise. Naomi had been all in.

"It's wonderful that the new librarian is here, but it's unexpected. I'll have my assistant set up a meeting to do a face-to-face debriefing with her about the Mindful Path Project and her role in it next week."

"She respectfully requests that you stop by this morning. She thinks someone was in her office last night during the event."

Aven took a deep breath, and Layka closed the refrigerator and moved toward her. She didn't want the surprise to create unneeded frustration for Aven. She wrapped her arms around her waist from behind, and Aven stopped her pacing.

"I'll go with you," Layka whispered near her ear.

I want to have the day with you, Aven mouthed silently, then spoke. "I'll be glad to discuss that at our meeting next week." She rubbed Layka's hands, still wrapped at her waist.

"She said you might not realize how important it was and to tell you that something is missing."

Aven collapsed onto the leather barstool. "That changes things," she said, looking over her shoulder at Layka, who gave her a kiss. "Layka and I will stop by while we are out."

"Thank you. That's perfect. Layka left her surprise for you here."

Layka smiled. The relief in Naomi's voice was palpable. She'd been excited when Layka shared her surprise but concerned that they wouldn't be able to pull it off. The woman was a gem for helping her create this special moment with Aven. She had a lot on her plate, fulfilling essentially two jobs, and Layka was grateful for her as a worker and now a friend.

The drive was quicker than Aven expected, and she was grateful for the time they'd saved by it being a Saturday. Traffic hadn't been quite a nightmare, and the building was closed so they could deal with this issue, meet the head librarian, and be on their way back home. Their time was limited.

"I'll let you in," Naomi said, lifting a set of keys from her desk when Aven entered the main office.

Aven didn't think it was wise or necessary to tell Naomi that, as the lead principal research investigator on the Mindful Path Project, she had a set of keys to the office till they were turned over to the head librarian. She entered the office space. "Thanks, Naomi." It was then that it dawned on her that the office should be open if the head librarian had arrived, and she realized Layka wasn't behind her. She was about to say as much when her eyes scanned the space. The office had taken on a new look, so obviously the head librarian had been here. "Did she step out?" Aven asked, hopeful she would have an excuse to come back later.

"She's just down the hall," Naomi said.

Aven nodded and took a seat in the chair across from the desk. Layka was probably in Naomi's office picking up Aven's surprise, which Naomi had said was on her desk. The furnishings were now unboxed, uncovered, and seated beautifully around the spacious room. Flashes of the night before flooded her mind, and she smiled. *Too bad that wasn't there last night*, she thought, noticing the antique fainting couch near the fireplace. There was a soft blanket draped at the foot, and she pulled her eyes away, pushing back against the images of her and Layka in here the night before. She didn't even care at this point if they had left evidence—a sock, an earring, or anything that might make her or Layka suspects for whatever was stolen. She would agree to making a report to the police if it meant she could leave and get home. She couldn't imagine what might be missing. Hopefully, it was just something small that may have been misplaced, and the new librarian would be content with changing the locks.

She was reaching for the phone she no longer had in her pocket when the door creaked, and she tapped her back pocket, making a mental note to put getting a new phone on the list of things to do today. She tapped her temple with her index finger as if the gesture would store the reminder, then looked up. "Layka? What's that?" she asked, pointing to the book-sized box in the hand not holding her huge purse.

Layka took the few steps between them with a flourish and lifted Aven's hand to her lips. She kissed her knuckles the way Aven so often kissed hers and pulled her to her feet, leading her over to the beautiful, tufted leather sofa.

Aven swallowed. If Layka's surprise for her was making out again in this office while the new head librarian wandered the building somewhere, she was going to love it and probably lose her mind at the same time.

"Sit down," she said, lifting Aven's legs up onto the sofa as she sat. She placed a soft throw pillow beneath her head. "I know you're exhausted, but as you know, the head librarian is scheduled to move into her office next month. She thought it would make the transition easier if she brought some things early."

Aven's eyes went wide. "You're the new head librarian for the antiquities library?"

"Yes, and I'll continue to be principal manager for the Mindful Path Program. I wrestled with the decision, but after last night, I knew I didn't want to leave you again." Layka stroked Aven's hair from her forehead, causing the long blond strands to fall. She pushed them behind Aven's ear. "I wanted to share my surprise in person," she said, running the back of her hand down Aven's face, then down her chest and stomach. "I'll be closer to my lead principal research investigator."

Aven closed her eyes at the touch and the words. *Layka is going to be here.*

Layka didn't stop her trailing hand till she reached Aven's ankle. She circled the small bone she had traced for the first time so long ago.

Aven opened her eyes and watched as this beautiful woman she loved so much—*Yes, loved,* she thought—removed her tennis shoes.

Layka removed the blanket behind her and laid it over Aven's stomach as she slid back on the couch and pulled Aven's feet to her lap.

"Where is home going to be for you?" Aven said, not holding back the moan as Layka pressed along her heel and up toward the ball of her foot.

"Wherever you are," she said. "I'm going to make an appointment next week with a real estate agent to look at some housing options. That's my other surprise. I'm not just taking the job. I'm staying here." Layka laughed. "It's funny how much of this I had planned in my head but wouldn't let myself believe I could live it. The celebration for all three Wheelhouse builds is scheduled for July in DC, three months away. I thought maybe we could fly back together then. I can get my car, and you can drive the U-Haul with all my stuff loaded inside."

"What about Brillo?" Aven asked.

"Sam and Farrah are traveling cross-country in two weeks. Farrah's position has her collecting data and visiting areas for potential new Wheelhouse builds. They said they would bring Brillo out here to us."

"Do you want your own place because you still think I will run away if things get hard?"

"You didn't run away this time." Layka rubbed up Aven's calves, and the tight muscles started to release. "You followed your dreams and gave me time." She slid her hands up along Aven's thighs, placing one knee between hers to balance as her thumbs and palms worked deep into Aven's thighs, then softened the pressure as she reached the apex. She stroked gently across Aven's core with her thumbs. Aven held Layka's eyes as she felt the throbbing in her core start to wash away her fatigue. Layka leaned in and kissed her lower lip, pulling on it gently. "Now, I'm following mine." She kissed down Aven's jaw to her neck near her ear, where she whispered, "I want my own place because you're worth waiting for, and when you're ready, we will make plans together."

Aven felt the tears forming, and she didn't want to wipe them away. They were happy tears, and she lifted her head to press her lips fully to Layka's. She didn't want to wait any longer, but she did want to soak up every second and take the time to be present to experience each new step for them. Her body hummed, and she deepened the kiss with this woman she loved.

Layka sighed just before parting her lips. Aven felt the vibration like a ripple through her entire body. "I am so glad you are here, and I don't want to wait a moment longer," Aven whispered.

Layka pulled back enough to lock eyes with Aven, just inches from her lips. "I'm here because the woman I love is here, and I don't want to spend any more of this lifetime distanced from her."

Aven's hand was making circles with her thumb at her jaw. "We're going to be an us. Fully?"

"Yes, if you want that too."

Aven answered by pulling Layka back into a deep kiss, then whispered against her lips, "I say we officially christen this office space."

"That sounds wonderful. I brought the strapless so we can pick up where we left off last night."

Aven smiled. "Seeing you in that strapless dress is an absolute tease, but it isn't necessary. I want you right now."

Layka grinned and walked to the office door where she'd hung her purse. She gave the lock a confirming nudge and then picked up her purse. Aven was certain Naomi had left and no one else was in the building, but seeing Layka lock the door stirred something primitive in her. She was watching Layka's long arm disappear into her purse when the word *strapless* turned over in Aven's fatigued mind.

"Yes," Layka said as if knowing Aven's mind was making the shift. She gave a flip to the short, flowing light blue dress that ruffled just above her knees.

Aven's hand stroked up Layka's leg when she reached the couch and slid up to her thighs as Layka straddled Aven's hips and placed her satchel of a purse by the couch. "You're not wearing panties." Aven's words hitched as her fingers traced Layka's bare hips and buttocks beneath the skirt.

Layka leaned close to Aven's ear, bringing their bodies to full contact and causing Aven's top to slide up as Layka lifted something from her purse. "I brought your strapless, not mine."

Aven heard the sound she made but could not describe it as her mind recalled images of Layka leaned over the desk last night. Layka worked Aven's pants and panties down and off, then slid the curled end of the strapless against Aven's wet folds, then clit, before sliding it inside her. Aven moaned with the feel of it as Layka rubbed the length of the shaft with Aven's wetness.

"I want you to take me here the way you did last night. I don't want gentle." Layka's voice went low. "I want you deep. I want you buried inside of me," Layka said as her movement down the shaft rocked the base against Aven's clit. She moved her hand back up the girth, tugging at the curled edge inside Aven. She licked her lips. "But make it slow."

Aven did a half crunch, grateful for the core workouts that made the movement possible because the shift made the shaft angle toward Layka's glistening wetness. The sight of her pink and wet made currents pulse through Aven, and she pushed at Layka's thighs to widen them as she stroked Layka's clit with her thumb. "You're so wet."

"That's what you do to me, Aven Summerhouse," Layka whispered, guiding the tip against her clit before pushing it inside her and pulling back slow. "Mmm, I've missed doing this with you."

"You make me crazy." Aven kissed her, biting and tugging Layka's lip as the tug of Layka's muscles on the shaft pulled the curled end inside Aven against the back of her pubis, and she clenched every muscle to hold it in that perfect place. "Fuck." The sensation was its own thrill, but the ability to hold Layka's face with both hands and kiss her lips while feeling the gentle slide of her along the shaft as it rocked inside her was indescribable. Slow was going to be hard, but she would give Layka anything she wanted.

"Oh God, yes," Layka moaned. "Deeper, Aven."

Aven slid her hands up and down Layka's thighs, then slowed her rocking with her hands on her hips. Finally, she stopped her movement and slid out, moving to her knees. The pulse between her legs, now a throb of need, was determined to take every inch of this woman for herself.

"Aven?"

Aven rubbed Layka's hips. "Turn over."

Layka bit her lip with understanding, then pulled her hand along the girth of the toy as she rotated to her knees and braced her hands on the arm of the couch. "Tell me what you want, Aven. What you've wanted since our first night together."

Aven moved in close. "I want you naked, vulnerable..." Aven said, her voice a husky whisper. "...and your body revered." Her hands traced the line of Layka's body as she unzipped her dress and pushed it up and off over her head. She squeezed the firm breasts that fell from the built-in cups of the dress. "I want you exposed and trusting me to take care of you." Aven felt her clit pulse against the base of the toy. "Something primal in me wants to pound deep inside you and protect you at the same time."

"Do it." Layka moaned, putting her hands over Aven's hands now pinching her nipples and backing into Aven as her muscles gripped and pulled against the shaft with every stroke.

Aven took in the form before her. Layka's body was perfection to her. She paused, squeezing Layka's breasts and pulling the shaft out to run it between Layka's thighs as she ran a fingertip down from Layka's breasts along her ribs and to her core.

Layka shivered, and Aven could feel her wetness along the shaft. Aven moved back and forth, knowing the length of it made it slide just across her clit at the top of the stroke before she pulled back.

"I don't know if I can handle slow," Layka breathed out, pushing back into Aven's movement.

Aven was on her knees and rubbed the soft skin of Layka's round bum as she continued her rocking along her folds before sliding just the tip in as she used her hands at Aven's hips to tease the way she knew Layka liked.

"Aven, yes. Take me."

Aven reached around with her right hand and circled Layka's clit, making Layka jerk.

Layka breathed out a little cry when Aven's hand moved away. "Stay."

Aven ran both hands up her side and ribs to squeeze her full breasts before circling and pinching both nipples as she slid completely inside the silk of Layka. She felt her own clit pulse with the pressure of the base.

"I want you," Aven said, rocking in and out. "Only you." She kept one hand teasing a nipple and slid the other back to Layka's clit. Circling then pausing, she leaned in to kiss along Layka's back, causing the shaft to slide with each movement. She was pulsing herself and wanted to pound against Layka's firm ass, but Layka had asked for slow. "Make yourself come for me."

Layka rocked into Aven's hand at the words, and the friction across Aven's fingertip made her own clit pulse. The movement caused the shaft to slide with its natural rhythm, giving Aven exactly what she wanted as Layka's beautiful ass pounded back against her.

"Make me yours, Aven."

Aven rocked hard and solid into Layka, pinching her taut nipple and keeping pressure at Layka's clit. Aven felt Layka's hand cover hers as her movements quickened. "That's it, come for me. Naked, vulnerable, exposed, and safe in my arms." Layka bucked, and Aven held her tight.

"I want more." The words were a barely audible gasp.

"Take more." Aven's voice was gravel with her own need, and Layka was close—Aven could feel it in the frantic movement and the tight squeeze around the shaft she felt with every pull.

"Aven! I'm yours."

That was it. The sound of her name on Layka's lips as she exploded and her body convulsed in Aven's arms made Aven topple over the edge with her. She cried out, then held Layka close, both of them breathing hard as Aven braced them upright with her elbow against the back of the sofa. She would never tire of hearing those words, and she gently rocked her hips side to side to pull out carefully.

"Stay inside me," Layka whispered. "Hold me." Layka pushed with trembling legs back into Aven when she started to pull out.

Aven lifted her hand from Layka's core and wrapped her arm around Layka's waist. She stretched the hand at Layka's breast across Layka's chest to rest below her ear so her thumb could brush Layka's cheek, and she could support her head. The cross-body position of her hands kept Layka close to her. Layka's arms were resting on the high end of the fainting couch, keeping the angle perfect for Aven to savor the intimacy of their bodies in the exquisite sensation of connection along every point of contact. Layka's body, relaxed in her arms and resting on her thighs, created a very real reminder against her clit that they were interlocked.

"You are the safest place I've ever been," Layka said, breaking the silence.

Aven placed a kiss on Layka's spine. "I want to always be your safe place." Aven felt Layka's smile at her thumb where it still traced Layka's jaw. Layka leaned her head into Aven's hand, then shifted slightly, lifting up on her knees from her half-seated position. Aven released her and guided the toy free as Layka used the sofa arm to balance as she stood.

She turned and sat on the blanket that touched the floor from its crumpled position underneath Aven's bent knees. She stroked down the shaft of the toy once, giving a little pressure to push the base into Aven's center before easing it out of her. Aven's breath caught at the spiral of shocks that shot through her with the movement. Layka laid it aside and wrapped her arms around Aven's waist. Their eyes locked.

"I love you." The words were perfectly in sync when they both spoke them. Aven laughed, and Layka smiled.

Aven's core pinged with the thrill of Layka being here. She ran her hand through Layka's hair, pulling gently to ask her up for a kiss. This moment meant everything to her. Layka pressed her body to Aven's and kissed her gently. Aven felt the tear leak out as she whispered, "We're creating a forever *us*."

EPILOGUE

THREE MONTHS LATER

Layka looped her arm through Aven's when the hotel porter whisked away their luggage. "I've always wanted to stay at the Hay-Adams Hotel." She bounced on her toes, too happy to fight her excitement as Aven led her from beneath the awning to the left, where they could take in the historic hotel away from the main entrance. "I never dreamed it would be for the Fourth of July!"

Aven squeezed Layka's arm with her opposite hand, then lifted her hand to kiss it. "What is your favorite historical story about this hotel?"

Layka stared at Aven's bright blue eyes as the brush of Aven's lips lingered on her knuckles. She breathed deeply, taking in the moment. She felt her feet settle as if Aven's kiss had grounded her to this beautiful moment frozen in time. Slowly, she pulled her eyes from Aven and let her gaze travel up the expanse of the stone walls, then over toward the main entrance accented with warm wood doors and black iron lantern lights. "I'll have to think about that a while. This area was the hub of intellectual conversation for so many people, like Mark Twain, Amelia Earhart—the list goes on." She squeezed Aven's hand, now laced with hers. Aven was looking up at the flags whipping in the wind. Layka watched her face. The wind blew wisps of her loose blond hair across her cheek. She was beautiful inside and out. Layka knew she was full-on in love with Aven Summerhouse. "I think my favorite history will be the history we make this weekend at this historic hotel celebrating a Fourth of July anniversary with a historic United States Madam President in office."

"I have to agree," Aven said, looking back at her with that smile that made her blue eyes seem to sparkle. "Shall we head inside?"

As they reached the door, a car pulled through to the valet. They both paused when a familiar face appeared from the back of the car.

"Thank you," Mildred said to both the porter and the driver as they lifted her suitcase from the trunk.

"Mildred, you're here!" Layka embraced the woman as she turned. "I thought you weren't going to be able to make it."

"Me too, sweet child, but I was able to hire the property managers for the Kansas branch with just two interviews. It's a wife-and-husband team that I think will be perfect. They'll live on-site."

Aven leaned in for a hug. "I still can't believe you flew out to Kansas to do the interviews in person."

"I believe it," Layka said, giving Mildred an additional side hug as the three of them moved toward the large, warm brown, welcoming doors. "Mildred taught us when we were on the streets about the value of face-to-face time with people."

Mildred squeezed her back. "And, this one was a quick study. She did most of the work scoping out their environment while her sister focused on finding resources." Mildred paused their movement once they were beyond the entrance. "Where is Sam? I haven't seen her for a month now. She usually stops by the second week of the month for lunch."

"She and Farrah took a cruise," Aven said.

Layka watched Aven's face. It was such a joy of hers that the history of hurt between Aven and Sam had created a balm for their dynamic group of four, healing more than just the two of them.

"They just returned a few days ago and should be here sometime today. Right, Layka?"

"Yes, you're right." The three of them stood in the foyer, taking in the opulence of the space. "Did you ever dream we would be here, Mildred?"

"This isn't the big dream come true for me," Mildred said, turning in a circle and taking in every detail with her keen eye before taking Layka and Aven by the hand. "The big dream come true for me is the Mindful Path Project." She squeezed their hands. "Thanks to you two, we have three fully constructed Wheelhouse centers creating true opportunity for the unhoused population."

"Not just us," Layka and Aven said together, then smiled at the moment of being so fully in tune with each other.

"No," Mildred said with a firmness Layka recalled hearing more than once when they were struggling to survive from day to day. "You two were the seeds. Everyone else was sunshine and rain, food, and support—yes—but without the seeds, none of those things could have impact."

"Thank you, Mildred," Layka said as they both leaned in and kissed Mildred's cheeks.

"I'm going to see if they have our party's early check-in available," Aven said, moving toward the desk.

"Thank you." Layka gave Aven a smile and forced herself not to watch the way Aven's jeans hugged her cute little tush as she walked away. She knew she failed when Mildred laughed. Layka grinned, knowing she was caught. "Speaking of impact, what about the success of the Wheelhouse here in DC? It was your ideas that facilitated us finalizing an occupational connection with the libraries. I am so grateful for that."

Mildred beamed. "I'm proud of what that has produced. We have twelve literacy graduates."

"Twelve—that's incredible, Mildred! I know the numbers are on my desk for review Monday, but please tell me about them."

Mildred moved them toward a seating area away from the bustle of the entrance. Layka recognized this was Mildred protecting what she called the sacred privacy of the inhabitants of the Wheelhouse. "Four of them are from domestic violence situations—three women and one man."

"Are their stories similar to yours?" Layka asked, reaching out to cover Mildred's clasped hands on her lap. Her heart had broken anew for Mildred when she learned during the DC Wheelhouse build that Mildred had found safety in the anonymity of the streets when restraining orders hadn't protected her from an abusive partner.

"In ways," Mildred said, unclasping her hands to give Layka's a strong squeeze that reminded her how determined this woman was to forge a path forward. She had done it for herself and was now doing it for others. "Learning to read as an adult was difficult but was the most empowering thing I ever did for myself. I'm excited to see it doing the same for others."

"You two absolutely glow when you're together," Aven said, kneeling beside Mildred on the bench and turning her phone screen so she and Mildred could see the picture she had snapped of them while they talked.

"I love that picture," Layka said, and Mildred reached out, touching the screen.

"It's beautiful. Please send it to me."

"Absolutely." Aven brought the phone back and tapped the screen as she stood. "They have our rooms ready, and Reynolds texted and said she, Sarah, and Steve ran into Dr. Sudha checking in. They're at the Smithsonian." Aven looked up, and Layka heard her and Mildred's phones ping with the photo. Mildred opened her phone, but Layka couldn't pull her eyes from Aven, who was staring at her with the most beautiful smile. "They'll be back this afternoon in time to meet in the restaurant for the kick-off dinner."

Layka smiled. That was more than enough time to unpack and have some well-deserved alone time with Aven before she had to share her as the co-partner on the Mindful Path Project at the first annual anniversary dinner.

Mildred stood, breaking the eye contact between them. "That sounds perfect. I'm going to unpack and rest for a little while. I'll meet you in the restaurant." She gave Aven a pat on the cheek, then turned to Layka and gave her a wink. "You should get a little rest yourself."

Layka blushed, and Mildred smiled before turning for the elevators.

Aven was still on a high from their "nap," but she tried to focus as she scanned the hotel restaurant, searching for Reynolds's distinct red hair. "There they are."

She tilted her head toward a table at the back. Sam noticed them and gave a wave. Aven's heart lifted at how easily things had slid into place for the four of them. Sam gave an additional two-finger salute that told her Brillo was here and now resting in Sam and Farrah's room. *One more piece in place for our special night,* she thought. She had helped get Sam and Farrah connected for the cruise from Los Angeles to Alaska, and they had planned it so that Sam and Farrah could bring Brillo with them on their week-long drive back from California while Layka thought Brillo was with a friend of theirs who had a vineyard in California. Several people from the table turned and smiled. There were fourteen people from the core team of the Mindful Path Project scheduled to be here with their plus-ones.

"I know we're on time, but we're late by our original plan to be the first ones here," Layka said in a whisper.

"I think we can technically call this being fashionably late since we had to dress twice." Aven grinned when her words brought a blush to Layka's cheeks and knew their thoughts were on the same undressing event.

Aven pulled a chair out for Layka when they reached the table, and the hum of conversation filled her with warmth. She checked her phone. They had about five minutes before Dr. Sudha was scheduled to officially toast the beginning celebration. Simon was the only one of their original group who had been unable to be here. He had taken a new position in Boston only one month ago and could not get away. So much had happened since the first Wheelhouse ribbon-cutting ceremony in DC. She was lost in her thoughts when Farrah lifted her glass. The movement pulled her from her thoughts, and she took in Farrah's wide smile as Sam leaned in and kissed her temple. Aven smiled, and her mind registered Dr. Sudha's voice at the head of the table. Mildred grinned next to Sam.

"I thank each of you for being here tonight. And even more than tonight, I thank each of you for your commitment to pioneer the Mindful Path Project into reality. I'd like to begin our celebration by reading a thank-you from our Madam President for the precedent the program has set for similar programs across the nation."

Aven closed her eyes at the prick of tears as Layka squeezed her leg beneath the table. She felt so much hope and joy in this moment. She covered Layka's hand with her own. Tomorrow was the Fourth of July, and she was proud to be an American hopeful for what a diverse group like theirs had created by working together across nationalities, beliefs, and differences.

The core group of their friends who had planned to stay at the Hay-Adams for the weekend had meandered down to the hotel bar. Layka stood at the black marble counter, now waiting on her drink. She leaned against the barstool, watching Sam and their handful of friends at the table. She listened to Sam's recounting of one of their childhood memories and noted how Sam's command of the table didn't create that nudge in her gut like it used to do. She smiled at how Aven had helped her see the value in who she was, and she no longer compared herself to her sister.

"Your Envy, ma'am." Layka accepted the green concoction from the bartender and smiled. She'd keep the envy in her cocktails.

She slid into the conversation with ease when she reached the table. Sam had left them briefly after dinner, saying she needed to take care of some business and she was glad to see she had made it back. She leaned into Aven, who sat next to her in the curved booth in the softly lit subterranean-level bar. She could smell her lavender jojoba oil shampoo when Aven shifted to plant a kiss on her nose. She could feel her face heat, realizing Aven knew what she was doing, but she couldn't help but breathe her in. Mildred chimed in with a story about Sam that had Farrah squeezing Sam's bicep and grinning.

Reynolds raised her cocktail glass. "Here's to enjoying a Fourth of July weekend with friends who make a damn difference in this world."

Everyone clinked glasses and took a drink.

"That reminds me," Sam said as everyone settled back into their seats. "We have the final word back from the FBI. Barton is being charged with multiple counts of campaign fraud, and the events with the unconstitutional translocation of the unhoused are being prosecuted under criminal trafficking."

"To Brillo and Amelia," Sarah said, raising her glass again.

Layka swallowed back the moment of grief. Amelia was gone, but her efforts had meant the difference for thousands of lives. Once Brillo's microchip confirmed the movement of Amelia and Brillo on the day that she and Aven had seen them loaded into the van, the FBI, the hospitals, the health department, CDC, and NIH had moved swiftly to isolate the virus variant and had dramatically reduced the transfer of the disease while also helping to generate structure for the medical component of the Wheelhouses being constructed. Necessity truly did generate innovation. The crisis of the viral variant created a need that fostered a medical management within the Wheelhouses that was unique and quickly identified patients at risk before they spiraled into sepsis. The thought reminded her of Brillo being separated from her mom before she had time to even know she was declining. Brillo had mourned Amelia's death as if she knew the moment the woman passed. She had recovered and was active and full of love now, but it had been difficult to watch the dog grieve.

"What are you thinking about?" Aven whispered in her ear.

"I miss Brillo. I won't have my nighttime cuddles."

"I know. I miss her too, but she does love running in the open space of Barbara's California vineyard."

"True. And it is away from the city with all the firework activity of the season."

"Maybe we take Barbara up on that weekend stay at the cottage there on the vineyard when we get back. We can spend some time with Brillo out in the wide-open space before the three of us head back to the condo in the city."

Layka leaned in and kissed Aven's soft lips. "That sounds like heaven."

Gradually, each of their group said their goodnights and headed to their rooms. She began to slide out of the booth, but Aven gave her a gentle tug, and she turned back into her.

"Can I have just a few more minutes with you here? I want to savor each moment of this weekend."

"Me too," Layka said, leaning in for a slow kiss. "I'm glad we planned to fly in and use these two weeks off to bring my car to Los Angeles with a cross-country drive back together. Sam said their drive was beautiful, and they did it in a week."

"Excuse me, ladies," the server said, pulling Layka from their conversation. He looked concerned. "The front desk tells me there is a dog loose on the roof. They're trying to catch it, but if you see it in the hotel, please call the front desk."

"Oh no," Layka started scooting from the booth. "We should go help them." She reached back for Aven's hand once she had cleared the table's edge and stood, but Aven was already out of the booth and behind her with a gentle hand at her back.

"Absolutely."

The elevator pinged on the rooftop floor, and the doors opened. She gripped Aven's hand and rushed out the door. She stopped immediately as she took in the beautiful space. There were candles and flower arrangements on every table, and each was full with seated friends and family.

"Hey," she said, pointing at Reynolds and Purdel. "You all said you were going to bed."

They shrugged and smiled as she continued to turn in the space, taking in the beauty of people she had seen earlier in the night as well as some additional familiar faces lit by only soft light. The sound of the space was a hum of servers passing out champagne flutes and chatting with tables quietly, but a single sound pulled her back to the reason they had come up here. "The loose dog," she whispered as she turned to the sound of a dog's whine. She spotted Sam and Farrah seated at a table with Aven's parents. Brillo pulled at the harness Sam held with a grin she had not seen since they were children. It was mischievous and full of love. She released Brillo, who barreled toward them. She knelt, and Aven joined her as they scratched Brillo's ears and rubbed the belly she immediately exposed. "What are you up to, love of my life?" she whispered, her eyes locked on those sky-blue eyes that told her everything with only a look. She stood when a server brought a small bistro table to the spot where they were knelt, and a second one brought a chair. Aven was straightening Brillo's harness, and then, before she could take her seat, Aven was on one knee, with Brillo sitting up next to her with her paw on Aven's hand that held a black box, open and displaying the most beautiful ring she had ever seen.

"Layka Corin-Silva, I love you. Will you marry me?"

"Yes!" Layka dropped to her knees, taking Aven's face in her hands and kissing her soundly. Brillo barked and circled them. She pulled back from the kiss.

"It's about damn time," Reynolds said by way of a toast.

Layka laughed, then smiled when Aven tilted her head in that way that made Layka feel adored. "We were waiting for each other," Layka whispered, giving Aven a gentle kiss.

"And now we have forever together," Aven said, stroking Layka's jaw and giving her a deep kiss as cheers erupted and glasses clinked across the expanse of the open roof.

Layka saw fireworks behind her closed eyes, and it wasn't even the Fourth of July yet.

Acknowledgements

Forever, when done well, is the ultimate Happy Ever After. You find forever people in your life at different places along the journey. This book is a culmination of inspiration from so many beautiful people across spectrums of my life that I could not acknowledge them all appropriately in a book given to just that task. However, I do want to say thank you.

Thank you first to the reader because without you this story would go unread. I am already excited about the growth of the relationships started with readers in this last year. It is beautiful and I am grateful for each of you.

Thank you to my writing colleagues and friends. The quiet conversations about creating good in the world, the loud celebrations with each other's success, the early morning writing sprints to make deadlines, the unselfish discussion of craft tools, and the steadfast friendship of knowing we are here for each other has been a constant renewal for me.

Thank you to my editor and my cover artist. I do not have words to describe the diligence and work ethic of these two people. I am forever indebted to you.

Thank you to my family for your patience, support, and cheers along this new journey. This year has felt exponential in the moments of growth and love.

www.ingramcontent.com/pod-product-compliance
Lightning Source LLC
Chambersburg PA
CBHW051241260626
47162CB00002B/550